LYNN MORRIS
GILBERT MORRIS

WHERE TWO
SEAS MET

BETHANYHOUSE
PUBLISHERS
MINNEAPOLIS, MINNESOTA

Published by Bethany House Publishers
A Ministry of Bethany Fellowship International
11400 Hampshire Avenue South
Bloomington, Minnesota 55438
www.bethanyhouse.com

Printed in the United States of America by
Bethany Press International, Bloomington, Minnesota 55438

ISBN 1-55661-437-3
ISBN 1-7642-2610-X (Large Print)

The Library of Congress has cataloged the trade edition as follows:

Morris, Lynn.
    Where two seas met / by Lynn Morris and Gilbert Morris.
        p.   cm. — (Cheney & Shiloh ; bk. 1)
    ISBN 1-55661-437-3 (pbk.)
    1. Duvall, Cheney (Fictitious character)—Fiction. 2. Women physicians—Fiction. 3. Quarantine—Fiction. 4. Honeymoons—Fiction. 5. Epidemics—Fiction. 6. Islands—Fiction. I. Morris, Gilbert. II. Title.
    PS3563.O874439 W48   2001
    813'.54—dc21   2001003785

DEDICATION

To Kay,
with love.

BOOKS BY GILBERT MORRIS

Through a Glass Darkly

THE HOUSE OF WINSLOW SERIES

1. *The Honorable Imposter*
2. *The Captive Bride*
3. *The Indentured Heart*
4. *The Gentle Rebel*
5. *The Saintly Buccaneer*
6. *The Holy Warrior*
7. *The Reluctant Bridegroom*
8. *The Last Confederate*
9. *The Dixie Widow*
10. *The Wounded Yankee*
11. *The Union Belle*
12. *The Final Adversary*
13. *The Crossed Sabres*
14. *The Valiant Gunman*
15. *The Gallant Outlaw*
16. *The Jeweled Spur*
17. *The Yukon Queen*
18. *The Rough Rider*
19. *The Iron Lady*
20. *The Silver Star*
21. *The Shadow Portrait*
22. *The White Hunter*
23. *The Flying Cavalier*
24. *The Glorious Prodigal*
25. *The Amazon Quest*
26. *The Golden Angel*
27. *The Heavenly Fugitive*

THE LIBERTY BELL

1. *Sound the Trumpet*
2. *Song in a Strange Land*
3. *Tread Upon the Lion*
4. *Arrow of the Almighty*
5. *Wind From the Wilderness*
6. *The Right Hand of God*
7. *Command the Sun*

CHENEY DUVALL, M.D.[1]

1. *The Stars for a Light*
2. *Shadow of the Mountains*
3. *A City Not Forsaken*
4. *Toward the Sunrising*
5. *Secret Place of Thunder*
6. *In the Twilight, in the Evening*
7. *Island of the Innocent*
8. *Driven With the Wind*

CHENEY AND SHILOH: THE INHERITANCE[1]

1. *Where Two Seas Met*

THE SPIRIT OF APPALACHIA[2]

1. *Over the Misty Mountains*
2. *Beyond the Quiet Hills*
3. *Among the King's Soldiers*
4. *Beneath the Mockingbird's Wings*
5. *Around the River's Bend*

TIME NAVIGATORS
(for Young Teens)

1. *Dangerous Voyage*
2. *Vanishing Clues*

[1]with Lynn Morris   [2]with Aaron McCarver

GILBERT MORRIS & LYNN MORRIS are a father/daughter writing team who combine Gilbert's strength of great story plots and adventure with Lynn's research skills and character development. Together they form a powerful duo!

Lynn has also written a solo novel, *The Balcony*, in the PORTRAITS contemporary romance series with Bethany House. She and her daughter live near her parents in Alabama.

CONTENTS

PART I: THE FAIR HAVENS

Chapter One: Locke Finally Comes Home / 10

Chapter Two: An Impudent, Saucy Fellow / 32

Chapter Three: Dr. Cheney / 50

Chapter Four: An Island Paradise / 71

Chapter Five: Skylarking / 86

Chapter Six: Friendly Duels / 112

Chapter Seven: All the Way From the Coast of Africa / 146

PART II: A TEMPESTUOUS WIND

Chapter Eight: Fear and Flight / 168

Chapter Nine: Number Six, The Flying Jib Inn / 182

Chapter Ten: For Richer, For Poorer / 200

Chapter Eleven: Bannister House, Bequia / 213

Chapter Twelve: *Bequia Breeze* / 229

PART III: NO SMALL TEMPEST

Chapter Thirteen: Storm Damage / 252

Chapter Fourteen: Becalmed / 271

Chapter Fifteen: Isolation / 291

Chapter Sixteen: Rats or a Little Blood / 304

Chapter Seventeen: Victims / 322

Chapter Eighteen: *Materia Medica* or Medical Matters / 345

Chapter Nineteen: Blood Always Tells / 361

Chapter Twenty: The Truth of Love / 391

Chapter Twenty-one: Death Is Strict in His Arrest / 417

Chapter Twenty-two: God's Hand / 430

PART IV: ALL THEM THAT SAIL WITH THEE

Chapter Twenty-three: Complete Conversions / 440

Chapter Twenty-four: The Hardest Honesty to Come By / 452

Chapter Twenty-five: Coffee / 458

Chapter Twenty-six: Beginning Now . . . / 473

And falling into a place where two seas met,
they ran the ship aground. . . .

And the soldiers' counsel was to kill the prisoners,
lest any of them should swim out, and escape.

But the centurion, willing to save Paul,
kept them from their purpose. . . .

And so it came to pass,
that they escaped all safe to land.

Acts 27:41–44

PART I

THE FAIR HAVENS

April–May 1869

*And when we had sailed slowly many days,
and scarce were come over against Cnidus, the
wind not suffering us, we . . . came unto a
place which is called
the fair havens. . . .*

Acts 27:7–8

CHAPTER ONE

Locke Finally Comes Home

CHENEY AWOKE IN STAGES. First her mind swam upward from deep, deep dreams. Then she felt her eyes grow focused, even though she kept them closed. Lastly she grew aware, with that primitive, half-forgotten sense humans have, that it was late morning.

Gentle rocking movement, odd faraway noises, a close rustle.

Cheney opened her eyes.

"Good morning, Doc."

Her eyes opened wider.

"We're married," Shiloh said brightly. "I'm your husband, Shiloh Irons."

"Oh yes, I remember you," she said with sleepy amusement. "What time is it?"

"Five bells in the forenoon watch," he answered, showing off. At the roll of her eyes, he said, "Aw, it's"—he took out the watch Cheney had given him so long ago, and it sang its tinny little tune—"ten thirty-eight. That would be A.M."

Cheney was reluctantly sitting up, gazing around in a bemused manner, stretching and yawning. She was in the owner's sleeping cabin of the clipper ship *Locke's Day Dream. Her* clipper ship. Hers and her husband's, that is, for he had given her half ownership of it for a wedding present. One of her wedding presents. She gazed down, still a little sleep-stupefied, at the giant ruby ring on the third finger of her left hand. Yes, it was true. She was indeed married to Shiloh, for—

"What day is it?" Cheney demanded.

Grinning, Shiloh lifted the heavy silver domed cover of the tray he had set down on the small table. "It's Wednesday, April twenty-fourth, the Year of Our Lord eighteen hundred and sixty-nine. You've been married for two whole days, three whole nights, and about twenty-one and one-half hours."

"That long? I'm practically a *hausfrau*. Is that bacon I smell? And hot coffee?" Cheney asked, finally becoming alert.

"Yes, *mon chou*. You want coffee in bed first?" Shiloh asked, fixing her first cup with two sugars and heavy cream.

"Mmm, no, I'm starving. I'm getting up," Cheney said, throwing aside the light coverlet.

"Want me to get Fiona?" Shiloh asked uncertainly.

"No, I can manage this much by myself," Cheney answered, amused.

"I still don't get all that lady's-maid stuff," Shiloh grumbled. "But I can help if you need it."

Cheney laughed, a rich, throaty sound.

"Shiloh, my love, after my long experience as your wife, I would say that helping me get dressed is not exactly one of your brighter lights."

"You've noticed?" He gave her a sly wink. "Anyway, I do think it'd be better to have breakfast at the table. Us expert sailormen have ways of making meals more efficient. See?" He pulled two straps from the side of the table, slid them over the two ends of the tray, and hooked the straps into tiny eyes underneath the lip of the other side, to keep the tray from sliding with the motion of the ship.

"Why, that's perfectly wonderful," Cheney remarked, sliding agilely into the small teak chair anchored into place at the two-seater table. The chair seats swiveled, but it still took a peculiar writhing, slippery move to get into them. "But it's hardly necessary, we're sailing so smoothly. Barely a ripple, is there?"

Shiloh eyed her anxiously, for in spite of her declaration, the ship was pitching—the natural fore-and-aft motion as waves passed bow to stern—just a little. "Feel all right, do you, Doc?"

"Mmm," she answered, partly in answer, partly in appreciation of the coffee. "Fine." She saw his half-anxious expression and added, "Really, Shiloh, I feel just fine. No seasickness at all."

"Good," he said with relief, somehow managing to fold his six-foot-four frame into the small chair with easy grace. They bowed their heads and Shiloh exclaimed, "Lord, thank you, thank you, thank you! Amen!"

"Sounds like one of my father's prayers," Cheney said, heaping her square, anchored plate with scrambled eggs, still steaming, three pieces of bacon, and a buttermilk biscuit.

"Good," Shiloh said with satisfaction. "I figure if I learn to pray as good as he does, I'll have a leg up, so to speak. With the Lord, you know."

Cheney's mouth was full, so she just shook her head with amusement. Casually he said, "I've brought some newspapers. And I know you brought some copies of *The Lancet* and some other stuff. Would you like to read while we eat?"

"Could we?" Cheney asked, childlike. "You don't think it's terribly rude?" At Duvall Court, she and her parents had always read at the breakfast table, in spite of the fact that generally persons of their social class had very formal meals, with only polite conversation. But Shiloh had stayed at Duvall Court enough to know how Cheney had been brought up and what she liked.

" 'Course not," Shiloh said indignantly. "Miss Irene reads at breakfast." He could not conceive of anything that Cheney's mother did as being rude. "What do you want?" He went to the twin armoires and from the bottom drawer of his took out the *New York Herald*.

"Mmm—the medical newsletter from the University of Pennsylvania, please," Cheney answered in a muffled voice. Perhaps that big bite of biscuit dripping with butter had been a bit too much. "The earliest one. I sort of got behind in the last few months, with the wedding and everything."

"Here you go, the February issue." Shiloh gave it to her and slid behind the table again and disappeared behind the newspaper.

They munched and read in silence for a while, in perfect ease with each other. Once Cheney looked up to get another biscuit, only to find that Shiloh had already split one, buttered it, put a generous dollop of raspberry preserves on it, and put it on her plate. "Thank you," she mumbled politely.

"Welcome," he said absently.

They were just mopping up the crumbs, sipping the last of the second cup of coffee, and Cheney was making a little triangle with her leftover bacon pieces when she exclaimed, "My goodness! This is just wonderful!"

"What?" Shiloh asked, putting down his paper.

"A German medical student named Langerhans has discovered that tiny cells in the pancreas—they're called the islets of Langerhans—produce two types of ductless gland secretions. There's a distinct possibility that they may be key diagnostic factors in the disease of diabetes," Cheney told him excitedly.

"Yeah? That would be great, if someone could figure that disease out," Shiloh said with unfeigned interest. "How is it diagnosed now?"

Cheney shrugged. "We can test for sugar in the urine, but that, of course, is a sort of hit-and-miss tool. Not all diabetics test positive for sugar all the time. And when the disease is advanced, you don't really have to test for sugar. Their breath smells sweetish, sugary, you know? And in an emergency—when they've fallen into a sudden coma—I saw Dev once just wipe his finger across the lady's lips, then taste. He said it was as sweet as if she'd just rubbed sugar on them."

Shiloh's eyes darkened to midnight blue. He leaned over, touched Cheney's lips with his fingers, and then tasted. "Mmm, your lips taste sweet too. But it could be 'cause you've got raspberry jam at the corner of your mouth."

Cheney put down the journal, rose, and walked behind Shiloh. Wrapping her arms around his neck, she bent down and nuzzled him. "I don't think you want to talk about the islets of Langerhans right now, do you?"

"Maybe later," he said, rising to take her in his arms. Again he was thinking, *Lord, thank you, thank you, thank you!*

Uli Sigiwald was captain of the forecastle-men, which meant that he was older (he was fifty) and more experienced (he'd been at sea for forty years) and that he made twelve dollars more per month than a simple-rated able seaman. He was also a qualified helmsman, and that was what he loved best, and that was what he was doing right now. He steered *Locke's Day Dream*, and when Siggy—his mates had always called him that—was at the helm, she never griped, never quivered, never had a jog in her ruler-straight wake. He knew her, this old girl, and loved her.

He was a taciturn man, rarely speaking but often grunting, with a locked jaw and farseeing blue eyes. He looked up at the towering sails, listened to the creaking of the rigging, the wind sighing through the shrouds. To him it was like a feast.

Then to his dismay he clearly heard a female voice, a cultured voice, raised high with mock indignation. "Twelve!" Cheney blustered. "You must be joking!"

Sigiwald saw the open transom of the salon skylight and considered whether to make some noise, call out—something so that the exalted owners of the ship might know they could be heard.

"Ten, then," Mr. Irons-Winslow's voice boomed out in deep amusement. "Ten?"

"Two," came Mrs. Irons-Winslow's voice. She spoke in a lower tone, but now that Siggy could hear them, he couldn't ignore their voices. It was as if a malignant sea breeze was wafting tales to him. Of all of the sailors on the ship, the single one who would never eavesdrop was Uli Sigiwald. He tried to block out the voices, knowing that his men wouldn't bother. *All the rest of the sods would break their ear-pans trying to hear, the bunch of gossipin' old women*, he thought.

"Two! Just two? Aw, c'mon, Doc. Eight?"

"No!"

They must be playing cards, Siggy realized with a slight lessening of discomfort.

"Seven," Mr. Irons-Winslow triumphantly announced. "Seven is the perfect number."

"Seven children?" Cheney repeated, and Uli Sigiwald now looked about in true alarm. "Oh! If only you could have four of them, then maybe I'd settle for having three!"

"You, Lott there!" Sigiwald roared out loud enough to shatter bone. Calvin Lott, the innocent forecastleman who was walking down the starboard side of the quarterdeck, dropped the block and purchase he was carrying with amazement. A helmsman *never* spoke, even if he was the captain of the forecastle. Especially Siggy— he just growled.

"Wot's up, Siggy?" Lott called out, fumbling to reassemble his machinery.

"Frap that backstay, can't you? Rigging all ahoo, the barky looks like a Frog lugger!" Sigiwald thundered, his face crimson. Poor Lott looked about in bewilderment for a frayed rope. Finding none, he nevertheless spit on his hands and smoothed down a stretch of thick backstay, shrugged, and walked on.

Silence from the salon.

Then Sigiwald, to his vast relief, heard first feminine and then deep masculine laughter. "Gentry," he grunted privately. "Who can tell of 'em?"

Cheney and Shiloh, in the owners' salon, were sitting at the long teak table, still staring up in amusement at the skylight with the opened transom. "Sorry, mon chou," Shiloh said contritely and quietly. "It kind of registered that the transom was open, but I just didn't think about the helmsman back there."

"Stuff," Cheney said stoutly. "Every servant we've ever had knew every conversation that went on in my house. You get used to it."

Shiloh regarded his wife with interest and vivid admiration. He had been worried that Cheney might feel crowded, smothered, without privacy, on a ship for their honeymoon. To his surprise he'd found that she seemed perfectly at home and relaxed. She treated the seamen with respect but without undue familiarity. Now it came to Shiloh that Cheney was used to living with people—strangers, really. All her life she'd been surrounded by servants, and even though Dally Clarkson and her family and Mr. Jack were hardly typical, it was still not like living a solitary life. He was the one who had always been alone.

"—the schedule today?" Cheney was saying.

"Want to go out and play?" Shiloh asked.

"I surely do," Cheney answered gamely. Cheney retrieved her parasol, for the sun was high. She was wearing one of her sailing costumes, as she called them. For her honeymoon voyage she had splurged and ordered twelve fine-linen blouses, simply made, and twelve lightweight muslin skirts. Today her blouse was cream with a sky blue ribbon tie, and her skirt was sky blue and mint green striped.

The sailing costumes, Shiloh thought, were so much less severe than Cheney's usual clothes, and she looked very young and pretty. Her hair glowed burnished copper, her green eyes sparkled, her exotic features glowed. Cheney was not exactly a pretty woman; her jawline and cheekbones were too pronounced, her mouth too firm, her gaze too direct to ever be considered peaches-and-cream pretty. But she was slim, lithe, animated, exotic—a striking, vital woman.

No one would ever know she's twenty-eight, Shiloh reflected with pride. *She looks even*

19

younger now than when I first met her four years ago. She's happier, lighter—she smiles more. I hope I can keep her this happy all our lives.

They came out of the salon, which according to the peculiar but ingenious construction of this deckhouse, meant that they walked up four steps to the level of the poop deck. Both Shiloh's father, Rory Winslow, and his uncle, Logan, were over six feet tall, and they had deliberately assumed the extra cost of building staterooms and the salon to accommodate their height. The superstructure rose above the deck six feet, but it was countersunk two feet, so the ceilings of the salon and stateroom were a luxurious, and unheard of, eight feet high. Shiloh was very glad of it. The other two deckhouses—the amidships one was the captain's stateroom and day cabin, and the forward one housed the galley, carpenter's shop, and apprentices' quarters—had six-foot ceilings, and Shiloh couldn't imagine living with the permanent stoop.

They stopped at the polished teak poop-deck railing and gazed out over the self-contained small city. To Shiloh's seaman's eyes, the ship had an orderly beauty, but to Cheney it was a wilderness of rope spider webs, bewildering machines both small and large dotted about the ropes and littering the decks, and other curious objects for which she had no name. No sailors were in the rigging—they had barely touched the sails since leaving New York, the winds were so kind—but about twenty sailors were on deck, busily working. Cheney had no idea what they were actually doing. "I'm amazed that men who seem so simple and, for the most part, uneducated can learn to operate such a complex machine," she said softly.

"It's not a question of education," Shiloh said thoughtfully. "It's not just a myth, you know, about true seamen having it in their blood. Sure, everyone has to learn the names of things and which rope is which and the difference between the quarterdeck and the poop deck, but a real mariner has an instinct that teaches him how to sail."

"Like you," she said, turning to him. "It's certainly in your bloodline."

He was still staring out over the ship, his eyes creased a little against the bright sun, a small smile touching the corners of his mouth. Cheney, with pleasure, simply watched him, admiring his broad shoulders, his muscled arms, the masculine grace of his stance. His eyes were sharp, a farseeing light blue, set in his wedge-shaped tanned face. His hair, tousled a little by the brisk wind, was sun-bleached white with just a touch of gold. *He's a heartbreaker, my husband is*, she reflected happily.

After a while Cheney went on, "So, Mr. Jack

Tar, what *is* the difference between a poop deck and a quarterdeck?"

His answer was eager, for Shiloh loved to talk about sailing and ships and *Locke's Day Dream* in particular. "We're standing on the poop deck. That middle part below us is the quarterdeck. Up at the front—"

"At the bow," Cheney said with satisfaction.

"Right, Doc, at the bow, the raised part is the forecastle."

"Poop deck, quarterdeck, forecastle," Cheney repeated.

"Now just so you'll know, we can go anywhere we want, since we own the barky—"

"But why does everyone call it 'the barky'?" Cheney interrupted. "It's not a bark or a barkentine. Even I know that much."

"It's just kinda an affectionate name— whatcha call a ship if you like her. That's the kind of thing us Jack Tars know in our blood," Shiloh drawled. "You can call her a barky too, if you want."

"Thank you, lord and master," Cheney remarked drily.

"Welcome. Now, as I was saying, just so's you won't be a grass-combing lubber, you see Captain Starnes out there, walking up and down?"

"On the quarterdeck," Cheney said smugly. "On the *port* side of the quarterdeck."

"You're pretty good for a girl. Now it's a tradition of the sea that the windward side of the quarterdeck is kinda reserved for the captain. So when you see him pacing up and down the windward side of the quarterdeck, see, and you don't want to look like an ignorant lubber, you don't go talk to him or even walk on that side of the quarterdeck," Shiloh expansively explained.

Cheney nodded. "I'll remember not to commit such a terrible sin. So the port side of the quarterdeck is also called the windward side?"

Shiloh stared at her, astonished. "Huh? No, the windward side is just the windward side. It could be either port or starboard. See?"

"No, I don't," Cheney said a little peevishly. "What is windward? What does that mean? The direction in which the wind is blowing *to* or the direction in which the wind is blowing *from*?"

"It's the wind from which the . . . it's which the direction is . . . it's to the . . . aw, great blue skies, today it's that way," Shiloh finally managed, pointing.

"Well, I know that, since Captain Starnes is on that side of the ship," Cheney said, exasperated. "Leave it to a seaman to make up some silly rule involving navigational principles before they can figure out where to walk."

Shiloh blinked. "It just never seemed that complicated to me before."

They stared at each other, and finally

Cheney began to laugh. "Oh, dear, I'm sorry, Shiloh! I just want so much to . . . to . . . I just don't want to embarrass you."

"You! Embarrass me! Never, never, Doc," Shiloh said, giving her an enormous bear hug that knocked her parasol askew. "Forget about it. With a captain, three officers, and forty-six sailors aboard, I don't think you'll have to worry about figuring out windward and leeward."

"Good," Cheney said with some relief. "I'll just be careful not to speak to Captain Starnes should I accidentally trespass on the holy windward side of the quarterdeck. I shall gather up my skirts and run as fast as I can for—*to* leeward."

"Good girl," Shiloh grinned. "Anyway, that's enough sailing lessons for today."

"No, I want to know one more thing," Cheney said. "We are going so fast, it's just—exhilarating! So how fast are we going? How many knots, I mean?"

"For that, we can presume on our exalted stations and bother the first mate," Shiloh said as he led Cheney, arm in arm, down the steps. "We have to be real nice to Captain Starnes, because he's the genius who's giving us such a fine sail, but we can torture the officers all we want."

"Mmm, if he is responsible for this fine sailing, I must send Captain Starnes a thank-you note," Cheney said, smiling as they promenaded slowly down the humble leeward side of the deck.

It was not just fine sailing, it was the best sailing. The sun was a perfect lemon yellow lozenge, high and cheerful, but they had not reached the tropics yet, so it wasn't too hot. The sea was a smooth, benevolent blue. The northwest trades blew steady and firm, and the clouds of sails billowed out like women's stiff petticoats. The rigging made pleasant creaks and whispers. It was a bright, clean-washed kind of day.

On their lazy promenade, Cheney and Shiloh passed two sailors sitting cross-legged by the mainmast, practicing knots and talking in low voices. As they passed the men Shiloh called out, "Lott, you've still got to teach me that masthead bend."

"Right you are, sir," Lott called out, knuckling his forehead in the old-fashioned Royal Navy salute. An Englishman through and through, his father had been a real "son of a gun"—born on the gun berth of a British man-of-war—and was a veteran of the Napoleonic wars. Lott had joined the British navy as a ship's boy when he was seven. Now forty-two years old, he was sea tough, swarthy, with heavy black brows and sharp black eyes. "Here, boy! Show some respect!" he hissed to the wide-eyed young boy sitting by him.

The boy gulped, then pressed his knuckle to

his head and mumbled, "Sir, ma'am."

Cheney smiled and nodded, and Shiloh said, "Pay attention, Redding. Mr. Lott's a hard task-master."

"Sir." Leith Redding gulped. He was barely sixteen, a thin boy with wispy brown hair and a perpetual half-terrified look about him. In Brooklyn he'd been a tailor's apprentice, but his father had decided that to toughen him up he needed to go to sea. He had joined as a sail-maker's apprentice, and he did work hard with the ship's sailmaker, Henry MacNair. But as so often happened on hardworking ships, a sea-soned hand would take a liking to a boy and be-come his "sea-daddy." Calvin Lott, in his long years at sea, had "adopted" thirteen boys; Leith Redding was his fourteenth. A more unlikely fa-ther figure than Calvin Lott there never was. He looked like a Barbary pirate, could swear like lightning bolts, and in the old days had both given and gotten some hard floggings. But still, he showed a rough kindness to the very young and even to ignorant landsmen if they were half trying to learn.

As Cheney and Shiloh passed out of earshot, Lott, with scarred and leathery but nimble fin-gers, tied a complicated knot so fast that poor little Leith barely knew which end was which when he'd finished. "Now this here is called by some a butterfly knot, and by some an artillery loop. I call it a manharness knot." His sun-blackened face screwed into an oddly prim frown, and he jerked his thumb toward Cheney's and Shiloh's retreating backs. "Like Her Ladyship there's got 'im all knotted up."

Innocent Leith asked, "Her Ladyship? You mean Mrs. Irons-Winslow?"

"Aye, the missus herself. But no, pardon me all to get-out, I mean the *doctor* herself," Lott grumbled.

"I heard she's a real, honest-to-goodness doctor," Leith whispered. "Not a barber-butcher kind of surgeon, but a real physical doctor, with schooling and papers and everything."

Lott sniffed. "That's as may be. But it ain't *natural*. Her being a woman and a physical doctor. She'll be a double Jonah, just you mind me, boy."

"You mean"—Leith swallowed hard—"you mean she's unlucky?"

"Some would say," Lott replied, his jaw tightening. "And it's a turrible shame if you would ask me, as he's the luckiest thing this ship ever could have latched on to."

"Mr. Irons-Winslow? Why is he so lucky?" the boy asked eagerly.

Lott looked surprised. "Where you been, boy, this last month you've been a *Locke's Day Dream* sailor? Sitting about with your fingers stuck in your ears? Why, that's Locke, that is.

27

Mr. Irons-Winslow *is* Locke."

"He is?" Leith's brown eyes widened like a startled doe's. "He's the Locke of *Locke's Day Dream?*"

"He rightly is too," Lott said forcefully. "And a might good thing it were when he got found and give back his rightful dues. This ship were hexed, she were with the other Mr. Winslow, Mr. Bain Winslow. Ever since Mr. Bain took Mr. Locke on, in sixty-eight 'twere, from San Fran to Hana." Lott nodded sagely. "Me and Siggy and Perkins, you know, knew who he were then. But Mr. Bain treated him real bad, he did, and did Mr. Locke say or do naught? He did not. He turned out to be a right seaman, he did, just like his poor dad. But after Mr. Bain ran him off, this here ship's been unlucky. I'm of the mind that if Mr. Locke hadn't come back to his ship, we might be splicing rope for Davy Jones right now."

Leith frowned a little and regarded Calvin Lott cautiously. When the sailor was in a talk-ative mood, Leith could ask him all sorts of questions, but when Lott got tired of talking, Leith knew he might get brought up right short if he was committing "impert-NANces," as Lott called them. But Lott seemed to be looking at him expectantly, so Leith plunged in. "I don't understand, Mr. Lott. I've heard about Mr. Logan Winslow, the big boss, and I've heard some of the stories about Mr. Rory and his ship."

With thinly veiled satisfaction, Calvin Lott said, "Ah, boy, that would take two watches to tell all about Mr. Rory. That were a sailing man, that was. I saw him, you know."

"You did?"

"That I did. I was just a little lugger like you, but I were already rated ordinary seaman. On the *Mongoose*, a trim little bark, Mr. Rory's first freighter. She's still sailing, did you know that? Still plowing along like the good workhorse she be, back and forth from Hawaii to Shanghai. But anyways, I was getting to Mr. Rory. I seen him twice. Once, when the *Day Dream*—his clipper, just like this here barky—was in Hana at the same time as the *Mongoose*." His sharp eyes narrowed. "T'other time I saw him were five year ago, in a bad storm off Honolulu. Saw Mr. Rory, his hands behind his back, his head bent, pacing the quarterdeck. Right over there."

Leith drew in a sharp breath. "But . . . but . . . I thought . . . Mr. MacNair told me . . . that . . . that . . . Mr. Rory and his wife and baby and all hands went down in the first *Day Dream* in . . . in . . . ages and ages ago!"

"So they did, in forty-three," Lott said in sepulchral tones.

Leith looked half wary, half frightened. There was a possibility that Lott was teasing him, for the sailors unmercifully practiced on ig-norant landsmen, and especially young lands-men. For instance, Mr. MacNair himself, an old man who, in Leith's opinion, ought to treat peo-ple better, had told Leith that belaying pins were called bobbins, just like lacemakers' spools. They were shaped a little like lacemakers' bobbins, only they were much bigger and heavier, of course. Leith had gone around calling them bob-bins, never understanding why everyone laughed so long and loud. But then it was Mr. Lott who had taken pity on him and told him the truth. Now he swallowed hard. "Are you joshin' me, Mr. Lott?" he asked.

"I am not," Lott replied firmly. "And I'm not the only one who's seen Mr. Rory Winslow on this ship, neither. You just go ask Mr. Perkins, who turned about one evil, foggy, wet dawn in the South China Sea and saw Mr. Rory running down the starboard quarterdeck. Perkins said he even heard the poundin' of his Hessian boots, loud and far apart bein' that he had them long legs.

"And if you can get him to grunt one way or t'other, ask Mr. Sigiwald. Ask him who he saw, up in the maintop one foggy night, looking out to sea with his golden glass. Lookin' for the *Day Dream*, is Mr. Rory . . . and his wife, and his son. His son Locke."

"Mr. Irons-Winslow? He's . . . he's Mr.

Rory's son? He didn't die on the first *Day Dream*?" Leith gulped.

" 'Twould seem not," Lott said sturdily. "He seemed to die, if you smoke my meaning, but then he didn't."

Leith tried to digest this for a while, but suddenly he cocked his head and scoffed, "Now, Mr. Lott, you wouldn't be playing me for a landlubbing fool, would you? I happen to know, from Mrs. Irons-Winslow's calling out so loud to him all the time when he's in the maintop, that his name is Shiloh, not Locke."

Lott was righteously indignant, which, more than anything he could have said, convinced Leith that he was telling the real cross-your-heart-and-hope-to-die truth. "Oh? And has it come to your noticin', Mr. Redding, that *he* calls *her* Monshoo?"

Abashed, Leith answered, "Yes, sir."

"Chinee name, wouldn't you say?" Lott relentlessly continued.

"Yes, sir."

"And is she a Chinee?"

"No, sir."

"There you are. There's no accountin' for no double-whammy of a lady Jonah with a Chinee name," Lott said darkly, "but he's Locke, all right. And how do I know? I know 'cause he's the spittin' mirror image of his dad. And that's why he's our luck. Locke's finally come home."

31

CHAPTER TWO

An Impudent, Saucy Fellow

CHENEY NIMBLY MADE her way down the small steps on the ship's side and climbed into the waiting gig, which bobbed gently in the waters outside of the harbor, while her husband watched anxiously. It never failed to amaze him how women could negotiate tricky terrain in such cumbersome clothing, and Cheney had an athletic grace that was even more unusual for women of the day. With a look of subdued triumph she sat beside him in the stern. "Now, I don't ever want to hear anything more about grass-combing lubber things like bosuns' chairs," she announced.

"Yes, ma'am," he said meekly. "I just thought Fiona might come if we rigged a bosun's chair for her." Cheney shrugged, and Shiloh turned to speak to the coxswain, behind them at the tiller. "Okay, Billy-O, this is it. Row dry for the ladies."

Billy O'Shaugnessy, the swaggering, handsome coxswain, said, "Sir! You heard 'im, mates, a nice smooth ride for the ladies."

Shiloh saw the furtive dark looks the six sailors exchanged and glanced at Cheney to see if she'd noticed. If she did, she gave no sign. Raising her parasol, she stared eagerly at the shore.

This was their first port of call. *Locke's Day Dream* had made a perfect run, from New York to the Bahamas in only eight days, with the crew's barely having to adjust the sails.

Nassau Harbor was a long, narrow strip of sea, crowded with small fishing boats of all kinds, so Captain Starnes had decided to anchor *Locke's Day Dream* in the roadstead just outside of the protected harbor. The six sailors expertly rowed—dry, as ordered—into the fast-moving sea stream. Mrs. Sketes, Cheney and Shiloh's cook and steward, sat primly in the bow. She was a stubby little woman, chubby and short, with a good-natured red face and jolly blue eyes. She smiled with pleasure at Cheney and Shiloh, such a handsome, happy couple laughing together in the stern.

"You look just beautiful today, Doc," Shiloh said warmly.

"Thank you, kind sir. But I do believe you're prejudiced."

"I sure am. But it's the plain truth anyway."

Cheney was wearing a traveling ensemble of sky blue with navy blue pinstripes. The jacket was close fitting—emphasizing her tiny waist—with a peplum, slightly tapered in the back over the small padded bustle. The collar and French cuffs were trimmed with a broad navy blue grosgrain ribbon, and the hem of the jacket sported a navy blue fringe. Her skirt was gathered, trimmed at the hem with the same navy blue ribbon. With her snowy white linen blouse and a low-crowned hat with a white ostrich feather, she looked crisp and dashing.

Cheney saw Shiloh appraising her appreciatively. "You're very gallant," she said. "Did you know that? It's gentlemanly of you to be concerned about Fiona. But I'm not sure we'll ever get her out in public."

"I thought at first it was me she was terrified of," Shiloh said wryly. "Then I realized she's just scared of the world. She's sure not like your other maids, Nia or Rissy. What's her story, anyway?"

Cheney frowned a little. "To tell you the truth, I don't know much about her. Victoria engaged her and trained her for me, you know, sort of as a wedding present. I barely had time to interview her before our wedding, I was so . . . distracted and busy."

"I know, you bein' so crazy in love with me an' all," Shiloh said impudently.

Cheney smiled brilliantly. "So I was. So I still am. Anyway, Victoria said that Mrs. John William de Peyster was almost bald, but her hair did always look so magnificent—"

"Wait—wait just a minute there, Doc," Shiloh interrupted, his brow wrinkling. "I wasn't through talking about how madly in love you are with me, and you're skippin' to some po[...] lady?"

Cheney elbowed him and said primly, "[...] tell you all about how I swoon over you later. But[...] now I'm trying to tell you about Fiona."

"She's *bald*?" Shiloh asked, astonished.

"No, silly! I *said*, Victoria said that Mrs. John William de Peyster was almost bald. But her hair was always done so well that Victoria said something to Zhou-Zhou about it—"

"Who's Zhou-Zhou?" Shiloh demanded.

"Who's Zhou-Zhou? Why, you . . . you man!" she spluttered. "She's Victoria's pert little French maid who's so in love with you! Heartless beast, to forget such a devoted admirer!" Chency teased.

"Oh, her. Yeah, I remember her. In New Orleans she wanted to put some kind of girl junk in my hair to keep that bloomin' crown on. Okay, I'm with you. Mrs. de Lan—I mean, Mrs. Buchanan told Zhou-Zhou that the bald lady's hair didn't look bald," Shiloh said with great concentration.

"Exactly. So Zhou-Zhou told Victoria that Pembley, who is Mrs. de Peyster's lady's maid, told her—Zhou-Zhou, that is—that she—Pembley—didn't do her hair. The third maid did."

"Uh-huh," Shiloh said blankly.

"So Victoria told me that she—Mrs. de Peyster—didn't even pay this third maid for

r so wonderfully. So Victoria stole
de Peyster."

id." Cheney nodded with finality.
silence Shiloh asked with hesita-
tion, "So this stolen third maid . . . is that
Fiona?"

"Of course. That's the point. I was telling
you what I know about Fiona."

"Oh. Oh, okay. I think I've got it now. But I
just gotta know one more thing."

"What's that?"

"Is poor Mrs. de Peyster running around
with a bald head?" Shiloh asked mischievously.

"I'm sure I don't know." Cheney sniffed.
"But if she wouldn't pay an expert *modiste* like
Fiona, then—on her own head be it."

Shiloh ducked under Cheney's parasol and
said in her ear, "You wanna hear the story 'bout
Sketes? It's not as good as Fiona's, but you'll like
it."

"Why, yes, I've been wondering about Mrs.
Sketes. She's such a jewel. Wherever did you
find her?" Cheney asked, her eyes sparkling.

"I didn't find her. She found me," Shiloh replied in his conspiratorial undertone. "See, she's
Mrs. Slopes's sister—"

"From the office? Dr. Batson's house-
keeper?" Cheney exclaimed.

"Right. So see, Mrs. Slopes told her sister

that I was looking for a cook and steward for us, so Sketes—she likes to be called just Sketes—decided to apply for the job. But . . ." Shiloh sighed. "You know Mrs. Slopes. She's so proper."

"I can't believe it. Slopes is like some fussy little blackbird, pecking and picking, and Sketes is so . . . round and fun," Cheney whispered.

"And such a good cook—and a good sailor. See, her husband was captain of one of the steam tugs on the East River, but he died three years ago in an accident on the docks. And Sketes had always crewed on the tug, cooking, cleaning, even lending a hand shoveling coal when they were short. After Mr. Sketes died, her sister tried to get her to come live with her and her husband, but she flatly refused. She went down to the docks, got a job as cook on a passenger clipper to Australia, and just worked her way around the world."

"Fascinating," Cheney said with admiration. "Doesn't it amaze you sometimes how strong people can be? Especially women like Sketes. I mean, she looks like . . . like . . . Mrs. Santa Claus!"

"Aw, now I'll never get that picture out of my mind. Hope I don't call her that," Shiloh groaned.

"No, you'd never do that. But I'm bound to," Cheney said with regret. "You never forget people's names, but I have to work at it."

"Anyway, there's just no telling what Mrs. Slopes told her about me," Shiloh went on ruefully. "You know Mrs. Slopes just always calls me and Troy and the other guys 'you young jackanapes.' When Sketes applied for the job I got the impression she was sizing me up, instead of the other way around. But we took to each other after a bit, even though I could hear Mrs. Slopes sniffing with disapproval in the hallway."

"I don't feel a bit sorry for you. Mrs. Slopes adores you, as do all women, no matter what she calls you," Cheney asserted.

"What's a jackanapes, anyway?" Shiloh idly wondered.

"William de la Pole, the Duke of Suffolk in the fifteenth century—"

"Are you talking to me? Is this the same conversation we were having a minute ago?" Shiloh interrupted.

"I'm telling you about why you're a jackanapes," Cheney patiently explained. "Anyway, he was an impudent, saucy fellow, and his nickname was Jack Napis. See? Jack Napis, jack-a-napes?"

Shiloh sat up straight with indignation, although the effect was ruined when he knocked his head on Cheney's parasol. After disentangling himself from the parasol's fringe, he managed to splutter, "Are you saying that I'm an impudent, saucy fellow?"

"I didn't say it. Mrs. Slopes said it."

"But do you think I'm an impudent, saucy fellow?" Shiloh persisted.

"Well . . ." Cheney gave him a sly, sidelong look. "Not saucy. That's too girlish."

"Gosh, thanks, Doc."

"Welcome," she answered mischievously.

He locked his arm with hers and whispered in her ear again. "But you're crazy about me anyway."

"Yes," she agreed serenely. "I am."

The gig came alongside Prince George Wharf as smoothly as if it were gliding on air. Shiloh helped Cheney up onto the dock and they began their eager exploration of Nassau. The town was crowded and noisy, as busy seaports are. Among the first things Cheney noticed were the flamingos. "Oh, I've never seen the real thing before," she said eagerly. "Only woodcuts. What delicious colors!" The birds were everywhere, flying overhead, stalking delicately along the piers and Bay Street, in riotous hues ranging from peach sorbet to flaming sunset orange.

The open market began right at the end of the wharf. Down both sides of Bay Street were three-sided stalls, rude wooden boxes that served as counters, and woven mats with goods spread invitingly on them. The islanders were mostly black, but as usual there were some prosperous-looking white women accompanied by their black maids and a few gentlemen strolling along in cream-colored morning suits and wide-brimmed straw hats. Cheney watched as a young woman walked by, carrying a tremendous load of fruit in a wide, shallow basket on her head. She was an exotic island beauty, with that striking Caribbean look of large lustrous eyes, lips fuller than most Europeans would admire, and wide hips moving seductively as she walked.

She cut her eyes to Shiloh, giving him an approving once-over, raven-winged eyebrows raised invitingly as she passed by.

Cheney pinched him.

"I didn't even see her!" he protested.

Cheney laughed.

Everywhere they looked, a smiling islander invited them to buy the fruits, the flowers, the fish, the baskets, the jewelry, the hats. Fragrant frangipani scented the air heavily as they passed by a woman with two children whose small mat was covered with flowers—frangipani, bougainvillea, anthurium, even great golden pear cactus blooms. The fishermen with their catches of the day, the women with cleverly woven baskets and hats, and the children with their conch jewelry and little carvings crowded around Cheney and Shiloh, but they were all smiling and courteous.

They made their way to a stall that had at

least twenty different kinds of fruit displayed. A very large black man with perfect white teeth smiled and bowed.

"We don't even know what some of these are," Cheney told him. "But they certainly smell delicious. What is this?"

"Sugarplums, madam," he answered—rather jarringly—in a cultured British accent. "A gift for you, lovely lady." He handed her one of the plump red fruits. Cheney took a bite, then smiled. "Mmm, it's delicious! I always thought sugarplums were candy, and this is so sweet it might be. Now what are these?"

In a singsong manner, as he might have done a thousand times for tourists, the man pointed and explained. "These are soursop—good, but not sweet, rather spicy. Hog plums, sweet but not as sweet as sugarplums. Sea grapes, sapodillas, mangoes, coco plums, papayas, tamarind, tangerines, coconuts, pineapples, bananas."

Shiloh tried the soursop, declaring that it tasted somewhat like a persimmon, and then the hog plums and sea grapes, a purplish cluster of fruit with a very mild citrus flavor. He paid the man a shilling, for it seemed no more "gifts" were forthcoming. "You have fine fruit. I'd like to buy a lot of it for my ship," Shiloh said, munching the grapes. "Can you arrange for a boat to take it out?"

"Oh yes, sir, my brother has a fine boat," the

man answered eagerly. "How much may I send?"

Shiloh turned to Cheney, who asked thoughtfully, "How many in the crew?"

"Forty-six sailors, three officers, the captain, Fiona, Sketes, me, and you," Shiloh answered.

Cheney smiled up at him. "How about all of it, then? Plenty for everyone?"

Shiloh grinned. "I hoped you'd say that." He turned back to the man, who was grinning very widely indeed. Shiloh engaged him in the usual barter, and finally the man said, "All right, sir, today is your lucky day. I will take ten pounds." He held out his hand.

Shiloh said good-naturedly, "I'll write a chit, sir, so Captain Starnes of *Locke's Day Dream* will pay you ten pounds and a pound for delivery."

Good-naturedly the man shrugged and bowed again. Shiloh wrote the chit, and he and Cheney moved along down the crowded, noisy street. "I wonder if I would have had sense enough to do that," Cheney mused. "He seemed so nice. I don't think it ever would have occurred to me that he might not be perfectly honest."

"Now that you've got me to watch over you, you don't have to worry about dishonest tradesmen anymore," Shiloh said lightly. Lifting his head, he sniffed. "Mmm, that smells good! Hungry?"

"I wasn't," Cheney answered, "but I am now that I smell that."

Following their noses, they found a stall—actually two wooden counters with an enormous thatched umbrella, its handle stuck into the sand, waving precariously over it. A handsome black couple manned the stall. The woman, wiping sweat from her forehead with a purple handkerchief, stood over a portable stove, while the man was attending to a pile of conch shells on the counter. He smiled at Cheney and Shiloh as they came up to watch. With a small tool he bored a hole in the conch and explained to them, "You must hit exactly the right spot to cut the muscle that keeps him in the shell. If not, this conch he never comes out."

The light-skinned man was small and spoke with a singsong accent. Slowly he extracted a rubbery brown-gray blob.

"Ooh, that's kind of—no, that's *really* ugly," Cheney muttered.

"He will make good conch fritters, though," the man said, waving to his wife. "Have some, pretty lady. Tastes much mo' better than looks."

Shiloh nodded. "Sure, they smell great. We'll take a dozen."

Cheney shook her head. "Not me, Shiloh. I don't think—"

"Oh no, Doc," Shiloh said firmly. "You eat oysters, and this is no worse."

"But that's different," Cheney said weakly. "Conchs are really, really ugly."

"Yeah? Well, I seem to recall saying something like that in New Orleans when I saw my plate *covered* with snails," Shiloh reminded her. "But you made me eat them anyway. C'mon, Doc, be a sport."

When the steaming little golden balls were delivered, Cheney didn't hesitate anymore. They were hot and crunchy, with a very mild taste. Cheney could only manage four, so Shiloh had to get down eight of them, which he did so quickly that the man eagerly tried to sell him more. But Shiloh declared that he was full.

They walked on, stopping to buy coconut milk and sitting on a wrought-iron bench underneath a stand of three graceful palm trees to cool off.

The market was noisy with the calls and cries and chants of the vendors. Several of them blew on conch shells, the wild high notes lingering in the air. But from somewhere behind them, wafting to them on the breeze, they heard singing.

"Pretty little song," Shiloh mused. "Want to go find the singers?"

Down the street, almost at the end of the market, a little old couple had a stall of woven goods. With wavering voices they were singing a simple chant in a minor key.

"Jamie Day, Anna Day,
Work the day,
Weave away.
Sun and sand,
Sea and strand,
Weave the day away."

As they neared the elderly couple, Chency looked up at Shiloh. "They look so sweet, so happy. Do you think we'll be that happy when we're old?" she asked wistfully.

He grasped her hand on his arm and caressed it. "I think you're the best friend and companion a man could ever hope for, Cheney. If you feel the same way about me, then I promise you we'll be happy all our lives."

"I do feel exactly like that," she said softly. "I always have."

"Good afternoon," Shiloh said to the couple. "Do I have the pleasure of addressing Jamie Day and Anna Day?"

"Yes, sir, it's our pleasure," Jamie said in island singsong, rising a little stiffly from his stool. Anna looked up and smiled but kept weaving. "My wife, Anna, and I am Jamie. What for your lovely lady today?"

"We liked your song," Shiloh said simply. "We just got married, you see, and we hope that one day we'll be singing together just like you and Mrs. Day."

He looked surprised but nodded sagely. "Sixty-two years my Anna and me have been together. It's been a good life, and I hope you are as blessed."

"Thank you," Shiloh said. "Now, Mr. Day, I've already spotted that clever picnic basket. Would you show it to me, please?"

Sitting on a box was what looked like a small rattan suitcase, except that it had a leather strap instead of two handles. It was open, and in the top were two glasses, two linen napkins with silverware rolled inside, a cut-glass set of salt and pepper, and two china plates, all neatly fitted and strapped into the top. The bottom had velvet-lined compartments, with a wedge of red-rind Cheddar cheese, two fish baked whole and wrapped in wax cloth, half a loaf of bread, a small bottle of wine, and half a seedcake.

"Perfect!" Shiloh said. "I'll take it."

Jamie bowed and said, smiling, "These are mine and my wife's plates and silver, and this is our supper. The basket is for sale, but I think Anna may be unhappy if I sell our plates."

Shiloh laughed. "And I wouldn't blame her. Do you have one empty so that I won't have to mess up your display?"

"Yes, sir."

Cheney was looking at all the items for sale, piled rather haphazardly around the couple's chairs. She picked up a wide-brimmed straw hat and tried it on. It fit perfectly. "I'd like to have this," she told Shiloh.

"But it doesn't have the gewgaws on it like ladies' hats do," he said.

"Oh, Fiona is so creative, she can trim it for me with birketts and spleckens and crosseyes, you know, things from the ship to give it a nautical flavor."

Shiloh grinned. "I just love your sailor-speak."

"Speaking of sailors, do you know what I'd really like?" Cheney asked mischievously. "A shipwreck kit."

"What? You planning on being in a shipwreck?" Shiloh rasped.

"No, silly, it's just that that clever picnic basket made me think of it. I've often tried to imagine what I would need if I *were* shipwrecked," Cheney said. "Haven't you ever played those little mental games, like, 'What three things would you take if you were marooned on a deserted island?' "

Shiloh answered, "Sure. You, you, and you."

Cheney giggled, and she saw a swift smile cross Anna Day's wrinkled face. "Well, I'm afraid I'm not quite so romantic, my love. If I were shipwrecked, I've decided that I'd want my Bible, a small sewing kit, writing papers and pen and ink, and chocolates. Lots of chocolates."

"That's four things," Shiloh objected. "And

chocolates? I'm not even on the list?"

"Sorry," Cheney said mischievously. "In a shipwreck you must keep your priorities straight."

"Did you hear that, Mr. Day?" Shiloh demanded, turning to the little man, who had sat back down on his stool by his wife and picked up his weaving.

"Yes, sir," he answered, looking up with a sunny smile. "With my Anna, I'm afraid she'd choose chocolates too."

"That I might," Anna murmured slyly.

"Well, we must give the ladies what they want," Shiloh sighed. "Look, Mr. Day, could you make a case for us like the picnic baskets, only smaller?"

"Yes, sir."

"Then here's what we need. . . ." Shiloh began to describe to Mr. Day the dimensions of the compartments, and Cheney noted with amusement that he knew the exact measurements of her Bible, a big worn one her father had given her for her sixteenth birthday.

Mr. Day nodded. "Can do it, sir, only not today. In the morning?"

"Could you make two?" Cheney asked eagerly, telling Shiloh, "I'd like to give one to Fiona."

"Sure, sure, pretty lady," Jamie answered.

"You want to stay overnight?" Shiloh asked her.

"Fine with me," Cheney answered. "It's not like we're on some rigid schedule."

"All right, then, Mr. Day, we'll be back tomorrow to pick them up," Shiloh said. He paid them for the picnic basket and Cheney's hat and gave them half the price of the "shipwreck kits" for a down payment. As they made their way to the quieter town center, Shiloh said lightly, "You know, Doc, you can't call it a shipwreck kit, or the crew might toss us both overboard. 'Naming calls,' you know."

"I've always heard that sailors are very superstitious," Cheney mused. "All right, then, we'll call it a 'deck kit.' Actually, that's more what I had in mind anyway. It will be so nice to have a little case with all those things I need when we sit out on deck in the afternoons."

"The Royal Victoria Inn is just up the street. It's supposed to be really high-hat. Would you like to stay there tonight?" Shiloh asked. His tone was careless, but his sidelong glance at her was sharp.

Cheney considered it, but then with a quick insight uncharacteristic to her, she realized that the question was very important to Shiloh. Though he rarely expressed it openly, he worried that Cheney might not love *Locke's Day Dream* and shipboard life as much as he did.

Impulsively she said, "Oh no, why should we? *Locke's Day Dream* is just as luxurious as any old inn, and so convenient. It's . . . it's like home," she added softly.

He stopped and turned to her in the middle of the cobblestone street. "You feel like that, Doc? Really?"

"Truly," she answered, gazing straight up into his eyes. "You're my home, Locke. Your dreams are my dreams. *Locke's Day Dream* is your home, and so it is mine."

CHAPTER THREE

Dr. Cheney

THE NEXT MORNING Shiloh magically appeared with breakfast, just as Cheney was starting to stir. She wondered how he knew just when she was waking, for with these luxurious guilt-free sleeping-in days, she never woke at exactly the same time. It was usually somewhere between nine and eleven. But whether it was nine-twenty-six or ten-seventeen, he was always there, with her hot breakfast.

"I'm just going to send Billy-O in the gig to pick up your deck kits," Shiloh told her as they were finishing. "Unless you want to go back ashore, that is."

"Not really," she answered. "Let's sail on.

The next island paradise awaits. Where are we going now? Jamaica?"

"That's the plan." He rose and gave her a peck on the lips. "I know Fiona's going to come in pretty soon with all the gewgaws and folderol, so I'm running away now."

Fiona did soon knock timidly at the door, to help Cheney dress and, of course, to do her hair. Fiona Kay Keane was an extremely shy young woman of eighteen, with a slight figure, thick ash brown hair, and soft brown eyes. She had a doll-like prettiness, somewhat marred by her tendency to duck her head and blush painfully. Always awkward around Shiloh, she had actually hidden in her little cabin, listening for him to leave, before she came out with Cheney's clothes, freshly ironed. "Miss Cheney? Are you ready?" she called timidly.

"Yes, come in, Fiona," Cheney answered a little impatiently. She had never had to deal with a servant who seemed terrified all the time, and sometimes she found it frustrating.

Fiona may have been awkward in some ways, but she could expertly tame Cheney's long, thick, unruly mane. In only half an hour—it usually took Cheney over an hour to dress and do her hair by herself—Cheney was up on deck, blinking in the brightness. To her surprise there were very few sailors about, though Captain Starnes was standing at the starboard side of the quarterdeck, looking overboard. Cheney could hear splashing, loud shouts, and boisterous laughter, and curiously hurried to stand by the captain.

"Good morning, Mrs. Irons-Winslow," he said formally, bowing slightly. Captain Starnes was an imposing man, barrel chested, with gray hair and a neatly trimmed mustache and beard and flashing black eyes. He was born in Portsmouth, England, and had joined *Locke's Day Dream* as soon as she'd been completed in the Aberdeen, Scotland, shipyard. He'd been twenty-seven years old then, commissioned as boatswain, which in American merchant marine tradition was the third mate. He'd made master and finally captain when the first captain had retired in 1855. "I trust you had a restful night?"

"Oh yes, thank you, Captain," she answered hurriedly. "They're swimming! How wonderful that must be!" Cheney was fascinated. The sailors had lowered a sail into the water over the side of the ship with an ingenious arrangement of ropes and pulleys to form a suspended swimming pool. "Why do they use the canvas?"

"Because most of them can't swim," Starnes replied. He didn't smile, but dark amusement lurked in his eyes at the boyish antics of the sailors. Even the older men, like Calvin Lott and Willy Perkins, the bosun's mate, jostled and splashed and dunked each other. "And it's a protection against sharks."

"Sharks!" Cheney gasped. She'd seen her husband out swimming, disdaining the "pool." She grabbed the railing and leaned over, squinting. It looked to her as if his blond head was miles away. "There are sharks?"

"We haven't seen any, ma'am. It's just a precaution because they're not unknown in these waters," he said hastily. "And, too, as I said, most of the men can't swim. Sailors rarely can."

"Oh? That's curious," Cheney remarked, relaxing as Shiloh swam closer to the ship.

"I can't swim," Captain Starnes said gravely. "I suppose we all have an odd notion that if we don't learn how to swim, we'll never have to."

"Ah, I see," Cheney said, smiling, recognizing one of the old superstitions sailors lived by: If I deliberately don't learn how to swim, then my ship won't founder. "It's not just seamen, you know, Captain. In my profession I see many people indulge in talismans and superstitions to ward off diseases. In fact, I think I'll invoke one right now. If I cross my fingers, it means there are no sharks. Shiloh and I had quite enough of them in Hana during the volcanic eruption."

The captain's roughhewn features immediately became steely, and he turned slightly away from her. "Yes, ma'am."

Cheney could have kicked herself. Shiloh

had warned her not to mention that terrible time to any of the crew of *Locke's Day Dream*, and had told her that Captain Starnes in particular was ashamed of the ship's part—or rather, the lack of it—in the tragedy.

Two years before, when Shiloh had first traveled to Hawaii on *Locke's Day Dream* at Bain Winslow's "invitation," Captain Starnes had been in Lahaina nursing his wife, who was dying of brain cancer. Captain Manning, the captain of the Winslows' bark *White Crow*, was filling in for Captain Starnes during those terrible months, sailing *Locke's Day Dream* for him. Just before *Locke's Day Dream* had reached Hawaii on Shiloh's first journey, Mrs. Starnes had died. Though Logan Winslow, and even Bain, did not insist on Captain Starnes's rejoining his ship, the captain wanted to, one month after his wife's death. It was the only home he had left.

But Captain Starnes's first voyage since his wife's death was ill starred. He had never forgotten that hellish night in Hawaii, docked in the solitude and silence of the Winslows' private bay, watching the monster enveloping the heights of Mount Haleakala. Captain Starnes had thought with dread that the long-sleeping volcano must be awakening.

And then Bain Winslow had come aboard in the middle of the night, demanding to set sail immediately. Captain Starnes had not, of course, questioned his temperamental employer, but something in the captain's look had prompted Bain to say sulkily, "My family is gone to Lahaina. Now let's get out of here."

It was a lie, and *Locke's Day Dream* had blithely sailed away and left the Winslows, Shiloh Irons, Cheney Duvall, and villagers and servants at the mercy of Mount Haleakala's fury. Captain Starnes had been bitterly ashamed of their departure when he'd found out the truth, and so had the crew, particularly when they had learned that the *Brynn Annalea,* their sister ship, had played such a heroic part in the rescue. Shiloh had warned Cheney that Captain Starnes and the old hands were very sensitive about the event, because they felt they had acted like cowards. It wasn't their fault, of course; short of committing mutiny, they were acting in good faith, under orders. But Captain Starnes knew that if he hadn't been so distraught by his wife's death, he would have discerned that Bain Winslow was lying, and then he would have disregarded his employer's orders, even at the risk of a mutiny and of losing his job.

But that knowledge had never made him feel any better. And Cheney understood as she stared at him with regret.

He managed to say politely, "Look at that husband of yours. He swims like a dolphin."

Shiloh, now close by, was cutting a path

through the green water. His legs churned powerfully, and Cheney could see the knotted muscles of his shoulders as he drove himself toward them. Alongside the ship, he stopped and treaded water. He shook his head and tossed his blond hair, bleached almost white by the sun, and shouted, "The water's fine, mon chou!"

Cheney merely nodded, and below her, treading water and staring up at her slim, straight-shouldered figure, he reflected, *Why, she can't do this—she could never just jump off the ship and take a swim whenever she wants. Just like the four thousand other things women aren't allowed to do. She's always been independent and daring, I guess. But still, her life is so . . . narrow, so closed in, so many rules. . . .*

Well, I can fix that, he told himself, diving deep and basking in the milk-warm water. *For a day, anyway . . .*

After Shiloh came aboard and got cleaned up, he hurried to Captain Starnes's stateroom. The door was open into the day cabin, and the captain and Nat Cadell, the first mate, were drinking tea and studying a chart of the Bahama Islands.

"Please come in, Mr. Irons-Winslow," Captain Starnes said cordially, rising to welcome Shiloh. Eyeing his hunchbacked stance in the low-ceilinged room, he added hastily, "Do sit down. Tea?"

"I'd love some, thanks," Shiloh said, and Tong Ten, Captain Starnes's steward, stepped up from the corner to serve. "Just lemon, please."

"We've been going over the charts, Mr. Irons-Winslow. Our tide is at eleven-thirty, you know," he added carefully. His former employer had been known to demand their sailing against wind and tide, and the fact that it was just about impossible never seemed to deter Bain Winslow.

But Shiloh Irons was not anything like his arrogant cousin, so he said, "So I understand. Tea's great, thanks, Tong Ten."

The young Chinaman, stone faced as usual, bowed.

Captain Starnes, with some relief, went on, "Mr. Cadell here has sailed the West Indies for many years now and has excellent navigational skills. His expertise is a great relief to me. As you know, I've never sailed the Caribbean before."

First Mate Nat Cadell was new to *Locke's Day Dream.* During the long idleness of the ship in New York, they had lost their first mate to a Norwegian herring brig, and Captain Starnes had been glad to find a solid seaman like Cadell. He was a short, muscular man, only twenty-six but already an able seaman, a fine helmsman and navigator. Redheaded and snub-nosed, he was generally cheerful, though he did have a temper and could roar like a freight train when giving orders.

Shiloh turned to Cadell and said in his friendly manner, "Then I'm glad you're aboard too, Mr. Cadell, because I've got a request for a change in plans, and maybe you'll know exactly what I need."

"Hope so, sir," he said confidently. Cadell, being from Brooklyn, was much less formal than the other members of the crew, who were mostly British. "What is it you need?"

"I need an island. Uninhabited. With palm trees. And a really good beach," Shiloh answered.

Silence ensued. The two seamen exchanged cautious glances.

Shiloh added easily, "Would there be anything like that in the Greater or Lesser Antilles?"

"Hundreds, maybe thousands," Cadell said, grinning. "When do you need it, sir?"

"Whenever you tell me I can have it," Shiloh replied.

"I know just the place you're looking for," Cadell said confidently. "And I can deliver it tomorrow."

———————

Fiona was reduced to speechlessness, almost tears, by Cheney's gift. Cheney suspected—

rightly—that Mrs. de Peyster, that stern Knickerbocker matriarch, had never bestowed gifts on her servants. Cheney regularly bought gifts for her maids and was a little embarrassed by Fiona's distraught gratitude.

"It's a shipwreck kit, you see, but my husband has strictly instructed me never to call it that. He said something about 'naming calls.' So evidently if we name it a 'shipwreck kit,' we will immediately founder," Cheney said lightly. "We must call it a 'deck kit.' "

"Oh, I'll never, never call it a shipwreck kit," Fiona said, clutching the basket to her chest like a shield. "Thank you, thank you again so much, Miss Cheney."

"You're welcome," Cheney said, smiling. "I'm glad you like it, Fiona. Now I'm going on deck to see if my husband's skylarking again. I have to watch him every minute. Perhaps later we might take our new deck kits out and sit in the deck chairs and play with them."

"Yes, ma'am," Fiona mumbled.

Cheney made her way up onto the poop deck, reflecting about servants. She was not normally a very analytical person, and she'd spent very little time thinking about such things. Her maids had always been the girls of the Clarkson family, who had been the Duvalls' servants since before Cheney was born, and they had never had the formal mistress-maid type of relationship. Rissy and Nia had seemed more like sisters. Cheney had never considered just how much power an employer had over their servants, power to make their lives miserable or happy. She determined to be more patient with Fiona and try to understand her better, though it was difficult for Cheney. She'd never been afflicted with shyness. Even when she was a child with a terrible stutter, her affliction had not made her bashful, only angry and frustrated.

On deck she breathed deeply, the strong hot wind stinging her nostrils. She noticed, however, that they weren't sailing very fast, and even as she was puzzling over this she heard Nat Cadell roar for all hands to "reef sail." Men swarmed up the rigging.

Shiloh was standing down on the quarter-deck, talking to Captain Starnes. He turned and saw her, waved, and hurried up to the poop deck. "Hey, Doc, I was just about to run up and take in the foretopsail."

"I think not," Cheney said severely.

"Figured you'd say that." Shiloh sighed. "Okay, I'll stay down here with the lubbers and be good."

"I doubt that. Where are we?" Cheney asked. "And even though I'm a lubber, I do know that we're taking in sail instead of making sail. Why is that, with this fine wind?"

"We're coming pretty close to a chain of reefs

and cays just northwest of Little Inagua Island. You can't see it yet, but it's just ahead, and it's a tricky passage," Shiloh answered. "Don't want to be just flying along and end up high and dry on a coral reef or a rock that you can't see except at low tide."

"But I thought you said when we left Nassau we'd be heading out to sea again," Cheney said, vaguely waving east.

"Yeah, but I lied," Shiloh said gravely. "I gotta quit that. Anyway, Doc, we're crawling right down the middle of the Bahamas 'cause I've got a surprise for you."

"You do? What is it? Where is it?"

"Over there," Shiloh said, nonchalantly waving. "You'll see this afternoon."

"But, Shiloh—"

His eyes widened and he jerked away from her. Only later did Cheney realize that Shiloh had been startled a fraction of a second *before* the tragedy happened.

She was turning to see what he was looking at.

Mainsails are enormous expanses of heavy canvas, taken in by small ropes called gaskets, which are wrapped around the bundled sail. The topmen stand on footropes, leaning against the yardarm, and securely wrap the sail as other men draw it in on ropes. In a strong wind the sail billows powerfully and must be secured first in the middle, the part closest to the mast. If the ends are secured first, the sail will act like a balloon, billowing up tightly in the middle.

Two of the less-experienced topmen on the starboard side of the sail blithely wrapped the end of the great maintopsail as soon as they got a good grip on it. The middle filled with wind and snapped up with the force of a tornado, knocking a seaman clean off the footropes.

He fell, striking the lower yard, bouncing, then crashing onto the quarterdeck in a broken heap.

Cheney ran. Shiloh was ahead of her, shouting. "No, don't touch him!"

A knot of men was already around him, but they moved aside for Shiloh and Cheney. She dropped to her knees beside him.

His eyes were open, stricken. He was a young man, with thick dark hair and rich olive skin, now gray. He was gasping. But he was, miraculously, alive.

"Don't try to move," Cheney said softly. "What's your name?"

"C-Castor Mylonas," he managed.

"Stay still, Mr. Mylonas. I can help you." She bent close to stare at his shattered leg, then abruptly jerked upright and rapped out, "Nobody move!" The men gathered around, frozen in what would have been comic positions under other circumstances, not even moving their hands or heads. "Shiloh—" She looked behind her, and he was already walking carefully around, his head down.

"Got it, Doc," he said grimly, then bent over to pick up something from the deck.

"Good," she breathed. "Go get my medical bag and then put that in carbolic acid."

"What is it?" Leith Redding whispered, afraid to look at the object Shiloh had in his hand. The shy teenager looked as if he were going to burst into tears.

"Be quiet, Mr. Redding," Cheney said crisply. What Shiloh had found, thankfully, was a two-inch piece of Castor Mylonas's shattered tibia, but she certainly didn't want Castor to hear about it.

Deliberately she leaned close over his face so he would have to look up and not down at his impossibly deformed leg. The cords in his neck were standing out, strained, as he tried not to cry out. "In just a moment I'm going to give you a shot for the pain."

"Hurts . . . really bad," he gritted.

"I know," Cheney said, taking his left hand. His right arm was obviously broken. He gripped her hand—hard.

Shiloh came running back and shoved the hypodermic needle loaded with morphine into her hand. Cheney gave Mylonas the shot, and immediately his face loosened, his eyes glazed.

Cheney stood up. "Captain Starnes, I need a firm support to tie him onto, not a hammock—a bulkhead or something. I need splints, two for his arm and two for his leg."

The captain growled, "Sigiwald, Upchurch, see to it."

"Where are we?" Cheney demanded.

Captain Starnes frowned. "I could give you the latitude and longitude, ma'am, but I—"

"No. I need to know where the closest hospital is, and when we can get there," Cheney interrupted. "This man needs immediate surgery."

He shook his head. "Nearest hospital—Cadell?"

The first mate's brow wrinkled. "There's a hospital in Kingston."

"Four days," Captain Starnes told Cheney.

"There's nothing nearer?" Cheney demanded.

"No, ma'am," Cadell answered sadly.

Cheney turned to her husband. Shiloh put his hands on her shoulders and smiled down at her. "You can do it, Doc. You know you can. And for my money he's better off with you, here, than in any hospital."

"I hope so," Cheney sighed. "I pray so."

"I know so, amen," Shiloh said firmly. "Now what do you need?"

"First, do we have surgical instruments?" Cheney asked.

"Yes, ma'am."

Cheney turned to the waiting crew. The men had finished reefing sail, and everyone on the ship was gathered around, except for the helmsman, who held a steady, slow course. "Captain Starnes, I can't operate while the ship is pitching, even this little bit. Is there a sheltered anchorage we could sail into, say, within an hour or so?"

"Cadell, what about Great Inagua?" the captain asked.

The first mate nodded. "Good northern bay."

"We'll get you there in about two hours," Captain Starnes told her. Glancing down at his sailor, he murmured, "Faster if I can manage it at all."

"I'll take the helm, sir," First Mate Cadell volunteered.

"Do so."

Cadell broke into a dead run.

Cheney knelt by Mylonas again, and Shiloh knelt behind him. The injured sailor was slightly turned on his side, his broken right arm twisted beneath him awkwardly. "I'll check his spine," Shiloh said.

"He has good reflexes in his left arm," Cheney told him. She leaned close over the young man again. "Mr. Mylonas?"

"I'm . . . awake," he said dreamily. "Doesn't hurt much now."

"Good. Please just lie still while Shiloh and I examine you," she said.

"Dr. Cheney?" he murmured quietly. "Are you going to cut off my leg?"

Her face tightened but her voice was even. "No, Mr. Mylonas, I'm not. I'm going to operate on it and repair it."

"You can fix it?" he breathed.

Her eyes met Shiloh's over the sailor's limp body. "Yes," Cheney said firmly. "I can fix it."

———————

Once they knew what was required, Cheney had never seen a more willing, quick, and efficient surgical team than the men of *Locke's Day Dream*.

David Upchurch was a giant black man from Georgia. *Locke's Day Dream* was lucky to have him, for he had learned blacksmithing and carpentry on the cotton plantation where he'd been born a slave, and now he was an expert at both. He was both ship's armorer and carpenter, two very important functions aboard ship. He and his apprentice, a tough fifteen-year-old from San Francisco named Solly Vaughn, set up a sturdy operating table right on the main deck, for Cheney decided that the cabins, especially those belowdecks, were too dark. Then Upchurch and Solly set up the little forge downwind, right on the quarterdeck. As Solly was working the bellows, making the coals grow bright red, he asked, "What's a doc need with a forge, anyhow? She gonna bolt him together?"

Looming over him, his massive arms crossed, Upchurch answered, "You just mind that fire, boy. When Dr. Cheney gets ready, I'm gonna be ready, and if I ain't, you're gonna be awful sorry."

"Yes, sir," Solly grudgingly replied.

The sailmaker, Henry MacNair, already had a number one lightweight canvas piece he was stretching over the table, measuring it. His apprentice, little Leith Redding, stood by, ready to start sewing the neat corners that would stretch the canvas taut.

Cheney had decided not to move Castor Mylonas any more than was absolutely necessary. His messmates—Cheney had come to know that this meant the man's closest friends with whom he ate his meals—gathered around her, humbly imploring her to let them do something. Castor Mylonas, she found out, was very young but was well liked and well respected for being a "right seaman." His messmates were five big, awkward, frightened men—Calvin Lott, the boatswain's mate Willy Perkins, the helmsman Uli Sigiwald, and the captain's coxswain Billy O'Shaugnessy. Cheney told them to erect an awning over Castor and then just sit with him and keep him calm. The awning was up almost before Cheney had finished speaking, and it was endearing to see these rough, coarse men's gentleness as they spoke to the boy. Siggy, the fierce German, even held Castor's hand.

Cheney and Shiloh got the instruments and supplies ready, standing out under the blinding sun and a gentle breeze that barely caressed their hot faces. "I think I want you to go ahead and anesthetize him while he's lying down there," Cheney said as they washed their hands up to the elbows in a basin of carbolic acid.

"Be best," Shiloh agreed. "I just hope I can get that leg stabilized enough so it won't do any more damage when we lift him. I've never seen a break that bad."

"I had one once in San Francisco," Cheney said quietly. "Same thing, compound fracture of the fibula, compound and comminuted tibia. But it didn't break off a two-inch piece of the tibia, so we didn't have to do this magic trick with the silver shilling pieces."

Shiloh stared at her, his eyes bright, sharp. "Upchurch is good. He got it perfect, Doc. Even the screws are perfectly turned and polished."

Cheney nodded. "I know." She glanced up and around, squinting, then smiled up at him a little. "Quite an audience we have." Every man who was free was standing around at a respectful distance, or perched up on the ship's rowboats, craning to get the best view of the table. About twenty men were up in the rigging.

"Nervous?" Shiloh asked.

"No, I'm not," she assured him. "It's not nearly as bad as that time we had to drill open Mr. Sanford's skull in front of every doctor in San Francisco."

"That was a hoot, wasn't it?" Shiloh agreed.

"Yes, a hoot," Cheney said drily. "Okay, Shiloh, get him sedated and get him up here. I'm ready."

Shiloh anesthetized Castor Mylonas as he lay on the deck, covering his face with a cloth with two carefully measured drops of chloroform on it. As soon as the boy was completely unconscious, he splinted Castor's right arm and leg, then told the men how to lift him onto the table.

Cheney made a long incision on his leg, and then, with something like awe, David Upchurch handed her the silver piece he'd melted down from two one-shilling pieces, measuring them exactly to the piece of splintered bone Cheney had given him, drilling two tiny holes in it, and then making two clever little screws. Cheney replaced the piece of shinbone, fitting it exactly, then placed the silver piece over it. The heads of the screws were necessarily tiny, but Upchurch had made a clean slot in them, and had even formed a thin sort of key that exactly fit in the slots so Cheney had a good tool to tighten the screws. As it turned out, Castor Mylonas was young and strong, and his bones were sturdy, so Cheney didn't have the strength in her thumb and forefinger to tighten the screws securely. She asked Shiloh to do it rather than try to make leading holes in what was already shattered bone. He finished the task in about half a minute.

"How is he?" Cheney asked.

"Respiration steady and strong, Doc. Pulse slowed but steady."

"Excellent," Cheney murmured, bending over to start the stitches on the incision in Castor's leg. "I'll sew. You set the arm."

"Right."

By four o'clock that afternoon Castor Mylonas was sleeping quietly in his bunk. His messmates gathered around him, looking down at him in awe.

"I have seen many a wonder in my life," Calvin Lott said, "but I've never before seen a female doctor slice open a leg, screw the bits of it back together, and sew it up like a right sailmaker."

"Dr. Cheney," Siggy grunted, "she's good."

The men nodded solemnly among themselves.

"Right good," Calvin Lott repeated. "I allus said she'd bring good luck on the barky. I allus did."

CHAPTER FOUR

An Island Paradise

"DO YOU SEE THAT white water breaking close to the cay?" Captain Starnes asked pointedly. "Those are coral reefs, Mr. Irons-Winslow, very tricky to negotiate. I think it would be much wiser if you'd let Mr. Cadell pilot and the gig crew row you and Mrs. Irons-Winslow in."

"And be stuck on that little island with seven sailors?" Shiloh said good-naturedly. "That's not exactly the kind of picnic I had in mind, Captain Starnes."

"They could return to the ship and come pick you up this evening," the captain argued.

"So you want to strand me and my wife on a deserted island with no boat?" Shiloh asked, his eyes sparkling. "Good way to get rid of meddlesome, landlubbing owners, I guess."

"Sir! I assure you I had no—" Captain Starnes spluttered.

"I know, I know, Captain Starnes," Shiloh said, suddenly embarrassed that he had teased the captain in such a manner. It was too close a reminder of the tragedy that had taken place in Hawaii—a blunder he knew Captain Starnes could never forgive himself for.

"I'm sorry, Captain," Shiloh went on. "I

didn't mean anything by that, but you see my point, I trust. I'd like to be *alone* with my wife, if I might."

Captain Starnes nodded. "Yes, I understand, but you must realize, too, that it's my responsibility to protect you." He stroked his gray beard thoughtfully. "I have it. We could send the launch *and* the gig, leave the gig with you, and bring the crew back in the launch."

Shiloh raised one eyebrow. "Send twenty men and two boats to drop us off on that island! Please, Captain, I assure you I can handle that gig by myself. I've used one before, in some pretty difficult circumstances. My wife and I will be all right."

Captain Starnes looked uncertain, but just then Cheney and a rather odd retinue came up from below and joined them on the quarterdeck. Cheney had insisted on checking on Castor Mylonas before she and Shiloh left the ship for the day. Behind her darted Fiona, holding a box of provisions for the beach, and Sketes, holding their picnic basket and another box stuffed with food. Both of them were talking, Fiona breathlessly and Sketes rather loudly. Following them were Castor's messmates—Calvin Lott, Willy Perkins, Siggy, and Billy-O—all looking mutinous.

"But, Miss Cheney, you might get sunburned," Fiona pleaded.

"And how, may I ask, are you two going to handle all this food by yourselves? And what about Mr. Irons-Winslow's gallons of water he needs every day? I'll just come along. You won't even know I'm there!" Sketes insisted.

"Dr. Cheney, no offense meant to Mr. Locke, but you need some right seamen to get you to that island," Calvin Lott said in serious tones. "What if there's reefs? What if you drift off course?"

"Mr. Lott, the island is right there," Cheney said, her eyes alight. "Even I could navigate to it. In fact, I don't see how we could keep from running into it."

"My point exactly, Dr. Cheney," Lott said stubbornly, crossing his hairy arms. The other sailors nodded somberly. "You might run aground on them reefs, knock a big hole in the gig, turn over, and drowned dead."

Cheney sighed. "Well, Shiloh. Do you think we'll ever get off this ship?"

"I'm beginning to wonder if we aren't being held prisoner," Shiloh retorted. Several other sailors had gathered around, their faces stiff with disapproval. Calvin Lott was still grumbling, Fiona and Sketes were talking together in accusing tones, and Captain Starnes and First Mate Nat Cadell were looking serious.

"All right, everyone, here's the deal," Shiloh announced. "I'm going to take the gig and row it all by myself to that island. I'm taking my wife with me. And she *is* my wife, remember, not the property of everyone on this ship. And I don't want to sight this barky until tonight. We'll be fine."

The captain finally relented at Shiloh's determined tone and nodded his consent. "Do as he says," Captain Starnes ordered.

Still looking defiant, the crew lowered the gig and fastened the rope steps to the side of the ship. Shiloh hurried down, grabbing the picnic basket and food box out of Skete's protesting grip. Cheney took the box of provisions from Fiona, handed it to Shiloh, and climbed down into the gig. Swiftly he cast off the pulleys and maneuvered the little boat away from the ship. When they were fifty feet away, Cheney turned around and saw that the deck was lined with sailors.

"Bunch of fretting old women," Shiloh grumbled. "They think I'm gonna 'drowned dead' their precious Dr. Cheney."

Cheney settled into her seat and raised her parasol. "Quite a different attitude toward me, I've noticed. It's rather touching."

Shiloh nodded. "Yeah, you're not the unnat'ral female doctor double-whammy of bad luck anymore. Since you fixed up Mylonas, they sorta think you're *Locke's Day Dream*'s personal saint, ship's doctor, and good-luck charm all rolled together. I'm surprised they didn't rub your head for luck before we left."

"And they seem to think that you are either your father come back from the dead, or the spirit and soul of the ship, or both," Cheney observed. "I heard Mr. Lott berating poor little Leith Redding for calling you 'Mr. Irons-Winslow.' It seems you must be addressed as 'Mr. Locke,' or else the ship—I mean the barky—will suffer some horrible fate that must remain unspoken."

"Yeah, I'm the great mariner, all right," Shiloh rasped. "Only they think I can't row this little toy boat all by myself. Like I'm some helpless pasty-faced lily-livered lubber."

"If only they knew." Cheney sighed. "I'll never, ever forget those terrible trips you made in that little dinghy from the *Brynn Annalea*, back and forth during the eruption in Hawaii, trying to get all of us back to the ship. Six crewmen couldn't have done better."

"Yeah? You really think so, Doc?" he asked, childlike.

"Of course I do, Shiloh," she answered gravely. "I've always thought that you are a brave and courageous man."

His eyes burned a brilliant blue, matching the exotic sea surrounding them. "Thanks, Doc. You just don't know how much it means to me to hear you say that. And now I'm gonna work real hard to slide right through these reefs, 'cause I'd sure feel silly if I drowned you dead now."

———————

The tiny cay was only about a mile long and half a mile wide, with blinding white beaches sloping down gently into the shallows. Right down the middle of the island was a skinny strip of volcanic soil, with palm trees and dune grasses growing thickly. They walked around the island, running in the gentle surf and gathering shells. When they returned to the gig, Cheney said, "Oh, I'm so hungry already! Are you ready to eat?"

"I could, but you're not supposed to eat before you swim," Shiloh replied. "You want to swim first and eat later? Or if you want, we could go ahead and eat and then nap a little."

"No, I want to swim," Cheney decided. "I think I'm going to love it. Would . . . would you excuse me? I'll just go . . . back there and . . . get ready."

Shiloh understood Cheney's modesty, but he couldn't resist teasing her. She was so pretty when she blushed. "I'll come, just in case someone sneaks up to try and see you." Surrounding them was an empty sea and sky.

"No, I don't—ooh, Shiloh! You're . . . you're incorrigible," Cheney said, stalking off to the privacy of the trees, where Shiloh had rigged up a canvas curtain for her to change behind.

"I am?" he called after her. "I thought I was impudent. See, I'm getting better already."

When Cheney returned, she was wearing her chemise, a loose-fitting cotton gown that reached her knees. "I feel so decadent," she said with some discomfort.

"I like it," Shiloh said, lifting one eyebrow. "A lot."

"Oh, come on, teach me how to swim," Cheney said, holding her hand out. He took it and they waded out. "I just hope I can do it."

"You can, Doc," he said confidently. "You can do anything you get into your head."

They waded out until the aquamarine water was up to Cheney's chest. "Okay, Doc, now you already know how to float. Remember? Just like in Hawaii, when we were swimming to the stream."

"*You* were swimming," Cheney stated glumly. "I was shrieking."

"You weren't. You never shriek. You just talk kinda loud sometimes. Anyway, here you go. I'm lifting you up. Just relax. . . ."

Shiloh put his hands under her knees and cradled her shoulders and lifted her up, laying her back. "Now remember? Take a deep breath . . . relax. . . ."

She felt him steady her for a few moments, and then his hands slowly moved away. "I'm floating!" she cried. "All by myself!"

"That's right. Did you know that women float better than men?"

"Why, no, I didn't," Cheney murmured, enjoying the warm cradle of the water. It was a sensation unlike any she'd ever felt before, and she thought she could float like this for hours. "Why is that?"

"I dunno, you're the doc," he teased, falling gently back to float beside her. She did notice that he had to flutter his hands and feet a little to keep them level, while her body effortlessly floated upright.

"Uh-huh," she said lazily. "And how is it that you know how well women float? How many women have you taught to swim? And were they all wearing only their chemises?"

"Aw, now, I just heard it or read it somewhere or something, or maybe someone told me—maybe Walker Baird. He tries to get everyone he meets to learn to swim—or maybe . . ." Shiloh spluttered a little, and his legs started sinking.

"You're right," Cheney mused. "I do float better than you. You're sinking fast."

"I noticed. Maybe we'd better move along to swimming," Shiloh grunted. "You ready?"

"I'm ready. What do I do?"

"Okay, I'm going to turn you over, and I'll hold you up." Easily he rolled her over onto her stomach, with his arms cradling her. "Don't tense up . . . just relax . . . I've got you. Get comfortable. That's it. Now I'm going to hold you, and you kick your feet."

Obediently Cheney kicked, and she could feel the additional buoyancy it gave her. "So I move my arms like this?" She took a stroke—powerful for a woman—and immediately glided out of Shiloh's arms into deeper water. Surprised, she took another stroke but lost her rhythm and dunked right under. Shiloh dove under and grabbed her, but Cheney sprang up by herself, laughing and shaking her head to clear her heavy hair from her face. "Oh! I swam! That was fun! Let's do it again!"

He pulled her back to where she could stand on the bottom again, and she struck out, churning up the water with her kicks and flailing her arms. She swam a few feet, with Shiloh right beside her, but soon ran out of breath. "Whew, this is very hard work," she gasped, righting herself and pushing her hair out of her eyes.

Gently Shiloh smoothed her hair away from her face. "Doc, you've already done more than most people do their first three times trying to learn to swim. Are you really tired?"

"No, I want to learn," Cheney said with a hint of impatience. "I can do this."

"Okay, then here's what you need to do," Shiloh said, resigned. He had known for a long time that his wife was particularly stubborn, and she never gave up. "You've got the movements down right, but the reason you're tiring so quickly is that you're fighting the water. What you gotta do is let the water work for you, help you. Take deep, even breaths."

"I've seen you and Walker keep your face down and turn your head to take a breath," Cheney said with concentration. "Can I do that?"

"Sure. Try it."

Cheney practiced her breathing until she felt comfortable.

"All right, now the only other thing is that you've got to make your movements smooth, and the way you do that is concentrate on using the right muscles," Shiloh instructed her. "See? It's these shoulder muscles you want to use to move your arms, not your wrists and forearms." He flexed his arms to show her how the shoulder muscles correctly pivoted the arms.

He stood there in the blinding sunlight, water droplets glistening on his tanned body, the sun gleaming on the smooth knotted muscles, and Cheney drew a deep breath and said softly, "Shiloh, I think you must be the most beautiful man I've ever seen in my life. Sometimes I can't believe how lucky I am, to have a husband that I love so much—and just for my enjoyment—who looks like a Greek god too."

His eyes widened and he swallowed hard. He tried to speak but couldn't. He stepped forward and swept her up into his arms and carried her to the beach, gently laying her underneath the palm trees, their fronds whispering in the warm Caribbean wind. Cheney quickly forgot the swimming lesson as Shiloh's gentle caresses enveloped her in his love—a love she returned with joy and abandon.

After falling asleep in the peaceful shade of the trees, they later awoke and finished the swimming lesson, splashing and playing in the sparkling waters until they were exhausted and famished. As they were drying off on the beach, Cheney, to her surprise and bemusement, noticed she was getting a tan instead of a sunburn. "It's scandalous," she said, gazing down at her coppery arms. "Oh, how I hope it fades before we go home and Dally sees me! And even worse, do I have freckles? Oh, Shiloh, please tell me I don't have freckles!"

His eyes crinkled with laughter. "Not a one, Doc. But you look like a Hawaiian with that suntan—a Hawaiian goddess!"

Blushing at his admiring gaze, Cheney pulled her towel about her and grabbed another of the thick, fluffy towels they had brought and began drying her hair. It was a hopeless mass of salty curls and tangles, so she decided to leave it down and let Fiona deal with it.

She settled back into his embrace, and in contented silence they watched the sun start its descent toward the western horizon. Looking up at her husband, Cheney thought that she could not possibly be any happier. She kissed him and said, "I just adored your surprise, Shiloh. Thank you so much for this perfect day."

"So you like swimming?" he asked. "'Cause you're really good at it, Doc. You learn quick."

"I love swimming," Cheney declared. "I'm going to swim every chance I get. But now we'd better get dressed and have something to eat." She disappeared behind the canvas curtain in the trees. It amused him greatly that she would still demonstrate such modesty with not a soul to see her other than her husband.

"You know, I've seen women swimming in Long Island Sound," she called out from her makeshift boudoir.

"Yeah?" he said with interest. "I didn't know ladies—real ladies, like you, I mean—ever went swimming."

"If you can call it that," she said, laughing. "They have those odd little bathhouses on big wheels, which you must hide in until they roll them out deep enough so you're hidden in the water. And still you must wear a knee-length bathing dress, a petticoat, thick stockings, and a mobcap. It must be as heavy as an afternoon costume—especially wet!" She stepped out from behind the curtain, demurely dressed, threw herself down on the blanket they had laid out on the sand, and hungrily bit into a rosy sugarplum from Nassau.

Shiloh frowned darkly. "I'm a liberal man and I want you to have all the fun you can have. But I'm telling you right now, mon petit chou, that you are not going to swim at Long Island in that little shimmy."

Cheney laughed and turned to him, her green eyes as bright as emeralds. "As if there's any danger of that! No, Shiloh, I'm not even tempted. But I must tell you that from now on you're going to have a hard time sailing by any little deserted islands with nice beaches. I know there are about ten thousand of them in the West Indies, and if we stop for me to go swimming at every one, we may be old and gray before we get back to New York."

"That'd be fine with me," he said, leaning back and closing his eyes. "I don't care where I grow old with you, Doc. I'm just glad that I will."

They ate until they were satiated, for Sketes had packed enough cold ham, cheese, fruit, and fresh-baked bread for the entire crew, it seemed. Then they lay back, staring up at the brilliant tropical sunset until the colors paled to gentle pastels and began deepening to cobalt blue. "Should be getting on back," Shiloh murmured.

Cheney turned so that her head was resting

on his flat stomach. "In a minute. It's so peaceful, so quiet."

"Mm-hm."

"Shiloh?"

"Hm?"

"I've changed my mind."

" 'Bout what, mon chou?"

"About my shipwreck kit," she said sleepily. "The three things I would take on a deserted island are you . . . you . . . forever you."

"Why, Mr. Locke, what can you be thinking of?"

Both Shiloh and Cheney awoke with a start. A circle of grim sailors holding lanterns stood all around them. Birr Dunstan, the boatswain of *Locke's Day Dream*, was a big stormy Irishman with thick black hair, flashing dark eyes, and a body like a granite column. He loomed over Shiloh accusingly.

"Huh? What . . . what time is it?" Shiloh asked, grimacing from the sand in his mouth.

"Why, it's near two bells in the first watch!" Dunstan growled. "Cap'n said you'd be back by sunset!"

"Went to sleep," Shiloh muttered, rasping his hand across his rough jaw.

"It's dark," Cheney said blankly, sitting up and looking around.

"It sure is, Dr. Cheney, and what's more, what about this here night air? Mr. Locke, what if Dr. Cheney should catch a chill?" Dunstan said accusingly. "You was supposed to be back by sunset!"

"I know, you told me, Dunstan," Shiloh growled, struggling to stand up. The sailor's righteous indignation had actually made him feel a little ashamed. "But we're all right, as you can see. You brought the longboat out?"

"That's right, sir, with the whole crew clamorin' to come and see about you," Dunstan said grimly. "Did you even bring a lantern in the gig? It's dark!"

"Sure I did," Shiloh blustered, stretching stiffly. "I'm not a complete idiot, you know."

Dunstan gave him a reproachful look. "What if there was sand fleas? What if there was pirates? What if there was sharks?"

"Land sharks?" Shiloh retorted, becoming amused at the situation. He turned and helped Cheney to her feet. "Your rescue party's here, Doc."

"So I see. Did you gentlemen bring out the big boat just to see about us?" Cheney asked, a smile pulling at the corners of her lips.

"Yes, ma'am, Dr. Cheney, and I think it'd be best if you—and Mr. Locke too—came back in the longboat with us," Birr Dunstan said sternly. "Lott and Perkins can bring back the gig." His tone brooked no nonsense.

"Okay," Shiloh said resignedly. "But I would've gotten us back to the ship, you know, Dunstan."

"Yes, sir," Dunstan said doubtfully. "But we'd all feel a lot better if you'd come back with us in the longboat. Just in case."

"I know, I know, in case of pirates and sand fleas," Shiloh sighed and offered his arm to Cheney. She took it and squeezed it as the men protectively surrounded them to escort them all of twenty feet to the boats.

"It was a perfect day, Shiloh," she whispered, "and as far as I'm concerned, we can be marooned together on a deserted island anytime you want."

CHAPTER FIVE

Skylarking

IN THE VELVET Caribbean midnight, *Locke's Day Dream* set full sail, lanterns blazing, and made for the Windward Passage. Shiloh stirred a little in his bunk as the ship raised her prow and began to ride the seas proudly like the thoroughbred she was. He was always in tune with the life of his ship, even when he was in the depths of restful sleep. He turned and threw his arm over Cheney, who moved closer to him and sighed contentedly. They slept on.

The next day was Friday, which meant, for the crew, sail drills. Captain Starnes was a stern disciplinarian, and even though he had a hand-picked, dedicated crew, he set rigid daily schedules. Particularly on an idyllic voyage like this, when the weather was so benevolent and the sailing so easy, it was important that the men keep busy. Sundays were reserved for the ship's inspection, a church service, and a free afternoon for the men; on Mondays they had sail drills; on Tuesday sail drills; on Wednesday small arms practice; Thursday was make, mend, and washing day; Fridays more sail drills; and Saturdays were for small arms practice. Today, immediately after swabbing the decks and polishing everything on the ship that was solid, the crew were shouting, running along the decks, hauling on lines, swarming up the ratlines, and reefing and making one sail after another.

Cheney and Shiloh, after breakfast and an impromptu Bible study that had begun with Shiloh asking Cheney about some interesting passages in Leviticus that dealt with medical principles, had gone to see about Castor Mylonas. *Locke's Day Dream* had no sickbay. When a crewman was ill or injured, the men set up bulkheads belowdecks to section off a cabin. Since they were carrying no cargo on this trip, belowdecks was relatively empty, and they had fashioned a fairly roomy cabin with Castor's sickbed and another bunk for a mate to stay with him. Luki Terrio, the cook's mate, was staying with him now, but he scuttled out when Cheney and Shiloh came in. Cheney had kept Mylonas heavily sedated for the last two days, but now he was conscious and alert.

"Dr. Cheney, my messmates told me that you not only saved my life but that you even saved my leg, even though Lott said it was busted all to pieces and scattered all over the quarterdeck," the pale young man said as soon as she came to his bunk. "Thank you."

"You're welcome," Cheney said briskly. "How do you feel?"

"Fine, thank you, ma'am."

Cheney gave Shiloh a wry look, and he shrugged. One reason Castor Mylonas was so popular on the ship was that he never complained, never grumbled. Shiloh had told her that one time the little cook's mate, Luki, a thirteen-year-old orphan, had accidentally spilled boiling soup on Castor's arm. Castor was kind to the boy, who was in tears, and made his messmates swear not to tell the grizzled old cook, Abel Penrod, who was known to cane the boy's backside when he made mistakes. Castor had slathered butter on his arm, had gone up to the foretop for his watch that afternoon, and had never said another word about it.

"No, Mr. Mylonas, I mean you must tell me *exactly* how you feel," Cheney said, picking up his wrist and timing his pulse. He grasped her hand lightly, and she smiled at him. He smiled back. He was Greek, and with his curly black hair and long, thick lashes and delicately sculpted face, he could almost have been called pretty. Shiloh had also told her—without going into detail—that Castor had had to prove to his rough mates that he was not just a pretty little boy; he was a grown man who could give as good as he got. Now, however, he did look like a young, delicate boy.

Cheney went on talking to him, coaxing him to tell her about his condition while she examined him. He did finally admit that he was in pain. "All right, Mr. Mylonas, I'm going to give you something for the pain and then we're going to check your splints and bandages," Cheney said calmly. "But I must tell you that I'm very pleased with your progress so far. Even though it's only been two days since your accident, you are already better than I could have hoped for."

"Good doctoring, ma'am," he said wanly. "Dr. Cheney, can I ask you a favor?"

"Of course."

"Do you think I could come up on deck for a little while? My mates could hoist me up. I . . . I love it when she's sailing fine to windward," he finished haltingly.

Cheney frowned. "I don't think it would be wise to move you right now, Mr. Mylonas."

His pale face fell. "All right, Dr. Cheney," he said in a low, tired voice.

Cheney watched him for a few moments, then took Shiloh aside. "What do you think?" she asked him.

Shiloh considered the young man. Finally he said thoughtfully, "I think, considering how young and strong he is, and that he's not feverish or vomiting or sick like when you don't want anyone to talk to you or touch you, he'd probably feel better if he could be up on deck."

Cheney nodded but said hesitantly, "But moving him so much, Shiloh. I know that the men would be as careful as if they were carrying a baby, but he'll be jostled. No one could help that."

Again Shiloh thought for a while, then suggested, "How about this? Down here it's quiet and solitary, but I really think that he'd be better off if he was closer to the . . . uh . . . heart of the ship. Why don't we ask him if he'd like to bunk up in the apprentices' quarters? There's only three apprentices this trip, and there are six bunks. We could fix up a sickbed. Then, instead of hoisting him up and down the hatches, he could just be moved a little back and forth from the deckhouse. It's noisy and busy up there, but I honestly think he'd be better off there than down here like he's on his deathbed or something."

Cheney stared up at him, her green eyes soft and warm. "You know what? You have such insight, and such empathy, with patients that I'm envious sometimes."

He took her hand and squeezed it. "Forget it, Doc. I'm flattered, but never forget that you're the healer. You always have been. I'm just a nurse. A good one, I guess, but still, there's a world of difference between my insight and empathy and your God-given gift for healing."

"You really . . . think that?" Cheney asked, her cheeks coloring a little.

"I know that," Shiloh assured her. "Now, how about we roust out those no-good messmates of his and get Mylonas out of this tomb?"

Once the sailors understood what was required, they went to work with a will, and again Cheney marveled at their quickness, cleverness, and efficiency. Castor's sickbed in the apprentices' quarters was rigged waist-high so that Cheney wouldn't have to stoop to examine him. Siggy figured out a way to attach handles onto a low, flat bulkhead, which served as the bed frame, with a light mattress set right on top. Then the sailors could just lift bulkhead, mattress, and Mylonas all at once to move him out underneath a small awning they'd rigged on the quarterdeck. Within half an hour Mylonas, seemingly a small, pale figure, dozed quietly beneath his scrap of awning, the wind ruffling his glossy curls.

Satisfied that her patient was not only comfortable, but that he did indeed seem to rest better in the noise and confusion of sail practice, Cheney retired to her own deck chair on the poop deck while Shiloh visited with Captain Starnes and the officers, observing the sail practice. It seemed to Cheney that the captain was working the crew very hard today. The first and second mates constantly roared orders and admonitions through their speaking trumpets. Then it occurred to Cheney that this was not just a mindless exercise to keep the men busy; Castor Mylonas's accident had happened because of some topmen inexperienced in the perilous business of reefing sail. That was exactly why clippers were often called "death ships"; the sails were so enormous, so complex, that accidents happened often. With a slight shudder, Cheney once again determined that the next time Shiloh decided to climb the rigging, she would stop him, even if she had to fall to the ground and hang on to his ankles.

Blithely unaware of his wife's dark reflections, Shiloh came up to the poop deck and threw himself down in his deck chair. "The captain's workin' 'em hard today," he said lightly. "Those boys that took a reef in the mainsail too quick are gonna be sick of canvas and gaskets before this day is over, I can tell you that."

Cheney glowered at him. "You are never to climb the rigging again, Shiloh. Never."

"Huh? But, Doc—"

"No! I—how am I supposed to feel, with you up there skylarking like an orangutan?"

He reached over and took her hand. She let him take it, but her fingers were tense. Absently he massaged them lightly. "Doc, I didn't fall. Castor Mylonas did. And I don't mess with the sails anymore. I wanted to see if I could do it, and I could, and I wanted to learn, and I did. Now I just climb up to the maintop—that thing there, just right up there, see? That big, roomy, safe platform. And what's an orangutan, anyway?"

"Don't change the subject," Cheney scowled.

"*You* said orangutan, not me," Shiloh remarked innocently.

"Shiloh, it scares me," Cheney said, dropping her head. Now she clasped his hand very tightly.

Quietly he said, "Look, Cheney, it's not just skylarking. It's . . . I love being up there. When you're up in the maintop, you can feel the ship, her . . . her heartbeat, her pulse. The wind sings, the rigging speaks, the sails seem almost alive. And you look at the horizon, so far away . . . but it's such a clear boundary of your world, so much clearer and secure than the boundaries you never see on land . . . and the sky, the enormous sky. It makes you feel small in one way, like a little speck, but in another it makes you feel like you're a part of the world, a significant part, because, really, you can see your whole world from that platform. You can see all of the sky, you can see all of the ocean, you can see all of your home just beneath you. It makes you feel . . . it makes me feel like I belong. Like it's my own special place God has given me to feel . . . secure."

She stared at him, spellbound. Shiloh rarely spoke so poetically, or so intimately. She realized that this quiet speech was difficult for him, partly because he had never had anyone to confide such heartfelt things in before, and partly because, even though they were man and wife, it was always hard to entrust such private things to any other human being. Softly she smiled at him. "That, my love, was pure poetry. I'm so glad you explained it to me. I had no idea you felt that way. Of course, you can go up into the maintop anytime you like, with my blessing."

He raised her hand to his lips, kissed it lightly, then released it and lay back, closing his eyes. "Thanks, Cheney. And I love you very much."

"I love you too, Shiloh. Today, tomorrow, forever."

"Here, you! Yeah, you, half-wit! You touch my paint work again and I'll fend you off with this here shark spear!" Calvin Lott shouted over the side, waving the deadly weapon. The big boatswain, Birr Dunstan, stood on the starboard side, a huge grappling hook in his hands and an ugly look on his swarthy, handsome face. He waved the hook menacingly in an effort to ward off the hordes of merchants who were descending on the ship. "Any o' you sods try to board, I'll knock you to Hispaniola!" Other sailors leaned over the railings, shouting and cursing at the swarms of boats surrounding *Locke's Day Dream* like horseflies torturing a nervous thoroughbred.

"What's going on?" Cheney asked, coming out of the cabin. She'd been getting dressed to go ashore. As soon as First Mate Nat Cadell saw her he raised his speaking trumpet to his mouth and roared, "Watch your language, you . . . you ruffians! And Dunstan, cut that line some . . . some . . . fool lassoed up into the backstays!"

Shiloh grinned down at her. "Kingston Bay, mon chou. Evidently the merchants aren't quite as genteel as they were in Nassau." From all around the ship Cheney could hear coarse voices yelling in English, Spanish, French, island patois, even German, calling out their wares and prices.

The more courageous ones tried to hook onto the side, calling for the men to drop them a line so they could send up samples. Cheney and Shiloh went down to the quarterdeck and leaned over, watching with amusement. All over the ship, sailors were shouting down at the cut-throats—almost unintelligibly, however, since they refused to use coarse language while Cheney was on deck. Some of them, so frustrated, just roared and growled.

The hull of *Locke's Day Dream* was painted a deep midnight blue and had a narrow curlicue trim of gold leaf. The crew worked all the time, painting and repainting the sides every time she sustained the least little scratch or wear, and they reverently polished the gold leaf each watch, as delicately and carefully as jewelers. They were not about to allow the yelling merchants to scrabble up her sides.

"It's not as if they could steal it," Cheney said, giggling.

A fruit vendor had looked up at the gleaming trim and craftily inquired, "That there's real gold, ain't it, mate?" and Lott had thrown a wet mop down on him, hard. Cadell roared, "That swab's coming out of your pay, Lott!"

"But, sir, them thievin' no-goods are just about to board and chew off the trim with their own rotten teeth, I swear!" Lott growled.

"You heard him," Shiloh shrugged. "If

there's a way to steal it, someone in Kingston is probably going to figure it out."

Captain Starnes joined them, his flashing dark eyes alight with amusement. "Sir, I'd like permission to take her back out to the mouth of the harbor while you're ashore. I'm not afraid we'll be boarded by any of these old pirates, but I *am* afraid that some of the men will have apoplexy over the trim work."

"Fine with me, Captain," Shiloh said. "And just for your own peace of mind, this time I think we'll take the gig *with* the crew."

"Very good, sir," Captain Starnes said with obvious relief. His former employer, Bain Winslow, had been a continual source of irritation and even grief to Captain Starnes, but this new owner's Wild West ways worried him even more, in a different way. Geoffrey Starnes was an educated, cultured man, but he was still a man of the sea, and somewhere deep in his mariner's heart he, too, believed that Locke Winslow's fate and well-being were inextricably entwined with that of *Locke's Day Dream*. The thought that some drunken ruffian might knock him on the head worried him extremely. And then, of course, Dr. Cheney was such good luck for the ship. . . . "Might I suggest, sir, that I give the gig crew shore leave to accompany you ashore as well?" he asked politely.

Shiloh gave him a shrewd sidelong glance.

"Think somebody's going to knock me on the head, do you? I assure you, Captain, I can take care of myself."

Starnes was startled at this echo of his thoughts, but he gave no sign. "Perhaps, sir. Port Royal and Kingston, I understand from Mr. Cadell, are very rough ports. Mr. Cadell tells me they're swarming with pickpockets and cut-throats. There'd be plenty who wouldn't think twice about accosting you, even in broad daylight." He glanced meaningfully at Cheney, who was still watching the rowdy show over the side and the distraught sailors with amusement.

Shiloh nodded thoughtfully. "You're right, Captain. All right, dress 'em up and trot 'em out."

Billy O'Shaugnessy, as coxswain, always piloted the ship's boats when Captain Starnes or the owners went ashore. In the navy, boat crews were strictly set, but the Winslows had always allowed any members of the crew who could "row dry" the honor of being the captain's or owners' shore crew, and Billy-O strictly rotated these men's privileges. Today Birr Dunstan, the third mate or boatswain, decided to go along, so Billy-O assigned three more men to the crew: David Upchurch, the ship's giant blacksmith and carpenter; Calvin Lott; and Auguste Bettencourt, the ship's master-at-arms. Cheney knew Billy-O, Dunstan, and Upchurch, but she had never spoken to Bettencourt except when they were introduced. He was a wiry, short Frenchman with thick, curly brown hair and heavy-lidded brown eyes. Cheney had noticed that he was fiery and high-spirited, dancing from one man to another and shrieking curses in French when the crew had small arms practice. Bettencourt had been almost hysterically happy when Shiloh had bought all new small arms for the ship—sixty brand-new navy Colt .44 revolvers. When Cheney was introduced to Bettencourt, he had been polishing revolvers and crooning over them. Twice she had noticed him practicing fencing with the second mate, an older man named Horatio Seaton.

The gig crew was rigged out in their shore-going attire, which consisted of spotless white duck breeches, white cotton shirts with wide collars and a navy blue neckerchief, and pea jackets with brass buttons. Cheney saw that the buttons on their jackets were monogrammed *LDD*. The Winslows always allowed enough canvas duck and cotton for the crew to make themselves two working outfits, and then provided each man with one outfit for going ashore. The crew was inordinately proud of their pea jackets in particular, for they were proud of their ship. Even Birr Dunstan, who was an officer, wore the same clothing, except that he wore a navy blue billed cap instead of the broad-brimmed sennit hats the seamen wore.

The reason Birr Dunstan wanted to come along soon became clear; as soon as the boat was lowered over the side, three small boats pounced. Dunstan, swearing under his breath, ran down the rope steps, picked up an oar, and pushed one of the merchants so hard he upended and went right over the side of his shabby little boat. "Any man jack of you touches this here gig," he roared, "will get that and worse!"

The boats backed off.

In their finery, the crew rowed Cheney and Shiloh to Port Royal, Jamaica.

"What's left of Port Royal, anyway," Shiloh was saying to Cheney. "Once it was called 'the wickedest city in Christendom.' Back when Henry Morgan was roaming the seas, plundering and raiding and pirating with the blessings of the British government, Port Royal was his base. Supposedly there were forty taverns in Port Royal, all doing a keen business."

"Forty taverns? On just this little spit of land?" Cheney asked, viewing the tiny peninsula jutting out from the mainland with disbelief.

"Unfortunately Port Royal's a lot smaller than it was in Morgan's time," Shiloh told her. "On June seventh, 1692, an earthquake dropped two-thirds of Port Royal right into the sea. Then a tidal wave blasted in. Sorta dampened their spirits, if you smoke my meaning."

Cheney rolled her eyes at the pun. "No wonder it looks so . . . jumbled. I guess about thirty or so of the legendary taverns must have washed away."

"Yeah, along with millions in pirate treasure," Shiloh said, leaning to stare down into the deep blue water over the side. "Y'know, I can hold my breath a really long time. Maybe I should just take a look around down there."

"I think not," Cheney said evenly.

"No, thought not," Shiloh sighed.

Billy-O glided up to a broken-down pier, which was faded to a dirty gray and tilted like a drunken sailor. When they tied up, Shiloh jumped out and helped Cheney, then the sailors swarmed out and immediately encircled them. After a quick look around at the sly-looking men and filthy sharp-eyed boys who hurried up to offer to look after the gig, Shiloh said in a low voice, "Billy-O, you better stay with the gig."

"Aye, sir," the coxswain said resignedly.

They started down the old cobblestone street. No lively open market here—only slovenly prostitutes, shabby, shifty-eyed men, and unkempt children. Most of the shanties lining the street had no signs. They were mostly wooden crates, some with doors, some not. Reeking garbage was piled on both sides of the narrow street. David Upchurch, Auguste Bettencourt,

Birr Dunstan, and Calvin Lott crowded so closely around Shiloh and Cheney that they could hardly see a thing. Finally Shiloh rasped, "Upchurch, even I can't see over or around you. And, Bettencourt, don't dance around in front of me like that. I'm gonna be walkin' up your heels if you don't give me some room. And, Dunstan, if you walk any closer to my wife, you'll be on the other side of her."

"Sorry, sir," Birr Dunstan said, clearly un-repentant. He swiped with his bosun's cane at a boy who made a face at them and muttered, "Hoity-toity, lookit the high hats!"

The sailors finally came to an understanding that they couldn't walk in front of Shiloh and Cheney. Dunstan and Bettencourt managed to stay on either side of them when the way wasn't too narrow, with Lott and Upchurch providing a grim rear guard. Though Calvin Lott kept tread-ing on the hem of Cheney's dress, she didn't really mind. Port Royal was, indeed, a grim place. She recalled the time when Bain Winslow had kidnapped her and locked her up in his New York brothel. Even then she hadn't felt nearly the same sense of lurking danger, of such vulnerabil-ity, as she felt in Port Royal.

The waterfront, however, was the worst area. Only one block over was a quieter, less grimy street with some small but clean cottages. Down the street was old St. Peter's Church, which had been built in 1725. Reportedly there was a silver communion plate there donated by Henry Morgan himself, and Cheney and Shiloh wanted to tour the church. But it was locked. "Can understand why," Shiloh muttered. "From the looks of this place, I'm surprised the stones are still here."

"Let's look at the graveyard," Cheney suggested. "Surely there will be old graves there. This place has a long history."

Many of the tombstones were so weathered it was impossible to read the inscriptions; some of them were tilted crazily, the graves sunken with the passing ages. They did see a number of small mossy headstones, many of which had only a name and year of death. "Mary May Lindsey," Cheney read sadly. "Seventeen-oh-one to seventeen-fifteen. She was only fourteen years old."

"Lots of children's graves here," Shiloh observed. "High mortality rates for children in the last century." He regarded Mary May Lindsey's marker thoughtfully. "You know what really gets me, Doc? I hadn't thought of it before, but at home, you know, the graves are new. The oldest is less than a hundred years old. It's odd to see this grave and think of this little girl. When she was alive, America was still just a vast wilderness, with only the Indians roaming around."

Cheney nodded. "We're a young country, very young. Something like this brings it home, doesn't it? And you're right, so many of our graves are new. Too many, and too new." Over half a million American men had died in the Civil War, only four years before. America was sown with new graves of young men.

Shiloh's look became faraway. He had fought in that terrible war. He had fought and killed men and watched friends die and he had bled. Nearby was a plot of ground that was obviously a grave, but it was overgrown with weeds. Shiloh walked over to it, then bent down and righted the marker. It was a roughhewn piece of stone, and if there had once been a name, it had been gone for a long time. Now it was black with fungus and covered with dull green moss. Still, he set it upright, digging around it with the heels of his old, worn cavalry boots and then tamping the dirt around the base. Then, slowly, he dragged his bootheel around the outline of the plot—twice. It touched Cheney, and she understood perfectly how he felt. For so long Shiloh had thought that he, too, might die and lie in some unmarked grave, unnoticed, for he had no family, no history. He would always feel an affinity for orphans, even long-dead nameless ones.

They wandered around the old churchyard a bit more, and Shiloh stopped in front of another headstone. This time he grinned back at Cheney. "Hey, come look at this, Doc. Lewis Goldy was swallowed up in the Great Earthquake of 1692 and spewed into the sea. He was rescued and lived another four decades. How about that? Only man I've ever heard of that died twice."

"Well, there was Lazarus," Cheney said, smiling.

"Huh? Oh yeah. He did, didn't he? Funny, you only think about the first time."

They went on back to the gig, walking quickly now. Shiloh and Cheney had seen enough of Port Royal. The sailors rowed them across the corner of the bay to Kingston. It wasn't nearly as grim and filthy as Port Royal, but neither was it as jolly as Nassau. Cheney noticed that though the port was every bit as busy as Nassau, the people weren't nearly as friendly. They hurried along, their shoulders pulled in tightly, their eyes downcast. No one smiled.

Taverns, inns, and shops lined the wharf, but most of them were dirty and dark. Still, Cheney and Shiloh and their tense guards made their way down the street. Once Cheney stopped to look at a stall that had a tall, imperious-looking black woman who was selling shawls, some of them skillfully embroidered with sun-bright colors. She was sullen, however, and Cheney decided against buying a shawl. The woman didn't seem to care.

They had almost passed a narrow, tall building with dusty barred windows when Cheney stopped and peered in. "Look, Shiloh. Those are fascinating!"

Displayed in the window was a green velvet-lined case with two handsome dueling pistols with silver fittings. The sun gleamed on the silver even through the filthy window. Impatiently Shiloh rubbed the window and bent to peer in. "Wanna go inside and take a look? Fool shoulda polished the windows while he was polishing the pistols. Can't hardly see them for this grime."

"Yes, let's," Cheney said enthusiastically. "I've never seen any like them, have you?"

"Sure haven't. All right, men, this place looks awful small and cluttered to bring in the whole regiment. I'll watch Dr. Cheney, okay? Trust me, I been watching out for her a lot longer than you mutts have."

The sailors obeyed, but they didn't look happy about it. Auguste Bettencourt hurried to catch a glimpse of the pistols before the owner took them away.

This fine establishment was Ricketts' Pawnshop, and Mr. Ricketts himself hurried forward, rubbing his hands together with delight, when Cheney and Shiloh came in, blinking in the semidarkness. "Welcome, welcome, sir, madam! Welcome to Ricketts' Pawnshop. I am Henry Ricketts, if I may make so bold, sir, madam." He spoke with a thick British accent and kept rubbing his hands together in an oily manner. He was small, with a sallow cast to his skin, one withered eye, and many missing teeth. He bowed rapidly, still rubbing. "What may I show you today, such a fine gent and lady, fine, fine, if I may be so bold?"

"We saw those dueling pistols in your window, Mr. Ricketts," Shiloh said. "May we see them?" Shiloh, though he watched Ricketts with a cool, discerning eye, was always polite.

"Such fine taste, such fine taste, sir, fine! One moment, one moment." He scurried, much like a rat, through the floor-to-ceiling clutter of pawned junk to retrieve the pistols. Hurrying back, he laid the pistol case reverently on top of a glass display case that held a jumble of cooking pots. He ran his fingers reverently along the barrel of one of the pistols. Cheney noticed that his hands were small and delicate and his fingernails were scrupulously clean. It seemed odd with his shabby appearance and crafty expression.

"These pistols are by Monsieur Nicholas Noel Boutet," he breathed. He pronounced it "mon-soor."

"Oh?" Shiloh said carelessly. "Frenchman, I take it." With a quick glance at Cheney's blank face, Shiloh said quickly, "Just a minute, Mr. Ricketts. I'd like for my man outside to take a look."

Shiloh stepped out the door and called, "Bettencourt? Could you give us a hand here?"

Auguste Bettencourt came in, and as soon as he caught sight of the gleaming pistols, he pounced, practically pushing Cheney aside as he bent over them. "Oh, such craftsmanship, such delicacy of line, such fine filigree. French, yes?"

"Froggee, yes." Ricketts sniffed and stopped rubbing his hands. Auguste Bettencourt did not impress him as having nearly as much money as Cheney and Shiloh. "They're by Boutet."

"*Non! C'est impossible!*" Bettencourt retorted and waved his hands. "Boutet! *L'arquebusier du roi!* The king's gunmaker. *Non, non.* Boutet's work is very rare."

"If you'd quit that fidgeting, mon-soor, I'll prove it to you," Ricketts said sourly. "And if you break something with that waving around, you'll pay."

"I can look at them for myself," Bettencourt grumbled. "I don't need you to show me a pistol by Boutet!" He picked up one of the pistols and looked closely at the silver filigree work. There were stars and oak leaves on the butt, and the base of the butt was covered with an etched silver medallion. Bettencourt held the pistol close to his face, squinting, and whistled low. "*Zut alors!* It's true! '*Boutet Directeur-Artiste. Manufacture de Versailles.*' This means he made these before 1816, when the Bourbons were restored to France."

"Really?" Cheney exclaimed. "But they look

brand-new! Even the velvet in the case doesn't seem aged."

"You like them, don't you?" Shiloh asked.

"I do," Cheney admitted. "They're so ornate, so elaborate. Absolutely beautiful work. But, Shiloh, I want to buy them. I saw them, I'll buy."

"Oh, no, mon chou," Shiloh argued. "I'll buy all of your guns. Just call it a man thing. I'd prefer to supervise your weaponry."

"Oh, you . . . you man. All right. How about if we go dibs? Right down the middle?" Cheney smiled, her eyes dancing with devilish green lights. "One gun for me, one gun for you. It's so romantic."

"Ain't it?" Shiloh grinned.

Ricketts quickly sidled up to Cheney. "Oh yes, madam, you have an eye, a fine eye, fine, fine. I do love these pistols dearly. I've had them for years, for I couldn't bear to let them go. But you are such a fine, lovely lady that I'll let you have them for only eighty pound."

"Eighty pounds!" Bettencourt screeched. It was about two hundred American dollars, a small fortune. "You little thief! *Non, non*, Monsieur Locke, these are only worth maybe twenty pounds. *C'est ça!* A scratch, right here! And this loading rod is filthy, with dirty oil! Non, non, twenty pounds only!"

"Twenty pound!" Ricketts shrieked. "I'd as

soon give my right leg than let my Boutets go for twenty pound, and—"

"That can be arranged," Bettencourt said haughtily, with a quick, graceful wave of his hand.

"There ain't no scratch on my Boutets!" Ricketts finished triumphantly.

Bettencourt went into a Gallic frenzy, his smooth cheeks flaming. Speaking very quickly, so that poor old Ricketts could hardly get a single insult edged in, he insulted the shopkeeper with every imprecation he could think of, slipping into French for some very heated terms, some of which Cheney had heard of, some of which she had not. Auguste Bettencourt obviously didn't know that Cheney spoke French, and Cheney carefully kept her face motionless, knowing that Shiloh would probably pluck the little Frenchman up by the ears if he knew the language he was using. As it was, Shiloh was very amused at the sight of the trim, elegant Frenchman and the little shopkeeper shouting at each other. It looked like a London wharf rat scrapping with a French bantam rooster.

Finally Bettencourt, still grumbling in French, agreed to take the pistols for forty-five pounds, about one-hundred-twelve dollars. As Cheney and Shiloh extricated themselves from Ricketts's oily hand-rubbing good-byes, Bettencourt whispered to Shiloh, "Any Frenchman would know this treasure and would have paid two hundred pounds for a Boutet. But that Ricketts, non! He knows nothing about Boutet! Pah! Englishmen, fools!"

"Bettencourt, you idiot," Calvin Lott muttered. "You're talkin' about Mr. Locke here too! You know, Mr. Rory's son, him what was in His Majesty's Royal Navy? His Majesty of England?"

"Oh, monsieur, please forgive me, non, non, I meant other Englishmen, like Ricketts, not like you, Monsieur Locke!" Bettencourt said, his cheeks flaming again. "*Alors!* I am desolated!"

"Nah, don't be desolated," Shiloh said good-naturedly. "Anyway, I forgive you, Bettencourt, 'cause you did such a good job in getting a good price for the pistols."

"*Mais oui*, I did," Bettencourt said with satisfaction.

"Yes, you did, Mr. Bettencourt," Cheney agreed. "And to show our gratitude, we would like to invite you to shoot the pistols anytime you'd like. Perhaps this evening, on the forecastle?"

Bettencourt, though still walking along, managed a very graceful bow. "*Merci*, Dr. Cheney. I am honored, honored."

"You won't be, Bettencourt," Shiloh warned, "when she outshoots you."

CHAPTER SIX

Friendly Duels

"AND I SAY THAT it's right nice, right fine of them to be buying fresh grouper not just for themselves and the officers, as is on most ships—you better know that not many owners, high-hatting it around like they do, put themselves out for the crew."

Sketes took a deep breath so that she could go on, but the ship's cook, Abel Penrod, took advantage of the break to grunt at Luki, "Boy, if you don't be hustling along to get me some more wood in this here stove I'm going to take you to the woodshed." Penrod was sixty years old, bow-legged, another old-style sailor with his coarse gray hair grown into a long pigtail and wearing an earring. Little Luki, his mate, scurried out of the galley.

It was a small room to begin with, and the bulk of the giant range and oven made only a narrow dogleg passage for the cooks. With Sketes, Abel Penrod, the captain's steward Tong Ten, and Luki Terrio all cooking at the same time, talking, and jostling and reaching around each other, it was indeed bedlam. The room was lined with open shelves holding the pots and pans, with a single scrubbed board mounted along two walls that served as a worktable.

Sketes was chopping red-hot bird peppers and limes to make pepper-sour sauce, a delicacy she had learned to make by interrogating a shopkeeper in Jamaica. It was wild tasting, with the kick of the peppers and the dash of the limes, but both Cheney and Shiloh liked it. Garrulously she continued, as she was wont to do even if Penrod and Tong Ten didn't listen to her. "But then Mr. Locke and Dr. Cheney, as far as I can tell, aren't ones to be a-snubbin' here and a-snootin' there, my sister says that Mr. Locke—that is, she calls him Mr. Irons-Winslow, as landsmen do—is a very kind gentleman always, to everyone, and she knew him when he was, as you may say, sowin' his wild oats, as young gentlemen will do until they find them a good woman to settle them down, like—Oh! Mr. Locke! You're up already!"

Shiloh stepped inside, stooping, of course, as the galley ceiling was only six feet high. He was wearing his usual dress, a pair of much-washed faded denims and a plain white shirt. "Surprised you, did I, Sketes?" he asked mischievously.

"Why, no, sir. I mean yes, sir," Sketes said, a little flustered. "Never mind, coffee's on, Mr. Locke."

While Sketes filled his covered mug with the thick black coffee, Shiloh wheedled, "You wouldn't have any papaya muffins left, would

113

you, Sketes? C'mon, I bet you stashed one or two of them for me, didn't you?"

Her lips pursed disapprovingly, but she plundered around in her box of supplies and came out with two muffins wrapped in a linen napkin. "There was one or two left that weren't as pretty as the others. I thought I'd throw them to the fish."

Shiloh snatched at the muffins. "Don't you dare throw your famous papaya muffins to the fish, Sketes! I'll take care of all the leftovers. Mmm, they're good, even cold."

"Thank you, Mr. Locke," Sketes said, pleased.

"Welcome."

Shiloh went on deck to lean on the rail and watch the sun rise, enjoying the coffee and nibbling the rich muffins. They had been at sea for more than two weeks now, and he and Cheney had fallen into a rhythm. Shiloh awoke just before dawn, and Sketes always had his coffee ready for him—hot and strong. Generally, as today, he filched something from the galley—yesterday's bread, butter-grilled, or leftover muffins, or a piece of fresh fruit—and climbed to the maintop to drink his coffee and snack and watch the sun come up. Later when Cheney began to stir, Sketes would have their hot breakfast ready, and he would take it to her in the cabin just as she awoke.

Dawn was his favorite time of day. A small brilliant fingernail of crimson showed on the eastern horizon, so hurriedly, Shiloh swarmed up the ratlines—the ladderlike expanses of rope that were for climbing—to the maintop. The faithful trade winds blew, ruffling his golden hair. He looked down at his world, recalling how he had been able to confide in Cheney the way he felt about his times, solitary in the small hours, in the maintop. He was so glad she'd been understanding. Shiloh reflected that he wasn't so sure *he* would be if Cheney wanted to climb up to the maintop. The thought gave him a little frisson of dread, as well as an insight into his wife and his marriage. *It's like people talk about all the time— marriage is a partnership, and in a partnership sometimes you have to give up things you want so the other partner can have the things they want. Compromising, learning to give and learning to take, accommodating your partner. Wonder if it'll be hard for me and Cheney. We've both been so independent. . . .*

Shiloh grinned a little as he thought of their first meeting—at least, their first formal introduction. He had already rescued her from two muggers—or worse—chased her, bled all over her, and then had to carry her home when she collapsed from shock and strain. But she'd certainly recovered her spirits the next morning when they actually "met." She had been expect-

115

ing the usual female nurse, and when he had showed up, all six-foot-four of him, she had been outraged.

He wondered how they had ever gotten past that first shock in their relationship. They had learned to tolerate each other, and then had become loyal business partners. Then fast friendship had come, and finally, deep and abiding love. Shiloh knew that next to finding God, his love for Cheney was the finest and most precious thing that would ever enter his life. He had known men who married more than once, but as he sat in this peaceful place, his eyes half shut against the brilliance of the risen sun, he knew that if he lost Cheney he would walk alone for the rest of his time on earth.

After a while he roused and reflected that Cheney would be waking up soon. Nonchalantly he slid down a backstay like a true seaman instead of climbing down the shrouds. The seamen who were on watch exchanged grins and approving winks, but Shiloh pretended not to see. He hurried to the galley, and Sketes, whose sense of Cheney's waking-up times was almost as honed as Shiloh's, had the tray ready. Shiloh took it to the cabin just as Cheney was getting out of bed and pulling on her morning gown, yawning hugely.

They sat down to an enormous breakfast of fresh eggs scrambled with sharp cheddar cheese, sourdough biscuits, chops, and papaya and mango compote. Shiloh handed her the *Boston Medical and Surgical Journal* while he studied Matthew Maury's *The Physical Geography of the Sea.* Cheney read for a while, then looked at his book curiously. "Is that a map of the West Indies?"

"Sure is, mon chou."

"Where are we?"

Shiloh pointed. "Our tide out of Kingston Bay was at about four A.M., so we're creeping along about here. The Caribbean is so calm it looks like glass. It's not much like blue-water sailing, that's for sure."

Cheney eyed him shrewdly. "That's true. There's hardly a ripple or ruffle. You say we're about here? And we're going to just dawdle across the Caribbean to Guadeloupe—here?"

"That's the plan."

"Hm. You know, I'd really like to see Grenada," she said nonchalantly.

"You would?"

"Oh yes. It's called the 'Spice Island of the West.' Doesn't that sound lovely and exotic? But I would also like to see a bit of this chain of islands rather than just dilly-dallying across the Caribbean. Do you suppose we could just sort of turn up into that little hole right there and go back out to sea and sail south to Grenada?"

Shiloh's eyes lit up. "That's the Mona

Passage, mon chou, not a little hole. Yeah, we could do that, if you want. You sure?"

Cheney nodded.

"Great!" Shiloh jumped out of his chair and headed for the door, clutching his book, but he turned around and said, "Sorry, Doc, would you excuse me?"

"Of course," Cheney said with amusement, and he hurried out.

Cheney looked after him with love welling up in her heart for the man she had married. She thought fondly, *He's like a small boy sometimes. . . . He does so love his ship and blue-water sailing. I'm so glad I thought of sailing back out to sea to Grenada. . . . I know he'd so much rather be flying along at ten knots on the open sea instead of crawling around on "The Spanish Lake." It's funny, Lord; it gives me such pleasure to give him things, to make sure he gets what he wants. I couldn't care less if we go to Grenada or Guadeloupe, as long as he's happy.*

Lord, please show me how to keep him happy always!

Cheney and Shiloh spent a leisurely day sitting on the poop deck under the awning. It was Tuesday, which meant sail drills, which also meant an inordinate amount of noise: gruff orders from blaring speaking trumpets, men running about and stamping, shouts and catcalls to the slowest crews. Somehow, however, for Cheney, the clangor was like a percussion section of the ship's orchestra—the deep creaks of the rigging, the crisp snaps of the sails, the soft hiss of the cutwater along the sides of the ship as it joyously sped along at eleven knots. Cheney slept off and on and saw with satisfaction that her patient, Castor Mylonas, had some color in his cheeks and was also lulled and dozing.

Shiloh was reading the Bible, and Cheney saw with amusement that he was studying Acts twenty-seven—the account of Paul's journey by ship from Caesarea to Rome. Shiloh was fascinated by this story.

"What are you reading?" Cheney asked politely.

"Acts twenty-seven again," Shiloh admitted sheepishly. "This story really interests me. I just wish I knew where all these places are. They aren't still named this, are they? Sidon, Cnidus, Pamphylia . . ."

Cheney frowned. She had, of course, read Acts many times, but she had never thought much about the geography. "I don't know. But your Bible has maps, doesn't it? Maybe of Paul's journeys?"

"Nope, I already checked."

"I think mine does. Here, I'll look. So nice to

have a shipwr—I mean, this deck kit," Cheney corrected herself hastily.

"Yeah, watch it," Shiloh said drily. "Naming calls. Did you know that when church is rigged, they never read this part of the Bible out loud? The description of the—er—mishap with Paul's ship is just a little too vivid, Captain Starnes said."

"It's funny, the way the crew is so devout about having a church service on Sundays," Cheney observed as she thumbed through the maps in her well-worn Bible. "Most of them don't appear to be dedicated Christians, but they are very reverent during the services. And I must say that Captain Starnes, though he doesn't actually preach, reads Scripture beautifully, with such heart. It's as uplifting as a sermon, in my opinion."

"He's a Christian now," Shiloh told her. "He wasn't, until after his wife died. He told me that he had real doubts about becoming a Christian, because he knew he couldn't carry on with Bain's little business enterprises. You know . . ."

Cheney nodded. Bain Winslow had, from time to time, bought girls in the Orient and brought them back to San Francisco for prostitution. He had also established a brothel in Manhattan, bringing in "island princesses" from Hispaniola. "But what did he do when Bain came down here and got his island princesses?" Cheney asked curiously.

Shiloh grinned. "The Lord works in mysterious ways. When *Locke's Day Dream* arrived in New York from Hawaii, she needed a complete refit. Bain put her in the yard to replace the copper bottom and flush and scour out the hold. Then he ordered some ironwork to strengthen the hanging knees. So when Bain got ready to go to Hispaniola to get his girls, *Locke's Day Dream* was dry-docked. Bain and Sweet evidently just took a passenger steamer, got his six island princesses, and paid their way back. Captain Starnes never had to face up to Bain about it, so he didn't lose his job. I'm ever so glad that he wasn't fired and had to go to another ship."

"That *is* good," Cheney agreed. "Sometimes things look so bad for us, but the Lord is faithful to provide. Captain Starnes was afraid that his becoming a Christian would cause him to lose his job—or as I can see how he feels about this ship, it would even mean losing the love of his life, at the worst time, after the loss of his wife. It must have been hard for him to come to the Lord and put his fate in God's hands."

"Yeah, must have been," Shiloh murmured. "I guess that's a good example of what that verse means—what is it? About if you lose your life, you gain it? What is that verse, Doc?"

"Mmm . . . in the Gospels . . . let me see. . . ."

Cheney and Shiloh searched through the Gospels, finding similar Scriptures in all four. Shiloh said, "I think I like this one in Matthew best: 'He that findeth his life shall lose it: and he that loseth his life for my sake shall find it.' That's exactly what happened to me. I found my life—my family, my past, some prosperity—and most important of all, I found my love for you. And then I lost it. I lost everything that night, even almost my life. But when I asked Jesus to save me and to be the Lord of my life and my heart, He gave me back all my life, so much better than before."

They talked about these Scriptures for a while and then went back to the apostle Paul's "mishap." Cheney's Bible had no maps of his journey, so she and Shiloh, like a couple of rowdy schoolchildren, went to Captain Starnes, who was supervising the sail drills, interrupted him, and insisted that he find them the ship's charts of the Mediterranean. Captain Starnes was always patient and cordial, but he clearly wanted to get back to the working crews, so Shiloh asked if they could study the charts in his day cabin. But as Shiloh and Cheney spread out the charts and began talking about Mediterranean ports, trying to make sense of the biblical journey, Captain Starnes got interested too and found himself getting out some of his antique navigational and sailing books to try to reconcile the ancient cities with the new. The three of them pored over the charts and old crumbling maps, finally tracing Paul's dangerous journey. When they had finished they were surprised to see they had been studying all afternoon, and it was already evening. Cheney and Shiloh had dinner with Captain Starnes and his officers. It was satisfying for Cheney, for by now the captain and officers had come to a very cordial relationship with her, instead of their previous air of strict formality.

The next day was Wednesday, which was small arms practice. The men formed themselves into groups of four, and four bottles were hung from a special rigging that the boatswain, Birr Dunstan, had concocted. Each man got six shots at the weaving, bobbing bottles. Then hay-stuffed man-shaped dummies got massacred over and over again. Cheney was always amused at the dummies. The high-spirited men dressed them up in old clothes, made straw hats for them, and even painted horrible faces on them.

Cheney asked, "You know, I've been wondering why the men even have small arms practice. Surely there aren't still wild buccaneers riding the seas, flying the Jolly Roger, and murdering and pillaging trade ships?"

"Nah, that day's long gone," Shiloh

answered, and Cheney thought with amusement that he sounded a little regretful. "Mostly I just have the men do small arms practice because they enjoy it so much. Crewing a clipper is tough, dangerous work. They deserve to have some fun."

"They do," Cheney agreed. "And they do have fun, don't they? Banging away and all the yelling and smoke. Boys and their toys."

Shiloh grinned down at her. "And ain't it just a lovely smell?"

She giggled, then sobered and stared up at him thoughtfully. "But . . . honestly, Shiloh, it doesn't remind you of the war? Especially the smell, I mean. Scent is so evocative."

He shook his head. "Nah, not the smell of the powder. In the war . . . it was the odor of blood and death, heavy and sickening, that got you. Nothing stinks like that, and I hope I never smell it again."

"You're a medical attendant. The smell of blood and death surrounds us sometimes," Cheney said in a low voice.

"It's not the same as in wartime . . . it's never the same," Shiloh said quietly. "Thank the Lord."

Cheney was curious, but she didn't push him. Sometimes Shiloh spoke about the war. When they were in Charleston, and Cheney had met General Nathan Bedford Forrest, Shiloh had talked about his memories quite a bit, reminiscing with the general and his half brother Shadrach. But though Shiloh always answered any questions Cheney asked him, she sensed his reluctance to talk of that terrible time. Her father, who had been a colonel on General U. S. Grant's staff, had the same gentle reticence.

"Anyway, there are still some pirates in the Orient," Shiloh said, rousing a little. "The Java Sea, the Banda, the Celebes. In those seas you have to creep along no more than a knot or two, taking continuous soundings, because Micronesia and Melanesia are thousands of miles of tiny little islands and narrow straits and uncharted cays and rocks and reefs. So they have these little boats—called proas—painted black, with crews of maybe twenty or so. The craft are small and fast, and they can hide behind any rock and dart out and board you just like that, in the dark. And the men paint themselves black and have knives in their teeth, and they just swarm up the side. The first four men aboard don't attack. They run right to the ship's lanterns and put them out. Then the fighters go to work in twos. One engages you in front while the other sneaks up behind and hamstrings you or grabs you by the hair and cuts your throat or stabs you in the back."

Cheney shuddered. "Good heavens, that's even worse than Caribbean buccaneers."

"That's the truth. And Captain Starnes tells me that those Oriental pirates' lives come really cheap. He said the first four men—the ones who head for the ship's lights—almost always get killed, because they're not supposed to stop and fight. Their job is to put the lights out. But still, they board first and head right into it. And they're always outnumbered and usually have heavy losses. But still they do it. So anyway, my men do need to have weapons and training for the Orient runs."

"They certainly do," Cheney agreed heartily. "I had no idea. And since I'm sure that one day you're going to drag me to Micronesia or Borneo or someplace like that, I think I'll go practice myself. Just in case, you know."

He turned to her, watching her sparkling eyes with pleasure. "Would you really go to Borneo with me?"

"Right now?"

"No. Someday."

"Any day," Cheney said softly. "Anywhere."

They joined the crew, who were now enthusiastically shooting away at the dummies. Master-at-arms Auguste Bettencourt was usually frenzied during small arms practice, rushing from one man to the other, calling them horrible Gallic names. Now polishing the new pistols, he hurried to Cheney and Shiloh. "Pah! These louts, they could not hit the sky!" he grunted.

"Dr. Cheney, Monsieur Locke, may I get your pistols and we will show these *imbéciles* how to shoot a pistol for to hit something!"

They practiced for a long while, for Cheney secretly enjoyed shooting at the dummies. She had always used bottles and cans for target practice. Shiloh had taught her how to shoot, and she was good. Now she reflected with satisfaction that, though she never planned to actually shoot anyone, if for some reason—such as scary pirates in Borneo—she had to shoot a human being, she could easily hit an arm or a leg and not any vitals.

"These pistols are pretty," Shiloh grumbled, "but they're not nearly as accurate as our forty-fours."

"I'm no firearms expert—like Monsieur Bettencourt—" Cheney said with a mock bow to the master-at-arms, "but that's sort of the point of dueling pistols, isn't it? I mean, they are designed for one gentlemanly shot at ten paces. Not for blasting away for hours at straw dummies. Our accuracy rate does seem to decline with each shot."

"So true, so true," Bettencourt said, taking Cheney's powder-smudged pistol with the motion of a mother taking back a delicate infant from a stevedore. "These are *objets d'art*, madame, not clubs. One shot, one death."

Shiloh shrugged and also handed his pistol to

Bettencourt, who practically snatched it out of his hand and laid it in the case, almost crooning. The pistols were too ornate, too pretty for Shiloh to truly appreciate. The clean, smooth, plain lines of the American gunsmith Joseph Manton were much more to his taste. Still, Cheney seemed to like playing with the pistols, so he practiced with her. And he had to admit that they were lovely in a dangerous, deadly way. Bettencourt cleaned them obsessively after Cheney and Shiloh shot them, and he polished the silver trim and fittings so assiduously that they glittered more than Cheney's jewelry.

"Monsieur Bettencourt, are you and Mr. Seaton going to practice fencing today?" Cheney asked.

"Oui, madame, always on Wednesdays I give Mr. Seaton his lesson."

"Good," Cheney said with satisfaction. "I find the sport truly fascinating. I have read of fencing and seen drawings of the various . . . um . . . does one call them poses? Exercises?"

"Positions," Bettencourt said eagerly, his eyes alight.

"Positions," Cheney repeated with relish, "but I had never seen a match until I had the opportunity to observe you and Mr. Seaton."

"These are not matches, *vous comprenez*, for Mr. Seaton is only a beginner," Bettencourt said sadly. "The true fencing match is a dance, as light as the air, as fast as the wind. *Mon grand-père* was a fencing master, with his own *salle d'armes*. He was *un bon artiste.*"

"Ah. And are you, too, a fencing master?" Cheney asked with interest.

"Non, non, Dr. Cheney," Bettencourt said sadly. "To become the true master takes years and years of dedication, of practice, of fencing with opponents who are more skilled than are you. Most of the salles are gone now, and one cannot find the opponent, worthy or not."

"I see. It's a shame. Not that duels are out of fashion," Cheney added hastily, "but that the art of fencing is no longer taught. It seems to me to be such a meaningful endeavor, such satisfactory exercise, and it teaches you grace and agility and concentration, does it not?"

"Oui, oui, madame, you have it," Bettencourt cried. "Dr. Cheney—I don't want to be presumptuous—but would you like to learn to fence?"

Cheney's eyes shone. "Oh, do you think I could?"

"*Certainement!* You have the head—*je m'excuse*, the brain—and the understanding already!" Bettencourt said excitedly. "It would be a privilege and an honor to teach you!"

Cheney turned to Shiloh, who was watching and listening with his arms folded, his eyes alight with amusement. "What do you think, Shiloh?"

He shrugged. "I think you're gonna do exactly what you wanna do, just like always, Doc. And I say go for it, if that's what you want."

"Ah, merci, merci, Monsieur Locke," Bettencourt said, grabbing Shiloh's hand and shaking it wildly, as if Shiloh had given him an extraordinary gift.

And maybe I have, Shiloh thought with understanding. *Everyone likes to share their passions, and the doc's so interested in everything, so eager to learn. My guess is that not many husbands would trust their wives with that fiery Frenchman. But he behaves himself with Cheney, just like all of 'em do. And I got no doubt she'll be good at it, just like she is at whatever else gets into her head. It'll be fun for her. Little enough I can do for her. . . .*

Cheney and Bettencourt went below, chattering together in French. Soon they returned, with the hapless Mr. Seaton in tow and two sailors carrying the gear. Horatio Seaton was rather old for a second mate—thirty-eight—and he looked even older, for he was portly, with sad dark eyes, and was bald on top with a salt-and-pepper fringe. Cheney had never heard his history, but she had observed that he seemed well educated, even cultured, and she suspected that at some time he might have been a schoolteacher. She also suspected that he was a heavy drinker, by his sallow complexion and the red veins on his nose and face. Still, he treated her with old-world courtliness and the men accepted him, though Cheney had once heard some of them call him "the schoolmarm" behind his back.

"Non, non," Bettencourt was saying to Cheney. "You will not fence without a mask, madame. In my salle no one even picks up the foil without a mask."

"But these swords have the little knobs on the tip," Cheney argued. "And the sides aren't sharpened."

"*Zut alors!*" Bettencourt said, outraged. "*Voilà!* This is *le fleuret*—the foil! This is *le bouton*—the button!" He twanged the fine, thin blade. "The foil, madame! Not the big fat sword *des imbéciles!*"

"All right," Cheney said begrudgingly. "But please tell me, Monsieur Bettencourt, if I cannot pick up the foil without a mask, and if I have no mask, and nowhere to get one, how am I to have a fencing lesson?"

He sniffed. "I will lend you my mask, madame, while you and Monsieur Seaton go through the positions."

"So you will go without a mask?" Cheney asked mischievously. "And will you, monsieur, touch the foil?"

"I must," he said grandly. "I am the teacher."

"I see," Cheney relented. Truth to tell, she had no desire to work with a foil without the wire-mesh mask. The slender blade may not have a sharp point, but the merest brush with the button—the small round of metal fashioned onto the tips of all fencing foils—could easily put an eye out.

She put on the mask, and Shiloh tied the fastening ribbons behind her head. He leaned down and whispered in her ear, "Knock 'em dead, Doc. You always do."

Grinning, she picked up the foil and did exactly what everyone longs to do the first time they pick up such a fine, sleek weapon: she swished it through the air in a quick figure eight, relishing the high-pitched whipping hum of the weapon. Auguste Bettencourt smiled. He had seen every student do that, and he admitted to himself that he still did it at times. The sound was just so satisfying.

Cheney first learned the salute, that ancient grand gesture of acknowledging respect for one's opponent. Then she and Mr. Seaton, in unison, practiced the *en garde* position. Setting up one of the target dummies—all of the men had finished their small arms practice by now and were gathered around to watch and call encouragement to Dr. Cheney—Bettencourt showed her the four sections of target area and the corresponding parries.

Cheney worked hard, imagining that the dummy—who had a tar-painted snaggletooth grin, a worn mop for hair, and fourteen bullet holes with sand trickling out in streams—had a sword and was threatening her four target areas. Crisply she made the tight parries, muttering under her breath, "Parry of sixte, parry of quarte, parry of octave, parry of septime."

"Excellent, madame!" Bettencourt praised her warmly. "You got them all the first time! And already, the grace, the finesse—"

"She's married, Bettencourt," Shiloh drawled from his perch on the boathouse. "Don't forget."

"I am desolated," Bettencourt said, his heavy-lidded eyes dancing, "but non, Monsieur Locke, I can't forget." He turned back to Cheney, who was wiping the sweat from her neck with a perfumed handkerchief. It was a hot day, and she was standing in the afternoon sun. "Dr. Cheney, this was a most successful first lesson. You have already—"

"But I'm not tired!" Cheney protested. "I want to learn more. Can't we go on? Or . . . of course. It's time for Mr. Seaton's lesson, so you must have your mask back. But please, couldn't I just learn the lunge? Mr. Seaton and I could practice that together."

"Oh, dear, I can only do two lunges," the second mate groaned. "I'm not as young as I once was, madame. Mostly I just stand still and let Mr. Bettencourt dance around while I try to parry one out of four hits. But I will lunge with you—until I fall down and am unable to get up, that is—and then I shall content myself with dueling with the dummy. I should be able to parry him, at any rate."

"Lunges," Bettencourt said doubtfully, staring at Cheney's skirt. It wasn't tight, but it would restrict the movement of the formal lunge, where a fencer thrusts all his weight forward on his right foot with the left leg extended straight behind.

"I can do it," Cheney said firmly. "Just show me how."

She could do it, but she first trod on her petticoat and then split the hem of her skirt about six inches. "Blue skies, this is annoying," Cheney said with irritation. "Why women must swaddle themselves in layers and layers of bulky, hot, uncomfortable . . . er . . . at any rate, Monsieur Bettencourt, please continue. Fiona can mend this . . . this straitjacket."

"If you're sure, madame. So the lunge— good—now back to en garde—oui, oui—and lunge—foil up, foil up!—en garde—"

Cheney practiced until her legs were trembling with fatigue and her arms felt as if someone had pummeled them. She retired to her cabin, with congratulations from Auguste Bettencourt and the crew, and soothed her tired muscles with a relaxing bath of lilac-scented water Fiona had readied for her. Cheney could barely stay awake through dinner.

As they readied for bed she told Shiloh, "But it's such a good kind of tired, you know? Yes, I feel limp and weak, and I know that tomorrow I'll be sore. But it felt so good to work hard, to be able to . . . to . . . exert myself, to breathe hard, to feel strong. But it's definitely not done, you know. Ladies must never exert themselves."

"Why is that?" Shiloh asked, yawning. He'd had a busy day, too, arranging for a surprise for Cheney. At least, he had conspired in it. It had actually been Auguste Bettencourt's idea, and before they were finished the entire crew and Fiona and Sketes were in on it.

Cheney awoke early the next morning, for a change, and felt perfectly wonderful, even though she was a little sore. "I think I'd like to have my fencing lesson first thing this morning," she told Shiloh. "I've heard that one can work the soreness out of muscles with exercise."

"That's true, mon chou. But I gotta tell you, Monsoor Bettencourt has a real job, you know. He's still a sailor on *Locke's Day Dream*."

Cheney made a face. "I know, I know. He has to rummage the briskets and belt down the bloomers and grackle up the noggins."

Shiloh grinned, and suddenly he knew, with one of his peculiar flashes of insight, that Cheney was just putting him on with her "sailor-speak."

She's an extremely intelligent woman—just think of how quick she picked up on those fencing terms and positions and movements yesterday! I bet she knows the name of every rope and sail and rig on this ship. She has an incredible memory . . . still can name all two hundred and six bones in the human body . . . but why does she make herself look so ignorant and helpless like that?

With an additional bit of wisdom, Shiloh thought he knew. Cheney didn't want to absolutely overmaster him in everything. She already could in medicine, in history, in manners and deportment, in general knowledge, and especially in biblical knowledge. With this—his greatest love, his ship—she was allowing him to be, in effect, superior.

She was watching him, for he was staring at her wide-eyed. "What?" she demanded.

"Nothin'. Oh, just one thing. Do you know I think you're just about the best, most generous, the kindest, and most thoughtful friend anyone could have?"

"You do?" Cheney asked, her cheeks coloring. "You really think that about me?"

"I do," he said emphatically. "All the time. I just . . . it's just kinda hard to say sometimes. Funny, isn't it? I can tell you I love you, but it's hard to tell you that I admire you . . . and like you."

"Why . . . that's . . . true," Cheney said

slowly. "How very odd. It is difficult to honestly and openly tell a person exactly how you feel about them."

"Let's always try to do that, huh?" Shiloh said. His tone was light, but his blue eyes were somber.

She nodded. "Yes, let's do that. Let's always do that."

They had a leisurely breakfast, and then Shiloh left while Fiona dressed Cheney. Cheney noticed that Fiona came in before Shiloh had left the cabin, and she could have sworn that they exchanged winks—at least, Shiloh winked at Fiona, who nodded and then turned her eyes away.

When Cheney came out on deck, she saw little knots of men standing around and grinning at her like idiots, but she could hardly walk up and demand to know what they were snickering about. Shiloh was nowhere in sight. She thought he might be up in the maintop, but she resolutely refused to look up. Even though she had given him her blessing, she still could hardly bear to watch him scuttle up the shrouds and especially could not watch him sliding down the backstays. Politely nodding to the grinning sailors, she made her way to her patient, Castor Mylonas, who was stretched out on his makeshift cot on the leeward side of the quarterdeck.

"How are you feeling today, Mr. Mylonas?"

she asked, picking up his wrist to gauge his pulse. It was strong and steady.

"Very fine, Dr. Cheney," he answered, and he, too, was grinning up at her like a baboon. "Very fine, thank you."

"You do look wonderful," Cheney admitted. The boy had color in his smooth cheeks—Lott shaved him every morning—and his black locks were crisp and shiny, and his liquid dark eyes were clear. She spoke to him a little more about his pain, his medications, his diet, and then wished him a good morning and retired to her deck chair on the poop deck.

She didn't see Shiloh until almost lunchtime. Then she heard a call. Shiloh was standing by Castor's cot and motioning to her. Cheney scrambled down the steps and along the deck at a dead run.

"What is it?" she demanded, then gave Shiloh a look that would have melted an iceberg. "You don't look ill, Mr. Mylonas." He was still grinning idiotically, as were the twenty or so sailors crowded around. Shiloh, too, was smiling.

Castor cleared his throat and said carefully—an obviously memorized speech—"Dr. Cheney, the sailors of *Locke's Day Dream* wish to thank you for your good care of the crew, and to tell you that we think you're the finest lady that ever graced the seas and that we are proud to have you as our ship's doctor, even though you are a woman, and also as owner of the barky. And so we wanted to give you some gifts with our . . . our . . ."

"Sincerest compliments," Lott whispered.

"With our sincerest compliments," Mylonas finished with relief.

Auguste Bettencourt and David Upchurch presented her with a fencing foil. "Madame, this foil is from my grand-père's salle, a student's practice foil. It is too light for me, and for most men, but you will find it a sweet blade, fine and true. As are you, madame." With a flourish he kissed her hand.

"She's married, Bettencourt," Shiloh growled. "You didn't forget, did you?"

"Our sorrowful loss," Bettencourt said, placing his hand over his heart and making a pretty bow. "Monsieur Locke's gain."

"He always says something poetical like that," Shiloh grunted. "He never just says, 'Yes, Mr. Locke, I know she's your wife and I know I can't even look at her sideways unless I want to die quick and hard."

"Frenchmen, sir," Lott said succinctly. "Kiss me hand and such."

David Upchurch grinned so widely at Cheney that it seemed his mouth would split at the corners. "I fixed the handle, Dr. Cheney, so's it's a little slimmer, and I give it some more curve, like Bettencourt said. So's it would fit your hand just right."

"Oh yes, it feels perfect," Cheney said, beaming. "Thank you, thank you both so much!"

Lott stepped forward and pressed something into her hands. "This here is the best number two sailcloth, donated by the owner of the barky, ma'am. Mr. Henry MacNair, the sailmaker, sewed it, and Mylonas did the fancy needlework." It was a fencer's vest, heavy enough to take the whip of a foil but with enough give so that Cheney could move around easily. Over the left breast, instead of the traditional heart, was embroidered *LDD* in gold and navy blue thread.

Next came Horatio Seaton, Uli Sigiwald, and Birr Dunstan. Dunstan had donated some soft Moroccan leather that he treasured and had intended to make into a vest and belt. Mr. Seaton had made the pattern, for he was clever in such things, and Uli Sigiwald had sewn the glove, for he had done some leatherwork in his wanderings.

Finally Fiona, blushing, came forward. "Here, Dr. Cheney. You need this for fencing. I . . . we . . . hope you like it."

Puzzled, Cheney held it up.

It was a skirt—but then, it wasn't truly a skirt. It was made of fine stout linen and was, in effect, loose breeches, gathered tightly at the waist to give them maneuvering room. In the front and back were sewn a flap, attached at the waist, also tightly gathered to give the skirt a look of fullness. But they were unmistakably breeches, albeit very modest ones. "Why, how clever! And how perfect! Oh, Fiona—and Sketes—I'm just thrilled that you thought of some way that I might work on my lunge and still be ladylike!"

Sketes nodded. "But it was Mr. Locke that designed it, Dr. Cheney. He thought it up hisself and drew it for me and Fiona to sew."

Cheney turned and threw herself into Shiloh's arms. "Oh, you're wonderful, wonderful, Shiloh!"

Bettencourt stepped up and, with a devilish grin at Shiloh, said, "I, too, am wonderful, Dr. Cheney. I started it, when I decided to give you the perfect little lady's foil."

"Don't forget, Bettencourt," Shiloh glowered.

"That she is married?"

"No. The part about dyin' quick and hard."

Bettencourt shook his head. "Englishmen! They have no romance in their souls."

————

They had left the calm of the Caribbean through the Mona Passage for the open Atlantic, with the wind never failing and the ship riding high. Cheney nagged Auguste Bettencourt into giving her at least one fencing lesson a day, and on Friday she asked, after dinner, if they might just "go over the octave parry and riposte one more time." Cheney seemed delighted with her new endeavor, and Shiloh was happy for her. She had asked him if he, too, would like to learn the sport, but he had declined, citing incurable laziness. Truth to tell, he knew he would be much better at fencing than Cheney. His reach and height would always give him an unconquerable advantage, and he wanted her to be better at something physical like this than he was. Women didn't have much of a chance to best men in sport, he observed comfortably, and this was something—small, admittedly, but important—that *he* could give *her*.

And, too, Shiloh was somewhat relieved that Cheney seemed to have lost interest in target shooting with the Boutet dueling pistols. He didn't like them much. Aside from the fact that he thought they were too ornate, they truly weren't very accurate after the third shot. And in his opinion—though he never expressed it to Cheney or Auguste Bettencourt, who thought the pistols were the ultimate in firearm artistry—one of the pistols had a cranky trigger pull. Shiloh disliked faults, however minor, in his firearms. To him target practice was a highly agreeable avocation, but it took all the fun out of it if the tools were faulty. He enjoyed shooting his faithful .44 while Cheney attacked, parried, and riposted.

Shiloh and Cheney had lunch with Captain Starnes, and as always Cheney wanted to see on the charts where they were. "About here, ma'am," Captain Starnes said politely, pointing to a spot on the open sea.

Shiloh pointed to Barbados, which stuck out from the Caribbean-encircling necklace of the Lesser Antilles. "Barbados, huh? You know, Doc, we could stop there—tomorrow, Captain?—if you'd like. I know we weren't planning on going there until we were homeward bound, but we're close enough to it to stop in for afternoon tea if you want."

"We could check in," Cheney said thoughtfully, then explained to the captain, "Barbados is the one island we were certain we wanted to visit, so we left instructions at home that any mail should be sent to General Delivery there."

"I see," Captain Starnes said agreeably. "*Locke's Day Dream* is at your service, ma'am. It would be no trouble to sail into Bridgetown tomorrow, and then"—again he pointed to the chart—"it would be an easy two-day sail to just ride the trades down the passage to Grenada."

"Would you like to stop?" Cheney asked Shiloh.

"Sure would," Shiloh answered. "But I gotta practice my British accent first. How 'bout some language lessons, Captain Starnes? You could teach me to say 'Cheerio' and 'Tally-ho' and 'Wot, wot?' "

"That's not too shabby for a first attempt," Captain Starnes said, deadpan. "But I'm afraid that learning the Queen's English would take more than one lesson, sir."

"If they can't understand me, then I'll just point," Shiloh said, winking at Cheney. "Like your father does to your new French cook."

Barbados was called "Little England" because, of all the West Indies, it had retained more of the British tradition and culture, perhaps, than any of the other Caribbean islands. Bridgetown was a lovely little port, fresh and clean and quiet. Cheney was intrigued by the whitewashed and pastel cottages with spotless windows, the port's own Trafalgar Square with a statue of Lord Nelson that predated Nelson's Column in London by two decades, a war memorial, and a three-dolphin fountain commemorating the advent of running water in Barbados in 1865. They found the post office, but had no mail as yet.

Cheney was reading a travel book as they sat in a lovely little tearoom, The Rose and Crown Tea Parlor, that could have been in St. James's Square in London. "Why, Shiloh, I didn't know this. It is said that George Washington worshiped at St. Michael's Cathedral—just on the other side of Trafalgar Square—in 1751. The cathedral has been rebuilt twice, in 1780 and 1831—damaged by hurricanes, you know—but some of the original cathedral still stands. I'd love to visit it, and we could have a prayer time."

"Yeah? But—a cathedral? Are we allowed to worship there?" Shiloh asked, puzzled.

"Of course, my love. We can worship God anywhere. And though I'm glad that we . . . um . . . what's the word? Fix church. . . ?"

"Rig church," Shiloh said, smiling a little.

"Rig church on Sundays on the ship, I do miss going to a real church."

"Well, if it's good enough for George Washington, it's good enough for me."

They found St. Michael's a little dusty but majestic nonetheless. No one was there, no priest or other worshipers. "It's teatime," Shiloh whispered to Cheney.

They sat quietly holding hands enjoying the hush of the magnificent cathedral. The sun reflected through the stained-glass windows, and they prayed together, at first silently and then aloud. Finally they left and returned to the ship to spend the night in calm, serene Carlisle Bay.

The next day was clear with gentle breezes and a blue sky right out of a poem by Keats. The barometer was steady. Captain Starnes and the officers agreed that the weather seemed perfect and was likely to remain that way, so it would be an easy sail down the channel between Barbados and St. Vincent to Grenada.

But just as they cleared St. Vincent, creeping down the leeward side of the hundred-plus reefs, rocks, cays, and tiny islands of the Grenadines, a small line of darkness, like gunpowder smudges, appeared on the eastern horizon.

"What is that?" Cheney asked, narrowing her eyes to stare eastward.

Shiloh's tone was grave.

"Trouble."

CHAPTER SEVEN

All the Way From the Coast of Africa

"ALL HANDS, ALL HANDS, all hands! Ready to make sail!" First Mate Nat Cadell roared down the main hatch. A stampede of men followed, some running to their stations on the lines, and many climbing the shrouds as easily as if they were teak staircases. Captain Starnes stood on the quarterdeck, watching the men with narrowed eyes.

Shiloh nodded with satisfaction. "Good move, Captain Starnes," he muttered. Cheney started to ask him what he meant, but Shiloh took her arm, saying, "We'll just be in the way on deck. We'd better go down into the cabin."

Cheney cast one last apprehensive look to the east. The wide, thin swath of indigo cloud seemed very far away, but she could now see tiny flashes of lightning on the underside. The sky overhead was still innocent blue with no clouds, but the sinking sun was taking on an ominous, bloated crimson appearance. The breeze was steady enough but was tempered with odd cold drafts.

Shiloh hurried Cheney into the salon. Fiona and Sketes were there, for their tiny cubbyhole cabins were just off the salon. Fiona was pale and kept biting her lip, but Sketes looked solid and comfortable. "We're in for a blow," Shiloh said cheerfully. "But it might be a couple of hours yet. How about some tea, Sketes?"

Sketes wiped her hands on her apron in a habitual gesture. "Yes, sir. Galley fires will be put out soon, I suppose. You and Dr. Cheney must eat something hot and not just have tea and cakes. Might be a while before we have fires again. . . ." She hurried to the door, mumbling to herself.

"Sketes?" Shiloh said, catching her at the door.

"Yes, sir?"

"Why don't you go ahead and fix enough for the four of us? If you and Fiona would be good enough to join us for supper, that is."

Sketes's round face flushed with pleasure. "Why, we'd be honored, Mr. Irons-Winslow. Right kind of you."

As Sketes made her exit Shiloh turned to Fiona and spoke very gently, for the girl dropped her head and blushed every time he spoke to her. "Fiona, you're going to need to batten down everything that's loose in our stateroom and your cabin. Check Sketes's cabin too, but I'm pretty sure she's already battened down. She's quite an old hand, isn't she?"

"Yes, sir," Fiona whispered, not looking up.

With a wry look at Cheney, Shiloh added, "Make sure all of Mrs. Irons-Winslow's glass gewgaws are padded good. And don't forget to rig the armoire doors and all the drawers so they won't fly open. Cords to wind around the knobs are stored in the locker over there."

"Yes, sir," Fiona murmured, on surer ground now. A long window seat on the port side of the salon was actually a storage locker with a padded seat. Sketes had already shown her the lengths of stout twine stored there and how to batten down her own cabin just before Cheney and Shiloh had come in. With a graceful little bob, she hurried to the seat, lifted the top, and rummaged around in the depths.

Shiloh and Cheney sat down at the teak table. Automatically Shiloh reached across and took her hands in his, smoothing her long fingers, admiring their grace. Then he asked, "You aren't scared, are you?"

She shook her head. "It's kind of hard to be

scared, right now when it's so calm. But I expect I will be when it hits us."

"Don't be," Shiloh said seriously. "Honestly, Doc, this ship is as seaworthy as they come. And I believe Captain Starnes is one of the best clipper captains on the seven seas. We're lucky to have him."

With interest, Cheney asked, "And what was it he did up on deck? When you said he was a good man?"

Shiloh started to answer, then hesitated, as though he were groping for words. Cheney watched him quizzically. Then she realized what the trouble was and grasped his hands tightly. "Shiloh, dear, I'm really not afraid, not at all. I trust you. I've always trusted you, with everything, even my life."

Shiloh was not given to romantic gestures, but he pressed a long, warm kiss onto her hand. Then, eyeing Fiona still fiddling with the cording at the other end of the salon, he released Cheney's hand with a mischievous wink. "Okay, Doc, here's the scuttlebutt. We're hard up on a lee shore, see? Captain Starnes had to decide whether to pack on and crack on and tack round west and north into Admiralty Bay, or whether to head out to blue water and scud along under close-reefed tops'ls and maybe the flying jib."

"Ahh," Cheney said, nodding wisely. "And which did he decide?"

"We're gonna sail into Admiralty Bay like a racing Thoroughbred," Shiloh answered lightly.

"All jibbims and blaskets flying," Cheney noted.

"Sure enough."

———

Sketes, Fiona, and the Irons-Winslows barely had time to finish their early supper before the first great rollers started. The powerful waves lifted *Locke's Day Dream* so that her great jib-boom pointed toward the sky, then dropped her down so that great torrents of green water and yellow foam washed over the forecastle. Cheney and Shiloh went outside for a last look round before deadlights were fastened over all the port-holes and skylights. Overhead the twilight sky, usually a peaceful lavender in the tropics, had darkened to an odd gray-green hue, and the eastern horizon was a livid purple-black bloated cloud bank with jagged lightning bolts flickering under it continuously.

"Are we going to make it?" Cheney asked, watching the Isle de Quatre looming up, a big rock surrounded by dots of smaller rocks.

"Sure we will," Shiloh assured her. "But we've got to go in right now," he said, eyeing the western horizon. Holding on to the bulkheads to keep their balance on the pitching ship, the two left the poop deck and went below. The wind blew stronger and erratically, with manic gusts that made the rigging shriek. They felt the ship tack sharply north, then box right around west, and they heard the loud flaps of the sails as she spilled her wind. They could make out hoarsely shouted orders to the helmsman behind, followed by the pounding of men running across the deck. A muffled thunder reached them as the great stern anchor chain veered out, vibrating the whole ship as she drifted along it, and then the slighter vibration and creak of the fore anchor.

"We're moored now," Shiloh nodded, releasing a long breath of relief. "But it's not over yet."

In a few short minutes the storm hit the ship in all its fury. It came out of the east, unchallenged all the way from the coast of Africa, a long virulent hissing sound and then rolling, deafening growls of thunder. *Locke's Day Dream*, like a great stunned animal, heeled far over, and Fiona fell right off the window seat. Shiloh jumped up and helped her to her feet. "You okay?" he shouted, for the tumult was terrific. She nodded, and he noted that her face was pale with fear.

Since the ship was anchored in such a sheltered bay, the water was relatively calm, with some jerky pitching and rolling. It was nothing to riding out a storm on the open sea, but to the inexperienced, it was terrifying enough. The wind steadily rose from a low growl to what sounded like an unending detonation of cannons. The storm was loaded with a mass of rain, so thick that the hands on deck had to struggle to get a breath that was not half water. In the salon the tumult was terrific, with the roaring wind and the crashing flood.

Fiona seemed terrified, wedged into a corner of the bench seat, her eyes wide, her mouth tight. Her eyes rose to the graceful four-armed lamp above the table. It was gimbaled so that it would stay level with the normal movement of the ship, but with the now erratic jerks of the tossing vessel, it swung wildly and threw crazy shafts of light this way and that. Sketes, who was sitting at the other end of the bench calmly sewing, scooted close to the girl, patted her hand, and said something in her ear. Fiona gave a tremulous smile but did seem to relax.

Cheney and Shiloh sat at the table, obliged to yell at each other for conversation. Cheney smiled at him. "We certainly are watertight," she said, nodding at the skylight above and the ports above the bench seat. "No leaks."

"She's a tight ship. But we're bound to get water—"

Even as he spoke, the ship heeled to port, and it sounded and felt as if a herculean bucket of water had been dashed onto the ship. Water came sloshing under the door, spreading through the cabin in jerky little waves. "Yeah, that's the water I was talking about," Shiloh said to Cheney. "No way to prevent it."

Cheney shrugged and tucked her feet up onto the long leather bench seat, noting that Fiona and Sketes, too, perched up onto their seats. She watched Shiloh carefully. He was not nervous, but he seemed restless. He gave her an absentminded smile, but his eyes kept straying toward the door. She leaned over, touching his hand. "You don't have to stay here and baby-sit us, Shiloh."

His eyes lit up, a keen flash of blue. "I don't? I don't mind, you know."

She shook her head and made a shooing motion. "Go on, Mr. Flying Dutchman. You're very poor company for the ladies' salon."

Shiloh rose at once and shrugged on his old "fishskin"—his canvas overcoat. With a fleeting bow to the ladies, he turned to the door. When he opened it the wind howled hungrily down the stairwell and a solid sheet of water soaked him, but he threw his head back and ran out, slamming the door behind him as he headed out into the maelstrom. Fiona watched him incredulously—as if she thought he were a lunatic howling at the moon.

Cheney said as carelessly as she could, "He likes storms."

Fiona nodded, utterly blank, but Sketes looked knowing. "Sailors do," she told Cheney. "Sailors generally do."

The force of the wind did not weaken, and the rain pelted the ship with a continuous pounding drumbeat. The ship still lurched fore and aft and sometimes pitched and heaved, for in such a wind and with a chopped-up sea it must have some leeway. Sketes sewed steadily. No fine work could be done in this upheaval and uncertain light, but Sketes was not one to sit idle. She could always use another canvas apron, which didn't require small, invisible stitches. Amused, Cheney saw that she was using a sailor's palm to sew the heavy fabric instead of a thimble. Fiona had calmed down enough to display some interest, and Sketes showed her the repetitive movements of placing the needle and pushing it through with the metal disc on the mitt.

Cheney sat for a while, contemplating seasickness. She was monitoring herself carefully for the first cold salivation, the first nauseating roll of a stomach that feels as if it has become detached from the rest of the innards. Seasickness was a treacherous and inimical affliction. Cheney had been on ships several times in her life, both steamers and sailing ships, and sometimes she had been prostrate with seasickness, while at other times she'd never felt a qualm. She had never been able to find anything to alleviate the nausea once it began. In fact, the only remedy she'd ever found that some victims could keep down was weak chamomile tea. She wondered if there was chamomile in the ship's stores.

Then she scolded herself. *I of all people should know how sickness is often either purely in the mind or greatly aggravated by mental upset! If I sit here anticipating it, I'll surely get it!*

With determination she rose from the seat, ignoring Fiona's protests, sloshed into the cabin, retrieved her deck kit, and returned to the salon. Fiona watched her reproachfully, but Cheney just opened the little case and greedily popped a chocolate into her mouth. She offered the box to Sketes, who looked surprised, and then to Fiona, who steeled herself and waded over to pick out one for herself and another for Sketes.

Cheney considered getting her Bible, but she didn't think she could read by the wildly swinging lamp. She thought writing might be a little tumultuous too, so she placidly picked up her spool of what looked like cotton thread but was actually fine silk. Cheney, for all her dexterity, was a dismal seamstress and had never tried to improve her skills, for needlework bored her extremely. All except one unique kind, however: she liked practicing making surgeon's knots. She had always been skilled at making the delicate knots of stitches with needle and forceps. She still practiced conscientiously at least once a week, mostly on a pig's foot, which was very like human skin. She had assisted at several of Devlin Buchanan's operations. Her adopted brother was a highly skilled surgeon of international renown. Compared to Dev's fine neat stitching, Cheney's was coarse and messy, and she was much too slow. So she had determined to make surgeon's knots as well as Dev's. She was very proficient and was teaching herself to do it one-handed. She was fairly good with her right hand, but her left-handed knots were slow and clumsy. With a patience unusual for Cheney, she sat, maneuvering the thread between the fingers of her left hand, over and over again.

———

Shiloh was gone a long time, it seemed to Cheney. When the door finally banged open, flung by the tempest, he almost fell into the cabin. He hurried to close it, then stood, shaking prodigious amounts of water from his hair and clothes. Fiona, more confident now, slipped into the adjoining storeroom and brought him two luxuriously thick Turkish towels. He thanked her but made no move to dry himself off as he stood, studying Cheney.

"What is it?" she asked, staring up at him.

"We made the bay before the storm hit, but the men were taking in the sails just as it came crashing in," he told Cheney soberly. "We got

156

everything reefed, but since this is a great howler, we had to strike the t'gallant masts down on deck. It's done, but . . ."

"Injuries?" Cheney asked calmly.

Shiloh nodded. "Always, in a blow like this. Nothing life threatening, though."

"I'll come," she said, rising.

"The men wouldn't ask you to, but they'd feel better," he said soberly. "And I figured you'd want to." He followed her into the cabin as she hurried to her armoire, where her medical bag was securely stowed.

"Do you know what sort of injuries?"

"Not really," he answered, pulling a long black macintosh out of his armoire and throwing it over Cheney. "Two of the foretopmen got hurt, so I had to help strike down the mizzen t'gallant. Wear this. You'll probably still get soaked. We don't have far to go on deck, though, so maybe you won't get half drowned."

"Where do I go?" she asked, obediently fastening the raincoat closed.

"We've got man-ropes rigged, so I'll carry your bag. We're going to go to the quarterdeck and take a right, over to the booby hatch. You know where that is?"

"Yes."

"It's battened down, so you'll have to hold on as tight as you can to me while I get the frame

157

up," he said severely, "and then I'm going to stuff you down it."

She laughed. "Now I know why you want me to do this. You'd better enjoy it, Mr. Irons-Winslow, because you're not going to have many opportunities to throw me down the hatch."

He sobered and said, "It's pretty bad up there, Doc. You're all right, are you?"

She met his critical gaze squarely. "I'm fine, and I'm ready."

He nodded and they left the relatively warm and secure salon.

The tumult and waterfall of the stairwell was nothing compared to the pandemonium of the deck. The wind was a steady mass blowing forty-five miles per hour, and the rain was a flood, horizontal and thick. The night was as black as the deepest cave sunk in the earth. When they stood on the poop deck, Cheney felt small, helpless, like a little leaf caught in a whirlwind, and she ducked her head to gasp for breath. Behind her Shiloh was a solid pillar, and he took her hands to guide them to the ropes. Blindly she went down one step, then another, each a struggle. Shiloh clasped her around the waist tightly. In this torturous way they finally reached the booby hatch. Cheney flung both arms around Shiloh's waist, and he somehow managed to lift the heavy hatch, then maneuver her down onto the steps, which were really more like a stepladder than a proper stairwell. Cheney hurried down, out of his way, and when he threw himself down and shut the hatch, it was as if he had shut out a raging monster.

"Whew! This is a fine blow," he said, again shaking himself like a wet dog.

"Yes, very fine," Cheney said sardonically. "Now where are my patients?"

The crew quarters were in the forecastle on the lower deck. But though the accommodations were roomy for a sailing ship—neat rows of double bunks with generous aisles between—there were still forty men quartered there, and the sick and injured needed quiet. Shiloh said, "We've rigged up one of the storerooms with hammocks."

As they hurried down the lower deck, Cheney asked, "Hammocks?"

"Seems like they're more comfortable in them," Shiloh answered thoughtfully. "Come to think of it, most sick people do lie on their backs. And rolling around in a bunk with wooden sides . . ." He shrugged. "Here we are."

The room was a simple square. To one side were the ship's medicine chest and a plain wooden table. Eight men were in hammocks, and two men sat on the chest. Cheney smiled as she came in. "Good evening, gentlemen. May I be of assistance? No, no, please, don't get up. First doctor's order: In my sickbay you do not hop up and down when I come and go. Understood? Good. Now, Shiloh, would you please find some clean sheets to put on this table, and I'll do a quick assessment of the injured."

Sailors were frequently injured when dealing with the monstrously heavy sails and treacherous rigging in a storm. The grizzled bosun's mate, Willy Perkins, told her sonorously, "It were a Dutch triple fiddle block, Dr. Cheney, and it looked like it done it a-purpose. Just lashed right out and dealt me one to the chest!"

"You have two cracked ribs, Mr. Perkins," Cheney said, pressing very gently with exploring fingers. "I know it's painful, but it's good that yours is the worst injury. The damage could have been much, much worse."

Perkins grimaced as she worked over him, but he seemed singularly satisfied with his dire prognosis as the most gravely injured man aboard, swelling with pride. "You hear that, mate?" he said to Calvin Lott, who was not injured but had come down to see about his messmates. "I'm hurt worsen than anyone, Dr. Cheney says."

"Good thing for you that . . . that . . ." He searched for an adjective suitable to use in the presence of a lady, scratched his head with frustration, and finally came out with ". . . that horrid old block didn't knock your head, Perkins. You'd be a dead 'un, you would."

"Aye, so I would," he agreed with satisfaction.

Cheney, hiding a smile, told Shiloh, "Give him twenty drops of laudanum and get him on the table, will you? He needs a good cingulum, and I don't think I can do it while he's in the hammock."

"Sure, Doc." Shiloh had naturally fallen into his old position as Cheney's assistant.

"I'll do the cingulum," she said quietly. She knew that Shiloh could wind a tight linen strip around Perkins' chest perfectly as well as she could, but she also knew that these men valued her attending them as highly as if she were the most esteemed physician alive.

As she attended the men—and listened to them—she tried to understand their attitude toward her. They treated her with a curious mixture of extreme, almost holy, deference and with a personable familiarity. All of them confidently gave her long, involved explanations of the event of their injury, and described their symptoms with a wealth of detail, mixed with remembrances of other injuries and storms and injured friends and relatives. But always, as they gazed at her with the innocent trust that most people gave their physicians, they spoke politely, using the best manners they had.

Cheney was amused—but also gratified. These were hard men, some of them shameless rogues, yet they obviously respected her and trusted her implicitly. It was much better treatment than she'd received from some more well-bred quarters.

Young Luki, the cook's mate, had sustained a painful second-degree burn. Cheney examined it, then asked, "Luki, how did you ever get burned here?" The burn was to his upper left shoulder.

He sighed and gazed at her with round, soulful eyes. "First the barky knocked me to my knees and then she threw me right aback. Into the range, before the fires was out."

"And how many times do you think Mr. Penrod's told you, you little swab, one hand for you and one for the ship," Lott grunted but not unkindly. He had appointed himself to make the rounds with Cheney.

" 'Bout a million," Luki admitted. "I'll 'member next time."

Cheney nodded sympathetically. "I want you to take some medicine that will relax you and make you sleepy. But don't go to sleep until I see the other men. Just rest, and then I'll come back and clean that out and bandage you up, and then you'll sleep like a lamb all night."

"Thank you, Dr. Cheney—and don't you hurry, now. I'll be just fine." He was only thirteen, but he was already toughening up.

Cheney worked quickly, taking time to speak

encouragement to each man. Two of the men had rope burns from some complicated disturbance in the arrangement of the rigging, and Lott excoriated them for being green lubbers if he'd ever seen the like, but they seemed to accept this with almost as much grace as they accepted Cheney's ministrations. One man had his hand crushed, but no bones were broken. Two men had been knocked sprawling; one had wrenched his shoulder, and one had sprained his wrist. Cheney and Shiloh repaired the dislocated shoulder with a teamlike expertise that awed the sailors. But the injured man, an able seaman named Spence, seemed mightily disappointed that he had been cured so precipitately. Cheney kindly suggested—since all the work was done and both watches were below, with all made fast—that he should take some tonic and rest, and with relief he groaned a little and settled back in his hammock.

One sailor named Daniels was rated landsman, though he had been a fisherman all his life. He had fallen down the main hatch and banged his head and cut his lip. "I'll stitch you up, Mr. Daniels," Cheney told him, "but I really need to attend to Luki's burn first."

"That's all right, Dr. Cheney," he said, nodding. "I can wait."

"You mustn't be falling down the hatches, Daniels," Lott said in the slow, careful, slightly loud tone one used for ignorant landsmen. "You could get hurt serious-like."

Daniels, a long-suffering, cheerful man, nodded. "I'll try to remember that, Mr. Lott, I sure will."

———————

It was very late, and still the wind raged and the rain poured down in torrents, with spectacular crashes of thunder and vivid lightning. Cheney and Shiloh sat at the table in the salon, both of them yawning prodigiously. Sketes had brought out a spirit stove, which she had mutinously lit to fix them hot tea, and it was very good indeed.

"It's so funny the way they are," Cheney mused. "I don't mean ha-ha funny—I mean so sweet and gentle for such rough men."

"They're only that way with you, you know," Shiloh said. "Now, I don't mean they go about assaulting Fiona and Sketes all the time, or cursing or spitting in their presence, or anything like that. They treat them well too. It's true, Doc, most seamen these days are a rum lot, but clipper men are often cut from a little better cloth. For one thing, to work a clipper you have to *want* to work a clipper. Other sailors call them 'death ships,' and so they can be. But there is a sort of prestige that goes along with clipper men. They're the real men of the tall ships, the true sailors. But to get back to you, you're different," he finished rather lamely.

"Different how?" Cheney pressed him. "Aside from the obvious choice of profession, I mean."

"It's kinda hard to explain," Shiloh said, frowning. "They themselves couldn't ever explain it. And they wouldn't if they could, because they think it would be unlucky to talk openly about it. But I'll try . . . see, they think that since you did so good with Castor, saving his leg and all—and you did, Doc, do a great job on him. That was a hard thing, under those circumstances. Anyway, so here you are, a virtuous Christian woman, a real doctor, not a barber-surgeon, with supernatural powers, and you're my wife, and I'm Locke, and this is *Locke's Day Dream*. So you're their patron saint on the one hand, but you're also part of the ship's luck. See?"

Cheney stared at him. "I don't know."

He tried again. "You're one of them. One of us. You belong here on this ship. And because of that, you belong to them, in a way."

"I think . . . I see," Cheney said slowly.

Shiloh reached across the table to caress her face. "Just don't forget, Dr. Cheney, that first you belong to me. Yesterday, now, and forever."

PART II

A TEMPESTUOUS WIND

May 1868–May 1869

But not long after there arose against it a
tempestuous wind, called Euroclydon.

Acts 27:14

CHAPTER EIGHT

Fear and Flight

MR. DENYS WORTHINGTON, ESQUIRE, and his servant Sweet stood outside a fairly respectable boardinghouse on Corlear's Hook, shivering. "Freakish weather," Mr. Worthington muttered, pulling his wool greatcoat closer around him. "I hate New York. I'm glad to be leaving it."

Mr. Denys Worthington looked, spoke, dressed, and carried himself like a British aristocrat. An elegantly slim man of twenty-seven years, his dark brown hair was always carefully styled, his full, smooth features always meticulously shaved. Perhaps the only clues to his true character could be found in the feral sharpness of his light brown eyes and the telltale crow's-feet of dissipation at the corners. His real name was Bain Winslow.

His companion, a man named Johann Zenger but always called "Sweet," could not have made a sharper contrast to Winslow. He looked like a German peasant farmer, with a fair complexion and massive rough hands and thick build. His long, fine yellow hair somehow did not match the rest of him; it seemed effeminate. His eyes, too, were jarring, both in the odd gray-ish blue tint that really was no color at all and in the blankness of them. He should have looked fierce and savage, but instead he looked like a portrait done by an indifferent painter who could not capture the spark of life.

Now he asked in his flat voice, "Mr. Worthington, where do we go now?"

Irritably Bain replied, "Not to Bermuda on the *Day Dream*—that much is certain. As usual my plans have come to naught." Twirling his ebony cane, he glowered up at the second-floor window of Captain Geoffrey Starnes's rooms. "That idiot Starnes says that the *Day Dream* can't sail for perhaps two weeks, maybe more. I'm not staying here for two weeks. I'm not staying in this blighted place for two days, not even two hours. Right."

He climbed back into the waiting cab, calling harshly, "New York Bank and Trust, Wall Street. And get that nag to do better than a crawl, can't you!"

Sweet climbed up beside the ancient toothless driver. "Your gent's got a temper on 'im, ain't he?" the man grumbled.

"Mr. Worthington is in a hurry," Sweet said evenly.

Sweet really didn't know what they were going to do, and he didn't care much. He knew that Mr. Worthington wanted him to come along, and Sweet, with his bulldog loyalty, was content to go wherever and do whatever his employer said.

He did know that he and Mr. Worthington needed to get out of New York. Even Sweet was smart enough to know that since they had kidnapped a woman—a woman of good family, a doctor—the night before and had imprisoned her in Sweet's House of Exotic Island Princesses, very likely the police would be looking for them. Sweet was unclear as to what exactly Mr. Worthington had done to the actress Minette York and her companion, a man named Shiloh Irons-Winslow. But he had gathered from Mr. Worthington's relentless insistence that they leave New York immediately, leaving behind everything but what Sweet could carry, that Mr. Worthington had done something to them as well that the police might be interested in.

The cab wound its way tediously through the traffic. The old hack wasn't quick, because no man or horse could make his way quickly through the streets of Lower Manhattan. Bain fumed, realizing that the time was slipping away too rapidly, and here he was, still jittering about Manhattan when he should have been halfway to the West Indies by now. And he would have, were it not for the incompetence and laziness of Captain Geoffrey Starnes. Perhaps Bain really knew the truth, that one could not ready a clipper ship for a journey with a crew of four dozen men at one hour's notice, particularly if the owner was unable to finance it.

Locke's Day Dream—Bain had changed the name to just the *Day Dream* because he despised his cousin so—had been laid up for months. She wasn't victualed or watered, her copper bottom was fouled from lying in the filth of the Perth Amboy wharves in New Jersey, and many of her crew had taken other ships during the last idle months. But if all of these compelling reasons to excuse Captain Starnes's refusal to sail occurred to Bain, he never considered them. He cursed inwardly and reflected bitterly that Sweet was the only servant—Bain regarded all of his employees as servants—he'd ever had that he could depend on. All the rest of them—captains of the ships of the Winslow fleet, their officers, the seamen, employees of the Winslow plantation, the house servants, the prostitutes he brought to his brothels—were against him. They always had been. Except for Sweet.

They finally reached that grand edifice, New York Bank and Trust, and Bain hurried in, tossing a coin to the cabbie and demanding that he wait. Bain fidgeted while the youthful but dried-up bespectacled clerk went through the machinations required to actually let one of their customers have his money. Evidently withdrawing the entire sum and closing the account was in the nature of a cardinal sin, for the clerk was obliged to dodder all about the bank and whisper to other men and get signatures and then visit other loftier personages before finally asking Bain to sign this and that.

All this nonsense for two-hundred-twelve dollars, Bain thought savagely. *You'd think it was two hundred thousand—and don't I just wish it were!*

Then a thought occurred to him: it was already ten-thirty and the bank had been open for an hour and a half. Perhaps the Duvalls, or maybe even his cousin Locke had somehow found out where he banked and had alerted them. Maybe even now, while the moron was flitting around, speaking to other men on the banking floor, they were calling the police. Bain licked his lips and furtively looked around, but saw no one eyeing him suspiciously. Just then the man came back with Bain's cash. One last signature and he was free.

Bain stalked back out to his ragged cab. "The Port Authority, and get that nag to trot faster, can't you?"

When Bain and Sweet finally arrived at the Port Authority after a tortuous trip across town, it was just after noon, and the terminal was crowded and deafening. The Port Authority of New York, on the southeastern tip of Manhattan, was a cavernous building whose acoustics raised the normal din inside to thunderous levels. The first floor was a long room with uncomfortable wooden benches here and there, always filled with people arranging for passage overseas, families waiting for the arrival of loved ones, sailors locating their ships, and stevedores looking for work. Posted on two walls were the schedule of sailings. Some ships or lines had big artful posters, some small handmade notices, some just one line posted by the Port Authority on plain scraps of paper. On the other side of the long room an immense sign read *HARBORMASTER*. Beneath it stretched a long row of glassed cubicles, stations for registrations and inquiries. The harbormaster himself had fine offices on the second floor, accessible only by a stairwell behind the cubicles.

Bain started fighting his way to one wall, which seemed to have mostly departure notices posted. He told Sweet, "Go over there and see if that wall has departures. We're looking for anything going anywhere in the West Indies, as long as it's today."

Sweet just shrugged and dropped his head.

Bain growled, "I forgot, you can't read. Well, at least make yourself useful and help me get close to the boards."

Sweet started clearing a path for Bain—with his massive build he was good at that, at least—when Bain stopped dead and grew pale.

A tall man stood at one of the cubicles, and Bain immediately recognized him as Richard

Duvall. Beside him was Dr. Devlin Buchanan. Bain froze, feeling trapped, exposed. He didn't think either man had ever seen him before, but certainly Dr. Duvall and Locke would have given them good descriptions of both him and Sweet. The two of them together were surely noticeable. Richard spoke to the nondescript clerk behind the cubicle and handed him a card. Hurriedly the man motioned down to Richard's left, and he and Dev disappeared down a long, bare hallway beside the cubicles.

They're looking for us. They've probably got every policeman in Manhattan down here, searching the docks. Now they must be checking all the passenger manifests.

Bain was right about one thing and wrong about another. Richard Duvall and Dev Buchanan were indeed checking with the harbormaster for any passengers by the name of Denys Worthington or Bain Winslow or Mr. Sweet.

But they did not have the police looking for Bain. They didn't even tell the harbormaster why they were looking for Mr. Worthington or Winslow. Both Cheney and Shiloh had been reluctant to press charges against Bain, though Richard and Dev would dearly have loved to see the police drag him off, preferably in chains.

Cheney had not said much to her father about her ordeal, only that Mr. Winslow truly hadn't hurt her and that she felt a little sorry for him. Shiloh had only said that since he wasn't the only person injured by his cousin, he would leave it up to Cheney and her family to decide how to handle the situation. But he was clearly reluctant to hunt down his cousin. Because Richard had such great respect for Shiloh, and also because he understood that to pursue charges would result in a shabby little scandal for his daughter, he had decided to try to find Bain Winslow and see if he could persuade him to at least come talk to Shiloh. And, of course, Richard also hoped that he could find *Locke's Day Dream*. She was, after all, Shiloh's ship.

But Bain Winslow had no notion of such charitable feelings toward his cousin, so as soon as Richard Duvall's tall figure disappeared, he frantically shoved through the crowd to search the departure notices. Only one passenger ship was leaving for anywhere in the Caribbean that day—the SS *Blaze of Glory* for Aspinwall. The coincidence shook Bain, for his only hope for passage out of New York was the very ship he had told Minette York that his cousin Locke was taking, running out on her. Bain thought it was an evil omen, a symbol of how at every step he took, some malevolent force was fighting him, blocking him, thwarting him. Bain thought it was because his cousin Locke Winslow had come into his life, bringing him misfortune. It never occurred to Bain that he himself was his own worst enemy.

But he had to run—he had to get away—and if the ill-used SS *Blaze of Glory* was the only means of escape, then so be it. But then his heart plummeted. He saw the prices of the berths. The *Blaze of Glory* was an enormous luxurious steamship; staterooms were $250, third-class berths $50. It hit Bain with force that, including the amount he had just withdrawn from the bank, the only ready cash he had, and was likely to have for a long time, was $284. Also, the ship was leaving from the Hudson River docks, all the way across town, at one-thirty exactly. They would never get there in time. Steamships didn't have to wait for the whims of tide and wind.

Frustrated, furious, frightened, Bain grabbed Sweet's arm and muttered, "We have to go now." He almost ran out of the terminal, followed by Sweet, and went straight into the first filthy, reeking saloon he saw. Bain downed two shots of kerosene-tasting whiskey, gasped a little, and shakily wiped his mouth.

Sweet finally asked, "We have nowhere to go, Mr. Worthington?"

Bain gritted out, "Don't call me that. I don't even want these drunken sods to hear it, and it's not my real name anyway."

"Yes, Mr.—yes, sir."

Bain sagged. "And yes, you're right, Sweet.

176

We have nowhere to go. I saw that woman doctor's father and her adopted brother in the terminal, going up to the harbormaster's office. They'll be watching the passenger manifests, and there are probably police crawling all over the docks looking for us right now."

Sweet nodded calmly. "Then we can't stay here, right by where they're looking for us. Come with me, Mr.—sir."

They walked out onto the East River wharves. Bain felt battered by the swarming crowds, the enormous din, the reek. Gruff, hard men shouted and cursed and shoved; hundreds of iron horseshoes struck the granite Belgian blocks of the streets; omnibuses and cabs clattered; the stench of horse manure, sour whiskey, and rotten fish overwhelmed the senses. Still Sweet walked surely and steadily, and men cleared the way for him. Though he was too vacant eyed to look dangerous, there was still a solid no-nonsense air about him. Numbly Bain followed behind.

Finally Sweet stopped and, shading his eyes, watched a ship's crew working on the jib rigging. He turned to Bain and pointed to a nearby shanty. "What does this say?"

The hand-lettered sign read,

HANDS. OFFICE 117 WALL STREET. FOR THE WEST INDIES.

Sarcastically Bain asked, "You don't actually think I'm going to crew a ship, do you?"

"No, Mr.—sir. But this brigantine, she is leaving soon, maybe two hours." Sweet waited.

Bain considered the ship. The brig was old but clean, and she had new copper. The men on the jibboom worked quickly and efficiently while the captain barked orders in German. The ship was obviously not for passenger trade, but it did look clean and seaworthy. "Perhaps he might take two passengers," Bain said uncertainly.

Sweet nodded. "Wait here, Mr.—sir." Nimbly he dodged the booms that were loading huge bales of tobacco onto the ship, went to the end of the pier, and spoke to a man holding a clipboard and wearing a watch cap. The man nodded and pointed to the rope ladder. Sweet mounted it and called out something in German as he reached the rail. The captain nodded, and Sweet went forward to him.

Bain was watching with curiosity and surprise because he didn't know that Sweet could speak German. Sweet did have an accent, and his English was riddled with the odd little mistakes foreigners often make, but Bain had never thought much about what Sweet's native tongue was. For some reason he had assumed Sweet was Swedish—something about his name. With a start, Bain realized he didn't know Sweet's real name. If he had ever known it, he had forgotten it.

The stern captain came to the side and stared down at Bain, then returned to Sweet, shaking his head. They talked more, however, and finally Sweet returned to Bain.

"This ship, she is *Wotan*. She leaves at three o'clock for Kingston, Jamaica," he told Bain.

"So? Will he take passengers? No questions asked?" Bain demanded harshly.

Sweet looked confused. "He will take us, yes. But no passenger . . . uh, passenger . . ."

"Accommodations?" Bain asked drily. "I thought not. But he'll take us?"

"Yes, sir," Sweet answered hesitantly. "You will have one pillow, one sheet, and one bunk with the crew. Eat with the crew. But I will be there too, Mr.—sir. *Wotan* will take us both."

The hard-driving Captain Berlyn had initially refused to take a passenger. They always caused much more trouble than the money they paid. But because Sweet volunteered as an unpaid able seaman for the journey, Captain Berlyn reluctantly took on the passenger, whose name he never asked. He charged Bain fifty dollars and stuck it right in his own pocket.

The journey took three weeks. Bain was sick

from the second day. Sweet nursed him, cleaned his clothes, prepared and served his meals, cleaned and changed his bedding, and shaved him. Bain was barely conscious most of the time, though he did recall thanking Sweet once or twice.

Once Sweet caught two of the sailors breaking into Bain's two trunks, which were stowed underneath his bunk. With shocking quickness Sweet turned from a dull nonentity into a savage fighter. He had almost killed both men before several other sailors broke up the fight. No one bothered Bain or his trunks after that.

So Sweet earned fear from his mates, but during the passage he also earned respect. A sudden squall overtook them off Abaco Island. Captain Berlyn was trying to lash himself to the mast when the brig almost broached to and the captain was close to getting washed overboard. Sweet saved him and lashed him to the mast. He and one other giant forecastleman were the only ones who could get manropes rigged in the fierce wind so the crew could work the ship.

Captain Berlyn was not only grateful, but he recognized that Sweet was a true seaman. "I'm paying you a third mate's wage for New York to Kingston," he told Sweet as they made their way into Kingston Harbor. "I'd like for you to stay on, Sweet, as bosun."

Sweet shook his head, staring at the shore.

With frustration the captain asked, "Look, Sweet, is the passenger a member of your family?"

"No, sir. I work for him."

"Working for him is one thing—being his nanny's another," Berlyn rasped. "He can't be paying you enough for that. Why do you stay with him?"

Sweet turned solidly, like a pillar, and fixed his peculiar ash-colored gaze on the captain. He struggled to speak, trying to find the words. Not being an articulate man, Sweet couldn't think how to express to the captain that Bain Winslow had chosen him, trusted him, made him feel valued. Maybe Bain was cruel sometimes. But Bain had taken Sweet with him on his trips to the West Indies, had named his House of Exotic Island Princesses after him, had asked for his advice about a woman to oversee the girls, and had taken his advice about Alana Patterson. Bain had bought him two suits, and even though at the time he'd made some caustic comment about Sweet looking like a ragpicker, he had still paid for them and not docked Sweet's pay.

No one had ever before in his life bought Sweet anything. No one had ever asked Sweet's advice about anything. No one had ever wanted him to accompany them anywhere, even if it was just as a paid servant. No one had ever noticed him much at all.

"He . . . he's a good man, I think," Sweet finally said with difficulty. "Anyway, I owe him."

CHAPTER NINE

Number Six, The Flying Jib Inn

THE *WOTAN'S* ARRIVAL in Kingston was little remarked, for that busy port saw the arrival of merchantmen by the score. Sweet left the ship, his wages for the voyage tucked away in his pocket. The wharves were crowded and the open-air market busy, but Sweet barely noticed. He was not a very observant man, for the antics of human beings were of little interest to him. A stolid, unimaginative man was Sweet, not subject to emotional tides. He had never known loneliness or despair or fear or ecstasy, nor had he ever felt the dizzying heights of love or the fiery depths of hate. The highest emotion he had ever experienced was his stubborn sense of obligation to Bain Winslow. And that was why he wandered the wharves now—on behalf of his employer.

He walked down the narrow street that bordered the wharves, looking for an inn but seeing only taverns and ships' stores and shipping offices. He knew, however, that where there were sailors, there would be inns. He finally found one that fronted the wharves. He stood still, staring up at the inn with empty eyes, trying to deter-mine if it was suitable for his employer.

The inn was nicer than most right on the harbor, a three-story white-plastered building, gleaming in the bright June sunlight. Red tiles covered the roof, and an extended bay window on the second floor jutted out over the street. Through the mullioned windows, Sweet watched two men eating, and one of them looked up and caught his eye. Sweet stared blankly at him until the man dropped his gaze.

A wooden sign was mounted just above the old mahogany front door, but of course Sweet could not read it. However, he recognized the emblem for the inn: a model jibboom, with furled sails and rigging.

Sweet stepped inside, and after the bright sunshine, the dark interior blinded him. A thick fog of raw alcohol, stale tobacco, and crowded humanity assaulted his nostrils. Finally his eyes adjusted to the light so that he could see the tavern. It was much like all taverns that multiplied like fleas around busy ports: old wood paneling blackened with age and smoke, a dozen or so tables, a long bar with bottles behind and glasses overhead, a man in a white apron wiping a mug with a dingy bar towel. At one big, noisy table, sailors drank out of tall pewter tankards. Another table was occupied by two prosperous-looking men in white suits reading newspapers, their white straw hats pushed back, long thin cheroots clenched between their teeth. A harried-looking woman with wispy hair and dirty apron hurried to another table, skillfully weaving among the crowd, a heavy tray full of slopping beer mugs held over her head.

The barkeep was a thin man with a small waxy black mustache. Sweet walked up to the bar, planted himself in front of him, and said simply, "I need a room."

The barkeep studied Sweet critically. "How long?"

"Maybe two weeks."

"Pay in advance."

"I'll see this room first."

The barkeep sneered a little—or perhaps it was just the mustache—and then nodded amicably enough. "My name's Jenkins. This is my place. And you are—"

"Sweet."

Jenkins waited, but no more was forthcoming, and he shrugged a little. He wasn't going to interrogate the man, no matter how sea worn and stupid he appeared, if he had the money to pay up front for two weeks. "That's my wife, Mary Mae. Go tell her to show you up to number six."

Mary Mae led Sweet up the stairs at the back of the pub to the third floor. The second floor, she showed him with pride, had a smaller, more fashionably appointed bar with a private card room. On the dark and stifling third floor she opened a nondescript door and stepped back.

The room was fairly large and light, with a high ceiling and long windows with sturdy shutters, thrown open to air the room, he presumed. In front of the windows was a small table and two chairs with woven-cane seats and backs. There were two small beds hung with mosquito nets, one scarred teak chest of drawers, one washstand, and two movable woven screens to serve as privacy partitions for the beds. As always in the tropics, a woven straw mat covered the floor rather than a heavy woolen carpet. The plastered walls were bare except for one amateurish painting of a ship in a storm at sea. Sweet glanced at it, thinking, *That fellow can't draw ships.*

The only thing Sweet checked closely was the mosquito netting swathed over the beds. Sweet had no conception of whether a room was finely furnished or not; all furniture looked alike to him, so he could not judge the price of a room by its appointments. He could, however, make a judgment as to whether the room was clean or not, and this one was. He also noted that the mosquito netting had no tears. Without another look at the woman, he turned and stumped back down the stairs to the tavern.

Once again he stood in front of the barkeep and waited with his oxlike patience until the man had drawn two tankards of beer. "How much for this number six?"

Jenkins cut his eyes to Sweet's blank face. "Six pound a week for such a fine, clean gentleman as yourself, sir."

"How much in American dollars?"

"Fifteen dollars a week."

"Too much. Five dollars a week. In advance."

The regular argument ensued, with Jenkins objecting shrilly and Sweet remaining stolid. Basically Sweet was an honest man, so he told Jenkins there would be two occupants. Jenkins finally insisted on twelve dollars a week and Sweet had to agree. It was much more than he could afford, but the place was decent and he knew that Mr. Winslow would never consent to stay in some filthy beetle-ridden pit.

Jenkins made a clucking sound of satisfaction and took the dollar bills Sweet painstakingly counted out and handed over. Jenkins tucked them into his shirt pocket and became more cordial. "Have a drink, Mr. Sweet, on the house, of course." He poured a thick, dark brown liquor into a small glass.

"It is just 'Sweet.' And I don't drink spirits. But when Mr. Wor—Winslow comes, you will give it to him." Sweet headed for the door but turned back and asked, "What is the name of this inn?"

"Huh? Why, it's the Flying Jib Inn, o'

course," Jenkins answered, scowling again and downing the drink himself.

Sweet nodded and left.

He returned to the *Wotan*, which was deserted except for the third officer and two hapless crewmen who stood watch. The rest of the crew, he knew, had drawn their pay and gone ashore looking for liquor and women. Down in the dark, stinking crew quarters, Bain lay limp in his hammock, his face pale and almost skeletal, he had lost so much weight. "Where the blazes have you been, Sweet?" he snapped.

"I found us a place, Mr. Winslow."

"What kind of a place?"

"The Flying Jib Inn. Number six."

Bain watched with little interest as Sweet gathered his meager belongings and stuffed them into a canvas bag. Bain had two large chests, but Sweet had already packed them after he'd fed and shaved Bain that morning. "If you're ready, we'll leave now," he said.

"Am I ready? I never want to see another seagoing vessel again, not even the *Day Dream*," Bain said with weak spite. "I swear this hulk is cursed. I've never been so seasick in my life. Well, help me, Sweet. Don't just stand there staring like a moonstruck calf."

Bain struggled to sit up and had to make two tries at getting out of his hammock. He swayed as the room whirled sickeningly around him, and

Sweet held him up as he shakily stood. "It's no good. You're going to have to help me out of here," Bain groaned. "What about my trunks?"

Sweet answered, "I'll take you to the inn and then I'll come back for the trunks."

"Leave them here for these cutthroats to steal?" Bain blustered. "No, sir. You just toddle back out and get a porter, Sweet."

"Mr. Wor—sir, the men are on shore leave, and I think they wouldn't bother your trunks now. They know I would make them give them back," Sweet said, his colorless eyes narrowing slightly.

Bain frowned, then managed a weak grin. "Oh yes, I'd forgotten. I was so sick it was rather like a delirium. You're right, Sweet, no one would dare take you on again. All right, then let's go. But—stop—don't manhandle me like that, I can put one foot in front of the other, so quit pawing me."

The blazing afternoon sun made Bain blink like a bat suddenly thrown out into the daylight, and contrary to his grumbling, he could barely walk. Sweet half carried, half dragged him to the inn, with Bain complaining all the way.

When they reached the inn, Sweet helped him up the stairs—it took them a long time, for Bain had to stop and rest every two or three steps—and led him to the room. "This is number six, our room, Mr. Wor—Winslow. I'm sorry, but I only had money for one room. I will be quiet, though, and I won't bother you."

Bain collapsed onto the bed in the darkest corner, lying back with exhaustion. "It's not a bad room, Sweet," he said begrudgingly. "You did well. And I don't mind sharing a room with you. You've had to wait on me hand and foot for weeks now anyway. I despise illness, especially when it's my own," he finished with the weak fretfulness of a patient who had been sick for some time.

Sweet nodded. "I'm going to get you some food and then you can sleep."

"I'm not hungry," Bain fussed.

"You have to eat," Sweet said as he left. Soon he returned with a tray, which he put on the table. He asked Bain hesitantly, "You want me to feed you, Mr. Winslow?"

"Of course not, you idiot! That was only because we were on that tub that sailed like a great thumping crate," Bain responded irritably. His aggravation gave him a little energy, so he managed to get out of bed without Sweet's help and sit down at the table. To his surprise, the clear chicken soup was quite good, and the bread was freshly baked. He managed to finish a large bowl of soup and two pieces of bread. As he ate, Sweet stood silently, staring out the open window down at the busy street below.

Only when he had finished his meal did Bain

think to ask, "Aren't you going to eat something, Sweet?"

"Later. You sleep now."

Bain stood and offered no further protests as Sweet helped him undress. It gave him an odd feeling. The big man was not a manservant or a gentleman's gentleman, but throughout the three-week voyage he had fed Bain and helped him wash, shaved him and kept his clothes clean and pressed. Now as Bain lay back on the bed, he felt the heaviness of exhaustion wash over him, but thankfully he was no longer nauseated.

His last conscious thought was of Sweet. *Why does he do all this for me? Certainly not for the pay. . . . What kind of man is he, really? I thought he was just a cipher, a nobody—that there simply wasn't anything to know about him. . . . Hmm, maybe I was wrong. . . .*

———————

For a moment Bain did not know where he was, and fear swept over him. He was accustomed to the swaying of the ship and the give of his hammock, and the very rock solidness of the bed he was in confused him. He threw his arm up over his face in a motion of self-defense. The physical movement brought him to full consciousness, and his memory came flooding back. He sat up to see Sweet coming in with a pitcher of water in one hand and a dark bottle in the other. "I've been asleep again," Bain said with some lingering confusion.

"Yes, sir, you look better."

Bain had rested for the better part of two days. His appetite had returned, and Sweet had brought him three full meals a day—good, plain, solid food. The big man had also washed, mended, and ironed all their clothes and cleaned their room continually. That was a funny thing about Sweet: he was compulsively, almost fanatically, clean and neat. Bain wondered if his mother had taught him this and reflected again that he knew nothing about Sweet's history.

Bain sat on the edge of the bed and eagerly took a long drink of the cool water. It was hot in the room, but then it was hot everywhere in Jamaica. He reached up and touched his face, his fingers rubbing against the bristles. He hated having beard stubble; Bain was always exquisitely groomed.

Sweet said quickly, "I'll get water and shave you."

"That would be good."

Sweet left. He moved very silently for such a heavy man, making almost no noise as he closed the door behind him.

Getting to his feet, Bain noted with satisfaction that much of his strength had returned. He had always been a quick healer. He stretched, then sat at the table, popped the cork of the misshapen brown bottle, and poured himself a generous drink.

He held the glass up to the light that filtered into the room through the cracked shutter, stared at the dark amber liquid for a moment, then tossed it down in one gulp. The island rum had a sweet syrupy taste in his mouth, but, as always, it bit at his throat and hit his stomach with a powerful force. "It's like drinking cough tonic," he muttered. Bain's taste ran to expensive old brandy and crusted bottles of port. Still, he poured himself another drink, sipping it more slowly this time, letting the warmth and alcohol-induced feeling of well-being slip over him like a kid glove.

Out on the street he heard two women singing a brassy, rhythmic island chant. He shifted restlessly, thinking of Alena Zeiss, his illegitimate half sister. Alena was lovely, half Hawaiian, and she sang like an angel. In his mind he contrasted this dirty, noisy, raucous place with the cool nights, the emerald greens, the blazing flowers, and the heavenly sunsets of Maui. The memories pained him. Savagely he downed the dregs of his drink and poured another.

Sweet finally returned with a steaming pitcher of water and poured it into the basin. "We'll shave now while water's good and hot," he muttered, half to himself.

"I'll shave myself," Bain said. "I'm getting

tired of being coddled like an infant." Bain got up and washed his face carefully, then worked the soap in his shaving mug into a froth. As he spread the thick lime-scented lather on his face, Sweet stood by woodenly, saying nothing, merely watching. Gratitude was not one of Bain Winslow's strongest traits, but now he thought back on how Sweet had gotten him onto a ship, had cared for him, had found this place. Clearing his throat, he said gruffly, "Sweet, I must thank you for all you've done for me since we left New York."

Sweet's eyes widened a little, a reaction comparable to anyone else jumping up and whooping. "It wasn't much, sir."

Bain shrugged. "I think it was. You're a good man."

Sweet stared for a little longer, then abruptly turned and walked out of the room without a word.

Bain shook his head and rolled his eyes heavenward. "And a very strange man," he added.

Taking the straight razor, he firmly pulled it down one cheek, then wiped the blade on a towel. He moved carefully but swiftly. He was adroit with his hands and had good coordination, which made him an excellent man with a sword and a pistol. Not that he had ever been obliged to use either, but his mother had carefully schooled Bain as a young English gentleman, providing him with fencing lessons and plenty of opportunities to go on hunting trips when he was young. He hated hunting—so dirty and messy—but he had enjoyed his fencing lessons. He ought to take it up again . . . and then he snorted as he thought of the unlikelihood of finding a reputable fencing master in this benighted part of the world. Cutthroats and thieves, more like.

Bain finished shaving. Wiping the lather from his cheeks, he studied his reflection. He had an elegant, aristocratic look, he knew, and he cultivated it carefully. He critically noted his dark brown hair, which still looked dull from his illness. But at least there was no sign of gray, that first harbinger of age. Bain had always been pleased with his smooth complexion, and he saw with satisfaction that, though he was still pale, he didn't have that sickly yellow tinge the ill generally get. His eyes were a light tawny brown, wide and well shaped, and the brows over them were arched more than those of other men. Faint lines of dissipation had begun to show around his eyes and mouth, and he wondered, *What will I look like in five or ten years?*

He frowned at this thought, then dressed quickly in the costume of the prosperous men of the islands: a fine cream-colored linen three-piece suit. He was careful to get the string tie even, then from a peg by the door, he snatched his low-crowned wide-brimmed straw hat. He settled it on his head, studying himself in the mirror and finally adjusting it to give it a rakish tilt. His three canes, carefully cleaned and polished by Sweet, stood against the wall. He chose the ebony one with the vulture's-head handle, twirled it gracefully, and went out.

Kingston, like many port cities in the Caribbean, was an odd combination of the ugly and the beautiful. He passed by wretched shacks surrounded by raw garbage and swarming flies, and he also stopped to admire beautiful, gleaming white houses with red-tiled mansard roofs.

He passed a man sitting on a cane chair who was occupied with making such tiles. The man was young, no more than twenty, and muscular. He greeted Bain with a smile and said cheerfully, "Good morning, sah."

"Good morning."

Bain watched as the man pulled a viscous blob of red mud from a wooden tub beside him. The mud was so thick the man could hardly handle it as he spread it over his upper leg and shaped it halfway around his thigh. When he had worked it to the proper thickness, he very carefully picked it up and placed it in the sun beside a row of other newly shaped tiles.

Bain was fascinated. "So the tiles are all different. If a man with a smaller leg made tiles, they wouldn't be like yours at all, would they?"

"No, sah, every tile is different." His white teeth gleamed against his dark skin. "This is Master Frobisher's house. It is fine, is it not, sah?"

"Very beautiful."

The house was finished except for the roof. The tile maker went on with satisfaction, "It is good to be a part of Master Frobisher's house. Even when I am dead, part of me will still be here. That makes me feel ver' proud."

Bain nodded and continued on his way. *He's proud of what he's doing—and he's leaving something behind, even if it is only some tiles on a rich man's roof. What am I leaving behind? Nothing!*

These dreary reflections troubled him as he walked the streets of Kingston. Bain was unhappy, uncertain, for the first time in his life. He had always been rakish, a brash man with a privileged life who did whatever he wanted without a thought of consequences, either to himself or to others. Now not only did the future seem melancholy, but Bain felt that his past—his history, his very existence—had been aimless and useless. Bain Winslow had never been bothered by critical self-analysis, and now with a stormy frown he shoved the unwelcome thoughts away.

All morning he roamed the streets, watching the people, then finally coming to enjoy the hot, brisk breeze and the sunshine. He had been weak for so long, and so virulently ill, that he felt his spirits rising with the return of his strength.

He wandered down the waterfront and stopped to watch some stevedores loading a ship. Sweet was among them, having gotten a job on the docks. Bain watched as his servant picked up an enormous coil of rope that must have weighed at least two hundred pounds and threw it over his shoulder as if it were made of air. Sweet always worked hard. A dark little worry flitted across Bain's mind—Sweet had taken such good care of him, had even paid for the hotel, and now he was doing hard labor on the docks to help pay their expenses while Bain continued to live as a gentleman of leisure. But Bain was not the kind of man to let such a worry trouble him for long. Dismissing the thought, he turned and walked away.

Bain was getting tired, but he was loath to return to his room. This was the first time he'd been out-of-doors in almost a month. He wasn't an outdoorsy type of man, but he was enjoying his walk, and when he wasn't painfully comparing the West Indies to the paradise of the Hawaiian Islands, he enjoyed the sights and sounds of the bustling tropical port. It was late in the afternoon, and on a whim he hurried back north two streets, to a respectable tearoom he had passed, and had an enormous high tea. It was very British, with hot buttered scones and crumpets and thin little sandwiches and seedcake, and Bain ate till he was satiated. By the time he finished the meal, the soft tropical evening was creeping in.

He walked slowly back to the inn, reflecting that he would take a hot bath, rest for a couple of hours, and then perhaps visit the tavern. As he passed a grimy pawnshop, the crimson-orange of the setting sun's rays caught a bright flash in the window. The pawnshop was closed and dark, but Bain stopped idly to peer in. He saw that the dying rays had caught the gleaming silver fittings of a fine pair of dueling pistols. Bain recognized them immediately as the handiwork of the famous French gunsmith Boutet. His eyes narrowed as he reflected savagely on how much he would like to have those pistols, and that not too long ago he would have just bought them without a thought. Now, however, he had very little money and no more coming in. What was he going to do? How did he ever get into this pathetic situation?

My cousin Locke, of course! He took everything I had, even my family. And that woman—that doctor—

Oddly, a memory came to Bain of the night he had kidnapped Dr. Cheney Duvall. Sweet had come to him after Bain had had his scene with her and had showed him that she carried a Colt .44 in her medical bag. Bain reluctantly admitted to himself that he admired her a little. The dueling pistols somehow reminded him of Cheney—ornate, lovely, but of steely purpose. But his bitterness refused to let him feel any admiration for her or for anything or anyone who had anything to do with his hated cousin. He turned and walked away without a backward glance.

He walked out to the end of a long pier lined with small fishing boats, now empty and rocking slowly in the swell. A school of dolphins leaped across the horizon. Gulls gathered overhead, calling hoarsely, hoping for a handout. It came rushing in on him now—a dark and suffocating flood of worry, the certainty of how devoid he was of any earthly help. He had no prospects, no idea of any endeavor that he could attempt to support himself. All he had ever done was to sail around in grand style on *Locke's Day Dream*. His father had always set up the trade routes and merchants and contracts. The only thing he had ever done on his own was to import prostitutes and open brothels. True, he had taken steps toward setting up a legitimate shipping business in New York, and had even had some modest success. Bain had, uncharacteristically, felt very good about that.

But what good would that do if he didn't have a ship?

Once again Bain thought of Locke and his

Day Dream. A burning anger rushed through him, a bitterness like fire in his soul.

CHAPTER TEN

For Richer, For Poorer

BAIN WINSLOW WAS NOT structured to handle idleness well. Not that he'd ever actually *worked*—such a plebian concept—but at least he'd always been involved in plenty of activities, sailing around the world in his own private clipper, spending money, finding lovely women for his brothels, lording over Winslow Plantation.

The pale tropic sun poured a relentless heat through the cracks in the closed shutters, and Bain awoke, sweating and gasping, to another sterile, fruitless day in Kingston, Jamaica. As he went through his morning ablutions—alone now, for Sweet always went to his job at the docks before dawn—he was already contemplating having a drink. Just to lighten his depression, he told himself. Deep down Bain knew that he was drinking way too much, and he rather despised himself for it. He had never in his life been subject to that kind of weakness, but now before shaving he recklessly poured three fingers of rum into the water glass and downed it, shuddering a little as the hot syrup coursed through his gut. "So what?" he muttered to himself. "It's not as if

I have any pressing appointments."

He shaved and dressed, immaculately as usual, and went down to the tavern for breakfast. Jenkins greeted him with oily warmth—in spite of Bain's near poverty, he tipped well to preserve the illusion of wealth—and offered him American newspapers, newly brought in by a New York merchantman. As he ate, Bain read a month-old *New York Herald*, surprised at how eager he was for news from his former home.

He read a full account of the acquittal of Andrew Johnson, and a full two-page exposition about Ulysses S. Grant, the Civil War hero who was the Republican presidential nominee and was evidently confidently expected to be the next president. Incredulously, Bain read about General Grant's "close friend and former aide, Colonel Richard Duvall, who often received General and Mrs. Grant at Duvall Court in Upper Manhattan." With consternation, Bain thought, *I had no idea the Duvall woman was from such an influential family. . . . How could I? He's just a tradesman, after all, and a female physician—how vulgar can you get? I knew they had money, but to be close friends with the president of the United States? It's a wonder they haven't hounded Sweet and me into the ground and hung us from the highest tree!*

Bain was again filled with dread and paranoia, and actually glanced furtively around, as if General Grant himself and Colonel Duvall might be lurking in the shadows of the tavern, waiting to pounce. Then suddenly Bain chuckled, a dark gritty sound. "Come and get me, then," he muttered. "It's not as if I have anything left you could take away."

As the days had crawled by, Bain had spent a great deal of time in the pub of the Flying Jib Inn. He had quickly exhausted the sights of Kingston and found that drinking in the tavern, and talking to the constant stream of men who frequented it, offered some diversion. This particular tavern had a higher-class clientele than the other public houses on the wharves; most of the patrons were plantation owners, officers from the Royal Navy, and prosperous merchant seamen.

What really attracted Bain was the gambling that took place in the second-floor bar and card room that wealthier gentlemen had come to regard as a sort of private club. Jenkins, the innkeeper, had introduced Bain to several prominent men of Kingston, and Bain had ingratiated himself with them enough to become a part of the "club." In every society, he had thought cynically, an inner ring rules. If you did not belong to it, you did not matter a whit. Once you were inside, you were free to look down on others from this exalted pinnacle. Bain had been aware of this principle all his life and had always expected membership in the "inner ring" as his privilege.

If the other members of this exclusive little clique had known of Bain's current financial position—or, rather, the lack of it—he would have been coldly cut. But Bain Winslow was no fool, and since he had arrived in Kingston, he had been very careful to maintain appearances. He had given his acquaintances the impression that he was on a tour of the tropics, a British gentleman of leisure, a rather well-to-do one at that. He used his real name and managed to drop into the conversation that his family owned a shipping concern in the Pacific. He also had let drop a hint or two that he was considering the West Indies trade. He stayed rather vague about the details and spent just enough of his slender hoard of cash to seem to have ready money.

He was quite a skilled card player—Bain had spent many, many nights in expensive gambling dens in Shanghai, Rangoon, and Macau—but, like all gamblers, he sometimes lost. Still, he bore his losses cheerfully, with the proverbial "stiff upper lip," and the gentlemen he played with noticed such signs of British gentility.

Although he did sometimes win, Bain, to his intense frustration, found that he could never quite get ahead. Finally he found it necessary to go to a pawnshop, and decided to go to Ricketts', the one where he had admired the Boutet dueling pistols. It was a sort of self-punishment, he thought with embarrassment and anger. He clenched his jaw as he again admired the beautiful, unattainable pistols—and pawned two silver snuffboxes, his gold cigarette case with a diamond inset, two gold fountain pens, and his silver watch inlaid with a ruby encircled by diamonds on the case.

He had been able to talk the greasy, tight-fisted Ricketts out of twenty pounds, which was just enough to pay for room and board for him and Sweet for another week. Sweet, of course, had paid for the room for the first two weeks, and Bain had paid for all their food—as well as his rum and gambling debts. Out of the $284 he'd left New York with, he still had $41—a little over sixteen pounds.

Sweet put all the money he made from his hard work on the docks into the common stash, but still things were tight enough to keep Bain perpetually frustrated and even fearful. He found that as the days wore by, with nothing to look forward to except eventual ruin, he was drinking more and more and caring less and less. He grew reckless.

It was on a Saturday night, the twenty-seventh of June in the year of 1868, that Bain reached a desperate conclusion. "I can't go on like this," he muttered as he dressed for his evening at the card room. "I'm going to have to find something to keep myself and Sweet too. I'll have to win enough from my three 'friends' to give me a stake."

He had no illusions about the so-called friendship with the three men he played cards with most often. They were gentlemen, but they were also gamblers. It wouldn't bother them in the least if Bain Winslow lost every cent he had to them.

"And it won't bother me," he said with a reckless flash of his tiger tan eyes, "if I take every shilling of theirs. And so I will."

His dark three-piece suit was immaculate, his hair carefully styled, his manicure perfect. His lips twisted cynically as he stared at himself in the smoky mirror. "I'm ready. Winner take all." A grim fatalism gripped him. He took up all of his remaining money, hesitating as he reflected that he ought to pay for the room for another week. But he stuffed it all into his coat pocket and went down to the card room.

"Good evening, gentlemen," he said courteously. "I hope this is my seat." The three men looked up at him with sharks' smiles.

Roger Shanklin was the youngest son of a wealthy English plantation owner, only twenty-three years old. He lounged in his chair, a sorry specimen indeed. He had thinning blond hair, heavy-lidded, washed-out blue eyes, and thick, drooping lips. He was stoop shouldered, as if he hadn't the energy for manly posture. He also had a potbelly that he attempted to cover with expensive tailoring. Despite his poor showing, however, he was an aggressive, skillful gambler. It was his only consuming passion.

Across from Shanklin sat Lawrence Nevis. *A different kind of fish altogether,* Bain thought, *and much more dangerous.* Nevis was forty-five, a British solicitor. He had mousy brown hair and extremely sharp brown eyes that darted about, constantly wary. He was a compact man, not fussy or prim, but rather feline. He dressed well and had the air of careless superiority that intelligent and wealthy men always seem to exude.

The third member of the trio, Captain Medford Haller III, Royal Navy (retired) also had a wealthy background. He had captained the HMS *Irresistible,* which had been stationed in the West Indies for twenty years. Five years previously he had retired to Kingston with his large family. He was a big, bluff man with leathery features cooked by the tropical sun, bald on top with dark fringe around his ears and the back, and a prodigious mustache. He was a good card player, relying on instinct rather than on reason and logic, as did Lawrence Nevis. "Sit down, sit down, Winslow," he grunted. "We were beginning to wonder if tonight we should have only three hands. Dislike an odd table. What about Van John, eh? How about it, Winslow?"

Bain smiled at the British corruption of the French game *vingt-et-un*. Americans just called the game twenty-one, a fast, simple game of chance requiring little skill, where the players tried to draw cards adding up to twenty-one without going over it. Captain Haller, a John Bullish sort of man, liked it very much.

Bain agreed, for he was usually lucky at twenty-one. With only the barest wisp of regret, he put fifteen pounds on the first hand. He won and won again, then won the third hand. He was holding one hundred twenty pounds now, though the players would never have seen the exultation Bain felt.

Shanklin eyed Bain coolly and, perhaps, a bit suspiciously. "Let's double the stakes, shall we? Give us a chance for our revenge on Winslow in quick time."

The others agreed, so Bain, with preternatural calm, bet one hundred pounds on the fourth hand.

He won, scoring twenty-one exactly.

Captain Haller mumbled, "Gentlemen, these stakes are a little beyond me."

The solicitor, Mr. Nevis, pronounced, "I don't care for vingt-et-un enough to lose such sums. It's too fast and too chancy. No satisfaction when you win."

Bain privately disagreed but only inclined his head slightly.

Shanklin said with an unattractive pout, "But I want my revenge. Let's play *écarté*—a gentleman's game that involves a little skill. And if the stakes are too high for you, Captain Haller, Mr. Nevis, of course you may bet on the players." Écarté was generally a two-person game, and it was common, in a large dinner party, for instance, for the spectators to bet on the players.

Bain felt a slight reluctance, for he had only played the game once or twice at just such polite gatherings, with negligible results. But then the reckless courage that had seemed to rule him this night washed over him, and he took a long drink of the brandy his companions always drank— and supplied, so Bain wasn't obliged to pay for his own liquor when he played.

"Fine with me," he said carelessly. "If Captain Haller and Mr. Nevis agree, of course. I do owe them their chance for revenge too. Of course, I always find it somewhat of a letdown to lower the stakes during the games, so I should want to keep to at least a hundred-pound minimum."

Captain Haller and Nevis politely declined, but they did sit at an adjoining table to observe the play and to place bets in whispers. Neither of them could resist the chance for betting on the faithless Lady Chance.

It was Shanklin's deal, and as he took a few moments to remove the twos through the sixes from the deck—a requirement for écarté play—the oddest notion washed over Bain, making his throat constrict. He felt that he was on the brink of a climactic moment; his entire future was going to be determined and set firmly on this night. He had already begun the course, and there was no turning back. The words of the marriage ceremony, of all things, came into his head: ... *for better, for worse, for richer, for poorer* ... And now his troth was plighted.

Bain lost the first hand, but he still felt the fatalistic calm. He won the second and third. Shanklin won the fourth, and Bain was back to the same stake with which he had begun the game: about four hundred pounds. An insistent voice in his head nagged that he could quit now with no shame, but he stubbornly ignored this little voice of reason and nodded at Shanklin to deal the cards.

On the fifth hand, Bain looked at his hand. His vision grew strangely sharp; the cards themselves seemed to be outlined in lurid red. His skin felt hot, and his fingers tingled. Somehow he *knew* he would win. Even though his hand was good, it could still theoretically be trumped, but that made no difference. Bain *knew*.

He put everything he had on the table, which came to some six hundred pounds.

Shanklin, a seasoned card player, gave no sign, except that perhaps his heavy eyelids rose a bit. At the other table, Nevis and Haller whispered furiously; Mr. Nevis had been betting on Bain's bit of luck, while Captain Haller was banking on Roger Shanklin, who generally won if he played long enough. The two observers were now about even themselves.

In a bored drawl, Shanklin said, "I've only got four hundred pounds on me, Winslow. You'll take my marker for the other two hundred, of course."

Bain said politely, his heart thumping, "I'm afraid, Shanklin, that I only play with—and for—ready cash."

Shanklin stared at Bain's face, which was impassive. "You're bluffing," he said.

"It seems, Mr. Shanklin, that it will cost you six hundred pounds to find out," Bain said with a tiger's toothy grin.

Shanklin took out a pen and a card from his pocket and began to write. Bain watched him cautiously. "Let me say again, I'm only playing for cash."

Shanklin disdainfully shoved the card at him. "You'll take this, I'm sure."

Bain picked up the card and read the words: *To transfer title and all rights to Bannister House, Bannister Plantation, and all properties attached.* He looked up with a frown at Shanklin. "What's this?"

"That? Why, that's the title to my spice plantation in the Grenadines," Shanklin replied carelessly. He felt safe, for he had a very good hand. "Nevis there is my solicitor, and he'll witness the marker. If it should be necessary, he'll immediately transfer the title."

"All true, Mr. Winslow," Nevis said quietly.

Bain didn't even study his cards again; he just laid them down.

To Roger Shanklin's credit, he took the shock like a British gentleman. "I say, Winslow, you're just too lucky tonight," he said, stifling a yawn. "I believe I'm going to have to retire from the field."

"Certainly," Bain said, gathering his money and the precious marker. He stood up and bowed. "Gentlemen, your servant. Mr. Nevis, shall I call on you Monday morning?"

"Certainly. Our offices open at eight o'clock."

"I'll say good evening, then, gentlemen." Bain left, his shoulders squared, his gait light.

Captain Haller frowned at Roger Shanklin. "Your father's not going to be happy that you've gambled away the family estate, old man."

His words amused both the other men. Shanklin chuckled while Nevis managed a tight smile.

"Hardly, Captain Haller," Shanklin said carelessly. "You see, my father snatched up Sir Guy Bannister's holdings when he died intestate two years ago; everything reverted to the Crown, you know, and he picked up the entire estate cheap. He got a coffee plantation on Barbados, a cacao-and-citrus plantation on Dominica, and a spice plantation on Bequia in the Grenadines. My two brothers got the other holdings, curse them! I got Bannister Plantation on Bequia." His face turned sour. "It's a small, dirty, deserted place, and poor as a low church mouse. I've only been there once, and I told my father I wouldn't ever live there, that it would be just a drain of money to try to make the place work. After speaking with Mr. Nevis, here, he agreed with me. He's tried, halfheartedly, to sell the place, but no planter in their right mind would be interested." Lifting his glass, he shrugged and took a long drink, smacking a little. "My father will be glad I didn't lose any more cold, hard guineas."

"Mr. Winslow won't be so happy," Nevis said drily. "What was that marker for? Two hundred pounds? Bannister Plantation never made more than sixty pounds a year, even when old Sir Roger was there fussing with it. And the taxes are twice that. And by now even the old cottage is probably in ruins. When a plantation is unoccupied, the natives steal everything that can be moved, you know, even bricks."

Shanklin shrugged. "It's Mr. Bain Winslow's problem now."

"I'll do the paper work to transfer the title

tomorrow so it's waiting for Winslow when he arrives on Monday morning," Nevis said darkly, "and then I'm not going to be available to see him in case he wants to ask a lot of questions." His thin mouth twisted in a cynical smile. "You really took him, Roger."

Shanklin shrugged. "He won, didn't he? I lost."

Nevis grunted. "More like you lost an albatross."

CHAPTER ELEVEN

Bannister House, Bequia

BAIN AND SWEET STOOD in the prow of the mail packet *Caribe*, their gazes fixed hungrily ahead.

The sea was blue-green and the waves leaped up as if they had life in themselves. Overhead the azure sky was decorated with amorphous clouds that drifted lazily with no purpose. A flight of pelicans formed a V-shaped flotilla to the east, and the gulls dived recklessly on the packet, uttering an endless cadence of coarse cries.

"This is fine anchorage, Mr. Wor—I mean Mr. Winslow," Sweet remarked, his curiously colorless eyes narrowing as the sprightly little schooner drove straight into the generous bay.

Sweet still had problems forgetting "Mr. Wor-thington" and remembering "Mr. Winslow," but at least he had stopped calling Bain "Mr.—sir," as he had for weeks after Bain had told him to call him by his real name.

"So I hear," Bain replied. "I just hope we have a fine plantation house too." Images of the gracious white pillars of Winslow House, and of the many fine colonial plantation houses he'd seen in the islands with their pastel colors, wide airy verandahs, and cool, shady gardens filled his mind.

Bain had studied the Grenadines carefully on the maps, of course, but now they were before him. They formed a necklace of more than one hundred tiny islands stretching between St. Vin-cent in the north and Grenada to the south. All of them seemed to have been born at the same time, by the same violent mother-volcano. They were much alike, according to the reports of the sailors—mountainous, with volcanic-enriched soil, lush tropical flowers, hearty shrubs, and towering royal palms.

Bain was most interested in Bequia, of course, for it was on this particular island that he would make his home. According to what he could discover from the charts and the sailors' reports, a ridge ran the length of it from north to south, separating the rowdy Atlantic from the placid Caribbean. It was a relatively small island, about five crooked miles long and not quite two miles at its widest points. It was irregularly shaped, as if God had splashed down a heavenly fountain pen to form Bequia and the blotches of tiny uninhabited cays dotted around it.

The only notable facet of Bequia, Bain had heard repeatedly from the sailors he had questioned, was that Admiralty Bay was the finest, most secure anchorage in the Caribbean, easily accessible to even the largest ships, a fine shelter from the violent tropical storms and hurricanes that ripped continuously through the West Indies. In previous centuries the Royal Navy had used Admiralty Bay as a base, but since there was no Spanish Armada roaming the seas like hungry dogs, or French warships threatening the British Empire, the Royal Navy had eventually centered in the larger ports, such as Kingston and Barbados. Bequia and Admiralty Bay had been forgotten.

It was a beautiful and secure harbor, Bain noted. The bay was securely banked by hilly arms on both the northern and southern sides, with a comfortably wide entrance into the generous harbor. The beach was pristine white sand, not the coarse black volcanic grit of so many of the Grenadine beaches, and was ringed by thick belts of coconut and royal palm trees. Lifting his eyes, he studied the lush volcanic ridge on this, the peaceable leeward side. It was covered with lacy palms, sprawling bougainvillea, enormous frangipani bushes, and dark glossy-leaved bread-fruit trees.

Bain narrowed his eyes to study the town. The miniature village, whimsically called by the grand name of Port Elizabeth, was a huddle of wooden, palm-thatched huts in the center of the beach, set back from the high-tide mark in groves of towering palms. He saw only one sub-stantial stone building, just at the southern end of the village. A tall man stood outside it, and Bain could see the gleam of his silver hair. The beach was decorated with weathered racks bear-ing lacy seines and nets drying in the sun. Sev-eral small boats, from little two-man jolly boats to sturdily built longboats, were drawn up on the sparkling beach.

"Makes a pretty scene, doesn't it, Sweet?"

"What does, sir?"

Bain glanced at the big man, then sighed im-patiently. *What does he think about? Or does he ever think?* Bain found Sweet to be monstrously dull company. He was accustomed to being sur-rounded with people of his own class, and he generally sought out companions—especially women—with some intelligence, culture, and wit. Bain felt a sort of kinship with Sweet, as one would feel to a particularly loyal and friendly dog, but the big man bored Bain to distraction.

Bain, dismissing his impatience with his

companion, stared upward with hungry concentration, beyond the beach and the little village, to the green heights of the ridge. He couldn't be sure, but he thought he saw the outlines of a house close to the summit. "That house up there might be our new home—Bannister House," he murmured. "But I don't see any fields of spice."

Troubled, Bain searched harder. The title to Bannister Plantation stated plainly that it was 642 acres, or a little over a square mile. Such acreage was surely large enough to be seen at this distance. But the entire mountainside appeared to be covered in the semijungle of tropical trees and plants.

Two small fishing boats, handled expertly by two black men each, dashed close up to the *Caribe* and backed water. One man sang out, "Ahoy, *Caribe*! Mail for Bequia?"

"Ahoy, Rikke! Mail for Bequia and two passengers!" Captain Smithers bellowed, tossing a very small packet down into the first boat.

"Passengers?" the young man said uncertainly, eyeing Bain and Sweet.

"Can you take us ashore?" Sweet asked.

The young man shrugged. He was a handsome mulatto, muscular, with chestnut skin and light brown eyes. "Yes, sir, we can take you."

Bain boarded the first small boat, with the man named Rikke. Sweet loaded Bain's two enormous trunks onto the second boat and came along behind. Rikke and the other young man stared curiously at Bain but said nothing. Bain ignored them and kept his eyes on the island as the small boat sped forward. The sound of the surf breaking on the white beach grew louder, and the rich smell of fish, hot sand, ancient salt, and black dirt filled his nostrils.

The boat grounded in the shallows, but Bain sat still. Raising one sardonic eyebrow, he demanded, "Surely you don't expect me to wade in?" With dark looks both men jumped out, seized the rope tied to the bow and pulled the boat up onto the shore. Bain stepped out and said carelessly, "My man will see to you. Where is Bannister House?"

Surprise crossed the face of the young man called Rikke, but quickly his expression became stony. He turned and pointed up to their left. "About a mile up there, sir."

Squinting against the brilliant sunlight, Bain could see a thread of a path—not a proper road—winding upward. "Is there a carriage for hire?" Bain asked, frowning.

Rikke grinned, a wide, sunny smile that lit his face, but he quickly sobered when he saw Bain's stormy features. "No, sir. No carriages."

"Horses?"

Rikke shook his head. "No horses either, sir."

Bain stared at him. "Then how do you propose that I get up there? Ride one of those blasted goats?"

Expressionlessly Rikke answered, "No, sir. But we've had no horses here on Bequia since old Sir Guy died. He had two, but someone came and took them away."

Bain grimaced but said nothing more. He merely turned, in effect dismissing the man and disdainfully ignoring the spectators who were gathered along the beach and in front of the cottages, watching him curiously. He searched along the ridge, eyes narrowed, until Sweet had unloaded the trunks.

"Bannister House is up there somewhere," he said shortly. "There are no carriages and no horses. Only goats. Tip the boatmen and see if you can arrange for some bearers to bring up the trunks. I'm walking on up." Without waiting for an answer, he turned and moved swiftly toward the narrow path.

———

By the time Bain reached the summit, he was soaked with perspiration and gasping for breath. He paused and pressed his hand over the painful stitch in his side, muttering acidly, "What the devil is this—the caretaker's cottage?"

But even as he stared at the structure before him, he suddenly knew with a sinking sensation that this wasn't the house of a servant. He now remembered clearly the lightning-quick flash of humor in the eyes of Roger Shanklin when he'd lost the hand. Bain had thought he'd seen it, but then he had not wanted to see it, so he had ignored it. But now he knew.

"Shanklin did me in!" Bain said bitterly. With his vulture-headed cane he slashed viciously at a hibiscus blossom, sending the petals flying.

This was Bannister House. Bain felt slightly sick, for he had been enjoying expansive dreams of a new life in a splendid, gracious plantation house. His blistering gaze raked disdainfully over his new property.

The building, a two-story square made of reddish, sharp-edged native stone, frowned down. No gracious verandah, no airy French doors leading onto shady balconies, no generous expanse of creamy island pastels or cool white plaster work. Even the shutters over the precisely spaced four small windows were painted a foreboding leprous gray.

The massive oak door was locked, and woodenly Bain made his way around a stone walk to the rear of the house, noting that even the gardens were shabby and looked defensively huddled, like the house. The back door, at the end of a roofed stone portico leading to an outside kitchen, opened soundlessly.

Hesitantly Bain went inside, blinking in the gloom. The house was dark, for all of the shutters were tight over the windows. Leaving the door open, he waited until his eyes adjusted to the shadows before making his way inside.

The servants' workroom was on his left; the back end of the entrance stairs loomed directly in front of him. To his right was a closed door, and fumbling a little, he pushed it open and went in. It was a combination study and library, with a fireplace, dark but clean. The room was cluttered in the Victorian manner, and ghostly white canvas sheets shrouded the crowd of furniture.

Bain stood still, listening, lifting his head in an unconscious primitive scenting action. Something troubled him, and he suddenly knew what it was—the house did not feel empty. It was as if he had accidentally wandered into a home, a place where people lived and cried and fought and laughed.

Sensitive to such things, Bain noticed that the house didn't smell empty either, no moldy or dull dusty smell. On impulse he went to one of the canvas shrouds and pulled it off. It was a roll-top desk, a fine one made of mahogany. On it was an ink bottle, long dry, a letter stand, and two slim leather-bound journals. "Even personal items . . ." Bain murmured.

The rooms were all floored and paneled with some dark wood, and the effect was a dusky mass of shadows. The heavy smell of spice hung in the air, and Bain started as he made his way upstairs. He realized that the entire interior was paneled with cinnamon wood of a dull reddish color. *Odd . . . priceless, but useless. You'd tear it up if you tried to tear it down. . . .*

Upstairs were two enormous bedrooms, furnished adequately, but they were curiously anonymous after the masculine, cluttered study.

Returning downstairs, he checked the other two closed doors: a dining room and parlor. Both of them had mounds of swathed furniture crowding them. In the entryway was a long-case clock, dark with age. On impulse Bain opened the case and set the weights. It began a deep, melodious incantation: *tock—tock—tock—*

Hastily he stilled the weights. The sound was ghostly and eerie in the quiet but not dead house.

Moving to the front door, he unbarred it and stepped outside. He was deeply depressed. Bitterly he thought of the high expectations he'd had—and now they all lay shattered. He moved around the house, looking at the neglected gardens and grounds, the line of shanties in back of the kitchen, the small—very small—groves of flowering bushes to his right.

He turned the corner and was startled to see a woman standing in the kitchen doorway, watching him. Startled, he blustered, "Here! Who are you? You're trespassing!" striding down the portico toward her.

She was young, with glossy, curly hair, blue eyes, and golden skin. She was much shorter than Bain, only a few inches over five feet. As he came nearer, Bain realized that she must be a quadroon or perhaps an octoroon, because her features had a hint of the black race, with full lips, high, rounded cheekbones, and a strong jaw. But her skin was lighter in color than many Hawaiian women Bain had seen, and her hair looked more like a Spanish woman's than the tight curls of African peoples.

She watched him coolly, undisturbed, until he was near her. "My name is Imri Ten Eyck," she said in a low, rich voice. "And I am not trespassing, sir. My family and I are servants of the house."

———

"Oh, sit down, Sweet," Bain said with disgust. "Stop hovering over me like some anxious hen. I'm just exhausted and filthy. On second thought, go see if you can get some of those people to prepare me a hot bath."

Every night since he and Sweet had arrived—for eight nights—Imri Ten Eyck and her two sisters had prepared hot baths in the kitchen for Bain, but every night he complained as if no one had ever heard of a bath before. One of the first instructions Sweet had given the servants was for his and Bain's nightly baths, arranging for the women to start heating the great pots of water directly after supper. Of course, Sweet attended Bain first and then took his own. In the fog of his mind a few things stood out clearly. One of them was that a man couldn't sleep unless he was clean.

"The bath is fixing now, Mr. Worthington," Sweet said woodenly, standing there, his hands down at his sides, the permanently vacant look stamped on his face.

"Then sit down," Bain repeated irritably. "Have a brandy. You do drink, don't you?"

Sweet sat as commanded, shaking his head. "Just beer sometimes."

"Oh? Why didn't you tell me? Buy yourself some next trip to St. Vincent," Bain said absently. He rolled his brandy expertly in the fine snifter—presumably the late Sir Guy Bannister's—and stared into space.

"Thank you, Mr. Worth—Mr. Winslow," Sweet said.

"We've landed in a pit this time, eh, Sweet?" Bain asked, his gaze still faraway. "Stuck in this jungle, on this wretched island in the middle of the ocean." He drained his glass and slammed it down on the table. "Stuck and broke."

Sweet's wide brow wrinkled. "But you own this farm, Mr. Winslow. All of this is yours."

Bain laughed, a sour sound, and swept his arm around in a lavish gesture. "Oh yes, all of this is mine! All six hundred and forty-two acres. Unfortunately, they are canted at a sixty-five-degree angle. Twenty whole acres of nutmeg and mace and cinnamon, and this fine, palatial house! And goats—and cats too! I hate cats."

"Without cats you have the rats, Mr. Winslow," Sweet said, glancing, puzzled, at the skinny but arrogant tabby cat that was seated on another leather club chair in the study. Her green eyes stared back at him, defiant. Bain just called her "Fiend"—but he let her stay in the house.

"Yes," Bain muttered. "Rats are the only things I hate more than cats. I hate goats too. In fact, I'm hard put to find anything I don't hate about this miserable place!"

Sweet looked perplexed. Bannister Plantation and Bannister House seemed to him to be fine properties. Sweet knew he would never in his life own a two-story house with servants and acres of sweet-smelling spices.

Bain settled in the leather club chair—it was very old, but it was still solid and comfortable—and sighed. "I went through Bannister's private papers today," he said in a low voice. Talking to Sweet was much like talking to a rock wall, but it was better than talking to himself. "The Ten Eycks—this part of them, anyway—were old Bannister's servants for years. They've been staying here, working the plantation by themselves for the last two years because the Shanklins never paid them, I guess. They harvest the spices, and Rikke and their father take them in that little skiff all the way up to St. Lucia and Martinique and sell them in the open markets. They just stayed on in the servants' quarters. Seems that once, about a year ago, some agent of Shanklin's came out here with Roger, looked around, took some of the financial records—and the horses—thumbed their noses, and disappeared without another word. No instructions to the servants, no word to the field workers, no word to Verbrugge, who had been Sir Guy's foreman."

"You mean one of the Verbrugges who live in the old chandlery?" Sweet asked.

Bain nodded.

"Which Verbrugge?" Sweet asked.

"Who knows? Kort, I think. The older brother. How many of them are there? A hundred?" Bain said drily, taking a drink of his brandy.

"I don't think so, not one hundred Verbrugges," Sweet said, frowning darkly. "Maybe twenty, maybe more, live in that big house. Many more Ten Eycks and Dekkers than Verbrugges. But not one hundred of any."

Bain sighed. Wry remarks were lost on Sweet. "I know, Sweet. I was just exaggerating." He stared down into his brandy, thinking of the racial makeup of the island. "Did you know that everyone in the village is a descendant of three Dutch sailors who were shipwrecked on Baliceaux? Baliceaux, that's that little—well, the bigger of the two little islands you can see from the Old Fort. By the way, I've been meaning to ask you, are you Swedish?"

"No, sir. Bavarian."

"Are you? Funny, I thought someone told me you were a Swede," Bain said carelessly. "Anyway, these three Dutch sailors made a raft and came to Bequia. Guess the French were the only ones here then, except for the African slaves. Anyway, the Ten Eycks and the Dekkers intermarried with the slaves, but the Verbrugges have always married white people—mostly other Dutch from Saba, I believe."

Sweet said, "They still speak Dutch. The Verbrugges, I mean. When they are by themselves. Alone."

Bain half grinned at Sweet's simplicity and started to ask him how he knew what they did when they were alone. But, of course, Sweet wouldn't catch on, and he would struggle to give Bain an explanation. So Bain just nodded. "Anyway, the Ten Eycks and Dekkers seem to just kind of marry each other, and then they pretty much just decide whether to be named Ten Eyck or Dekker. The Verbrugges, though, trace their line strictly back to that first Verbrugge. He was the bosun, Dekker was the ship's carpenter, and

Ten Eyck was the carpenter's mate."

A slight flicker of interest showed in Sweet's dull gaze. "Maybe that is why all of them are such good seamen and build such good boats."

"Maybe so," Bain agreed. "Anyway, most all of the Dekkers and Ten Eycks in the village are illiterate, but Imri and her family can read and write, thanks to Elena Verbrugge. She fancies herself as a teacher."

Sweet sat dumbly, as Bain's statement seemed not to require any comment from him. He never knew, in conversation, whether he was supposed to say anything or not. And when he felt that he should, he didn't know what to say. Sometimes Bain was sarcastic to him, but this time he seemed not to notice, or care, whether Sweet spoke or not, and Sweet relaxed just a little.

Bain was saying expansively, "Anyway, I'm going to make Rikke manager of the general store, and make Pieter and Ama—that's the parents, you know—manage the tavern. Right now they've got some fools of Ten Eyck cousins or something running those little ramshackle nothings. But I'm going to clean them up and stock them up, and see if maybe we can at least get some decent supplies and tobacco and liquor on this island. I'll probably be the only paying customer"—he laughed bitterly—"but who knows, maybe they can at least pay for themselves instead of being filthy shacks stocked with nothing but coconuts and those cursed spices and that sickening sweet island rum."

But Sweet had lost the thread of Bain's business plan; he would never interrupt Bain, so he waited until he finished before going back to the beginning of the speech. "But if Rikke and the parents go to the village, who will be servants and field workers here?"

Bain shrugged. "Ten Eycks and Dekkers can work the fields and the spice shacks. And as for house servants, Imri's younger sisters Chika and Mandisa can cook and clean."

"And Imri?" Sweet asked with his customary lack of inflection or expression.

Bain dropped his eyes and answered in a low, harsh voice, "Imri stays here."

CHAPTER TWELVE

Bequia Breeze

BAIN WINSLOW AWOKE one bright morning at the end of August and realized, to his shock, that he had already spent two months on Bequia. They had gone by quickly, for he had been very busy, and he admitted to himself with wonder, he had even come to enjoy a measure of contentment. When he had first arrived, he had prepared himself for a dreary siege of boredom at best, but it had not been like that. August had come and was now almost gone, and not only had he survived, he had actually thrived.

He laughed and groaned at the same time as he got out of bed. Yesterday he had made a royal fool of himself. The old Bain Winslow would never have worked like a poor tenant farmer in the fields. But somehow Bain Winslow of Bannister Plantation could, and would, if he took the notion to.

Bain was amazed at how much he had learned about spices—and at how fascinated he had become with his tiny kingdom. Knowing full well that he had no other options, he had thrown himself into absorbing every scrap of knowledge available about growing nutmeg and cinnamon. He had learned how mace is processed and nutmeg extracted, and he had been shocked to discover how slow the process of building up a field of nutmeg and mace could be. Only the females produce, and it requires five or six years before a nutmeg tree puts out its first blossoms. At that point the male trees must be removed and the bearing females spaced. When he learned that it takes at least fifteen years to reach full output from a field, he had understood, with a sinking heart, that expansion to produce more nutmeg and mace was not an option. He didn't have fifteen years to realize a profit, and neither did he have any more arable land. Bannister Plantation, it turned out, encompassed half the hillside, including the village, but the only acreage level enough to cultivate was the twenty-two acres that Sir Guy Bannister had already formed. Still, Bain had doggedly thrown himself into learning how to most efficiently produce and process the spices that he had.

The production of cinnamon, he had also learned, was not easy either. A wild cinnamon tree grows as high as thirty feet, but cultivated trees are severely pruned. The ideal plant is a shrubby affair with many slender stems. When the shoots are about six feet high, they are ready for harvesting. The previous day, about two acres of the cinnamon groves were ready, and so Bain had closely observed this, his first spice harvest.

With quick, practiced movements, the workers—most of them women—slit along the length of the cut stems on each side with a sharp knife and then pried loose a strip of bark and peeled it off. This, Bain had learned, facilitated the stripping later, after the shoots had been stored and covered with sacks to promote fermentation, which loosened the corky outer layer of bark. It was the heart of the tree that contained the precious spice.

Later, in the spice shacks, when the bark had separated somewhat, the workers took curved knives and scraped the shoots, holding the bark rigid by pressing it tightly against a smooth stick. The scraped inner bark was dried into what were called *quills* and bailed for export. The broken quills were ground up into powder and tied in linen bags.

Bain had decided to try it himself—the women's quick, sure motions looked pretty easy. He had strong hands, but after struggling mightily to cut straight along the side of the corky stem, his fingers were sore and he had cut his palm. Stubbornly he worked and picked until he had managed to open a jagged strip in the outer layer, reflecting that this work was not nearly as easy as the women made it look. They gave him curious sidelong glances, but of course they would never comment or laugh. Stubbornly, mostly because he was embarrassed at his lack of skill, Bain worked the entire afternoon in the cinnamon grove, cutting and stripping stems. When the sun sank low that day, he stood up and pressed a hand to his aching, burning back. Then, along with the other cinnamon workers of Bannister Plantation, he piled his cinnamon shoots up to take them to the shack.

Long shafts of pale afternoon sunlight slanted through the nutmeg shack as Bain stood, watching his workers with satisfaction. Fourteen women and children processed the nutmeg and its attendant spicc, mace. The clatter as they rhythmically cracked the nuts reminded Bain irresistibly of castanets. The rich aroma of nutmeg and the stinging scent of mace intertwined heavily on the air.

The shed was sweltering, the air suffocatingly heavy with the scent of spice. In particular, the heavy scent of raw mace made Bain's nostrils burn. Thoughtfully he reflected that he ought to make some windows in the shacks. He could install locking shutters. Processed spice—a small, portable crop—could easily be stolen, and that was why the shacks had only a sturdy door, which was padlocked at night. But it was so hot and stifling, Bain thought he might make lockable windows if he could gather up an extra dollar or two.

"Let's go outside," he said shortly to Sweet.

Leaving the shed, the pair walked back through the grounds to what Bain had taken to calling the Overlook. It was an enormous flat rock just down the path that juttcd out over the slope, with a wide, clear view of the bay and the village. It was a favorite perch of Bain's. Often in the cool evenings he and Imri would bring a blanket to sit on and a bottle of rum, and would watch the sun set.

In the past weeks Bain, sometimes with Imri, sometimes alone, had wandered all over the island, even over to the barren windward side.

He'd rather enjoyed exploring the old French fort and staring out at the endless expanse of the gray, wind-whipped Atlantic. He had also walked down to the village every day, enjoying the recognition of the villagers. He was, after all, the "big boss" now.

The exercise had been good for him. He was leaner than before, hardened and more substantial looking. He had lost the tavern pallor, and his face was tanned, his eyes bright. The tropical sun had tinted his brown hair with dark golden streaks.

When they reached the great flat rock, Bain stopped and gazed out at the sea, noting a line of dolphins playing about a quarter of a mile out. He especially liked to watch them, and he had strictly forbidden the islanders to kill a dolphin for any reason.

He was silent for a time, then turned and saw that Sweet was frowning, obviously trying to frame some sort of difficult idea. Bain waited with only a hint of impatience. He'd had only Sweet and Imri to talk to for so long, he felt his mind had grown almost as slow and plodding as Sweet's.

Finally Sweet muttered, "More cinnamon, maybe, sir? More . . . more . . ."

"More acres for cinnamon and less for nutmeg and mace?" Bain asked idly.

"Yes, sir," Sweet said gratefully.

Bain shook his head. "Won't work. I've already thought endlessly about it, trying to work around those little squares of spices to make them yield more money." He sighed. "Besides, we're just too close to St. Vincent and Grenada. Both of them have miles and miles of spice plantations and spice-processing plants, fine shipping-and-port facilities, and distribution networks. Our little twenty acres can't possibly compete with them."

Sweet nodded, though a little doubtfully. He didn't understand the concept of big organized industry versus small-yield farms.

Bain, who had realized that he disliked wearing hats and always had, wore no hat even in the hottest tropical sun. Shading his eyes with his hand, now toughened by honest work, he stared out into the bay. He muttered a curse, then asked Sweet, "Is that those Dekker brothers? Hauling in a whale?"

Sweet took one glance and nodded. His eyes were very sharp. "I think it is Willem and Pieter Dekker, yes, sir. The village will be glad for the whale."

Bain had been amazed to find that almost all of the men on Bequia hunted whales. True they didn't get many, usually only two or three humpback whales, but they had only small boats and handmade harpoons. Usually four boats a day went out, with six men to a boat. The boats themselves were wonders, Bain had discovered, with seams so close that a piece of paper would hardly go between them. When they did kill a whale, the entire island shared in the prize.

Bain saw three boats bringing a small humpback whale toward shore. At once he raised his voice, "Devil take them! That last beast they brought in—the stench! And the bloody, greasy mess on the beach for days! I'll not have it on Bequia! Get down there right now, Sweet, and tell them to haul that thing to Baliceaux or Batowia for flensing!"

Sweet took off, running down the zigzagging path to the village. His thick legs were like pistons, and he could run for hours without taking a deep breath. Bain was satisfied that he'd reach the boat before they beached the whale. Disgusted, he started to turn back to the house, but he stopped and gazed out to sea again. The Bequians were expert boatbuilders, that much was certain. The bay was dotted with small, nimble fishing boats, larger whaling boats, two-man jolly boats, even little dugouts that the children used.

"I wonder . . ." Bain whispered to himself. "I wonder why they couldn't build something bigger. Something fine. Something like . . . a schooner!"

August waned, giving way to September and October—glorious months, as was every month in the Caribbean.

Ever since Bain had seen the Dekkers bring in the whale, he had been deep in thought. One late afternoon he summoned Kort Verbrugge, Rikke Ten Eyck, and Willem Dekker to his house for tea. They met in the formal parlor, obviously ill at ease. Kort Verbrugge was the tall, blond-haired man Bain had noticed when he first arrived on Bequia. Willem Dekker was twenty-eight and looked like a white man but was actually one-eighth black—an octoroon. He seemed to be the acting head of the Dekker clan. Sweet was there too, and though he lived in the "big house," he still had the uncomfortable air of a man caught in a situation above his station.

They finished tea, served silently and gracefully by Imri, who then withdrew. Without much small talk, Bain launched into his agenda.

"I've been considering a project for a while now, and I'd like to discuss it with you men." They exchanged wary glances, but Bain said bluntly, "This island is poor. You are poor. I'm not poor, but I soon will be. I hope you all realize that all this plantation really does is provide work for you. It's impossible for me to make any money from it."

Kort Verbrugge shifted restlessly, then said in a low voice, "But . . . Sir Guy made money, Mr. Winslow."

"He did not, not from Bequia. Were you aware that he owned two other plantations? Both of them were large and wealthy holdings. I know he lived here most of the year—why, I cannot fathom—but his money came from his other two holdings, not from Bequia. It seems that Bannister Plantation was just a sort of charitable concern for him. But *I* am not a charitable institution," Bain finished drily.

The men's faces looked wooden, and they dared not exchange glances, much less protest.

Sighing, Bain went on, "I might have a way for you and me and all of the villagers to make a better life for ourselves. I think it can be done, but I can't do it alone."

Kort Verbrugge looked up with interest. "You mean we can help?"

"I certainly hope so. Tell me, Verbrugge, could you build a schooner? A fine one, I mean, not a crude Bequian fishing boat. More like a yacht. Could you do that?"

Verbrugge frowned. "Maybe. Maybe. But I'm no shipwright, Mr. Winslow. I think I could follow plans—I draw out rough ones sometimes—but I don't think I could design such a craft."

Bain smiled broadly. "Well, *I* have plans,

but I can't build it. I think that you can. And I know, Rikke, that one of the Ten Eycks has a little forge and you do blacksmith work sometimes, making the iron fittings for the whalers. And, Dekker, I know you and many of your relatives make sails and cordage and do fine decorative carpentry work." He sat forward, uncharacteristically animated, and spoke in a low, intense voice.

"You see, if we could make something of the village, have an industry, we already have the best anchorage in the Caribbean. If we could build private island-hopping schooners and have ships' stores—sails, cordage, rigging, tools—and a couple of good wharves, we might be able to have a nice little marine industry here in Port Elizabeth."

Verbrugge slowly asked, "But, sir, how can we do all this just by building a schooner?"

With exaggerated patience, Bain said, "Because, Verbrugge, if you build me a schooner, and I contact some of the wealthy plantation owners in the islands and sell a few schooners for island-hopping, then they will know Bequia is a center for fine yachts—and fine marine stores. First we sell schooners, and then we get men coming to us for the best rigging and the finest sails, as well as for cleaning, repairs, and overhauls . . . and then we have a marine industry."

A long silence fell on the room. It was broken when Kort Verbrugge finally asked, "Sir, may I see these plans for the schooner?"

Bain Winslow lost track of the passage of time after his meeting with his three "partners" in October 1868. Now it was May 1869—almost a year since Bain had come to Bequia. He truly thought of himself as an islander now, though he would never openly admit it. He was the "big boss," that was certain. He owned the entire town, except for the old ship's chandlery, which the Verbrugges owned and lived in. He had twenty-four hands on the plantation, and almost every able-bodied man in the village had had a hand in building his schooner.

Bain and Imri stood on the beach, watching the *Bequia Breeze* come in. Oh, she was lovely! And, of all people, Sweet had thought of her name. It was perfect, for she was swift and graceful on even the lightest wisp of wind.

All of this Bain absorbed with pleasure, and now as he watched the *Bequia Breeze* approach, he found himself feeling something like affection—even love—for her. He had loved very few things, and would have been embarrassed if anyone had known of this feeling. Rather guiltily he glanced down at Imri, for at times she had shown a surprising insight into his emotions. She merely looked back up at him and smiled her mysterious smile.

Bain, who had just discovered the one true love of his life, now reflected with some confusion that he had never spoken to Imri of love. He had, honestly, never thought about being in love with Imri. Was he? Was it possible? She was so simple, so lacking in the skills of acquiring and keeping a man that Bain had so often seen displayed in other women. Imri was a simple island girl, naïve in many ways, though she was no saint. Bain had wondered, sometimes, about her and old Sir Guy Bannister. But Imri had never said a word, and somehow Bain found that Imri's innate dignity kept him from intruding on her privacy. It was an odd thing, since they had lived together for almost a year now. But that was the way it was between them.

She was barefoot, wearing a brightly flowered dress, and with her long, gleaming hair blowing in the breeze, she looked lovely. She was generally a grave, reserved woman, but when she laughed it was purely childlike.

Imri had never presumed on their relationship, or demanded special attention, and certainly not expensive gifts. Bain had given her some coral jewelry and several bolts of fine muslin and one of crimson silk. A few days later she, her sisters, her mother, and two of her cousins had turned up with crimson silk skirts. Imri was a very good seamstress.

With amusement Bain recalled an incident a few months previous. On a visit to the bustling port of Kingstown on the island of St. Vincent, Bain had spotted in a dressmaker's window four pretty little dolls from France that were clothed in the latest French fashions. These dolls were exported from France to the rest of the fashion-crazed women in the world to show the latest *haute couture*. Bain had bought them for Imri, along with several yards of materials and laces similar to the ones fashioned for the dolls. Imri had thanked him gravely. "No one has ever, ever given me such a wonderful gift before, Bain," she said, her blue eyes glowing. "I am so very grateful."

Later Bain had heard squealing and giggling in the servants' workroom and had investigated. Imri and her two sisters, Mandisa and Chika, were sitting on the floor, playing with Imri's new dolls.

Somehow Bain never had the heart to tell Imri what the dolls were really for. *Besides*, he had thought, with some discomfort at his strange reluctance to hurt Imri's feelings, *she would look silly in those complicated, bulky frocks. She looks like a vision, barefoot, her hair flowing, in a simple wrap skirt and bright blouse. . . .*

Coming out of his musings, he again paid

close attention to the *Bequia Breeze* as she came home.

Sweet, Kort Verbrugge, his brother Konrad, and Rikke had sailed the schooner out of the bay, north, around Baliceaux and Battowia, come back around south, and back. Bain and the crew had already taken her on several short hops: to Mustique, Canouan, Carriacou, and north to St. Lucia. On this last trip north, it seemed that she had been pressed down at the forefoot a little when the schooner had joyously hit twelve knots!

Sweet, however, had frowned and said, "Shift ballast, Mr. Winslow. Lighter in the bow, heavier at the stern." He was truly a good sailor, handling the schooner with such grace and ease that Bain was envious. He had designed her, yes, and she was beautiful, but he was not a good sailor, and he handled her so awkwardly that even this dream of a yacht jigged and grew petulant when he took the helm.

But now she swooped into the bay, all sails rigged and full-bellied. Just before she hit low water, Sweet pulled her around in a perfect curve for anchorage. Pieter Ten Eyck, Rikke's father, had already taken out one of the boats to bring them in.

"Doesn't seem as if she's pressed down now," Bain remarked with satisfaction. "Sweet may be stupid, but he is a right seaman."

Imri said calmly, "He isn't really stupid,

Bain. He just takes a little longer than some, is all." She, too, spoke like a Britisher of the working class.

Bain shrugged, ignoring her defense of Sweet. "I think it's time for some real sailing. I think I'll take her to Jamaica and look up my old friend Roger Shanklin." He smiled, a wry twist of his mouth. "Show him what a prosperous planter and fine yachtsman I am. Serve him right. Who knows? Maybe even he can afford a Bequia schooner."

Bain had spent every last pound he'd had on the schooner, as well as every shilling he could wring out of the plantation, the store, and the tavern. He'd ordered the finest teak for the deck, the finest canvas for the sails, and he had made the Ten Eycks work overtime at the little forge, fashioning the best and most polished ironwork.

Imri stared out at the schooner, rolling gently in the calm turquoise bay. "May I go with you, please?"

"What? Oh no, no, that won't do, Imri," Bain blustered. Bain wasn't ashamed of Imri—not on Bequia, anyway. All of the islanders, even the pure white Verbrugges, were a close community, with little sense of hierarchy according to color. Bain had observed that in the West Indies, the Europeans—French, Dutch, Spanish—thought little of taking women of color as mistresses. But the British were exceedingly disdainful of associations with a woman with any trace of African blood, even what could be called the high-caste octoroons. He certainly had no intention of letting his British friends know of his relationship with Imri Ten Eyck.

She remained unmoved, merely nodding.

But Bain went on uncomfortably, "It's business, you see, not really a pleasure cruise, Imri. I'm going to start trying to create some interest in wealthy planters buying their yachts from us, so it's . . . business," he finished lamely.

"I see," she said quietly. "In my life I've only been to St. Vincent, you know."

"I know, and I'm . . . sorry. Some other time, perhaps."

"Perhaps," she agreed with a shrug.

A short, uncomfortable silence fell. Bain truly had a strong inclination to grant her request. She asked him for nothing, and he felt a stab of guilt for his selfish treatment of her. But Bain, being the kind of man he was, quickly shrugged off his discomfort and put his arm around Imri's waist.

Imri turned to him and started to say something, but then she looked back at a woman who was sidling up behind them. The woman was Opal Dekker, Willem's wife. She alone among all of the two hundred plus Bequia islanders was prejudiced. When Opal, who had been a prostitute in St. Vincent, had married Willem Dekker, she hadn't known that he was part black, and that he had cousins and aunts who had even more black blood than he. She was a blowzy, rather slatternly-looking woman, but she did have fine white skin, and she kept herself and her little daughter, Bonnie, out of the sun to preserve this pitiful symbol of her supposed racial superiority. Now she was sidling up to them, apparently about to speak to Bain, when Imri turned.

Opal stopped, fidgeted for a moment, then spun on her heel and hurried back toward their hut.

Imri, with a long-suffering roll of her eyes, looked back to Bain. "I think Mrs. Dekker was coming to ask you about Willem. She won't speak to me, however, so she could hardly throw herself on your mercy and snub me at the same time."

Bain frowned. "I'm not letting Willem out of jail. I told them and explained to them and ordered them, over and over, that they may not cut down any more *gommier* trees on this island. How difficult is it to understand that if they cut down all of the deep-rooted trees, the land will soon be barren? Palm trees will not anchor soil. Neither will shrubs. Only good, solid trees like breadfruits and gommiers. And I caught that fool Willem cutting down one of the half dozen left on Bannister land! No. He stays in jail for at least another week."

Imri said gently, "But he's already been in that awful hole for a week, Bain. And he's sick." Bain had designated the cellar of the old chandlery storehouse as the jail. It was airless, stiflingly hot in the daytime, chilly and damp at night, a stone box with only straw for bedding. Not for over a hundred years had it been used as a jail, but Bain had exploded when he caught the man cutting down one of the few precious trees, evidently to make a dugout for his nieces and nephews. On Bain's orders, Sweet had thrown the man in jail, and no one on the island would dare oppose Bain's decree.

"He stays," Bain said shortly, already forgetting the conversation, for the dinghy carrying the *Bequia Breeze* mariners had ground up on the beach.

Sweet, actually smiling, came running up to Bain. "Mr. Winslow," he said proudly, "she sails as sweet as an angel. A pure angel."

"Good, good," Bain said. "Tomorrow, Sweet, we take her out and let her show us her best."

_____

Bain rose early the next morning. He had come to be an early riser, though he was not very happy about it until he'd had at least three cups of scalding hot tea. He dressed and went down to the dining room, where Chika and Mandisa

247

served him tea and toast at the smaller tea table situated in front of a wide side window overlooking the spice fields. He stared out the window at the cloudless deep blue sky and knew the day would be blistering hot. Sweet came clumping in, looking glum. He stood motionless by the table, as always, waiting to be addressed.

"Why can't you just come in and sit down and start talking like a normal person?" Bain said irritably. He was, after all, only on his first cup of tea.

Obediently Sweet sat down, his face working as he tried to speak.

"Well?" Bain asked. "What is it?"

With great effort, Sweet said, "Something with the wind, sir."

Bain stared at him. "The wind? What are you blathering about, Sweet?"

Sweet shook his head with frustration. "It feels not right, Mr. Winslow. The wind, it feels . . . not right."

"Not right?" Bain repeated blankly. Then his eyes narrowed. "Have you checked the barometer?"

"No, sir," Sweet replied. The barometer, a fine instrument, was in Bain's study, and Sweet would never, never go in there without permission.

Bain rose, followed by Sweet, and went into the study. The barometer was dropping. Bain frowned, then took his captain's glass from the case and went outside. Without speaking, he and Sweet hurried to the Overlook.

The day seemed perfectly benevolent. The sky was clear, a careless blue, and the sunbeams in the bay were like silver sprinkles. "It does feel a little, just a little . . . damp, perhaps," Bain murmured. Carefully he fit the glass to his eye and began a careful sweep of the horizon, perhaps twenty miles distant from this vantage point. To his right—north—clear, crisp. Bringing the glass around very slowly, he swept meticulously west, south, and east. "Nothing," Bain said, lowering the glass. "It seems as clear and fine a day as we ever have."

But Sweet, he saw, was facing to the east— toward the Atlantic. "Mr. Winslow, we can't see it, but there is a storm out there, sir," he said in a low, intense voice. Of course, they could see nothing but the ridge towering over them and mild blue sky above that.

Bain considered the situation, watching Sweet's face. Then he nodded. "All right, Sweet, I believe you. Go batten down *Bequia Breeze*, will you? Strike down the—but what am I saying? You know more about it than I do. And tell the villagers—if they need telling. And let that fool Willem Dekker out of jail. Imri's driving me mad about him. And especially—this is important, Sweet—bring Imri's parents and Rikke up to the house. Can you remember all that?"

"Yes, sir, Mr. Winslow," Sweet said slowly, repeating his instructions under his breath. He turned down the path, but Bain called, "And, Sweet—"

Sweet turned, the whole of him, like a great gorilla. "Yes, sir?"

"You . . . you did well, Sweet. Very well."

PART III

No Small Tempest

May 1869

*And when neither sun nor stars in many days
appeared, and no small tempest lay on us,
all hope that we should be saved
was then taken away.*

Acts 27:20

CHAPTER THIRTEEN

Storm Damage

FOR TWO DAYS and two nights the storm poured out its fury, then on Tuesday, May fourteenth, just before dawn, almost as if a switch were thrown, the sky miraculously cleared and the rain ceased. The sun rose as innocently as ever. Except for a fitful breeze, the wind that had lashed the seas to a froth hid itself.

Shiloh and Captain Starnes stood side by side on deck, studying Port Elizabeth through telescopes. They had not been able to glimpse the shore since mooring in Admiralty Bay, but now the small village and the outlines of the island were clearly discernible.

Shiloh peered through his telescope, searching the tiny village, then turned to face his companion. "Captain Starnes," he began resignedly, "do you think we could sneak out of here—like maybe in the next five minutes or so?"

The captain dropped his telescope to regard him quizzically. Captain Starnes was an authoritative individual, rather stiff at times. His sense of humor generally extended only to an occasional dry sarcasm, and although he respected Irons-Winslow, he had some difficulty gauging his new employer's broad, flamboyant exaggerations and self-deprecations and ironies. He was fairly certain that Shiloh knew they were becalmed and the tide was coming in—but then again, one never knew about landlubbers. Or owners.

"Hrmph, Mr. Irons-Winslow, I'm afraid that would be quite impossible. Er . . . the wind, you see—or the lack of it. Often after these tropical gales, you're becalmed a day or two, and I'm sorry to say that right now the tide is unfavorable for us. Later we might perhaps be able to warp out on the outgoing tide, but then I'm afraid we'd just be wallowing around out in the channel."

Shiloh sighed deeply. "Don't guess it would help if I rowed, huh?"

Captain Starnes looked amazed but quickly recovered. With his stern, dark eyes twinkling a bit, he replied, "Sir, you own this barky, and if you wish to row, we'll make the arrangements."

Flashing him a half smile, Shiloh collapsed his telescope, leaned up against the railing, took his watch out, and checked the time. "Eight-forty-nine. No, it wouldn't do any good now, even if I rowed with all my might. We're bound to get caught."

Captain Starnes frowned. "Caught? I'm sorry, sir, I don't understand."

"Yeah, well . . . that's 'cause you don't know my wife like I do. You see that little village?"

"Of course, sir, and again I must thank you for this most excellent glass," Captain Starnes said, bowing a little. Shiloh, grateful to Captain Starnes for writing the letter that essentially "gave" *Locke's Day Dream* back to him, had given him a new gold telescope, a new barometer in a teak stand with gold trim, and a substantial raise in pay. The captain continued, "Certainly I saw the village, as clear as if I were standing on the shore, with this fine telescope."

"So you saw the two huts with missing roofs, and the one that a palm tree had crashed down on, and the other one with the door blown off?"

"Of course," Captain Starnes answered, mystified.

Shiloh waited but could see that Captain Starnes really had no idea what he was talking about. "You see, Captain," he said in his lazy drawl, "my wife is a doctor. You knew that, o' course."

"Er . . . yes, sir. Of course."

"Well, she's a good one too. She thinks that it's all-fired, almighty important, being a good doctor. And when she comes out here, and you know how doctors—'specially women doctors—are so know-it-all, fix-it-all, and when she sees those smashed huts and downed trees, you know what she's going to do?" Shiloh finished with exasperation.

"Er . . . no . . . but, Mr. Irons-Winslow . . ."

Captain Starnes said, his eyes narrowing.

But Shiloh went on, oblivious. "Is she going to say, 'Oh no, I'm on my honeymoon, and I'm having such a great time with my new husband that we ought to just sail off into the glorious sunset'? No, sir, she will not. She'll—"

Desperately—for Captain Starnes had been sadly fidgety for the last few moments—he interrupted rudely and called out much too loudly, "Good morning, Dr. Irons-Winslow!"

"Oh no," Shiloh muttered.

"Hi!" Cheney said brightly from right behind his right shoulder.

"Hi, Doc," he said, turning to face the music.

She looked knowing, with her eyebrows raised and her green eyes flashing with amusement. "May I borrow your glass, sir?"

He handed it to her with resignation, and his broad shoulders sagged as she perused the wreckage. "Captain Starnes, I assume we can't sail out of the bay at this time. Even though I am a grass-combing lubber of a woman, I can tell there's not a breath of wind," she said gaily.

"Er . . . no, ma'am," he answered with a guilty glance at Shiloh.

"Told ya," Shiloh muttered.

Cheney snapped the telescope closed and turned to him. "There may be people hurt, Shiloh, and that village doesn't look as if it would have a doctor."

"Yeah, yeah, I know, Doc," he said a little sulkily. "But it's our honeymoon, you know. 'Member me? Your husband, Shiloh Irons?"

She softened. "I know, I remember you very well. You're kind of hard to forget, actually." She blushed a little and took his hand.

Captain Starnes slipped away with some relief.

Looking up at her husband in the strong, blinding sunlight, Cheney asked a little hesitantly, "Do you mind? Really?"

He grabbed her, pulled her to him, and kissed her soundly . . . warmly, for a long time. It startled Cheney at first and embarrassed her a little—normally she and Shiloh both avoided such public displays—but after all, it was her honeymoon, and this was their ship. She returned his kiss ardently.

He released her but kept his arms close around her waist. She was blushing vividly now but was smiling. With mock severity, he said, "No, Dr. Irons-Winslow, I do not mind if we waste our honeymoon doctoring people we've never met, and who probably won't do what you say anyway, and that we'll probably never see again. Matter of fact—just to keep the record straight and all—I'd be disappointed in you if you didn't."

The sailors who ferried Cheney and Shiloh ashore weren't decked out in their best shore-going outfits because it seemed that there would not be much to dress up for in this tattered little back of nowhere. Coxswain Billy-O, Calvin Lott, David Upchurch, Fausto and Flavio, Siggy, and Auguste Bettencourt pulled at the oars. The longboat, crammed with the twenty men who'd been granted shore leave, followed the gig closely.

The rowing was easy, for now the bay had returned to its normal calm. Shiloh was admiring a fine schooner battened down and moored in the bay close to shore. "Look at that schooner, Doc," he said. "It's a fine craft—look at that shallow draft."

Cheney duly admired the schooner until the prow of the gig ground onto the sandy beach. Shiloh lifted her out so she wouldn't get the hem of her dress wet, and they walked up toward the village.

In all the huts, people were opening the storm shutters. She noted that few of the huts had glass windows, only openings, and now the villagers were arranging new mosquito netting over them. In almost every hut the front door was open, and women and even small children were shoveling out watery mud. A number of women were stringing lines between the trees and hanging woven floor mats in the sun to dry.

With some furtive, guilty glances at Cheney, the sailors passed her and Shiloh, heading down the beach. Cheney curiously watched them and saw them go straight to a hut. It had no sign, but it was obviously a public house, with men lounging on the shady front porch, talking and swigging from brown bottles. The people seemed friendly enough. Almost every young woman waved and called out gaily to the sailors, and several of them joined the men and went to the tavern with them. Though they gave Shiloh and Cheney curious glances, no one spoke to them.

The two made their way to the three damaged huts, which were close together. They saw no signs of life in them, and Shiloh gave Cheney an uncertain look. "Well, Doc, where do you want to start?"

"At the meetinghouse, of course, over there," she answered, pointing her parasol.

"Doc, that's a tavern," he said with exasperation.

"No, really?" she replied, wide-eyed. "Oh, Shiloh, what do you think? That I want to go knock back a few with the mates?"

"Er . . . no, guess not. Do you?"

"Maybe later. For now, why don't you make yourself useful and just go ask some of those men if anyone was injured in the storm or if anyone needs a doctor."

"Okay," he said slowly, "but what are you

going to do? Where are you going to be?"

"Shiloh, of course I'm not going in there. I'll just wait for you outside in the shade. See, they have all those nice tables and stools right outside."

Shiloh considered this. It wasn't the usual or proper thing for a lady to sit in a tavern unaccompanied. But then again, he realized that if anyone should approach Cheney or insult her, any one of the twenty sailors on shore leave would likely take care of that little hitch in a hurry.

"I guess it'll be okay." He installed her at a smooth, clean table with a sturdy bench and hurried into the tavern.

Cheney settled down, grateful for the shade. She was wearing one of her sailing suits, a pale peach linen blouse with a sprigged muslin skirt and only one light cotton petticoat. Still, it was hot, brutally hot. She was wearing white gloves, of course, for no lady would ever go out in public without gloves, and she was carrying a small lace reticule, a peach-colored parasol that matched her blouse, and the inevitable fan hung from her wrist. Shiloh had been carrying her medical bag for her, but he'd set it down on the table.

Cheney opened the bag to give it an automatic check, though she knew it was in perfect order. Shutting it with a snap, she noticed two young women, draped around the boatswain Birr Dunstan and his mate Willy Perkins, watching her with open curiosity from another table about ten feet away. The two sailors—particularly the older, more settled Willy Perkins—looked a little shamefaced and dropped their gazes. Cheney was amused and smiled at the two girls. "Good morning, ladies," she said brightly. "Lovely day, after that terrible storm."

They giggled but didn't answer. Birr Dunstan, with a resigned and guilty look, heaved one of them from his lap and walked over to bow deeply before Cheney. He was a rough-looking man, with his heavy beard shadow and flashing black eyes and great rough hands, but he was the third officer, and technically only officers should approach ladies unbidden to speak to them. "Dr. Cheney, may I get you something?" he asked respectfully. "Sharik there . . . that . . . lady . . . tells me the tavern has fresh ginger fizzes."

"That sounds wonderful, Mr. Dunstan," Cheney answered gratefully. "If you would be so kind."

"Be happy to, ma'am," he said, hurrying away. Soon he came out, carefully holding a pewter stein, and set it on the table with another deep bow.

"Thank you, Mr. Dunstan," Cheney said warmly.

"You're very welcome, ma'am," he said,

hurrying away with some relief.

Cheney was amused. She knew that the men regarded her and Shiloh as Bible-thumpers, and they were well aware that many Bible-thumpers did denounce the evils of alcohol and loose women with great rigor. She and Shiloh believed that sometimes the Lord did give some men a measure of righteous anger and indignation, and that they might denounce sin loudly and vigorously at times. But it simply wasn't their way. Neither one was a fire-breathing evangelist, and Cheney thought it funny that the men of *Locke's Day Dream* seemed to think that she might suddenly jump up onto the table and start railing at them. *They just feel guilty,* she reflected. *It's so funny how uncomfortable lost people feel about their sin when they're with Christians—even if we would never condemn them.*

She sipped the ginger fizz, regretting that it was lukewarm but enjoying the tart spice of the fresh ginger. Languidly she opened her fan and managed to stir up a breeze onto her face as she studied the little settlement. Huts were clustered all around in no particular order, with no streets as such. She glimpsed several more dwellings in the thick palm groves behind, where the land rose up from the flat beach.

From the tavern she heard several voices— one in particular, a man's very deep, booming voice with a singsong kind of accent repeating

"Winslow." It startled her, but of course that was her husband's name. And hers, she realized with an odd feeling. She wasn't used to it yet, and Shiloh was even worse. *Like this morning,* she thought, *he keeps saying "I'm Shiloh Irons, your husband" . . . and sometimes he forgets and introduces himself that way. No wonder I can't get used to it. . . .*

Her gaze moved down the beach to a fairly large hut. Perhaps it might have been called a cottage, for it had glass windows and wooden shakes for a roof instead of palm thatch, and it was bigger than the other huts in the village. It had a generous wraparound porch, and a little girl was standing alone on it, staring at the tavern and the men milling around. Cheney thought she looked a little forlorn.

Cheney got up and walked slowly to the cottage, and the girl's gaze shifted to her. Solemnly the girl watched Cheney walk up. "Hello," Cheney said. "I'm Dr. Cheney Du—Irons-Winslow. What's your name?"

"Bonnie," the girl answered. She was a pretty little girl, about six years old, Cheney judged, with glossy black curls and round dark eyes with long velvet lashes. What was so striking about her, however, was her creamy white skin. Cheney had, of course, seen that most of the islanders were blacks or mulattos, except for a couple of blond men. But this little girl didn't even have the glow of a tropical suntan, as most white people did in this climate. Cheney herself was scandalously tanned.

"That's a pretty name," Cheney said warmly. "Is this your house?"

Bonnie nodded, then cocked her head to one side and moved closer to the porch railing to stare up at Cheney. "Did you say you was a doctor?"

"Yes, I am."

"A real doctor?"

"A real doctor, with papers and everything," Cheney said, amused.

Bonnie shifted from one foot to the other, frowned, and considered Cheney. Cheney bore it with equanimity. Finally Bonnie said, "Would you come see my mama and daddy? They're sick."

"I certainly will," Cheney answered. "That's why I'm here. But if you would excuse me for a minute, Bonnie, I must go back over there and get my medical bag and let my friends know where I'll be."

Bonnie nodded, so Cheney hurried back to the table and grabbed up her bag. "Mr. Dunstan, I'm going to go over to that house—the one with the little girl on the porch—so when my husband comes back out, would you be so kind as to tell him where I am?"

"Er . . . but Dr. Cheney . . ." Birr Dunstan

said uncertainly, jumping up and spilling Sharik unceremoniously from his lap.

"I'll be fine," Cheney said crisply. "And no, I don't need a nanny, though I thank you kindly." She bustled off.

"But . . . but . . ." Dunstan said helplessly, but it was to her back, so with a feeble shrug he sat and pulled Sharik back onto his lap.

"You think maybe we ought to go with her?" Perkins asked uncertainly. "Mr. Locke, he's going to be right upset if she gets herself into something."

"I dunno," Dunstan grunted. "But for my part I'd ruther bear Mr. Locke's dressing-down than herself's. Wouldn't you?"

When Cheney arrived back at the cottage with her medical bag, Bonnie took her hand and led her inside. Cheney blinked, for the shutters were still over all of the windows except the two on the front porch. She noted the generous front room, with a long rectangular table with four chairs upended onto it. To the side was a plain upholstered sofa and two planter's chairs. She was surprised to see that the furniture was finely made of mahogany, with a deep, satiny shine. The walls were whitewashed, and there were two surprisingly good watercolor seascapes hanging on the wall over the sofa. The place had a scrubbed, polished look, except for the floor.

Cheney's heeled boots sunk into a full two inches of slushy, stinking mud.

"Bonnie?" A weak, querulous woman's voice called from the darkness of the back room. "Bonnie, come here."

Bonnie took Cheney's hand and led her into the bedroom. "Hullo, Mama. This lady is Doctor . . . Doctor . . . a doctor."

"I'm Dr. Cheney Irons-Winslow." Cheney introduced herself as she went to stand beside the bed. "But, Bonnie, you may call me Dr. Cheney. How do you do, ma'am?"

"I'm sick," the woman said listlessly. "And so is my husband. Would you go see about him, please?"

"In a moment." Cheney felt her forehead—she had a low-grade fever—and took her pulse, which was weak but steady.

"Who . . . who did you say you are?" the woman asked, confused.

"I'm Dr. Irons-Winslow," Cheney explained patiently. "Our ship was sheltered in the bay during the storm, and my husband and I have come ashore to see if we can offer any assistance. Bonnie told me that you and your husband were ill."

"I'm Opal Dekker. My husband, Willem, is in the bedroom down the hall. Would you see about him, please?"

"Of course." Cheney went into the other bedroom. Willem Dekker was awake. Cheney introduced herself, but he said nothing and seemed not to have the energy to speak. He was about twenty-eight years old, she estimated. His brown hair was plastered to his skull, he was deathly pale, and his eyes were clouded with fever. She took his pulse, frowned, and said, "I'd like to take your temperature, Mr. Dekker."

Still he said nothing, merely opening his mouth obediently for the thermometer. His fever was one hundred two, high for an adult.

Cheney returned to Opal, and the woman told Cheney that Willem had gotten sick when he was in jail—he didn't really know how many days ago he'd started feeling bad—and she had been sick for three days. Both of them had fevers and headaches, and the light hurt their eyes. Cheney was most concerned and puzzled about their lethargy. Willem would hardly speak or move, and his wife was not much better. They seemed overly listless for the symptoms.

A knock sounded at the door, and Bonnie was sitting with her mother, so Cheney answered it. It was, of course, her husband.

"Can't leave you alone for a minute," he complained. "Somebody hurt?"

"No, ill. A couple, Willem and Opal Dekker. They have a daughter, but she seems fine."

"What's wrong with them?" Shiloh listened attentively as Cheney related the couple's symptoms. She finished with, "So they both have fever and headache, but no respiratory ailments or other symptoms that might be attributed to influenza or catarrh."

"So what's the diagnosis?" Shiloh asked intently.

Cheney bit her bottom lip. "I don't have one yet. The symptoms are worrisome. These people are almost lifeless, but neither one has been sick long enough to be so weak."

Shiloh nodded, looking around with an assessing gaze. "Did you notice how clean the house is apart from the mud on the floor?"

"Yes, and Bonnie's clothes are well-made, clean, and carefully ironed. But they haven't made any move to clean up the mud, and they obviously are not as attentive to the child as it seems they normally would be. And the room is so clean and neat otherwise, but just look at the filth covering the floor—oh, horrors!" Cheney hurried to a corner, and Shiloh followed.

They stared down at two rats, fat and huge. "They're dead," he said, leaning to study them closer. "Hey, they're covered with sores, open sores."

"Anomalous lesions," Cheney absently corrected him, wrinkling her nose.

"Yeah, you know, there are dead rats everywhere," he said, eyeing them with disgust. "In the tavern there were an old man and a young boy shoveling out the mud, and I saw the boy pick up a dead rat and just throw it out the nearest window. I yelped like a scalded cat and scared him to death, but I think I managed to communicate to him that he shouldn't pick up those stinkin' things with his hands—he should use the shovel. And I'm going to go help them find a good place to build a fire pit to burn them all, instead of just throwing them out anywhere."

"Good heavens, yes, do that, Shiloh," Cheney said fervently. "And make sure the pit isn't close to any wells—oh, but pardon me, Mr. New York Metropolitan Board of Health High Hat! You know the rules, probably better than I do." Cheney referred to the cholera epidemic in New York, when Shiloh had been a much-esteemed medical assistant at the quarantine hospital, and even the haughty and aloof physicians of the Board of Health had taken Shiloh's earthy, commonsense advice.

"That's me, the expert on filth and rats," Shiloh agreed cheerfully. "Wish Jeremy Blue and Spike were here, though. They'd have this whole island cleaned up before you could sing 'Three Blind Mice.' Anyway, listen, Doc, I got the scuttlebutt in the tavern. This island's a real tight little place, mainly made up of three extended families—Dekkers, Verbrugges, and Ten Eycks."

"So this couple would have people here?"

"Bound to be some cousins or aunts and uncles to help them out."

268

"Were many people hurt in the storm?"

"No one was. The people who lived in the damaged huts just moved to a cousin's or auntie's or uncle's. Everyone here is a cousin or auntie or uncle. Reminds me of the hill people in Arkansas."

"Well, the Dekkers must have some help," Cheney said firmly. "A nurse to sit with them, and someone should really take Bonnie for a couple of days. Probably all they need is some fresh fruit juice to take some salicylic acid with, some clear broth, and rest."

"Are you going to make my mama and daddy well?"

Cheney was startled, for she had not heard the child come back into the room. "Don't worry, Bonnie. They're going to be fine. Do you have an aunt or uncle who might come help with your parents, and maybe take care of you for a night or two?"

Bonnie hesitated for a long moment, then finally answered, "Maybe my aunt Elena would. Mama likes her."

Cheney nodded. "Now, why don't you go get another of your pretty dresses and put on your sandals, and then we'll go find your aunt Elena."

As they left, Shiloh said in a flat voice, "There's one more family here on Bequia, they tell me. One man, at least, living in the Big

House. You're never going to guess what his name is."

"Mr. Winslow lives in the Big House," Bonnie piped up. "Mr. Bain Winslow."

Bain stood on the Overlook, sweeping the village with his telescope. "Looks like some minor damage to a couple of roofs," he said to Sweet and Rikke Ten Eyck. "No huts down."

He lifted the glass to see the *Bequia Breeze*, but then he clearly saw a much larger ship anchored at the mouth of the bay. "No, no! I don't believe it! If that's not just my ill-starred luck! It's Locke! *Locke's Day Dream*, curse her, right there in my bay!"

Sweet looked upset, while Rikke looked mystified. Finally Bain snapped the telescope shut and turned to them. "And there they are, with their long noses stuck right into my business. Locke and his female witch doctor!" He turned to Sweet, his face grim, his jaw rigid. "I don't want them here, Sweet. I don't want to talk to him or see him. You understand?"

Sweet didn't, but he nodded woodenly just the same.

Rikke said uncertainly, "I need to go down to the village, Mr. Winslow. I need to see about all my aunts and uncles, and just look! There's already a horde of sailors in the tavern. Uncle

Helmond and Hansen can't take care of business like I can."

Bain shrugged carelessly. "Go ahead. But my cousin Locke Winslow is there, and we are what you might call estranged. So don't bring him up to the house, don't direct him here, and don't tell him anything about my business or me. You understand, Rikke?"

"Yes, sir," Rikke answered subserviently.

Sweet said, "I'll go, too, to help. Big dirty mess down there with the flood."

Acidly Bain said, "And no wonder, since the fools have almost stripped the island of trees. What do you care, Sweet?" The big man shrugged and Bain muttered, "Suit yourself." Turning on his heel, he marched back to the house, his shoulders squared and defiant.

CHAPTER FOURTEEN

Becalmed

CHENEY STIRRED, and Shiloh was there, along with the heavenly smell of steaming coffee, fresh eggs with cheese, fried ham, and bread right out of the oven. "How do you always know when I'm waking up?" Cheney asked a little grumpily. "It's not fair. You always catch me all frowsy and foggy eyed."

Shiloh shrugged. "It's my job. I gotta watch

you every minute, you know. And when you first wake up you look dewy eyed and soft, not frowsy and foggy."

"Do I?" Cheney responded, yawning hugely. "Oh, I don't either. You're lying, and thank you so much."

"Welcome. Want some breakfast?"

"Of course."

They munched for a while, not reading and not talking much. "I talked to Captain Starnes this morning," Shiloh said, pouring her another cup of coffee. "I told him I wanted to go ashore for a bit, to go up to Bannister Plantation. Turns out we're still becalmed. He asked if we might let the other half of the crew take shore leave today and see how the weather shapes up tomorrow."

"It's fine with me if it's all right with you," Cheney said.

Shiloh nodded. "The men behaved really well yesterday, I must say. They helped with the rat killing and burning and even helped clean up the tavern and some of the huts that were flooded."

"Ah yes," Cheney said gravely, but her eyes twinkled. "I'm sure they were concerned about the tavern. Can't have the saloonkeeper wasting his time killing rats and shoveling mud instead of serving rum. And I'm certain the young ladies appreciated all the help with cleaning out their cottages."

"Uh . . . yeah. They were real nice," Shiloh said lamely.

Cheney nodded, but her green eyes were focused on a distant point just behind Shiloh's right shoulder. His eyes narrowed, and he reached over to take her hand. He loved her hands; he thought they were pretty but still so lithe and capable looking. He'd always said she had healing hands. "You thinking about the Dekkers?"

"Um-hmm. I haven't been able to stop thinking about them. Do you know, I've never seen those particular symptoms before. I should have taken a detailed clinical history."

Nodding thoughtfully, Shiloh said, "Okay, Doc. Why don't you come with me when I go ashore? You can go check on the Dekkers again."

"Yes, I'd feel so much better," Cheney agreed. She regarded him thoughtfully, chewing on her lower lip. "You . . . you're certain you want to go see Bain? I mean he probably . . . likely he won't . . . that is . . ."

"You don't think he'll be glad to see me?" Shiloh asked mischievously.

Cheney sighed. "I just don't want you to be hurt anymore, Shiloh."

He waved carelessly. "It won't happen, Doc. I'm all ready for him. And who knows? Maybe he'll be really glad to see me. Maybe he'll ask us to stay awhile, maybe even up at the Big House, as the villagers call it."

"Maybe so," Cheney agreed wryly. "After all, I've been his guest before, in his 'big house' in Manhattan."

"Don't remind me," Shiloh groaned. "I'm just now getting to where I don't want to wring his scrawny little neck."

Once ashore, Shiloh escorted Cheney to the Dekker cottage, then began the climb up the steep hill to the Big House. He stopped on the road as soon as Bannister House was in sight. Built of native stone and black-shuttered, the two-story house had looked forbidding and cold to Bain Winslow on his first sight of it. To Shiloh, however, it appeared to be a dignified, inviting place, which fit in perfectly with the tropical surroundings and the sharp red ridges in the far background.

Squaring his shoulders, he marched up to the front door and knocked. A sultry young island woman answered, cracking the door and staring up at him with liquid dark eyes.

"Good morning, ma'am," he said cordially. "My name is Shiloh Irons-Winslow. Mr. Bain Winslow is my cousin. I'd like to see him."

She nodded, obviously expecting him, and opened the door. "Come in, please," she said in a pleasant, though husky, voice. "This way." She led him to the study. "I'll let Mr. Winslow know you are here."

"Thanks." Shiloh turned to study the room curiously. He was hungry to know anything the room could tell him about his cousin. He hadn't seen Bain for over one and a half years. The thought jarred him. Ever since he had first met Bain Winslow on that fateful night of the party at Steen House in San Francisco, Shiloh's life had changed dramatically. In these last two years his life had been so inextricably entangled with Bain Winslow's that it seemed impossible they had actually not been face-to-face for so long.

It was a comfortable room, Shiloh thought. A man's room, with heavy furniture and leather armchairs and comfortable fat hassocks. He noted the desk in the corner, littered with papers and journals, and had to restrain himself from looking more closely. Shiloh, though he could hardly contain his passion to know and understand his cousin better, would never intrude on anyone's private papers for any reason.

He studied two paintings on the wall behind the desk, watercolor scenes of the fishing boats and nets lined up along the strand on Admiralty Bay. One of the scenes was in a golden early morning, and the other was of a crimson evening. They were very good, Shiloh thought and wondered who the artist was. He also wondered if his cousin had hung them, or if the previous owner had left them.

The door opened and Bain came in.

Shiloh turned. The two men stood, studying each other.

On the surface they looked nothing alike. Shiloh was tall, fair, deeply tanned, scarred, broad shouldered, rough fisted. Bain was slender, of undistinguished height, elegant, rather feline.

But an impartial observer might have noticed the same cut of the jaw, the same slender high-bridged English nose, the same tension carefully controlled by the set of their shoulders and the tilt of their chins. Though Shiloh and Bain were unaware of it, they both had their left eyebrows raised just a bit at the outward corners in a peculiarity that both of their fathers had passed down to them.

Finally Bain said acidly, "So you've found me. What now, Locke? Clap me in irons, throw me into the hold, haul me off to jail?"

Carefully Shiloh controlled his already rising exasperation and shook his head. "I didn't hunt you down, Bain, and I'm not here to accuse you of anything or haul you anywhere. I just want to talk to you."

Cynically Bain eyed him. "Is that so? Then I suppose we'd better sit down. Brandy?"

"No thanks," Shiloh said, seating himself in

one of the fine leather armchairs.

Bain poured himself a good shot of brandy and seated himself all the way across the room, on the sofa. Leaning back, he tossed off about half the shot, all the time eyeing Shiloh warily. "Talk, then."

Shiloh leaned forward, resting his elbows on his knees and clasping his hands. He seemed perfectly relaxed, though he was intent. "I didn't come here looking for you, Bain. But I am glad I found you. I just want to tell you that what's in the past is over and done, and I'd like for us to start all over again."

"Start all over again doing what?" Bain asked bitterly. "You've already taken everything I had. Do you mean you'd like to start over taking away what little I have now?"

"No, no," Shiloh said hastily. "I don't want anything of yours. I meant—"

"Oh?" Bain said, sitting up stiffly, his tawny eyes flashing. "You don't want anything from me? Then are you going to give me back my ship?"

"*Locke's Day Dream* is not your ship, Bain," Shiloh said as gently as he could.

"She was, until you appeared like some evil wind," Bain rasped. "You ruined my life, Locke. You just walked into my life and stole everything away from me."

"I didn't," Shiloh protested. "I've never taken

anything away from you, Bain."

"No? Are you so sure?" Bain demanded. "Are you really?"

Shiloh sat back, feeling slightly stunned. Had he? Had he really crowded his cousin out of his life? *No, I didn't. . . . Bain just threw everything away and ran away. It's not my fault.*

Maybe it wasn't his fault; at least it was not intentional. But Shiloh, being the fair and just man he was, suddenly tried to see things from Bain's point of view. It was true that, regardless of the reasons and the logic, Shiloh was now master of Winslow Plantation in Hana; he owned *Locke's Day Dream;* he had taken over Winslow Brothers Shipping; and he had an uncle Logan, and a cousin Brynn, and yes, even an aunt Denise, while Bain seemed to have lost his father and sister and mother.

Confused, Shiloh stared at Bain, who was looking back at him with something like pure hatred. His long, elegant fingers were tightened with tension on the now-empty brandy snifter. Shiloh sighed deeply. "Bain, all I can say is that I never meant to take over your life. Your life is all still there. You can walk back in anytime, and be . . . be a part of the family again. Maybe before I was too judgmental, too harsh. Or would have been, if I had found you before. But you see, now I'm a Christian. I've changed. I've forgiven you for everything, all the things in the past, and—"

Bain interrupted in a guttural growl. "You've forgiven me? *You've* forgiven *me*? So now you're a Bible-thumper, and a self-righteous one at that! Oh, that is rich! Before you were just a vulgar brute, but now you're a crashing pious bore!"

Almost defeated, Shiloh tried another tack. "Okay, maybe you're right, Bain. I mean, in the Bible it says that if you have anything against your brother, you need to go to him and ask forgiveness. It doesn't say anything about who's right and who's wrong, just that you have to make it right with him. So I guess what I'm trying to say is that I used to be . . . be angry at the things you did, and I had a lot of resentment after . . . last year, in New York. But it seems like instead of me forgiving you . . . I guess all that stuff in the past is really between you and God . . . that maybe I ought to ask you to forgive me. So I'm asking. Can you forgive me?"

Bain stared at him, now with disbelief. "No," he answered with relish. "No, I'll never forgive you for what you've done to me. And I couldn't care less what you think of me, or whether you ever think of me at all."

"I really am sorry about that," Shiloh said quietly. "I'm married now, to Dr. Duvall. We're on our honeymoon. Both of us hoped that maybe you would at least have dinner with us."

"You're married to Dr. Duvall?" Bain asked with some surprise.

"Yes," Shiloh answered, now warily. He knew suddenly that if Bain said anything—*anything*— the least bit disrespectful about Cheney, he would lose his temper. And if he lost his temper, he would certainly take it out on Bain. And if that happened, Bain would be in very big trouble indeed. Shiloh stiffened, and his fists clenched. A muscle in his jaw tensed.

But Bain missed these clear signs of danger, for he was staring off into the distance, his eyes blank. It seemed as if he had forgotten for a moment that Shiloh was even there. "So you married her," he said absently, softly. "She's a remarkable woman. I have to give you that. The most curious thing . . . I saw some pistols, some fine, ornate dueling pistols by Boutet in a pawnshop in Jamaica. They reminded me of her. Cleverly wrought, ornamental, but of such stern purpose . . ."

Shiloh was amazed, and unexpectedly something like hope flared up in him. "Yes, she's beautiful, and she's strong," Shiloh said eagerly. "She never held anything against you. She's always been better like that than me. We'd like to make it right with you, cousin. Cheney too."

Bain focused his bitter gaze again. "If you really want to make it right with me again, Locke, then the best thing you can do for me is just leave me alone. Just get out of my life, once and forever, and leave me alone."

Defeated, Shiloh stood slowly, as if he were much older and a little sore. "All right. Cheney and I will pray for you, always. There's just one more thing I have to ask you, Bain. Why, why can't you at least write to Uncle—I mean, to your mother and father and sister? They miss you; they've been frantic about you; they worry about you all day, every day. Aunt Denise has been half crazy ever since you disappeared."

Bain shot up and his arm caught the brandy snifter, sending it hurtling into the wall and shattering into a thousand shards onto the plush wool carpet. "How dare you!" he shouted. Two painful streaks of scarlet marred his smooth cheeks. "How dare you lecture me about my mother and father and sister! You stole them away from me just as surely as you stole my ship, and you're going to stand there and tell me that I ought to do this and I ought to do that? Get out! Get out of this house, and get off this island! *My* island! I want you, your wife, and *Locke's Day Dream* away from here tonight!"

Shiloh didn't bristle at Bain's temper; in fact, it just made him feel even wearier. He nodded. "All right, Bain. Just know that I am really, really sorry for . . . for everything. Good-bye."

Shiloh put out his hand.

Bain turned on his heel and stalked out of the room.

———

Depressed, Shiloh returned to the village and made his way to the Dekkers' house. He came in just as Cheney was settling down to tea. "Shiloh, I don't believe you've met Mrs. Elena Verbrugge," Cheney explained. "She's the Aunt Elena who Bonnie told us about, and she's come to take care of Mr. and Mrs. Dekker."

"I'm honored to meet you, Mrs. Verbrugge," Shiloh said, taking her hand. "It's so good of you to help out with the Dekkers. My wife has been worried about them."

Elena Crozat Verbrugge was no more than twenty-two years of age but had the grace and poise of a far older woman. She was of French descent, and her hair was as black as the darkest shade in nature. She was a small woman with magnolia skin, and her figure showed few signs of bearing four children. "I'm happy I can be of assistance," she said quietly. She had the faint lilt of a French accent.

Shiloh sniffed. "Mmm, tea smells good. I could use a cup right now."

"Elena just prepared this," Cheney said, eyeing Shiloh anxiously. "Mr. and Mrs. Dekker are both asleep."

"I believe I'll go sit with Willem and fan

282

him," Elena said. "It's very hot."

"No, please join us, Mrs. Verbrugge," Shiloh said, standing again. The tea set had two cups, obviously for the two women.

"Thank you, but no," Elena said firmly and slipped into the darkened bedroom beyond.

Shiloh seated himself again at the plain but gleaming mahogany table. "Nice of her to let me steal her tea," he said wearily.

"Yes, she's a very nice lady," Cheney said quietly.

"How are the Dekkers?" Shiloh asked.

Cheney frowned. "Mr. Dekker's fever has risen a little. Mrs. Dekker is much the same."

"Were you able to get thorough histories?"

"Yes, but they didn't tell me much. They both had the usual childhood measles, mumps, chicken pox. Both are healthy—no chronic health problems, no family history of tuberculosis, and no heart problems. Neither of them have been anywhere—off the island, I mean—recently."

"So what do you think?" Shiloh asked curiously.

"I still just don't know," Cheney answered. "But I think that maybe Mr. Dekker is in the beginnings of a crisis stage. Perhaps I'll find the symptoms more readily identifiable."

"You'll figure it out, Doc," Shiloh said confidently. "You always do."

"Sometimes you're the one who does," Cheney said. "I'd really like for you to take a look at Mr. Dekker, talk to him. Sometimes patients seem to be able to communicate more to you than they do to me."

"Sure," Shiloh said, rising.

Cheney put her hand out and caught his. "Not right now, though, Shiloh. He is asleep, and besides, I want to talk to you. You—you're going to tell me about Bain, aren't you? I mean, you don't mind talking to me about it?"

He sat back down quickly and took her hand in both of his. "Mind talking to you? Never in this life, mon chou. It's just that it was kinda sordid and dreary. No good news."

Cheney said softly, "I'm so sorry, my love. I did so hope, and pray, that we could make our peace with him."

Shiloh's mouth tightened. "Not likely. He's just really got his back up against me, Doc. I tried, and I think I did pretty good. I mean, I didn't call him a scrub or yell at him or anything."

"Didn't hit him?" Cheney asked mischievously. "Not even once?"

"Not even one little tap."

"I'm very proud of you, Shiloh," Cheney said, only half joking. "Not too long ago I think that might have been how you opened the conversation."

His eyes grew thoughtful. "Yeah . . . yeah. You're probably right. But this time I really tried to make friends with him, to let him know that I hoped he'd come back to the family. But he wasn't having any of it."

Cheney said, "It's a shame. He's hurting you, and he's hurting his family. But the gravest hurts are the ones he's inflicting on himself."

Shiloh said with some pain in his voice, "You know, I can understand him being resentful of me, just showing up out of nowhere and inheriting everything—every rich man's worst nightmare, I guess. 'Course I think he's behaved like a scrub, but I mean I do understand that kind of anger. But what I can't get is why he won't write Aunt Denise and Brynn and Uncle Logan. He sounds like and acts like he's flamin' mad at them too."

Cheney was surprised. Usually Shiloh was the insightful one, with his almost mystical gift of seeing into people, sympathizing with them, his uncanny understanding. "But, Shiloh dear, don't you see? His anger with them has nothing to do with you; it doesn't even have anything to do with them. He's really angry with himself because he's ashamed for leaving Hana just before the volcano erupted, for leaving them. I'm sure he feels guilty, and like the worst kind of coward, and he has to bluster with anger to cover it up."

He stared at her, astounded, then grinned.

"You're so lucky I married you."

"What?"

"Just look how smart you've gotten since we got married. Have you noticed that?"

"Yes, I have," she answered drily. "Lucky, lucky me."

"Anyway, Doc, I couldn't make an inch of headway with my cousin. It's a shame too, 'cause I really did try hard."

"I'm sorry, Shiloh, truly I am," she sighed, touching his hand lightly. "I had hoped—I mean, it seems that he's been working, really trying to accomplish something here."

"Has he?" Shiloh asked, surprised. "No one's told me. Of course, yesterday just about all I talked about to the men was about the rats and the fire pit and checking the wells and the privies and everything. Not much about Mr. Winslow at the Big House."

"Well," Cheney said reluctantly, "it does seem that opinion is divided about Mr. Winslow. Elena told me that generally the Verbrugges and the Ten Eycks see that Bain is trying to build up an industry for the entire community. That pretty little schooner out there? Well, Bain designed it and hired the men to build it, and he's hoping to start selling schooners built right here to wealthy men in the islands. Then he hopes that Port Elizabeth will be able to build up a marine supply business."

Shiloh's troubled eyes lit up a little. "Yeah? That sounds like a good deal to me. So what's the down side?"

"Some of the villagers—many of the Dekkers—feel that Bain is . . . um . . . I guess you'd say, using them, ignoring the plantation, taking all the money out of it, and paying them a pittance for him to have his own little yacht," Cheney answered, frowning. "But Elena, who is such a sweet woman and tries so hard to be fair, said that Bain's property includes every single hut in the village, except for the Verbrugges' house, which did in fact used to be a ship's chandlery, owned by their grandfather back when the Royal Navy still had a big presence in the Grenadines. Anyway, Bain never charges any of the villagers any rent. Kort Verbrugge even asked him about it one time—Sir Guy Bannister, the previous owner, did charge them a nominal rent. But evidently Bain just shrugged and said it wasn't worth the trouble."

"He did?" Shiloh responded with pleasure. "That's pretty generous of him. These landowners on the islands usually would either take everything a squatter had down to the last coconut or else throw 'em in jail 'til somebody paid the rent."

"Yes, that's true, and Elena said that most of the villagers realize it," Cheney said. "But some of them still murmur and complain about him.

And Elena said it was true that Bain had invested a lot of money in that boat, using teak and mahogany and the best copper sheathing, and at the same time he had forbidden anyone to use any of the island's trees—some kind of special trees, I forget the name—to build their own boats. In fact"—she dropped her eyes—"Bain had thrown Willem Dekker into their dreary little cellar prison here for a week for cutting down one of these trees. He was going to leave him in there for another week, but evidently someone named Imri interceded for him and told Bain that Willem was sick, so Bain relented and let him out when the storm blew up."

Shiloh nodded thoughtfully. "Yesterday Kort Verbrugge—he's pretty much the top dog around here, except for Bain, of course—said something about the flood. They have lots of storms here, but Kort said this is the first time the village has ever flooded, and it's because the men have cut down so many of the trees that anchor the loose topsoil. He muttered something about the Dekkers being fools in paradise."

"Fools in paradise," Cheney repeated idly. "Aren't we all?"

"Yep," Shiloh agreed sturdily. "And what's more, we're officially trespassers in paradise. Criminals, you might say."

"What? What do you mean?"

"I've been ordered by Mr. Bain Winslow,

who evidently owns most of this island, to take myself off his property immediately, as in pronto," Shiloh answered carelessly. "He mentioned you too, so I'm not the only skulking criminal here."

"But . . . but . . . are you going to stand for that, Shiloh? I mean, are you going to let him order you around like that?" Cheney demanded indignantly. "After all he's done? Speaking of skulking criminals!"

He grew grave. "Sure he is, Doc. But like you said, it seems he's trying to make a new start. At least this island isn't one big brothel. So I kind of don't want to . . . to knock him down, if you know what I mean."

Cheney was stormy, but after a few moments she calmed down. "I guess," she said reluctantly. "I suppose . . . I suppose we should try to show him some respect."

"As much as we can under the circumstances," Shiloh said quietly. "I can't think of any other way to help him. It might give him a little bit of self-confidence, and it might show him that I really don't bear him any ill will."

Cheney bit her lower lip. "But, Shiloh, I'm really concerned about Willem Dekker. As I said, I think he may be going into another stage of this fever, and I'd really like to closely monitor him tonight."

Shiloh nodded thoughtfully. "Okay, Doc. I

mean, we're still becalmed. It's not like we could sail tonight anyway. How about if we go on back to the ship, have dinner and a nap, and then tonight we can come back and check on Mr. Dekker? Will Mrs. Verbrugge stay?"

"Yes, and she is a good nurse," Cheney said.

"Then our banishment can take effect tomorrow," Shiloh said heavily. "If my cousin finds out we're still trespassing on his precious island, he can just choke it up for one more night."

———

It turned out to be almost midnight before Cheney and Shiloh returned to the Dekker cottage. As soon as they stepped onto the porch, the door flew open and Elena said worriedly, "Thank God you're here. Willem is in terrible shape."

They hurried into the bedroom. Dekker's cheeks were crimson and he had a high fever. His skin was dry and burning, and he writhed on the bed, muttering with delirium. Elena whispered, "Here, Dr. Cheney . . . see . . ." and lifted his shirt. His abdomen and chest were covered with mulberry-colored spots.

Cheney blanched and turned to Shiloh. "Well, at least I know what it is now."

"Doesn't look like good news," he ventured warily.

"It's not," she said slowly. "It's not good news

at all, and I could just kick myself—but, anyway, Shiloh, it's jail fever. And it looks like a particularly virulent form of it."

"That means quarantine," he rasped.

"Yes," she said wearily, "and it means there'll be more people getting sick."

CHAPTER FIFTEEN

Isolation

"WILLEM DEKKER DIED about two hours ago."

Cheney tried to appear composed as she looked around the men gathered in Captain Starnes's day cabin. The first shafts of weak dawn sunlight crept in the portholes, but the primary light came from the overhead oil lamps. The pale, flickering reflections threw the craggy faces of the men into stark relief.

As soon as Cheney and Shiloh had returned to *Locke's Day Dream* Cheney had insisted on meeting with the captain and officers. Captain Starnes, as usual, was imperturbable, but the officers—First Mate Nat Cadell, Second Mate Horatio Seaton, and Boatswain Birr Dunstan— looked troubled. Shiloh, lounging on the bench seat at the table with Cheney, smiled to give her confidence as she prepared to break the news.

"And what did this man die of?" Captain Starnes asked steadily.

"Typhus," Cheney answered bluntly. "Sometimes it's called jail fever, or ship fever."

Captain Starnes nodded. "We've seen it before. That is—well, what about you, Mr. Cadell? You're new here. Have you ever seen this before?"

"No, sir," he answered. He was very pale and licked his lips.

"Two other villagers are sick," Cheney continued. "An elderly couple named Helmond and Kiffa Ten Eyck."

"Do you think they've got typhus too?" the first mate asked quickly.

"I can't be certain because I haven't seen them yet," Cheney answered. "Someone at the tavern just told my husband. But—yes, it is very likely."

Uneasily Birr Dunstan shuffled his feet, then blurted out, "Dr. Cheney, Leith Redding and Solly Vaughn took sick last night."

"What are their symptoms?"

"Just said they felt rotten. I sent them to the sick bay and told them to wait for you."

Cheney and Shiloh grew grave. "I'll examine them, of course, but I already know what it is," Cheney said quietly. "This disease is cruel and arbitrary, and we have no way of knowing who will come down with it next. We only know that where there's one victim, there will be more. I had hoped that it would just be in the village, though."

Shiloh asked, "Now we have to quarantine the ship too, right?"

"I'm afraid so," she replied wearily. She'd been up all night and had lost a patient. Now she was feeling guilty because she hadn't correctly diagnosed him. Cheney knew that the preliminary signs of typhus were puzzling, and that even if she had diagnosed it immediately, it wouldn't have done Willem Dekker a bit of good—just as it wasn't going to help the fifty to sixty percent of the afflicted who were going to die in the next few weeks. The thought didn't comfort her much.

Captain Starnes asked, "What do we do, Dr. Irons-Winslow?"

Cheney roused herself from her glum reverie. "First we have to scrub this ship from top to bottom with an antiseptic. Do we have any phenol, Shiloh?"

Shiloh had personally stocked the medical stores for the ship. Naturally he had included plenty of the antiseptic that he and Cheney always used, a prepared mixture called Carr's Carbolic Compound. But he hadn't stocked up on phenol, the base acid in bulk powdered form. "No, 'fraid not," he said thoughtfully. "I didn't think of having to sanitize the whole ship. What about vinegar?"

"It'll do in a pinch," Cheney said hesitantly. "Do we have enough of that? And, Shiloh, you know that every house in the village is going to have to be scrubbed. Do we have enough vinegar?"

"Three gallons," he answered. "We'd have to dilute it fifty times."

"Too weak to do any good," Cheney said worriedly.

Thoughtfully Horatio Seaton asked, "Would borax be anything like what you need?"

"Why, that would be wonderful, if there's enough of it," Cheney said.

"We have, if I'm not mistaken, eleven fifty-gallon barrels," Captain Starnes said. "The men use it to wash their clothes, and so I buy it by the barrel and use it for ballast."

"Powdered, or boracic acid?" Cheney asked hopefully.

"Powder."

"Wonderful! That will be plenty for everything," Cheney said. "Now, Captain Starnes, we're going to have to isolate the sick men. And Shiloh and I should be isolated too. The sick bay won't do; it's too close to the crew quarters. How can we do this?"

Captain Starnes regarded Cheney and Shiloh

doubtfully. "You mean, total isolation? No contact at all?"

"As little as possible. None if I can manage it," Cheney said forcefully. Shiloh nodded in grim agreement.

"But how *are* you going to manage?" Captain Starnes asked, troubled. "I mean, you're going to be attending to the villagers, and I assume you're going to be attending the crew. How are you going to get back and forth to the village? You'll need a boat crew. How will you cook, how will you provide for the sick men?"

Cheney frowned, and Shiloh said smoothly, "I'll figure out a way, Captain Starnes. Believe me, the doc knows what she's talking about. It's important to keep the victims away from the ones who don't catch this vile bug. And the attendants have to stay in strict isolation too."

He nodded. "Then I suppose the best way would be to quarantine the stern section. That would include your stateroom, and belowdecks it's the officers' quarters." He turned to the three men, asking, "Can you handle that?"

Birr Dunstan, Nat Cadell, and Horatio Seaton exchanged quick glances. Nat said, "No problem, Cap'n. Little enough to do."

Captain Starnes nodded approvingly. "So we move the officers into the crew quarters and use their quarters as the sick bay."

"What about the helmsman?" Cheney worried.

"Ma'am, it seems to me that we're not going to be going anywhere for a while," Captain Starnes said drily. "So none of the crew would have to go past the quarterdeck for any reason. I won't even post lookouts on the mizzenmast. But my question is, what about the galley? How are you going to get food?"

"That reminds me," Cheney said, ignoring the captain and turning to Shiloh. "We're going to have to move Fiona and Sketes out. Where can they go?"

"They can bunk in the apprentices' quarters," Shiloh answered. "There'll only be Luki in there now." The other two apprentices, Leith and Solly, were the ones who were sick.

"No, Mr. Mylonas is still bunking there," Cheney said. "But he's hardly in any shape to terrorize Fiona. Since Sketes will be there too, I think it will be all right. That reminds me, gentlemen, I will need two or three men to commit themselves to caring for Mr. Mylonas. I'll leave instructions and medications for him."

"His messmates will take care of that," First Mate Cadell assured her.

"Good. As for food, Captain Starnes, I don't care a whit right now. I'm so tired," Cheney murmured.

"You sure are," Shiloh said quickly. "Don't

you worry, Doc, I'll get this train going, here and in the village. Go get some rest."

She nodded, stood up, and stretched. "I will," she said in a low voice, "because for the next few weeks, sleep is going to be hard to come by."

———————

Locke's Day Dream, though a clean ship at all times, now absolutely sparkled. The crew had not only vigorously scrubbed every visible surface with borax dissolved in almost-boiling water, they had pumped out the bilge twice and emptied an entire barrel of the borax into the hold.

The village, however, was a different story. Shiloh and Cheney had simply halved the village, with Shiloh taking the south end and Cheney the north end. They planned to go to each house to ask if anyone was ill and try to find the sick couple Shiloh had heard about the day before. Then they would inform them of the preliminary symptoms of typhus and tell them to go down to the beach and get two buckets of borax solution to scrub their houses. Shiloh had ordered the sailors to mix up four barrels of it, which they had then brought to the island in the gig.

Exhausted, Shiloh and Cheney had finally met back at the tavern late in the evening.

Cheney sipped a lukewarm ginger fizz, and Shiloh thirstily drank bottle after bottle of mineral water. He'd always been a big water drinker, and Cheney wondered again if perhaps that might contribute to his high level of health and general stamina. But such idle scientific musings couldn't hold her interest for long right now. She had other, more pressing worries.

"No one I talked to seems to be infected—right at this moment, at least," she said. "Did you find the couple?"

He shook his head. "Sure didn't. There's about a hundred Ten Eycks, and they all shook their heads and slammed the door in my face. It's funny, Doc. They almost seemed . . . afraid of me. No, not afraid. Resentful, maybe."

"Yes, I know. It's the old ploy of shooting the bearer of evil tidings. But you understand the real implications of this particular human folly, don't you, Shiloh?"

"Guess so. It's denial, plain and simple. If I just ignore all this unpleasantness, it'll go away," he rasped.

She sighed deeply. "And the worst part of it is that they'll ignore the prodromata, and that means—"

"The who?" Shiloh interrupted wryly.

"The prodromata. The early indications," Cheney explained and waited with some detachment.

Though he did not know all the medical terminology doctors used and had no formal education, Shiloh had an innate sense of the courses of disease and the effects on patients.

His clear brow wrinkled as he sipped his water and stared out into the purple shadows of the deep palm groves. "That's bad. That's really bad," he muttered. "This fever, it's not like cholera or yellow jack, is it?" He and Cheney had been through those terrible plagues together.

"No, it's not. It's very different, and in a way, it's much worse. You're beginning to see why, aren't you?"

"I'm afraid so," he answered slowly. "The first symptoms are pretty mild. Low-grade fever, headache, listlessness. With cholera you just get knocked right down to your knees first thing, and with yellow fever too, though the symptoms are different. But with this . . ."

"Yes, it's so easy for people to ignore that first little headache, that first little touch of a chill. And typhus typically has a latent period of anywhere from four to fourteen days," Cheney said worriedly. "Anyone with a persistent headache or with the least bit of fever should be quarantined immediately. But I can tell that these people aren't going to do that, Shiloh. They just won't, and that means they'll be wandering around in the general population, possibly spreading the infection everywhere."

"How does this fever spread?" Shiloh asked without much hope. He was well aware that the science of medicine was still in its infancy. Physicians were just beginning to realize that diseases weren't caused by miasmas or the upset of the four humors of the body. But this realization didn't automatically shed light and reason on every disease and disorder. The science of medicine was progressing in bits and pieces, and he doubted that the mechanism of typhus was even close to being completely understood.

"I don't know—probably evil miasmas," Cheney answered drily, echoing his bleak thoughts. "It's as good an explanation as I can give you. But listen, Shiloh—and this is very important. Don't let anyone—not even Captain Starnes—see that we don't understand this disease. Always be confident. Never show any doubt or hesitation in your diagnosis or in administering the prescriptives."

"I don't get it," Shiloh said, puzzled. "That's kind of like lying to the patient, isn't it?"

"Yes," Cheney replied brusquely. "But it's very important, particularly with this fever, that the patient has the utmost confidence that we know all about this disease and how to cure it. Call it a white lie if you wish, but it's necessary because of a peculiar and persistent symptom of typhus. You recall, of course, that I was concerned with the extreme lethargy, the listlessness that Willem and Opal Dekker were exhibiting?"

"Yeah, that's what gave you the heads-up, wasn't it? Not the fever or the headache but the fact that they seemed so depressed and were neglecting Bonnie."

"Yes, and I wish I had recognized it earlier," Cheney murmured distractedly. "Anyway, typhus has a psychological symptom that seems to be almost as life threatening as the physiological trauma. The victims always get lethargic, listless, then steadily deepen into dark depression. They get so they just don't care, and they won't fight—and then they die."

"Why?" Shiloh asked, appalled.

"I don't know, and neither does anyone else," Cheney replied gravely. "It must affect the brain, but you certainly know that that field is still the darkest of mysteries."

Shiloh nodded. He had been obliged to explore the new fields of neurology and psychiatry the previous year when trying to care for his aunt, Denise Winslow, Bain's mother. He had found that the workings of the mind were the least understood field of medicine. Now he shifted restlessly and frowned. "Look, Doc, I'm getting confused. I need to know . . . I need to figure out . . ."

She reached over and grasped his hands. They were warm and strong and rough. "I know, Shiloh. I'm going to have to explain to you the course of the disease, the kind of nursing care required, and—" she blew out an exasperated breath—"I myself am dreading working out the prescriptives. They're complicated and dangerous. Anyway, you can do it. You're the best medical attendant I've ever seen. Even if I weren't here, I know you'd probably give better care to these people than any physician or trained nurse."

His grin was crooked. "That's my speech. You stole it."

"We're married," she said primly. "I can steal anything of yours I want."

"Sure can," he agreed happily. "Anytime."

Bain narrowed his eyes as he looked his cousin up and down. "You promised to leave, Locke."

"I don't think I did, Bain," Shiloh said quietly, standing at the front door of Bannister House. "And now I can't."

"What do you want?"

"Can't I come in?"

Bain shrugged, whirled, and marched angrily down the hall to the library. Shiloh stepped into the foyer, closed the door quietly behind him, and followed his cousin into the library.

As always Bain poured himself a generous snifter of brandy, then turned to Shiloh, whirling the big balloon glass impatiently. "So please be gracious enough to explain why you will not leave as I've ordered. You are trespassing on my property."

Shiloh shifted his weight tiredly; Bain had not asked him to sit down. "Did you know Willem Dekker died?"

The brandy snifter stopped whirling. "Died? How?"

"Of typhus."

Bain stared at Shiloh blankly. "So what do you expect me to do about it?"

Shiloh rubbed his hand across his forehead. "It means strict quarantine, Bain, which is why we haven't left—and now can't. Both the ship and the island. The ship, that's easy. But it's going to be hard on the island. You could help."

Bain blustered, "What could I do? I'm no doctor."

"You're the most important man here, Bain. The villagers respect you," Shiloh said awkwardly. He was concentrating so hard on trying not to offend his volatile cousin that he didn't notice the look of mildly pleased surprise that washed over Bain's face. Slowly Shiloh continued, "You could explain to them about the disease, the medications, and the sanitizing procedures."

Bain listened but with growing wariness. "I'm no one's wet nurse. And if you and your wife insist on imposing yourselves here, where you're not wanted, then you can just do all that dirty work yourself."

Shiloh nodded wearily. "All right, we will. But listen, Bain, you need to have your servants sanitize the house. We've brought borax solution from the ship, big barrels of it down on the beach."

Bain shrugged. "Sweet and Imri will attend to that. Is that all?"

"Just . . . listen, Bain, if anyone feels the least bit sick—headache, fever, lethargy—you'll send for us, won't you?" Shiloh pleaded.

"I don't need your help, thanks," Bain said curtly. "You've helped me quite enough for one lifetime, Cousin. Now, if you're finished, I'll say good afternoon."

Shiloh left Bannister Plantation, defeated once again.

Chapter Sixteen

Rats or a Little Blood

"WE MIGHT BE ABLE to catch a couple more hours sleep," Shiloh said as they wearily climbed up the ship's rope steps.

"Maybe," Cheney said doubtfully.

They had gone to bed at about ten o'clock, after checking on Opal Dekker, Leith, and Solly, and then rose again for the 2:00 A.M. checks. Shiloh rowed Cheney over in the jolly boat and they went together to the Dekker cottage. Sure enough, Opal Dekker was worse. Like all medical attendants, Cheney and Shiloh knew that the hours from 2:00 to 4:00 A.M. were always the worst hours for grave illnesses. For some unexplained reason they tended to be the death hours. People and animals died most often in those bleakest minutes that were neither full night nor sweet dawn.

Elena Verbrugge was still faithfully attending Opal, so after Cheney gave the patient a light dose of salicylic acid for the fever, Elena insisted that Cheney and Shiloh return to the ship and get some rest. She could sponge the patient and would send for them if Opal grew any worse. With relief Cheney and Shiloh agreed to leave Opal in Elena's capable hands.

But Cheney's feeling of foreboding was true enough. When they returned to the ship they found Second Mate Horatio Seaton, his face as pale as death, sitting in their salon, waiting. "Good evening," he said calmly. "I'm sorry to say that I don't feel well. And this time"—his round cheeks puffed up with a little smile—"I'm afraid it's not a hangover, Dr. Cheney."

Cheney, though bleary-eyed and heavy-hearted, smiled at him. "You've come to the right shop, Mr. Seaton. I need to take a thorough medical history, and I need your height and weight, and I need to know, in as much detail as possible, exactly how you are constituted. This allows me, you see, to tailor your prescriptive exactly. Now, have you had measles?"

Cheney was taking the most detailed history Shiloh had ever seen, and he was paying close attention because Cheney hadn't yet fully explained to him about the prescriptives involved, which were evidently complex. But she had only completed about half the rough questionnaire she'd drawn up when a timid and halfhearted knock came at the door. Shiloh got up to answer it, and Billy O'Shaugnessy, probably the healthiest, strongest, most vital sailor on the ship, stood there uneasily, looking down at his bare feet. "Mr. Locke," he said quietly, "I got a headache."

Shiloh brought him into the wardroom, nodded at Cheney reassuringly, and sat with him on the padded storage benches at the end of the room. "Billy-O," he said lightly, "tell me all about your life. Start with 'I was born . . .' "

But before Shiloh or Cheney finished with their patients' medical histories, Sam Bowles came in, still with the angry rope burn on his forearm, which had been utterly forgotten as soon as he felt the fuzzy headache and the chill deep in his bones.

"Have a seat, Bowles," Shiloh said kindly.

"We'll be with you as soon as I get Billy-O fixed up here."

Shiloh had barely turned back to the coxswain when the door flew open defiantly—no knock this time.

Steadying the large, heavy tray in her hand, Sketes stamped into the salon, followed by Fiona, her head down, also carrying a tray.

Cheney jumped up, her face desolate. "Oh no—Sketes? And Fiona—you too?"

"Never you mind, Dr. Cheney," Sketes said defiantly. "I'm feelin' just fine, right pert, considering all this upset, barky all ahoo, and folk trying to rouse me out of my own little snug cabin. Here's coffee and tea."

"Fiona?" Cheney asked, her eyes narrowing.

"Dr. Cheney," she said softly, raising her pale face to Cheney's. "I just can't bear the thought of you doing your own hair."

"Don't be foolish, girl," Cheney rasped. But mindful that the sick men were listening—all of them registering some shock at Cheney's apprehension—she cleared her throat and said evenly, "Shiloh, why don't you serve these gentlemen? Tea with honey would be good. Fiona, Sketes, come with me, please."

Cheney marched into the stateroom, holding the door open for Sketes and Fiona to follow. Sketes looked defiant. Fiona had lowered her eyes again, but Cheney saw with surprise that there was a hint of stubbornness in the set of her slim shoulders and in the line of her jaw.

After closing the door she whispered—for the two rooms were hardly soundproof—"You shouldn't have done this. Those men out there have jail fever, Sketes. Sometimes it's also called ship fever. I'm sure you've seen it before."

"That I have," she answered heavily. "And a terrible fever it is too. But I didn't catch it in '62, when it seemed like half of everyone on the docks got it, and I didn't catch it in '53, when it seemed like half of everyone in New Jersey got it. And I'm not going to catch it now."

"You don't know that," Cheney said darkly. "There's no rhyme or reason as to who catches this fever. And you can't be inoculated against it."

Sketes raised her plump chin. "Beggin' your pardon, Dr. Cheney, but I don't think you and Mr. Locke can do this all alone. Do you?"

Cheney hesitated. "To tell you the truth, no. With just the two of us attending the ship and the village, I don't think we would be able to give the patients the attention they need."

"There you are," Sketes said, settling the matter.

Cheney turned to Fiona. "Fiona, why did you decide to do this? You have no nursing experience. It's not your responsibility, you know. I would never ask you to have anything to do with

308

my profession. You are a good lady's maid, and that's all I've ever expected."

Fiona wrung her hands as she struggled. She was not inclined to be a talkative girl. She and Molly Sketes had become good friends, but Fiona rarely spoke of personal matters even to Sketes. "Dr. Cheney, I know you don't expect me to help you with your . . . doctoring. And I suppose I won't be very good at it. But it's such a big part of your life, and . . . and . . . you've been so kind to make me a part of your life, not like Mrs. de Peyster at all. I . . . I wouldn't have anything to do if I didn't come and help you and Sketes."

Cheney made a wry face. "Fiona, I hardly think that exposing yourself to typhus is a good way to keep from getting bored."

"Well," she said with a ghost of a smile, "I do dislike being bored. I like to keep busy, to work hard. And it's a good thing I do, begging your pardon, ma'am, with your hair."

"Don't change the subject," Cheney said with mock sternness. "All right, you're both grown women. I'm satisfied that you know what you've gotten yourselves into. And I must tell you that I'm much relieved . . . and very grateful. Shiloh and I are going to need all the help we can get."

Sketes gave a dismissive shrug. "Now, Dr. Cheney, I know I can't be running back and forth to the galley, so I've got a little portable stove I can use to cook some easy things like coffee and tea and eggs and to heat up soup and the like. Tong Ten can cook pretty good, and he's going to cook for you and Mr. Locke. I've given him some instructions," she said darkly, "and if he knows what's good for him, he'll have Mr. Locke's steaks seared like he likes 'em, and the fresh fruit compote better be fresh and sweet like you like it. Or I'll have his head!"

"I'm sure he'll do very well," Cheney said lightly, then with a look at the woman's stiff face, added, "though no one can please me and Shiloh like you can, Sketes."

Sketes nodded, receiving the compliment as her due. "I've done lots of nursing in my time, Dr. Cheney. Don't you worry about that. And I can help Fiona."

"I feel so much better," Cheney said with obvious relief. "Patients need doctors, of course, but sometimes I think that good nursing heals them better than all our pills and boluses and concoctions. What I need right now, Sketes, is for you to take some tea down to Leith and Solly and sit with them until Shiloh and I can get down there. Tea with either honey or lemon is good, but no coffee for them and no milk."

Cheney turned to Fiona. "You have such good penmanship, Fiona, and right now that's just exactly what I need. I have made up a questionnaire—a medical history form—but I only have one rather rough copy. If we had been in civilization, I could have gotten them printed, but"—she made a helpless gesture—"here I'm afraid I'm going to have to ask you to be a scribe."

"I'll be glad to, Dr. Cheney," Fiona said stoutly. "How many copies do you need?"

Cheney answered, "Let's start with twenty, and let's pray that that will be too many."

They opened the door and Cheney came out, but Shiloh took her elbow as Sketes and Fiona came into the salon. "Hey, Doc," he said, "c'mere a minute, will ya? You gentlemen will excuse us for a minute—I'm just going to take my wife in here and smooch a little."

"Shiloh!" Cheney said, pinching him.

"Sorry," he said unrepentantly. They went into the stateroom and shut the door. "Doc, I don't know what I'm doing," he said gravely. "I'm just not clear what you're aiming for with this intense questioning, and what about the physical exam? What are you looking for?"

Cheney pressed her hands to her temples. "I know, I know. I should have stayed up and worked out the charts for the prescriptives and listed the critical indications. But I didn't. And by the time I get all of that done, it'll be getting late—or early—and one of us really needs to go back to the village. I just know there are other victims on the island, and maybe if one of us stays there, they might come to us. They'll never row out to the ship and rouse us out. And I need another check on Opal Dekker. I wanted to give her her dose as early as possible this morning. I haven't mixed it yet, and no one but me can do it. And I have to stay and see how well she tolerates it."

Shiloh's eyes narrowed and he stared at the wall, considering. "Okay, here's what we'll have to do. You go on into the village. Billy-O's not bedridden yet, and he'll probably rouse enough to row you over. I'll finish with the questionnaire with Mr. Seaton and . . . and then what do I do? Give him his physical exam? Or start with Mr. Bowles's medical history?"

Cheney answered, "Take Mr. Seaton down to the sick bay and get him in bed. Give him twenty drams of salicylic acid solution. I've already mixed up a carboy of that—did you find it when you were setting up the sick bay?"

"Sure did."

"Then just get him settled in. In fact, Sketes can do it—she's a volunteer now, bless her soul—and you can keep getting the histories," Cheney said thoughtfully. "Then when you finish the histories and start a chart for each patient, go on and do the physical exams."

"Okay," Shiloh said reluctantly, "but, Doc, you've got to tell me what I'm examining for."

"I'll write it down," Cheney said hurriedly. "It's necessary to give a very thorough exam and document it completely."

Shiloh nodded. "Look, Doc, about the sick bay. There are three rooms—the officers' quarters, I mean. I thought we could set up one of them for an examination room and the other two for the sick bay."

They heard another knock at the salon door.

"I hope they're big enough," Cheney sighed.

On the next evening Shiloh and Cheney rowed across to the village for what seemed like the hundredth time. Shiloh dug the oars hard, shooting the jolly boat forward through the green water. The sun was a golden globe in the west, seeming to balance on the horizon, and he rested a moment to admire the view. The sky was a sheet of dark blue and the west was decorated with tatters of clouds dyed crimson by the dying sun. Overhead a flotilla of pelicans veered from their flight, seeking land before the dark swallowed them. As always the hoarse cries of the gulls sounded above the moaning of the sea as it broke on the beach.

Cheney sat in the stern facing Shiloh, and as he rowed she admired his easy strength. "Husband, you are one fine physical specimen. If I could package a compound to give men the strength and muscles you have, we'd never have to work again."

He shrugged, just a little, so it wouldn't interfere with the rhythm of his rowing. "Just lucky, I guess. No, no, that's not true. Did I ever tell you, Doc, that Miss Behring—Miss Linde Behring, in New York—told me just before she died that my strength was a gift from God?"

Cheney's eyes lit up. "Why, no, you never told me. But I'm not surprised. The Lord gives us such diverse gifts. And though I hated it, and I will divorce you if you ever fight again for any reason, I admit that it's because of your strength that Behring Orphanage is such a wonderful, wholesome place." Shiloh had won a purse of ten thousand dollars for winning his fight with James Elliott and had bought a ninety-acre farm in Upper Manhattan and donated it to the orphanage.

"Don't worry, mon chou, I'm not going to fight again," Shiloh said, grunting a little with exertion. "That's part of the trouble with being a man with property and responsibilities and all that stuff. I'm gettin' soft as a wet noodle."

"You're not," Cheney said firmly. "I swear I think you're in just as fine a shape as when you were training for those awful fights."

His face clouded and he said in a low voice, "Maybe you're right. You know, Miss Behring said something else too, and it's kind of spooked me ever since. I even remember her exact words: 'For the Lord has shown me now that your body will be strong and hard and muscled, even until the day you die, and it is His reminder to you that your strength comes from Him.' "

Cheney was silent, absorbing this.

After a while Shiloh went on, troubled, "So you see, when I was all doped up and out in the rain and freezing and thought I was going to die . . . I thought, 'Yeah, this is it. Miss Behring knew . . . she meant I'm going to die young.' "

Cheney could see that Shiloh was troubled, very troubled. And she didn't blame him; no one likes to contemplate his own mortality. But instead of offering him thoughtless platitudes or scoffing, she chose her words very carefully.

"Shiloh, I was just saying that you do have great strength and health and physical stamina. If you look at it one way, it's almost supernatural. Because, though you are active, I know you aren't training your body to be this well-muscled machine, and haven't for some time. So you see, maintaining this top peak of physical form could very well be considered a God-given gift that will last you all of what I am sure will be a very, very long life."

He grinned a little raggedly. The great glowing ball dropping down toward the horizon lit his hair as if it were fine silver. "So you'll still admire my manly physique when I'm doddering around at a hundred and twelve?"

"I surely will. And don't think I won't still be fighting off all your silly women, even though I will be one hundred and fourteen," Cheney grumbled. "I've seen those island girls twittering around you. I'm considering a ball and chain."

Pleased, he smiled and his blue eyes sparkled. "Doc, there's not a woman in this world who could compare to you. I'd be a pure, plain fool if I took any note of another woman. Never happen."

"Better not," Cheney warned.

They glided toward shore on the incoming tide. Shiloh was really just riding it, mainly using the oars to steer. As usual in the tropics, sunset was abrupt and final. Shiloh had lit the stern lantern before they rowed out, and now he studied Cheney by the dim yellow light. Finally he said, "But, Doc, I brought up all that stuff about Miss Behring because—well, I guess because I'm uneasy about this fever. What are—" he swallowed hard—"what are the chances of me getting it? And . . . and you?"

Cheney made a face. "Who knows? No one, that's who. Because we don't know how people get exposed to it, so we don't know the odds of getting it once you've been exposed. Many times in typhus epidemics the attendants don't get it, but people who haven't been around the victims do."

"Like Tong Ten," Shiloh said thoughtfully. The captain's steward had been the last sailor to knock on the door last night. "He didn't even have shore leave, never left the ship. I was kinda thinking that this fever got started on the island, and Bowles, Mr. Seaton, Billy-O, even Leith and Solly, had all been on shore leave. I just knew it was those rats. So many of them were sick, some of them had sores and junk. But then Tong Ten pops up, and I know he hasn't even seen a rat. Not on my ship," Shiloh grunted.

"I do wish I had some laboratory equipment," Cheney mused. "I would love to dissect some of those vermin and study their blood. But even if I had a fully equipped lab, I wouldn't have time."

"Yeah, I sure do wish we could take some time off from doctorin' sick people to dissect putrid rats," Shiloh grumbled. "Some honeymoon."

"I'm sorry, Shiloh," she said, then added slyly, "I'll make it up to you when this is all over. I promise."

"I'll hold you to that, mon chou," Shiloh said, his eyes gleaming. "I sure will."

Shiloh rowed hard to ground the sturdy little boat as far up on the beach as he could and then leaped out to drag it up farther. He had gone back to wearing his faded denims and worn cavalry boots, swearing that the black three-piece suits gentlemen wore made him feel like a mortician. The only difference in his preferred wardrobe now was that his plain white shirts were of fine lawn instead of rough muslin or cotton.

He lifted Cheney out of the boat, and she linked her arm through his while they made their way toward Opal Dekker's cottage. Several men and some of the young women were sitting on the porch and at the tables outside the tavern. Shiloh called out courteously, "Evening. How's everyone feeling?"

No one answered. One of the men spat.

"Oh, dear," Cheney said quietly. "This is worse than I realized."

"They think we brought the plague," Shiloh told her reluctantly. "Even though they're not admitting there is a plague."

"It's odd, considering how superstitious sailors are," Cheney said, "that they've been so good to come to us as soon as they feel the first symptoms."

"The prodromata, you mean," Shiloh said airily. "I wish you would be more careful to use the proper medical terms."

"Ah yes. Pardon me."

"Sure. And gettin' back to the sailors—

that's 'cause of you, Doc. You're their good luck, you know. Of course they're gonna come for your help. They think you can raise the dead."

She squinted, trying to see his features in the soft darkness. "It's good that they have confidence in me, and in you, of course. But I'm not so sure . . . they need to be aware of the seriousness of this disease too."

He shrugged and covered her hand with his, squeezing it lightly. "They know, Doc. They've all seen these fevers before. And personally I think it's good that they have this kinda awe of you. Because of what you told me about the fever making you so depressed and all. It gives 'em an extra bit of hope."

"They'll need that," Cheney admitted. "But I tell you what I need, Shiloh. No matter how hectic it gets, no matter how busy we are, no matter how much of the day and nights we're apart, we've got to set aside some time to pray together. I need you to pray for me, and with me."

Shiloh nodded. "We'll do it, Doc. That's my promise to you. Because I know now that that's the most important doctoring of all."

Sharik Dekker was slightly drunk. She'd stayed at the tavern until midnight, hoping that

Birr Dunstan might come ashore from the ship. She liked the sailor very much, and he'd bought her all the Jamaican rum punches she'd wanted. Besides that, he was so handsome with his flashing dark eyes and black curls and thick arms and broad chest. Sharik wasn't a pretty woman, but her skin was nice, a dark buttery gold, and she was lithe and slender, for she worked hard, fishing with Isaac Dekker and his brother Emil. She held her own and provided for herself, not wanting to ever be totally dependent on a man. Neither had she ever wanted to take just one man. She was young, and she was going to live forever.

When she'd brought Birr to her little hut, he had even shoveled it out for her, slapping her on the behind and telling her to run on back to the tavern and bring him some beer, for it was going to be thirsty work.

It hadn't taken her ten minutes to run the errand, and when she returned he'd already had most of the mud shoveled out and was waiting for her, thirsty, as he'd said. They drank the two bottles of beer and then put out the candle. He'd stayed all night, snoring heavily and once throwing an arm across her, nearly suffocating her. She'd adjusted it gently, not wanting to disturb him, and he had slept on until morning. Then he'd returned to the ship, promising to come back. But he hadn't.

Now she slept uneasily, tossing and fighting drunken dreams in which she heard children screaming. Sweating, terrified, she bolted upright. Then she relaxed when she realized what it was.

Two rats were fighting in the corner of the room. Muttering to herself, she lit the single candle by her bed. "You stinkin' vermin!" In the candlelight one of them reared up, his eyes red and glowing malevolently, and then scurried underneath the ill-fitting door. The other lay motionless in the corner.

Blearily Sharik got up and stood over the rat. She swayed, the candle flame making wavy circles in her unsteady hand. The rat's eyes were still open, but Sharik was sure it was dead. Too sleepy and drunk to want to find something to scoop it up with, she bent down and picked it up by its naked tail.

She fumbled, trying to hold the candle and the rat and push aside the mosquito netting at the window when she felt a sharp, fearful pain on her hand. She screamed—a short, loud terrified yelp—and shook the rat loose. She was a strong woman, and as the rodent dashed against the wall, she heard the fateful cracking sound of its skull breaking. It fell limp, and she swallowed hard. "Dead now, ain't you, you devil?"

Now, shaking a little, she carefully set the candle down and examined her hand. The rat had gotten her on the soft meat at the side of her palm, just underneath her little finger. She was bleeding from both sides, from the two vicious puncture wounds of its top fangs and from the tearing wounds of its smaller ragged bottom teeth.

But Sharik Dekker was made of stout stuff, and she wasn't afraid of rats or a little blood. She wrapped her hand in a strip of red linen she'd been saving, cursing because she'd been intending to make a headdress out of it. Then she fetched her broom, a homemade affair made from a smoothed plank and a saw palmetto, and swept the rat out the door.

And then, yawning, she crawled back into bed and went to sleep.

CHAPTER SEVENTEEN

Victims

CHENEY SAT AT THE long table in the salon with papers, pens, pencils, and two books. One was *Cellular Pathology as Based Upon Physiological and Pathological Histology* by Rudolf Virchow, and the other was a slightly less solemn and less weighty tome, *Lectures on Materia Medica and Therapeutics* by John B. Beck.

Shiloh, who sat beside her, made a wry face as he searched the open pages of the books.

Might as well be written in Latin for all the good they do me!

Across from them sat Sketes and Fiona, but neither of them bothered to look at the books. Sketes was sewing a button onto one of Shiloh's old shirts, and Fiona was making little rosebuds by folding a one-inch-wide satin ribbon in a particular way.

Shiloh glanced up at Cheney, who was muttering to herself as she turned pages, pointed to a passage, then quickly made notes. Idly he turned his attention to Fiona, noting how her fingers moved quickly, surely, as she made odd little folds in the ribbon. She pressed the folds together, then more folds, and more pressing, on and on. Finally she held out the rosebud to Sketes, who picked up another threaded needle and quick-quick sewed two stitches and bit the thread. Fiona laid a tiny, fine little yellow satin rosebud down on the table. She saw Shiloh watching her, and her cheeks colored as always, but she didn't drop her eyes. He winked at her but said nothing, for the three of them were trying not to distract Cheney.

Finally Cheney shuffled some papers and nodded with satisfaction. "All right, I think I've got it organized now so that you can all understand what we're dealing with and how best to take care of the patients."

"That's not been hard at all," Sketes said,

323

laying down her sewing to pay close attention to Cheney. "They're just tired-like and a little melancholy. But they don't seem too sick. They're eating and drinking well if you prod them a little."

"I know, but that's because they're in the second stage of the disease," Cheney said cautiously. "Let me explain. Typhus has four distinct stages. The first is the initial contraction of the disease, when the patient has an elevated temperature, a headache, and usually feels a slight rigor in the abdomen—or sometimes in the arms or legs. Most of the time they'll just tell you they feel achy or stiff. That's why so many times a physician will think they have contracted influenza or may even have just a touch of catarrh. But on close physical examination, you can feel the spleen is palpable, and that tells you it's not influenza or catarrh."

Sketes's round blue eyes grew wide while Fiona looked horrified. "And pray tell, Dr. Cheney, what in the wide world is a *spleen*? And what does *palpable* mean? And once you tell us that, how are we to find one?"

Cheney managed a smile. "Don't worry, Sketes. Shiloh or I need to see everyone who has any medical complaint, no matter how insignificant. And likely there will be men with just an ache, or maybe a little cold, or even just indigestion, who might come, thinking they have the fever. It's very common, you see, and understandable. That's why I've told everyone to report to the salon instead of down in the sick bay. That way the ones who don't have typhus won't be exposed too deeply."

Fiona and Sketes nodded with relief.

Cheney turned and suddenly asked, "Shiloh, you do know how to palpate the spleen, don't you?"

"Sure, Doc," he said easily. "I just call it pokin' their guts, though."

Fiona giggled but pressed her hand to her mouth to stifle it.

"That's all right, then," Cheney went on, unnoticing. "So now we have the infected person, and the prodromata—I mean the initial symptoms—actually seem to lessen a little, and the patient enters a latency phase. This can last from as little as four days to as long as fourteen. Oh, how I wish I had my books here! I've been trying to recall so much from memory, and these two books don't have exactly what I need!"

Shiloh grabbed her hand. "Doc, you're doing fine. You'll remember."

She flashed him a smile and left her hand in his, Sketes noticed with warmth. Cheney continued, "So in this latency period the patient has a slightly elevated temperature and a continual but not severe headache. They are usually, as you noticed, Sketes, more melancholy than just their conditions can explain. So it's very important to stay cheerful, to smile at them, to do just as you said, Sketes—encourage them to eat and drink. Anything to keep their spirits up."

"We'll come up with something to entertain that lot, Dr. Cheney," Sketes said stoutly. "Don't you worry."

"I know you will, Sketes," Cheney said warmly. "Personally, I regret that you've been placed in this position, but I'm glad for my patients that you two are helping. Both of you, I think, will make excellent nurses." She sighed deeply. "But then comes the crisis stage.

"First the patient will break out in a mulberry-colored rash, usually starting with the chest and spreading all over the body. The patient's temperature will shoot up to a raging heat, and he will become delirious. Sometimes patients will become violent, because they're hallucinating, you see, as the fever rises. They'll usually either go back and forth between delirium and deep coma, or else they'll lapse into coma for a period of time. This may last anywhere from twenty-four to forty-eight hours."

"And then?" Fiona asked fearfully.

"And then about half or maybe a few more of them will die." Cheney watched her closely to see her reaction.

Fiona bit her lip and looked distressed, but she finally raised her chin and nodded firmly. "I can do this, Dr. Cheney. I *will* do this."

"Good girl," Cheney said quietly. "Not many people can or will deal with things like this. I'm proud of you. Now the survivors will come out of the coma, and their fever will drop to a manageable level. But the recovery stage is long, slow, and painful. They require, perhaps, the most careful nursing of all, because they're so weak and their bodies so ravaged that they become subject to pneumonia. And if they get pneumonia in the recovery stage, they will most certainly die."

"How do we prevent that?" Shiloh asked thoughtfully.

"I've designed a course of treatment for each stage of the disease, including preventive measures for the recovery period," Cheney said rather wearily. "Unfortunately it's a complex, painstaking, time-consuming program. We're all going to be working very, very hard for the next few weeks."

Shiloh eyed her sardonically. "Why'd we have to get such a tough sickness to deal with on our honeymoon? Why couldn't we have an easy one, like cholera?"

Fiona and Sketes looked shocked, but Cheney gave him a mischievous grin. "We can call it cholera if it makes you feel any better. But I'm afraid, Mr. Iron Head, that this time you don't get to just stride around terrorizing poor little nuns and bossing know-it-all doctors and holding the women patients' hands and sweet-talking them. You're going to have to do some real nursing now. Doctoring, even."

"Knew you'd get me into something like this," he grumbled. "I don't wanna be the doctor. You're the doctor in the family. I wanna be a sailorman."

"Tough," Cheney said cynically. "You've been drafted. Now let's go through this maze of materia medica—"

Vaguely they heard a commotion outside, somewhere far away down the quarterdeck, but dismissed it as some shipboard chores getting done. Then moments later the door flew open and Rikke Ten Eyck stood there, his dark face a sickly gray hue. "Dr. Cheney," he said distractedly, "you have to come. Hurry. Sharik Dekker—" He stopped, appalled, unable to continue. "You got to come *now!*"

"All right, just let me get my medical bag," she said calmly and hurried into the stateroom.

Rikke's dark, worried eyes went up to Shiloh. "Mr. Locke," he said, gulping, "I didn't come because of Sharik, but when I got to the village and saw her—" He shook his head helplessly. "Anyway, I was coming here to get you and Dr. Cheney. Because this morning my sister told me she has a headache, and she feels cold."

Shiloh nodded. "I see. Did my cousin tell

you to come get me? Mr. Winslow's my cousin, you know."

Rikke frowned. "No, he didn't. But I told him I would come get you, no matter what he said. And he didn't speak for a long time. But then, when I was leaving, he took me aside and told me to also bring Dr. Duvall. That's Dr. Cheney, isn't it?"

"It sure is," Shiloh said warmly, "and I'm glad to hear that my cousin asked for her."

Rikke, as soon as he had seen Sharik, had dismissed the idea of taking a larger, slower fishing boat out to *Locke's Day Dream* and had instead jumped into his little brother's dugout canoe. It was hollowed out of a single log of gommier wood and was light and fast. It had four seats, but they were made for children, so when Rikke, Cheney, and Shiloh squeezed into the dugout to ride back to shore, the sea reached to about four inches below the draft.

Shiloh grunted, "Better get a bailing bucket, Rikke."

The islander just smiled distractedly and shook his head. With a single touch of his oar, the little craft skimmed on top of the water from wave top to wave top, with very little water coming in. Shiloh noted Rikke's rowing technique with interest, watching his calculated dips of the oar to shoot the craft ahead to ride the waves, much like the Hawaiians did with their *nalu* boards. Cheney's thoughts were more focused on making it to shore without ditching. She gripped the sides with both hands, trying not to show her alarm.

After they beached the dugout, Rikke kept hurrying them, walking behind them and almost nipping at their heels. "Hurry, hurry, Doctor, she's bad, she's sick, sick!" he kept muttering.

He took them to a tiny one-room hut at the southern end of the village. Beside the doorway stood a tall, muscular black man, leaning up against the wall. He shrugged a little at Rikke's questioning look. "Nothing I can do," he said in a deep voice and dropped his eyes.

Rikke stopped at the doorway. "This is Isaac Dekker. He found Sharik, because she fishes with him and his brother Emil, and she didn't come this morning. He didn't know what to do, so he came to get me when he saw me heading for the boats." He, too, averted his gaze. "Go on in."

The little hut was shadowed, for though the shutters were open, there were only three small windows. Both Cheney and Shiloh involuntarily sniffed as they stepped into the hut. Then Cheney gave Shiloh a haggard look. "This hut hasn't been sanitized," she whispered.

His eyes narrowed. "I know, Doc, but that

smell . . . I remember it too well . . . from the war."

She nodded but said nothing else. Now they could see the little wooden bed in the corner of the room and the dark figure on the single white sheet. Cheney went over to her and then remembered: *Sharik . . . that young, laughing girl sitting on Birr Dunstan's lap. . . . How long has it been? Good heavens, the days and nights are already starting to blur!*

"Sharik?" she said pleasantly, bending over the bed. "Sharik, Rikke said you were ill. What's wrong?"

Without a word the girl, her eyes dark and dull, pulled her arm out from under the sheet and laid it across her abdomen, grimacing with pain as she moved it. "A rat," she whispered in a broken voice. "A rat bit me."

The arm was swollen to twice its size, all the way up to her elbow. The skin on her forearm was angry red, but her hand was a horrible shade of dark purple with black splotches. The skin was already peeling off the side of her hand and her little finger, leaving open lesions. Cheney looked closely at her arm but didn't touch it and made a little signal to Shiloh behind her back to step away. Then she straightened and smiled down at Sharik, who was watching her, it seemed, with dull hopelessness. "When did this happen, Sharik? When did the rat bite you?"

"Last night," she answered. "Sometime last night."

Shiloh shifted restlessly, jarringly, but Sharik didn't appear to notice. When she looked at anything, she looked at Cheney's face.

"Late? After midnight?" Cheney persisted.

"I . . . I guess so. I don't have a watch or a clock. But . . . yes, I stayed at the tavern until everyone went home. I think that was around midnight. And then I slept. But the rats woke me."

"All right," Cheney said calmly. "I need to examine you more closely, but first I'm going to clean up a little. I'm afraid my hands got soiled in the boat coming over," she said lightly. Sharik turned her head to the wall without answering.

Cheney pulled Shiloh out of the hut, and he looked stunned. "That happened just a few hours ago?" he asked, still whispering outside the open door. "Doc, I've never seen such putrefaction so fast! Have you?"

"No, I haven't," Cheney answered, frowning. "And, Shiloh, don't touch her unless you've just washed your hands in carbolic acid. You understand me? Even if it's only been a few minutes, keep dipping in the carbolic acid, the whole time."

"You're not going to get any argument from me, Doc. What are we going to do?"

Cheney answered slowly, "I have to have

better light to examine her. Find me some good lanterns—go to the ship if you have to and bring me a couple of those big Flying Dutchmen. But I'm pretty sure already that we're going to have to amputate that arm."

"Then I might as well go back to the ship, get the surgical stuff and the lanterns. You okay, Doc?"

"Of course," she said stiffly. "What do you think, I'm going to have the vapors?"

He regarded her with his steady blue eyes. "Some grown men would pass out just looking at something like that. But not you, Doc. Never you." He turned and hurried down the beach, where Rikke and Isaac and another man whom Shiloh assumed to be Isaac's brother Emil, for he was a smaller version of Isaac, were loitering under a palm tree. The three of them looked rather shamefaced and frightened. As Shiloh passed them, taking long, hard strides, he growled, "Rikke, come take me back to the ship in that little racer you brought me in on."

Rikke stumbled to catch up. "But . . . but what about my sister, Mr. Locke? You have to come—you have to help her."

"We'll come," Shiloh said with some frustration. "As soon as we can. But right now we've got to operate on Sharik. So step lively. I'm a man in a big hurry. Your sister will be all right for a few more hours."

Fearfully Rikke, now running to keep up, asked, "Does she . . . does Sharik have the fever?"

"I don't know," Shiloh answered briefly. "I'm not the doctor—my wife is. And that's why it's a good thing my cousin was smart enough to ask for her. She's the best, Rikke—the best there is."

———————

As Shiloh entered the hut after the amputation his gaze went at once to the figure on the bed. Sharik, her entire right side swathed in thick bandages, was still unconscious. Shiloh soundlessly picked up a straight-backed chair and placed it by Sharik's bedside, where Cheney sat watching the girl sleep.

"It's done," Shiloh said quietly. Cheney had decided that the amputated limb, with its poisonous effusion, had to be burned. Without a word, Shiloh had wrapped it in clean bandages and departed for the fire pit. "Was that gangrene?"

"I don't know," Cheney answered in a tired whisper, though she didn't think Sharik could hear anything. "I don't think so. I've never seen gangrene set in so quickly, and the tissue was more febrile and mortified than I've ever seen before. Did you ever see anything like it? In the war, I mean?"

"Never," Shiloh answered. "Is this a part of the fever? I mean, could it be that she has typhus, and that sort of—aggravated the rat bite?"

"I just don't know," Cheney said again, her shoulders drooping a little. "And we'll never know, because we have no facilities for clinical studies here. This putrid infection is an anomaly, and the arm should have been dissected and the blood and tissue carefully analyzed, and the rat should have been dissected and analyzed too. But that's impossible, I know. As badly as I'd like to—and as badly as the information is needed—I can't in good conscience transport any infected tissues or rats to a place with a well-equipped lab. That's the trouble with these tropical fevers; they occur in places where scientific investigation is impossible. When we have an outbreak of cholera or malaria in New York, it can at least be studied, and with each outbreak we gain some useful information. But here—" She made a helpless little fluttering gesture.

Shiloh took her carbolic-stained hand and raised it to his lips. "Maybe one day you can just lug your fancy microscope all over the world to wherever they have plagues and really study them. I know a ship you can have anytime you want."

She looked at him, a little surprised. "Why, there's no organization I've ever heard of that does clinical investigations like that. But it certainly is an intriguing idea."

"You could do it, Doc," he said easily. "I'm

335

ready whenever you are. Maybe at least one good thing will come out of this amonaly."

"Anomaly," she corrected him with a faint smile.

"Yeah, that thing." He jerked his thumb over his shoulder. "The villagers are lining up out there. They all knew that Sharik was in a bad way, and a lot of them followed me to the pit. I started to run them off—bad form, their ghoulish curiosity—but then I thought, why not? Maybe they'll get over this dumb idea that they'll ward off the evil eye or wicked miasma or palm-tree demon by ignoring what you're tryin' to tell 'em. And it worked! They got scared, all right, and there's plenty of 'em now figuring you might better check their headache or runny nose or whatever."

Cheney knew he spoke so carelessly to try to lighten the situation, but she was already so fatigued from lack of sleep and the heavy burden of responsibility that she could barely make herself speak. "Are there many of them?"

"Yeah, just about everyone's millin' around out there," Shiloh answered, "but I don't think all of them are sick. It seemed to me that they were trying to figure out how to take care of their sick. You know, there's no place here on this whole island that would make a good quarantine hospital. Except maybe the Verbrugge home—that's the big stone house, you know. But there's already sixteen of them living there, the two couples and their twelve kids. No, make that seventeen, because Bonnie's staying with them. Can't see setting up an isolation ward there."

"No, no, that would never do," Cheney said hastily. "But oh, Shiloh, this is going to make it so hard on us! Having the patients scattered around in different houses, I mean. How are we ever going to take care of them all?"

He stood and gently pulled her up into his arms. Smoothing her hair, he whispered, "Cheney, my love, we can do it. Together, like always. Haven't we always made it?"

Her voice muffled against his chest, she mumbled, "Yes, we have. Maybe this isn't so bad. At least there's not a volcano trying to burn us down."

"Or sharks trying to eat us," Shiloh added.

"Or big mean fish trying to poison us," Cheney grumbled.

"Or people shooting at us from the woods."

"Or *vaudou* queens cursing us."

Cheney leaned back and smiled up at him, genuinely amused. "You know, this really isn't so tough after all, Iron Man. Let's start this fight."

"First," he said firmly, leaning down to her, "let's smooch. You owe me, Dr. Cheney. This is my medicine." He kissed her long and passionately, and she clung to him, reveling in his clean carbolic and pine-scented soap smell, his warmth, his strong arms and body.

Finally she pulled back, slightly breathless. "Smooching in an operating room is hardly professional."

"Have to catch it where I can these days," he grumbled, then sighed with exaggerated impatience. "Okay, I know, Doc. Time to go back to work."

"It is getting late, Shiloh, and you know we still have to go to the Big House," she said as lightly as she could, straightening her dress and smoothing down her hair, which Shiloh had mussed a little.

He nodded. "Just sit down here, Doc, and rest. I'm going to go get you a ginger fizz, and I'll make arrangements for someone to come sit with Sharik. When we get back from Bain's, I'm sending you back to the ship to get some sleep. I'll get everyone organized, give instructions for her care, and I'll get the villagers who are sick lined up."

She started to protest, but he stopped her, raising his hand and shaking his head. "No, ma'am, I ain't discussin' it. Remember me? Mr. Iron Head, with superhuman strength and all? You said it, not me. It won't do anybody any good if you get sick with exhaustion. I'm not even tired. I would send you on back now but—" he faltered a little, looking anxious—"but I did think it was a really good . . . thing, Bain asking for you. You understand?"

"Of course I do," Cheney answered, taking his hands and squeezing them tightly. "I'm fine, really, and I will sit here and be a good little doctor. And thank you, I'd love a ginger fizz. I only wish they had some ice," she sighed. "But no matter. You just go on and do all your chores. And then we'll go see Imri, and maybe we'll get a chance to talk again to Bain."

By the time Cheney and Shiloh reached Bain's house, Cheney was exhausted. The uphill climb had drained her, and Shiloh muttered, "This is too much for you."

"It's all right," Cheney said shortly. "I'm fine."

Shiloh frowned but didn't argue. He knocked on the door, and after what seemed like a long wait, it opened. Bain stood framed in the doorway, his face fixed in a look of displeasure. "So you came," he said in a brittle tone. "You took your time about it, Dr. Duvall."

Cheney civilly inclined her head. "It's Dr. Irons-Winslow now, Mr. Winslow."

"Ah yes, it had temporarily slipped my mind," Bain mocked. "Please come in."

Without any more small talk he led them upstairs to what was obviously his bedroom. Cheney went to the bed, where she saw a beautiful island quadroon sunk into the soft bedding. She looked very small and very young. "How do you do, Miss Ten Eyck? I am Dr. Irons-Winslow, Mr. Winslow's cousin," she said with the merest hint of irony.

"I'm pleased to meet you," Imri said gravely, offering Cheney her hand. It was hot and dry. "Please call me Imri."

The social niceties over, Cheney turned to Shiloh and Bain, who hovered at the foot of the bed. "Would you two gentlemen excuse us, please?" she said formally, for Bain's sake.

He was staring at Imri with narrowed eyes. "What's wrong with her?" he asked impatiently.

"That's why I would like to do a thorough examination, to find out," Cheney answered crisply. "I'm sure you'll excuse us, Mr. Winslow."

Bain opened his mouth to reply but then clamped it shut. He whirled and stamped out of the room.

Shiloh rolled his eyes. "He does that a lot. Call me if you need me, Doc."

Shiloh followed Bain into his study, where he was, of course, pouring himself a stiff drink. He didn't look up or speak when Shiloh came in. But Shiloh saw a man—a big, thick man with long yellow hair—sitting hunched on the sofa. With hard eyes, Shiloh stood in front of him. "Shiloh Irons-Winslow," he growled. This was the man who had kidnapped Cheney.

Sweet stood up. Though not as tall as Shiloh, he was more thickly built, like a stone slab. "Sweet," he responded listlessly.

Shiloh stuck out his hand, and Sweet took it. Shiloh gauged the man as he gave his hand a hard shake, which was returned with no visible effort on Sweet's part. Sweet met his gaze squarely, but there was nothing there—no recognition, no guilt, no shame. Shiloh noticed that his eyes were slate gray, and they were shadowed and dull.

"He knows who you are, Locke, just as you know who he is," Bain said irritably, throwing himself into an armchair. "Just leave him alone, can't you?"

Shiloh shrugged and seated himself, not caring whether his cousin invited him to or not. Bain seemed not to notice; he was distracted and fidgety. To Shiloh's great surprise, a ginger cat stepped prettily up from the shadows, twitched her tail, and jumped into Bain's lap. Nervously he stroked her, and Shiloh could hear her pleased purr. Shiloh would never have thought that Bain would like cats.

"She's got it, has she?" Bain asked with a great effort at sounding nonchalant.

"Probably so," Shiloh answered evenly.

"What's . . . what's going to happen to her?"

Shiloh looked curiously at his cousin. Bain's

worry over the girl was obvious, and that, too, was a surprise. His cousin wasn't exactly a caring sort of man. "She'll probably feel pretty much the same as she does right now for a few days— she's got a headache? Feverish? Listless? Right. Then—" he shifted restlessly, and Bain watched him with burning eyes—"then she'll go into a crisis stage, with a high temperature, delirium, sometimes coma."

"And then?" Bain asked in a guttural whisper.

"Only time will tell," Shiloh answered. "But listen, Bain, while she's sick she's going to be real low, really depressed. She needs to feel as secure as possible, with . . . with something to look forward to, something to live for. You get me?"

The Winslow eyebrow rose coolly. "Yes, I *get you*. Vulgar Americanism. Anyway, her entire family is here. They'll know best how to take care of her."

"You could help," Shiloh said quietly. "You could probably help her more than anyone."

Bain rose, carefully placing the cat in his chair, and then started pacing behind Shiloh's chair. It's an awkward thing to have someone who is not particularly fond of you stalk back and forth like a leashed tiger behind your back. Wearily Shiloh rose to face him. Bain's face was flushed.

"You're always trying to get me to be a wet

nurse like you," Bain muttered. "But in case you haven't noticed, Locke, I'm not you, I'm nothing like you, and I don't wish to be."

"Okay, then, how about if we take her to the ship?" Shiloh asked as politely as he could manage. "Cheney and I are stretched pretty thin, with patients scattered all over the village and six men sick on the ship."

"No," Bain said curtly. "Imri stays here."

An uncomfortable silence fell while Shiloh tried to figure out how to persuade Bain to bring Imri to *Locke's Day Dream*. He knew that no untrained person could give a typhus victim the skilled care required.

But then again, Shiloh reflected sadly, *I can understand why Bain doesn't want to come to* Locke's Day Dream. *And he would want to, because he really does want to be with that girl. I can see he really cares for her. . . .*

Cheney came back in, wiping her hands with a clean cloth. "Mr. Winslow, I'm afraid that Imri has typhus," she said without preamble. "She's going to require a great deal of special care—"

"I know all that already. My cousin has been good enough to instruct me," Bain said harshly. "I'll go get her parents, and you can instruct them."

"But—" Cheney began, but it was to Bain's back as he stalked out of the room. "He does make quick exits, doesn't he?"

Sweet had slowly risen to his feet when Cheney came in and now stood dumbly, as he always did. Cheney steeled herself and went to him, holding out her hand. "Mr. Sweet, I believe? We've never been properly introduced. I am Dr. Cheney Irons-Winslow."

He took her hand, and Shiloh saw the faintest trace of confusion pass over his wooden features. "Sweet," he finally muttered, dropping his eyes.

Cheney frowned, then took his hand in both of hers and stepped closer to him. Shiloh came up, puzzled. Sweet glanced back up at Cheney—guiltily, it seemed. "Do you feel quite all right, Mr. Sweet?"

"Just Sweet," he mumbled. "No, ma'am."

"I see. I think I'd better examine you, and you really should be in bed," Cheney said briskly. "Do you have a house down in the village? Or one of the servant's cottages, perhaps?"

"Oh no," he answered, showing some signs of life for the first time. "Mr. Winslow, he gives me a bedroom here in the Big House. As big and as nice as his own."

"I see," Cheney said slowly. "Well, I'm sure Mr. Winslow would want you to go straight to bed."

"C'mon, Sweet," Shiloh said, giving Cheney a dark look. After all, this man had kidnapped her, and Shiloh didn't care if Sweet was a reformed character and about to die, he had no intention of letting Cheney be alone with him. "Let's get you upstairs and in bed, and I'll examine you. The doc needs to talk to the Ten Eycks as soon as they get here."

Sweet nodded. He turned as they reached the door. "Dr. Cheney, I'm sorry that Oona and I scared you."

"And drugged her," Shiloh added darkly, "and tossed her in a carriage like a butcher's cut and kidnapped her and left her alone and scared in a stinking whorehouse."

"Yes. Now I'm sorry," Sweet said humbly. "And not just because I'm sick. Because I think Mr. Winslow is sorry too."

"I forgive you," Cheney said softly. "I forgive you both."

CHAPTER EIGHTEEN

Materia Medica or Medical Matters

"CHENEY, YOU LOOK EXHAUSTED," Shiloh said with concern. "Have you been to bed?"

"No, and I'm not going to either, and neither have you," Cheney answered distractedly. Shiloh had just come in from the village after a round that had started at midnight. Seven of the villagers were now officially typhus victims—nine counting Imri and Sweet. There were six crewmen in the sick bay. After they had left Bain's house, Shiloh had stayed on in the village while Cheney had come back to the ship. Now it was three-thirty in the morning.

She sat at the table in the salon, again with her books and papers full of frantic scribblings. She also had the six sailors' charts, and a litter of colored bottles, some uncorked, some unopened but on their sides, along with an apothecary's balance, spoons, and a mortar and pestle with some grainy white substance spilled around it.

Cheney looked up at Shiloh, and he was shocked at her appearance. Her green eyes glittered brilliantly, but she had deep purple shadows under them. She seemed washed-out, and though some semblance of her tan remained, her skin was dull. Part of her hair, which Fiona had carefully dressed into a smooth, full French chignon, had come loose, and strands hung around her ears and shoulders, with one limp curl that kept escaping over her eye. She shoved it back with a nervous gesture. "Go get Fiona and Sketes," she said shortly. "I have to go over this materia medica with all of you."

"But, Doc," Shiloh began, but when he saw the flash in Cheney's eyes he shrugged and murmured, "Yes, ma'am."

When Shiloh returned with Fiona and Sketes, Cheney started talking—very fast—

before they had even sat down at the littered table with her. "All right, the only alteratives that empirically address the disease are heroic dosages of antimony, or I guess I should say tartar emetic, along with quinine salts, also in heroic dosages as a preventive, but contraindications are vital in postprescriptive monitoring—"

"Whoa, Doc," Shiloh said, easing himself down beside her.

Fiona and Sketes, who had stopped in amazement at this tirade, had identical round, startled eyes. Comically their heads swiveled right over to Shiloh. "Is she speaking English?" Sketes asked.

"Sketes!" Cheney said severely.

"Sorry, Dr. Cheney," Sketes murmured, easing her comfortable bulk into the bench opposite Cheney and Shiloh. Fiona slipped in beside her. "But I'm confounded, plain and simple."

"Well, then, you must listen and try to understand," Cheney said impatiently. "I didn't realize until I returned to the ship that it's been almost a week since we had the first typhus case, and I still haven't instructed you on the materia medica. Now all these people are sick, and I don't have the prescriptives ready, much less coherent written instructions for you."

"But, Doc, verbal instructions that we can't understand aren't going to do anyone any good,"

Shiloh said calmly. "Now, let's just take this one step at a time. Slowly."

Cheney took a deep, exasperated breath and began, "The only alterative empirically proven for typhus is antimony in heroic dosages. At least I remember that much, and these"—she motioned with disdain toward the opened books— "don't give any course of treatment for typhus. They only list the symptoms. I also remember that quinine is indicated for any tropical fevers, but I can't remember if heroic dosages are recommended or not."

Shiloh, who was beginning to see the problem, put up his hand to stop her. Turning to Fiona and Sketes, he said quietly, "What she means is that we've got to give the patients large amounts of dangerous drugs. Okay, Doc, go on."

She stared up at him with haunted eyes. "It's not that simple. Weren't you listening? You know that I've never adhered to the outdated belief in giving immense dosages. I've always thought that the assumption 'more is better' was false. And you know that antimony, if not administered with the utmost care, can poison a patient."

He kept his eyes trained intensely on hers. "Doc, I know all that. You're not arguing with me, you know. You're just arguing with yourself. And I don't think you should do that. You're a healer. Your decisions will be the right ones."

"Maybe," she said, ducking her head and rubbing her temples with her fingertips. It muffled her voice as she muttered, "But the fact is that these medications must be designed specifically, and exactly, for each patient according to a number of variables. And I don't have the charts for dosages. All I can remember is that it's ten drams of tartar emetic once a day for a healthy adult male."

"That's a start," Shiloh said easily. "We can figure out a mathematical calculation on that, Doc."

"And I don't know about heroic dosages of quinine," Cheney said dully, still holding her head in her hands.

"Let's start with ten drams," Shiloh suggested. "It's not as rough on the system as tartar emetic, so surely we can start the men on that, and if it goes down and stays down we can try small increases."

Cheney jerked upright and her fists came down, too hard, on the table. "But that won't work! There are so many variables, and any adverse side effects must be judged on a baseline, which won't exist without constants!"

Fiona and Sketes exchanged slightly alarmed glances. Shiloh sighed and took Cheney's hand, caressing it. "Doc, I don't know what that means. But if you'll just slow down—"

Cheney jerked her hand away and cried,

"Oh, why, why didn't you go on to medical school? You would know all this, and I wouldn't have to try to explain things beginning with the alphabet! You're not helping me at all, Shiloh!"

Now Fiona and Sketes both hastily looked down. Shiloh's face tightened for a moment, not with anger but with consternation. Cheney stared at him, her color reckless, her mouth tight. Softly Shiloh said, "Sketes, Fiona, would you excuse us for a few minutes? I dunno about the doc, but I sure could use some hot coffee about now."

"Sure, sure, Mr. Locke," Sketes said hastily, hauling Fiona up bodily. With cautious wide-eyed glances at Cheney, who ignored them, they scurried out of the salon.

Cheney sat unmoving, staring up at him defiantly. His face softened and his ice blue eyes grew gentle. "Doc, listen to me. This isn't you, and what you just said is not true. I can help you, and I will. So talk to me."

For long moments she just stared up at him. And then she seemed to wilt. Her shoulders sagged, her eyes grew dull, and with great weariness, she shoved the bothersome hair from her face. "Shiloh, I don't know what I'm doing. I've never had this sort of responsibility before, and I've never been without resort to other physicians, or at least to research literature."

He nodded. "Okay, I see that. So what are your options?"

"I don't have any options. I have to do it myself."

"Right. So let's just get that out of the way. Wishing for books and other doctors isn't going to help you. But Sketes and Fiona and I will help you, Cheney. Now I know that we're not trained, and I know it's hard for you to get down on our level. But the simple fact of the matter is that that's exactly what's going to have to get done."

"Yes, but . . . Shiloh, I could actually kill these people with these dangerous drugs," she said, dropping her head and pleating her dress between her fingers.

He put two fingers under her chin and lifted her face. "Cheney, you will not kill anyone. You're a healer. You have a gift from God. Do you think He'll suddenly take away that gift and turn you into some kind of well-intentioned murderer? No, no, no. Even I know that's not the way it works."

Cheney's eyes filled with tears. "But I could make a mistake."

"But God won't," Shiloh said gently. "So let's just pray and ask Him to tell you what to do."

Her brow crinkled, and then she smiled weakly. "But that's not in my materia medica that I've been slaving over for hours."

Shiloh grinned widely. "Then let's just get

one of your little chewed-up pencils here and put it in. Okay?"

"Okay. Shiloh?" She reached up and took his face in her hands. "Oh, Shiloh, I'm sorry, so sorry I spoke to you that way. Will you forgive me?"

"Of course," he said, turning to kiss her palm.

"Will you pray for me?"

"Always," he promised and bowed his head.

"Lord, thank you so much for giving me this wonderful wife," he prayed humbly. "And thank you for giving these sick people a doctor who is blessed by you. Now, Lord, she needs you to tell her about these medicines, and she needs you to tell her about each one of the patients. So we ask, in Jesus' blessed name, that you give Cheney this knowledge, and let her know for sure that you'll take this heavy burden of worry from her, as you take all of our burdens away. Amen."

———————

Sketes and Fiona, with dread, approached the salon door. They both came to a standstill just outside it. Sketes held a tray with the elegant silver coffee service, and Fiona held a tray with fruits and nuts piled artistically on it. They glanced at each other with clear reluctance.

Resignedly Sketes raised her foot to knock, as neither of them had a hand free, but just as she did, they heard a rich laugh from inside the salon. Cheney was laughing.

"He fixed her," Sketes murmured with wonder.

"Thank the Lord," Fiona whispered.

"Amen," Sketes said and tapped on the door with her foot.

"Come on in, Sketes. I thought I heard you two lurking out here," Shiloh said, opening the door and taking Sketes's heavy tray. He always did things like that, and it never failed to fluster Sketes.

"Here's ... here's coffee, Mr. Locke," she said, casting cautious sideways glances at Cheney.

Cheney smiled brilliantly at her. "Come on back in, Sketes, Fiona. Don't be frightened. I'm not biting anymore."

"I let her nibble on me a little," Shiloh said airily. "She's all better now."

"Shiloh! Oh ... just ... don't pay any attention to him," Cheney blustered. "Good, you brought four cups. You'll join us. And the fruit tray, Fiona—it's exquisite! It looks much too beautiful to eat."

"Forget that," Shiloh said, grabbing a chunk of mango and biting it voraciously. "And you eat something too, Doc. I mean it. That's an order."

"Mmm, I must say that those sugarplums smell heavenly. And are those fresh coconut chunks? Here, Sketes, I know you're very partial to these hog plums—such an ugly name for such a pretty fruit. Help yourself, I insist. . . ."

They each had two cups of strong coffee, the beans freshly roasted by Sketes that morning, and munched for a while, just talking about how delicious the fruit was, and how different fresh nuts tasted from imported dried ones.

Finally Cheney sat back, sipping the last of her coffee, and smiled. "Now, don't be afraid, friends, but I'm going to, once again, explain to you about the prescriptives for the patients."

"I'll translate," Shiloh assured Sketes and Fiona.

Cheney gave him a wry glance but went on, "All right, with prayer and with my husband's wisdom, I have decided that we're going to give the patients strong dosages of two drugs, tartar emetic and quinine salts, each morning. Then they will have to be monitored very carefully to see how they tolerate the drugs. Tartar emetic, if the dosage is too high, can cause antimony poisoning, which will bring on sweating, vomiting, and catharsis. We don't want that. So if any of the patients has any of these side effects, be sure to document it on the chart. Carefully, in as much detail as you can manage."

Sketes and Fiona looked uncertain. Finally Sketes said, "But, Dr. Cheney, sometimes these men, they're sweating any old way because of the fever. How are we to know which is the right kind of sweating and which is the bad kind?"

Cheney chewed her lower lip. "Actually, I don't think—no, I'm certain," she said, glancing at Shiloh with a smile. "The indication of antimony poisoning is excessive transudation and only occurs in conjunction with the other symptoms."

Shiloh turned to Fiona and Sketes and winked. "She means that if they're throwing up and sweating at the same time, it's the bad kind of sweat."

Like solemn little dolls, Sketes and Fiona nodded.

Hiding her amusement, Cheney continued, "Now, I've already given one—no, two—or is it one? What day is it? Oh, never mind. I've already given doses to the men who are in the sick bay—two days, isn't it, for Leith and Solly? And one day, yesterday, for the other four men. They have all seemed to tolerate the doses so far."

Sketes frowned. "Well, you know, Leith didn't want to eat his breakfast this morning, Dr. Cheney. He usually eats like an ox, even if he is just a little mite. You think maybe he was feeling sick from the . . . uh . . . medica?"

"Perhaps," Cheney answered worriedly. "It is a problem. Actually tartar emetic has a very mild sweetish taste, but the quinine salts are bitter. It might be that the taste of the drug alone will upset their stomachs."

Shiloh asked lazily, "Then why don't we sweeten it up for them, Doc?"

She said thoughtfully, "You can't disguise the taste of quinine with any aromatic or even a sweetener, like sugar or honey."

"How about rum?" Sketes asked solidly. "Seems like it wouldn't hurt those poor beggars to have a little tot of rum to get that nasty stuff down with."

Cheney stared at her. "Why . . . that might not be a bad idea, Sketes. Do we have any rum?"

Shiloh and Sketes laughed, and even Fiona giggled.

"What's so funny?" Cheney demanded with a touch of her previous impatience. "It was a perfectly logical question."

"Aw, Doc, sorry," Shiloh said. "It's just that we're in the West Indies. The Caribbean is practically made of rum. It's everywhere."

"On the ship?" Cheney asked wide-eyed.

"Uh, yeah, I would imagine that there's a bottle or two around," Shiloh admitted. "Normally Captain Starnes doesn't allow the men to have liquor stores, but since we're holed up here, I imagine he kinda turned a blind eye if, say, some wicked sailor sneaked a bottle in from shore leave."

"I see," Cheney sniffed. "Well, how was I

supposed to know? So . . . so, Sketes, go get us some rum, and we'll just have to cook up a new prescriptive for the morning dosage."

Sketes soon returned with a heavy brown bottle with no label, refusing to say where she'd gotten it. Cheney mixed up a man's dosage of tartar emetic and quinine salts in an ounce of rum and then dipped her finger in it and tasted. She made the most disgusted face Shiloh had ever seen, and he chuckled. "It's not funny, it's horrid," Cheney said, choking a little. "Goodness, I hadn't tasted this prescriptive. It's really repulsive. I don't know how the men got it down with just water. It's as if the slightly sweet taste of the tartar emetic makes the quinine taste that much worse. It's not doing the rum any good either."

Shiloh dipped his finger in and tasted. "Agh, that is bad, no joke. Here, Sketes, Fiona. Sorry, hazards of the profession. If you're gonna shove it down their throats, you need to know what you're inflicting on 'em. So, Doc, you think maybe increasing the amount of rum?"

"I hate to," Cheney said reluctantly. "I don't mind using any alcohol for medicinal purposes, but it is a depressant. And since this disease evidences a peculiar melancholy, I don't want to use any more depressants than I have to."

Fiona spoke for the first time, hesitantly. "Dr. Cheney? What about molasses? My mother used to mix molasses with spirits of wine to give us quinine powder when we had fever."

Cheney smiled. "Then let's give it a try."

They experimented and finally came up with a dose that was not exactly pleasant tasting but was at least a great improvement over swallowing down the bitter powders dissolved in water. The four of them started preparing doses for the men. Cheney measured the drugs carefully, Shiloh combined them with the mortar and pestle, while Fiona and Sketes mixed the molasses and rum.

Shiloh asked, "Okay, Doc, now what about something at night? You know sick people always feel worse at night. Their fever usually goes up, and their spirits go down."

"Oh . . . I see. You mean, something to treat the symptoms . . . yes, a febrifuge, along with a roborative . . . "

With a sigh, Shiloh turned to Fiona and Sketes. "She means something to bring down the fever, and something to perk them up."

"Ahh," Sketes said knowingly. "Now I don't know about febberfews and robotives, but I do know there's nothing like fresh ginger tea, good and hot, to lighten up your spirits."

Cheney stared at her balance with the little pile of white salts on it. "Yes, that's good, that's very good. Ginger infusion for the roborative, but we need to have a contrastimulant, even a sedative. Not laudanum, it's a depressant. . . ." She was muttering to herself now.

"She means—aw, listen, Doc. How about valerian? We've got lots of that for some reason. I didn't stock it. It was already in the ship's chest. Dried."

Cheney nodded slowly. "Yes, it is a truly effective sedative, with demulcent qualities. Very soothing to both the body and the mind. But, Shiloh, how could we administer it? I don't think even rum and molasses would disguise it."

At Fiona's questioning look, Shiloh said, "It stinks and it tastes like sour milk."

"Oh, dear," Fiona said.

"But, Shiloh, you are right. They are going to need something to remedy these symptoms," Cheney said quietly. She looked up from her powders to smile at Fiona and Sketes. "You see, that is what makes a good nurse. I was just thinking of how to cure the disease. Shiloh was thinking of how to make the patient feel better. He's always been the very best nurse I've ever seen."

"Thanks, Doc," Shiloh said with real pleasure.

"Welcome," she said briskly. "Now, since I've decided that I'm willing to try anything to help these people, I have a suggestion. What about brandy?"

Shiloh grinned. "That'd do it."

"Could we sneak in some salicylic acid, do

you think?" Cheney said slyly.

"The febrifuge," Shiloh told Fiona and Sketes with a supercilious air. "Sure, Doc. They'll never notice. Take my word for it." Again he spoke to Fiona and Sketes. "Once I drank some brandy with a drug that had one big wallop to it, and I never knew it. I think you could put a dead frog at the bottom of a snifter of brandy and you'd never know."

"Oooh," Fiona groaned. "I'm sure I'd notice."

"Butter," Sketes said succinctly. "Add a little hot butter, just a tot, and Bob's your uncle."

With surprise Cheney said, "Why, that's a really good idea, Sketes. Butter has definite demulcent properties."

Shiloh sighed. "She means that it'll be good for their stomachs."

"I mean," Cheney said quietly, "that I'm so grateful for such capable, knowledgeable assistants. Thank you all very much, for you've all been such a great help to me already. And the only thing that I want to add to our materia medica is this: Pray. Always pray. For your patients, for their families, for yourselves, for Shiloh, and for me."

Shyly Fiona whispered, "Maybe we could all pray right now? I'd feel so much better. Not so afraid."

Cheney said, "Fiona, after my husband prays

for you, I can promise you that you won't be afraid another minute. Believe me, I know. He's getting to be an expert, just like my father."

"Hey, thanks, Doc," Shiloh said, pleased.

"Welcome."

CHAPTER NINETEEN

Blood Always Tells

CHENEY REMEMBERED DREAMS.

She'd been in some nameless, formless place, running and shouting, for there was some urgent, perhaps desperate, task she needed to accomplish in this tiresome never-never world. But she had been running in painfully slow motion, as if she were entombed in some thick, viscous substance that obscured her every move. She had shouted, straining with the effort, but could never make a sound. She had felt such frustration because she couldn't run fast enough and she couldn't make herself heard.

To feel this way for an hour was terrible, but it was exactly how she had felt for what seemed like forever. She had hurried all through the days and most of the nights, but somehow it was never fast enough. She had talked and talked and could never say enough. She never knew the date, or what day it was, or what time it was. At sunset and dawn she never knew if one day was ending or another was beginning.

But in her dreams she didn't have Shiloh. And when she had a rare moment or two for introspection, she thought that the dreams, on the whole, were worse than the reality. Shiloh was her solid rock of security, her confidence, her joy, and perhaps most valuable in those dark days, her jester. He had made her laugh, even when she was so exhausted she could barely see and so low she wanted to hide.

And there had been bad times in the last days. Sharik Dekker had never regained consciousness; she had stayed in a deep coma, had broken out with typhus rash, and had died the night after her operation. Isaac Dekker and his brother, Emil, had volunteered to sit with her, and both of them had come down with typhus. Helmond and Kiffa Ten Eyck, the elderly couple, had died within hours of each other. Four other villagers had it, including Kort Verbrugge and his eldest son, Markus. Also, Elena Verbrugge, Opal Dekker's only faithful nurse, had gotten the fever. Kort's wife, Katrina, would have stayed with Opal, but when her husband and son had become ill she, of course, refused to leave them.

The dreams and the reality merged into one seemingly endless time, and Cheney endured, but at a high cost.

"I don't understand about Opal Dekker," Cheney said as she and Shiloh went down to the sick bay. It was about three-thirty in the morning on the twenty-first of May, and Shiloh had just come back from the village. Cheney had been asleep for a couple of hours, and Shiloh was determined not to awaken her, but she'd heard his voice on deck as he was talking across the forbidden space to Captain Starnes. She'd risen, still dressed—that happened a lot to her these days—and called Shiloh in for them to pray for a few minutes. They had to grab each other in passing to get a few moments alone together. Cheney had refused to go back to bed, so they had decided to do sick-bay rounds together.

She continued, "The villagers seem to be so close. They take such good care of each other. Opal is a Dekker, after all, but the Verbrugges seem to be the only ones who will care for her."

Shiloh went first down the booby-hatch ladder, then held up his arms to help Cheney. "Yeah, Opal really messed her own self up when she came here," he told her, neatly swinging Cheney down, holding her by the waist. "Seems like Willem didn't tell her he was part black—"

"He was?" Cheney said, surprised. "He didn't look like it."

Shiloh put his arm around Cheney's waist as

they walked slowly toward the officers' quarters, now two sick bays and an examination room. "I dunno, I didn't really notice one way or the other. Anyway, Opal was a lady of the evening over in St. Vincent, and Willem courted her over there. Well, one fine night they got married, and Willem swept her off her feet and took her away from all that. Kinda like me and you, you know."

"I beg your pardon?" Cheney asked indignantly. But her mouth twitched, and her eyes sparkled.

"Uh . . . wait. No, that's not what I meant. Not like you were a lady of the evening or anything like that. I meant I swept you off your feet," Shiloh spluttered.

"Did you? Well, you certainly didn't take me away from it all," Cheney grumbled. "Here we are, at our Honeymoon Sick Bay."

The largest of the quarters, which had been First Mate Nat Cadell's cabin, berthed Leith Redding and Solly Vaughn, the two apprentices, along with Willy Perkins, Sam Bowles, and another ordinary seaman called Jimmy Wooling. Horatio Seaton, the second mate, had been put in his own cabin, and Billy-O berthed with him. Birr Dunstan, the handsome boatswain, had gotten the fever the day after Sharik had been bitten by the rat, and he was in his old cabin too, along with Tong Ten. All three of the cabins opened into the officers' wardroom, which had a fine oak table that could seat eight, and this provided a good place for Fiona and Sketes to sit and sew and read when the patients were asleep. But now, as Cheney and Shiloh entered the wardroom, the sounds of a man shouting in delirium came from the first mate's cabin, along with Sketes's voice, low and calm but strained.

Cheney and Shiloh hurried into the cabin. Sketes was struggling with Willy Perkins, trying to hold him down. He was thrashing wildly, his face purple-crimson. "There's that black thief what stole my new brass buttons! He's getting clean away!" he railed, his eyes popping, staring wildly into empty space. He pushed Sketes hard and started to get out of bed. Cheney steadied her and murmured, "Get his chart."

Shiloh hurried to him, pushing him back onto the bed. "Perkins, it's me, Mr. Locke. Settle down now. I'll take care of it."

Perkins lay down reluctantly, but he still waved frantically with both arms. "Mr. Locke, that there scrub stole my buttons, he did! I'm going to get 'em back!"

Shiloh kept talking to the delirious man, trying to calm him, gently holding both his wrists. But Perkins, of course, was unable to reason, and he continued to fight Shiloh.

Cheney frowned as she hurried through the notes on Perkins' chart. Glancing up worriedly at the other men, she saw with satisfaction that

Sketes was already attending them, particularly the two boys, who looked pale and frightened. Sam Bowles was watching Perkins and Shiloh but seemed dull and only half interested. Wooling, the other seaman, was a dark, rather savage man, and Cheney had hardly seen him and had never talked to him. He was staring at Perkins with something like a sneer on his face and called out, "Shut up, you old fool! Man can't get a minute's sleep in this bedlam!"

Cheney went to him and adjusted his light coverlet. "Mr. Wooling, Mr. Perkins is unable to help himself. Please lie quietly, and in a few minutes he'll be sleeping."

"Hope so," Wooling growled. "He's just lookin' for attention, if you ask me. This here fever ain't so bad. He oughta take it like a man."

"Just rest now," Cheney said evenly. Quickly she went to the small table inset into the wall and opened her medical bag. Taking out a cobalt blue bottle, she measured thirty drops into a glass and went to Shiloh, who was still holding down the wildly flailing man as gently as he could. "Doc, you better let me," he said quietly.

She nodded and stood silently by the bed.

Shiloh pushed the man down hard and put his face close to his. "Listen to me, Perkins. It's Mr. Locke. You know who I am?"

His reddened eyes searched Shiloh's face. "Yes, sir, I do."

"I want you to take some medicine," Shiloh said sternly. "You understand?"

"Yes . . ." he said, his eyes narrowing and darting back and forth.

Still bending close over Perkins, Shiloh reached out to Cheney, who shoved the glass into his hand. "Sit up," he said, grabbing Perkins' shoulder. "Drink this."

Perkins stiffened and regarded Shiloh suspiciously, but Shiloh—brutally, it seemed—shoved the glass against his lips. After a moment of stubborn lip tightening, Perkins finally opened his mouth and Shiloh poured the cloudy amber liquid into his mouth, then quickly pinched his nose. Perkins swallowed automatically but then began fighting Shiloh again, raving about his brass buttons. This only lasted a few moments, however, and then his eyelids fluttered, and he sank back onto the bed with a soft moan.

Shiloh straightened and then gently rearranged the mussed coverlet and fluffed his pillow. Lifting the cover and Perkins' nightshirt, he glanced down at his chest. "It's starting," he told Cheney quietly.

She nodded, still thumbing through Perkins' chart. "He'll be calm for a while now. Let's make rounds, and then we'll talk in the wardroom."

They visited all the patients with Sketes, but so far everyone except Willy Perkins was still in the latent stage of the disease, and so were calm, though obviously all of them were miserable. Horatio Seaton, the second mate, was a gentle, courtly man and did rouse himself enough to say how nice it was for both Dr. Cheney and Mr. Locke to visit.

Cheney was careful to write down on each chart that she and Shiloh had at least spoken to the patients. She'd found that if she didn't do that, she couldn't remember the last time they'd made rounds. As usual, she studied each chart and whispered instructions to Sketes, who conscientiously wrote down everything Cheney said, while Shiloh talked to each man, sometimes giving them a drink of juice or water, joking with them, touching them, laying his hand on their shoulders or on their fevered foreheads. Watching him, Cheney was again amazed at the way patients invariably responded to Shiloh. When he was around, they calmed down, their eyes brightened a bit, and they seemed to take a little heart. Even the sour Jimmy Wooling told Shiloh he was feeling better and thought he would sleep for a while.

After visiting with the nine men, Cheney, Shiloh, and Sketes sat down at the wardroom table with the pile of charts.

Cheney was writing in Perkins' chart and murmured, "Shiloh, help me with this. I only gave him thirty drops of laudanum. For a man his size, the recommended dosage is sixty drops.

He'd had the night medication at . . . at . . ."

"Midnight," Sketes said. "When I relieved Fiona, I gave all the night dosages."

"Fiona's staying with the men by herself?" Cheney asked in surprise.

"Oh yes, Dr. Cheney. We both stayed down here for two nights and a day. Mr. Dunstan hung a hammock for us right over there, and we took turns napping. But Fiona got to where she was managing these swabs just fine, so we've been on watch and watch," Sketes said confidently.

"Good, I'm sure that's much easier," Cheney said absently. "But, Shiloh, I'm just not sure about medication for Mr. Perkins. I don't like to give typhus patients laudanum, because it does have a depressive tendency, and their prescriptives have liquor in them already."

"I know, Doc," Shiloh said quietly, "but Perkins, with those cracked ribs, has to be kept calm. He doesn't need to displace those ribs and have that to fight too, not to mention the pain when he comes to himself. You did the right thing."

She nodded, a little uncertainly. "Yes, he must be sedated. How unfortunate that his delirium took the form of agitation. Most of them are just restless and mutter nonsense to themselves."

"Well, that's good news to me," Sketes said. "I've nursed men—my own husband, God rest his loving soul—through ship fever, and none of them fought like Perkins did. And him being such a kind man when in his right mind too! If anyone was going to knock around and make a fuss, I'd have figured on Wooling. He's a sullen old swab, he is. Fair tortures those two poor boys, calling them little mewling kittens and telling them that they'll probably kick off in their sleep."

Shiloh growled under his breath. "Is he giving you or Fiona any trouble, Sketes?"

Sketes pursed her mouth. "He tried at first. But I told him that if he so much as looked crossways at me or Fiona, we'd go fetch you right quick, Mr. Locke, and that he might find his hammock hanging in the head, if you took such a mind. That put a stop to that nonsense! He's even civil to Fiona now."

"Maybe we should move him," Shiloh said thoughtfully. "No, Doc, I don't mean into the head. I mean, maybe put him with Dunstan. Birr still feels good enough to knock him on the head and put a stop to that mean mouthing. And Tong Ten would be good with the boys."

Cheney answered stubbornly, "Mr. Wooling is still my patient, and I don't care what his attitude is. I'm responsible for him and I need to consider what is best for him. I'm not sure that moving him in with Mr. Dunstan would be the best thing for him. It would seem to be ostracizing him. And I noticed that every single man here has gifts, presumably from his shipmates—except for Mr. Wooling. He has no fruit, no playing cards, no handmade pachisi boards, no books."

"He can't read anyway," Sketes said lamely. "And Captain Starnes sends down fruit and little sweet biscuits for all the men." She and Shiloh exchanged uneasy glances.

"What is it?" Cheney demanded severely. "I need to know. I keep telling you that I need to know everything about these men."

But surprisingly Sketes buttoned up her mouth stubbornly while Shiloh fidgeted with Perkins' chart and muttered, "Doc, it's nothing that would affect his condition. Now, how about movin' him? I mean, I know you ferociously defend all your patients, so think about Leith and Solly. Wouldn't it be better for them if Tong Ten was berthed with them? I mean, his quarters are up there right by the apprentices' quarters anyway. They mess with him most of the time."

Cheney understood the shipboard connotation of messmates—the close friends who usually messed together—and she considered the importance this could have to the patients. "All right," she said reluctantly. "But first I want to talk to Mr. Dunstan and Mr. Wooling. And, Shiloh, I want us to send down gifts to all the men, from us as the owners, not the attendants. Sketes, find out what food Mr. Wooling particularly likes, and if he likes playing patience, or perhaps—what do they call it when they carve things?"

"Scrimshaw," Sketes answered. "And I have seen Wooling carve some, I sure have. But as for food, he's more likely to appreciate a liquid treat, if you know what I mean."

"I'm not sending him whiskey," Cheney said impatiently.

"Rum, he likes," Sketes said airily. "And lots of it. But he did seem to show a particular liking for those sugarplums we got in Nassau."

"Do we have any of those left in our stores?" Cheney asked.

Sketes made a face. "Yes'm, there's four left, which was going to be your breakfast, and I'm of the mind that you and Mr. Locke should have them and not that worthless scrub who won't thank you for it anyway." Sketes was like a tiger with her stores for Cheney and Shiloh.

"No, they go to Mr. Wooling, Sketes," Cheney said sternly. "And, Shiloh, you make sure to find a good wood-carving knife, and maybe in the village they have some ivory or shark's teeth or whatever it is they . . . they . . . scrimshaw. I want Mr. Wooling to have a kit to-morrow."

"Yes, ma'am," Shiloh said obediently.

"Now, can we move on? Shiloh, you have to help me make these calculations for Perkins. I feel like my brain's made out of mush. . . ."

They had only started on the second chart, which was Jimmy Wooling's, when someone started moaning in the big cabin, and Sketes hurried in. She came back out in a few moments, frowning. "Mr. Bowles is broke out, and he feels like he's afire."

Cheney nodded wearily. "Cold-water affusions, Sketes. And, Shiloh, you really need to check Mr. Perkins' temperature. He may be sedated, but laudanum won't help the fever. If it's high, he needs cold affusions too."

Shiloh got up, but just as he started toward the big cabin Mr. Seaton called out weakly, "Sketes? Are you there? I . . . I don't feel well. . . ." Shiloh gave Cheney a rueful look and hurried into his cabin.

Cheney worked furiously on the charts, reading them, noting the patients' reactions to the medications, making the mathematical calculations necessary to adjust dosages, noting their food intake, changing diet orders, trying to gain an overview of each patient's condition from Sketes's illiterate scrawl and Fiona's closely written but uninformed observations. Sketes came bustling out of the great cabin, hauling a bucket of water, and Cheney called, "Sketes, don't forget to make your notes on the charts."

"Yes, ma'am," she responded hurriedly, "but look now, it's almost six o'clock. I should have been cooking up the medicine a half hour ago.

And Mr. Perkins is waking up, and he's a-starting in on them buttons again, and Bowles is burnin' like a house afire. I swear, he warms up the water 'stead of it cooling him down!"

"Get more ice," Cheney said. "All you need. But only use it on men whose temperature is over one hundred two degrees."

"All right, Dr. Cheney, but you'd better write it down. I swear, I'd forget my head if it weren't attached, and sometimes I wonder about that. . . ." She bustled out, and Cheney resignedly started making notes on Perkins' and Bowles's charts herself.

Shiloh came out and said, "Mr. Seaton's vomiting blood, Doc. You better come." Horatio Seaton had been an alcoholic for years, and Cheney had known that this condition was going to complicate his illness. She rose heavily, eyeing the charts. Just reading and updating them for nine men took hours, and it wasn't going to get done.

———————

The morning slipped by, with Cheney, Shiloh, Sketes, and now Fiona so busy they rarely had time to speak to one another. Sam Bowles had reached the crisis stage. Horatio Seaton's condition had worsened considerably, due to complications from the ravages of years of heavy drinking combined with the breakdown in mind, spirit, and body from typhus, and he required most exact attention from Cheney. Wooling had not been moved, and Cheney heard Sketes mutter a warning to Shiloh that the boys were upset, and Leith Redding had vomited up his morning dosage. Willy Perkins was growing agitated again, and Cheney had to leave Horatio Seaton to measure his medication and administer it, but once again Shiloh had to intervene and practically force it on him, and Cheney made a mental note that he was going to have to be monitored very carefully to see if she needed to increase the laudanum dosage again.

Or maybe if I increased the dose of rum in his morning dosage? she considered as she hurried back to Horatio Seaton. *I just don't know, and I can't know, because I can't observe him as I should. Oh, Lord, give me strength!*

Sometime later—Cheney had lost track of time passing—Shiloh came in and gently pulled her aside as she was hurrying between cabins. "Doc, it's almost nine o'clock and the men haven't had any breakfast. Look, with the patients going into crisis stage, Sketes isn't going to be able to fix any meals. How about if Mr. Penrod takes that over? Captain Starnes—and all the men—would really like it if they could do something, anything. It's hard for them, you know?"

Cheney stared at him. "None of them can come down here, Shiloh. You know that."

"Yeah, I know. But Mr. Penrod could fix the men's meals up in the galley, and they could bring the food down the main hatch up there. If you want I could set up a bulkhead just on the other side of the storerooms down there, stretching across to shield the hatch, and put a table on the other side of it. They could leave the food there, and we could go get it as soon as they've gone back up top. And then we could take the dishes and silverware and let them do the washing up. Fiona's been doing it, but she's not going to have time for that."

"All right," Cheney finally agreed. "But I want a bulkhead across the main hatch and also on the side facing amidships. And put a half barrel of borax water, mixed very strong, to put the dirty dishes in. They don't need to be touching the dishes and silverware unless they've been sanitized."

"You got it." He hurried up the rear hatch, and Cheney heard him above decks calling out to Captain Starnes. She would allow Shiloh to talk to the captain, as long as he stayed on the quarterdeck and Shiloh stood above, on the poop deck. It must have been hard for the men who weren't sick, she reflected, for this was a terrible way to get news about their mates, shouting it down half the ship to Captain Starnes. In a normal quarantine, the attendants, with careful sanitization procedures, were not isolated with the patients. But typhus was still such a mystery to physicians, and such a deadly disease that Cheney had imposed the strictest isolation she could conceive. Even if it kept only one person from contracting typhus—and she would never know whether it did or not—it was well worth it.

Sometime later Shiloh took her aside again. "Little break now, it seems like, so I'm going on into the village. You're doing good, mon chou."

Cheney smiled and gave him a distracted peck, then turned to the endless round of work. Fiona and Sketes were repeatedly giving Perkins and Bowles cold spongings. Cheney tried to monitor Horatio Seaton as closely as she could while still making rounds to each patient and noting charts and making desperate seat-of-the-pants adjustments to diets and medication.

When Shiloh came back—Cheney had no idea if he'd been gone an hour or all day—he took her aside. "It's no good, Doc," he said regretfully. "They got some problems over there that only you can handle."

"Go on," she said intently.

"The villagers just don't have enough education to make up those prescriptives, Doc. I don't dare leave the ingredients with them. They'd just drink all the brandy and rum and feed the drugs to the goats. So I guess we're going to have to figure out how to get over there and mix up the stuff ourselves. Or mix it here and haul it over."

"All right," Cheney said wearily. "We'll . . . figure something out. What else?"

"I was at Hansen Ten Eyck's hut. He was a lot worse, in a lot of pain, and seemed to be real feverish—and I know he's only had the fever for four days. I couldn't figure out what was the trouble. So I gave him another complete exam, and this time I saw it." He grimaced. "He's got an impacted wisdom tooth, Doc, a bad one. It's all swollen and fiery red and leaking pus all down his throat. He didn't tell me when I did his first exam. I checked his tongue, but I never saw that tooth."

She sighed. "I wouldn't have seen it either, Shiloh, because I wouldn't have been looking for it, just as you weren't. He didn't tell you during the history?"

"Not a word," Shiloh rasped. "He was too scared to have it pulled—the village butcher pulls teeth with pliers—so he's been putting oil of clove on it. But now it's really inflamed, and I don't know how to medicate him."

"All right," Cheney said, writing a note on a much-folded, tattered sheet of her mono-grammed notepaper. She had eight such pages stuck in her apron pocket. "Is there more?"

" 'Fraid so. After I saw Hansen I just kinda

ducked into the other huts and told them either you or I would be back soon. And when I got to Opal Dekker's hut, she was alone."

"What?" Cheney cried sharply. "Alone? But didn't some of the Dekker women say they'd stay with her?"

"Yeah, there was an old lady there this morning—I forgot her name, so I just called her Mrs. Dekker, and she told me it was 'Miss Dekker, thank you very much,' " he said wryly. "Anyway, she promised to stay until we came back for afternoon rounds. But there was no sign of her, or anyone else."

"How was Opal?" Cheney asked.

"She hadn't had any breakfast, and she'd drunk all the water in the pitcher by the bed and hadn't been able to get up and get more," Shiloh said, his eyes glinting like blue ice. "But her temp was still at about one-oh-one, and she said her headache was no worse. And, Doc, before you start in on me, I tried to get her to come to the ship. But she wouldn't have it, got real upset. And I guess I kinda understand," he said in a low voice. "That's her home, the only home she's ever known, she said. And she said when she starts to die, she wants to see Bonnie one last time, even if it's just out the window."

"She's not going to die—not if I can help it. I'm going into the village," Cheney said crisply, retrieving her messy pile of notes, then stripping off her dirty apron and throwing it into a bucket of carbolic acid. They didn't have enough aprons to burn them after each round, though Cheney would have loved to if they could.

"I'll row you ashore, mon chou, but I gotta tell you that every man on the ship has volunteered to row you back and forth. Lott said they'd all crunch up in the bow and hold their breath," he said, his eyes now crinkling with laughter.

Cheney smiled, but to Shiloh's surprise she seemed to be considering the sailors' offer.

She was indeed thinking, *I know Shiloh approves of my strict isolation procedures and would never question my judgment . . . but it is true that the logistics are additional difficulties. . . . I have to weigh the risks of loosening the rules against the advantages gained for the patients. . . .*

"Logistics," Shiloh said succinctly, and Cheney stared up at him, bemused. "Always a problem, in the war. Moving men and material. Balancing the risks against the advantages."

"Shiloh," she said with exasperation, "I'm not so sure it's to my advantage to have a husband that can so easily read my mind. Oh, never mind. Just you hustle yourself upstairs—"

"Above decks," he corrected her teasingly.

"Up there"—she pointed up—"and tell Mr. Lott to get the happy boat ready."

"Jolly boat," he said, grinning.

Ignoring him, Cheney muttered, "And he'd better be good at holding his breath."

Cheney was very tired, but she kept her eyes fixed on Opal Dekker's face. Opal was asleep, breathing heavily, her face dead white and glistening with sweat. Sometimes she moaned softly. The single candle on the small table by the bed had burned low and flickered uncertainly. Cheney's head was bowed, her hands clasped together but relaxed on the open pages of the Bible in her lap.

"You praying for me? That's not a good sign," Opal said dully.

Cheney looked up and smiled. "I pray for all of my patients, Mrs. Dekker. It's not a sign of anything at all, except that I care."

Opal's bloodshot dark eyes searched Cheney's face. "Why? Why should you care for me? I mean, I see you're the kind of doctor who feels responsible for your patients—you wouldn't be sitting here with me otherwise. I know there's others. . . ."

Cheney replied, "Yes, there have been fourteen cases on the island so far. And I'm happy to tell you that Bonnie is just fine. Both my husband and I take special care to check her every day. She's doing very well at the Verbrugges' house."

Opal nodded, grimacing with pain, and her eyes flickered toward the candle. Cheney leaned over and pinched it out, and they sat in darkness. The night was warm, but a cooling tropical breeze, scented with sea and fish and hot sand, came floating in through the western window. The sound of the sea lulled them. Cheney chose her words with care and spoke very quietly. "Mrs. Dekker, I do care about you as my patient, and I care, too, for your soul. Are you a Christian?"

Opal turned her head away. "You going to preach at me on my deathbed?"

"No, I'm not ... and you're not on your deathbed," Cheney said evenly. "I don't want to offend you, but I am a Christian, and I want everyone to know the joy of the Lord as I do. God's love is the most precious gift, the greatest joy, and the deepest security of the heart anyone could ever know. I can see you're unhappy, and I promise you that the Lord Jesus can give you a joy, and a peace, that you'll always have, all of your life."

She turned back to Cheney, her features haggard. "And how long might the rest of my life be? A few days? A few hours?"

Cheney met her frightened gaze and answered steadily, "I don't know. Only God knows that. But as your physician, I can tell you that you're young, you're strong, and you are responding very well to the medication. And, perhaps even more importantly, you have such a wonderful thing to live for—your daughter. That, I think, is helping you to fight this, and you must keep fighting—hard."

Opal seemed reassured, brightening a little as she thought of Bonnie. She asked, "So you're not trying to have a deathbed convert here?"

"No," Cheney replied. "That's not why I decided to speak to you about the Lord. I don't always, you know, to my patients. But while I was praying for you, the Lord impressed on me very strongly that you have a lot of bitterness and worries about the future, and of course you are grieving for your husband. All of that is a heavy burden to bear, and I felt that telling you about Jesus, how much He loves you and cares for His children, would give you hope. He will carry those burdens for you, Mrs. Dekker, and then you can just concentrate on getting strong and having a rich, full life with Bonnie."

"A rich, full life? You, ma'am, don't know what you're talking about, with your fancy dresses and millionaire's yacht and rich husband!" she said harshly. "And you don't know who you're talking to either. I'm . . . well, I *was* a whore. Did you know that, Miss Fancy Doctor?"

"Yes, I did," Cheney answered quietly. "And I don't care. And the Lord doesn't care. He loves you just as much as He loves me."

Opal stared at her defiantly, her face a white blur in the dimness. Cheney couldn't make out the expressions on her face, but when Opal spoke again Cheney could hear she was choking back tears. "But I'm going back to it if I live. I have to! That's all I know. That's all I've ever been. And I don't have any money. I don't have a rich husband. I don't even have a poor one now." She sobbed, a painful, choking sound. "I'm poor, I tell you. I can't think of any other way to support Bonnie. I can't sew or cook or be some fancy lady's maid. I wouldn't know the first thing about a real lady."

Cheney took Opal's fevered hand, and the woman clung to it. "You won't have to go back to your old life, Mrs. Dekker. I don't know right now exactly what will happen. But I know two promises that God gives His children, and God never lies, and He never breaks a promise. One is that His children will never have to beg for bread. And the other is found in the Old Testament. Over and over again God makes very special provisions for widows and for fatherless children. He will take very special care of you, Opal, and because of His very great mercy and pity for women like you and children like Bonnie, I think that means He will take even better care of you than He would of others who are not so lonely, so vulnerable, and so lost."

"Is . . . is that true, Dr. Cheney? You really

think that even though I've been so bad, so wicked, He would take special care of me and Bonnie?" she begged piteously.

"I know it," Cheney said. "He promised."

"What . . . what do I do?" Opal asked, crying openly now.

Cheney smiled. "Just pray, and admit to God that you are sinful and that you need forgiveness. Jesus came and died for you, you know, so that God will never remember any of your sins. He'll bury them in forgetfulness. Ask Jesus to save you from your sins by His blood, and you will be whole again, a new creature. And ask Jesus into your heart so that you will have peace, and the certain knowledge that He is your Lord and will care for you always, and then He will take you to heaven to be with Him forever."

Opal prayed, honestly and humbly, and asked the Lord to save her. Then Cheney prayed for her aloud.

Afterward Opal seemed to be more restful, but she didn't really want to talk anymore. Cheney knew her temperature was rising and she was in pain. She was trying to decide whether to give her weak ginger tea or to try a small dose of laudanum when Opal drifted off to sleep.

Cheney, too, sitting holding her hand in the dark, dozed.

But about an hour later Cheney started.

Fumbling, she lit the candle again and peered fuzzily at the watch on her waist fob. It was five minutes to midnight. Opal was staring at her, but her eyes had that all-too-familiar glazed, unseeing look, and then she started mumbling something about brushing Bonnie's hair. There were mulberry red spots on her chest.

"Sketes? I hate to wake you, but I need you."

Molly Sketes jerked upright, peering up at Shiloh. She'd fallen asleep at the wardroom table, her face right down on the chart she'd been notating. She hadn't even folded her arms to cradle her head; she had just, she reckoned, keeled right over onto the table head-on, her hands falling to her sides. "Don't you never sleep, Mr. Locke?" she asked irritably. He looked bright-eyed, cheerful, and he hadn't been asleep for two days, that Sketes knew for certain. "Don't you never even *get* sleepy?"

"Sure, I'm sleepy right now," he answered airily. "I'm just faking it."

"Well, you sure do it good," she grumbled. "I'd hate to play poker with you. Now what can I do for you?" She stretched painfully, and noted ruefully that her hands, dangling down at her sides, had swelled up and also gone to sleep. She bent her fingers, grimacing.

"Here, let me," Shiloh said kindly, taking one

of her rough, red hands between his and massaging first the palms, and then each finger at the joint, in the most relaxing way. Sketes was mortified, but she had to admit that Mr. Locke did have such a nice, soothing touch.

He frowned a little, still massaging, and said, "Rikke just came out, hollering to wake the dead. Imri's fever's gone up. He didn't know if she had the rash, and he didn't know what her temperature was. Seems like they don't have a thermometer, and they didn't understand exactly how to watch for the crisis stage." He finished her hands and sat down beside her, rubbing his neck.

Sketes tried to gather her woolly thoughts. She was so tired, and she, like everyone else— except for Mr. Locke, she reflected with rueful wonder—could hardly keep thinking clearly like a sane person. "How's Mr. Seaton? And Bowles, and Perkins?"

"Mr. Seaton's finally asleep, but his fever's high, and he didn't have his night dose. Bowles and Perkins are both slipping in and out of coma, and Perkins still thrashes around every once in a while. But that's not what's worrying me," Shiloh said, dropping his voice even lower than their usual half whisper. "Leith Redding's broken out, and his fever is sky high. Fiona and I have been bathing him, but we can't seem to bring it down at all. And what worries me more is that we can't get any liquids down him. I gave him a piece of ice to suck on, but he swallowed it and convulsed."

"Why didn't you wake me?" Sketes said accusingly. "I can help take care of that little mite. He practically thinks I'm his mother. I should take care of him when Dr. Cheney's not here."

"You have to get some rest, Sketes," Shiloh said sternly. "Doctor's orders. If you don't, you'll collapse. You know it's the truth."

Sketes nodded reluctantly, then was struck by a thought. "Oh, but . . . you or Dr. Cheney needs to watch over Leith, don't you? So . . . would you like me to go up to your cousin's house? You need me to go?"

Fiona came up, carrying an empty glass to fetch more ice from the owner's storeroom, which was just by the wardroom. She stopped to listen, slipping up behind Shiloh.

He dropped his head a little. "I . . . I don't know, Sketes. It's a hard decision. Cheney and I both know that we have to be with the most critically ill patients. I don't know if Imri is reaching the crisis stage, or if she's just having a little spike in temperature, which isn't unusual."

"But she's your cousin's lady, isn't she?" Sketes asked solidly. "And I know you have to want to take the best care of her, for your cousin's sake. It's cruel hard, Mr. Locke, for you to have to stay here, but don't you worry, I'll go see about that girl."

"No," Fiona said softly but firmly. "You're a much better and more competent nurse than I, Sketes, and you're needed here almost as much as Mr. Locke. I'll go."

Shiloh turned around and rose hastily. He could never sit while a lady was standing. "I don't know about that," he muttered, dropping his eyes. "My cousin . . . he's . . . I don't think . . . I think it would be better if Sketes went."

"Better for who?" Fiona countered with surprising forcefulness. "Not for these men here. And as far as your cousin goes, Mr. Locke, I don't know anything about him, but if he's anything like you, then I'm not a bit nervous."

Shiloh gave her a twisted grin. "He's not like me. He's . . . he's . . . uh . . ."

"Shorter," Sketes said thoughtfully. "And meaner."

"How do you know?" Shiloh demanded.

"Sailors talk like gabbling geese," Sketes said disdainfully. "And they say women are gossips."

"Oh yeah," Shiloh said helplessly. Of course, many of the crew of *Locke's Day Dream* had sailed with Bain for years. "Well, then, Sketes, you know why I don't think it's too good an idea for Fiona to go to his house."

"Mr. Locke, I'm not a child," Fiona said, though she spoke in a low, nervous tone and ducked her head. "I've heard talk too, about Mr.

Bain. I was just trying to joke, you might say, when I said that about him being like you, and—"

"Why, Miss Fiona, were you teasing me?" Shiloh interrupted, grinning at her. "That's some sass. But I'm not surprised. The doc's maids have always bossed me around from daylight to dark. She's a bad influence on 'em, I say."

"I wasn't really sassing you, Mr. Locke," Fiona said, blushing scarlet. "At least not on purpose. Anyway, don't you think it's true, what I said? About it being better for Sketes to stay here with the crew?"

"Well, maybe, but . . ."

Fiona lifted her chin. "Then it's settled. I'll go to the Big House. I'm not afraid of your big bad cousin. He couldn't embarrass me any more than you do, Mr. Locke."

"Oh, but you just don't know my cousin," Shiloh muttered. He eyed the girl with a critical gaze. "All right, Fiona, I have to say that it does make more sense for you to go. But you just don't take any nonsense from my cousin Bain. You tell him I'm coming as soon as I can, okay? And I'll want to hear from you," he added fiercely, "that he's treated you with respect. You tell him that."

She shrugged. "If I have to threaten him with your wrath, Mr. Locke, I will. But maybe I won't have to." She smiled shyly up at him. "After all, he's your blood, and so he must have some good in him."

"That's the plain truth," Sketes agreed solidly. "Blood always tells."

CHAPTER TWENTY

The Truth of Love

AS FIONA REACHED the top of the steep, winding pathway, she looked with some apprehension at the Big House. Beside her, Rikke Ten Eyck, who had rowed her over from the ship, said nothing. It was one-thirty in the morning, and in spite of the fact that Rikke had not been very companionable—he was too worried about his sister—Fiona was certainly glad that she hadn't had to walk up to this brooding house all alone.

Rikke didn't knock; he just opened the door and motioned Fiona to go in. A man stepped out of a door down the hall and came forward, his shoulders stooped with fatigue. "Who the devil are you?"

Fiona swallowed hard but managed to answer in a steady voice. "Mr. Winslow? I'm Fiona Kay Keane. I've come to take care of Miss Imri. Mr. Locke and Dr. Cheney send their apologies, but they couldn't come right now. They'll be here just as soon as they can."

Bain had not shaved for two days, and his clothing was stained and wrinkled as he critically examined the slight girl who stood before him. She was fair skinned, with delicate pink flushing her smooth cheeks. She was very shy, he could see, and was a little coltish.

Abruptly he stepped back to allow her to pass. "Are you a nurse?"

"Not really, sir, but I've had some experience lately helping the sailors on the ship."

"Wonderful," Bain growled. "You'd better come on, then."

He led her upstairs to his bedroom. Imri's entire family was gathered around her bed—her mother and father, her two sisters, and Rikke, who had hurried to join them.

Fiona was dismayed; it was going to be difficult to care for the woman with all of them hampering her every move. Bain glanced at her face and announced, not unkindly, "All right, everyone, the nurse is here. Clear out and let her get to work. You can visit Imri later."

"Maybe . . . maybe just one or two at a time," Fiona said faintly.

"You heard her," Bain said. "Go on down to the kitchen. Make yourselves some tea or something."

Meekly they filed out.

Bain watched as Fiona went over and felt Imri's forehead. She stirred slightly, mumbling.

Her forehead was blazing hot. Fiona lifted the sheet.

"That rash . . . what does it mean?" Bain asked in a low voice.

Fiona answered, "She's reaching the critical stage of the fever, Mr. Winslow."

"I know that, Miss—what did you say your name was?"

"Fiona Kay Keane," she answered faintly.

"Miss Keane, but what I want to know is . . . what . . . what you can do for her. What we can do for her," he corrected himself.

"Her fever's high, so I need to sponge her with cold water," Fiona said rather tremulously. "And . . . and do you have ice? Oh, I hope so . . . I didn't think . . ."

"My cousin Locke sent up four tubs of it," Bain said with some bitterness. "I can't afford it, but evidently he's sailing around with tons of it."

The rich man's luxury, ice, was hauled by ship from either the North Atlantic or the uppermost reaches of the Scotia Sea. Ice freighters hauled in enormous chunks of icebergs, packed in metal tubs with sawdust, and took them all over the world, a most lucrative cargo. For his and Cheney's honeymoon, Shiloh had filled half the hold with ice just to make sure that they had enough—Cheney was accustomed to iced drinks—and also for ballast.

But Fiona didn't notice the bitterness in

Bain's tone. "Oh, thank the Lord. I need to give Miss Imri ice chips to suck on when she's awake."

"All right," he said shortly. With one more quick, worried glance at Imri, he left. Fiona was expecting another servant or perhaps one of Imri's sisters to return with her supplies, but Bain came back in himself, bringing a pitcher of clean water, clean cloths, and a bucket of ice set down in a bigger bucket lined with sawdust. Without a word he left again.

Fiona went to work, sponging Imri continually, speaking softly to her, smoothing her tangled hair. When Imri was unconsious, Fiona moistened the clean cloth and dabbed her lips. When she roused a little, Fiona had her suck on the small shards of ice.

Bain returned with a clean sheet, a light cotton blanket, and a pillow. "I don't have a guest bedroom. You'll have to sleep on the love seat." One corner of the generous room was furnished as a reading nook, with an armchair, a love seat, and a small tea table. "That's . . . that's fine, Mr. Winslow. Thank you."

He made a curt, dismissive gesture. "How is she?"

"About the same," Fiona said. "She woke up a little while ago and sucked on some ice."

A haggard, desolate look ravaged his face, making Bain look ten years older. "If she wakes up again, come get me immediately," he said thickly. "I'm just in the other bedroom, across the passage."

"Yes, of course, Mr. Winslow," Fiona said softly.

As he left again Fiona thought, *Why, of course, I'd forgotten, there's another man sick here . . . some funny name . . . Mr. Winslow must be taking care of him. He's awfully upset. But I'd be curt and speak sharp too, I guess, if the one I loved was dying. . . .*

Does he know Imri's dying?

Fiona didn't know if Bain Winslow knew it or not—but she did. She'd found that she somehow had a sense about this—about when the patients were going into crisis stage and which ones were going to have a harder time than another. And she was fairly certain that Imri Ten Eyck was going to die. *Oh, if only Dr. Cheney or Mr. Locke would come!*

But the time passed, and they didn't come. Bain, however, came often, standing by Imri's bed and looking down at her. He asked Fiona no more questions. At some time in that interminable night, Imri's parents came in and sat for a while quietly, their eyes wide with fear. And her sisters came once with Rikke. None of them interrupted Fiona with her ministrations; they just sat quietly by and held Imri's hand.

Imri's fever kept rising, and her breathing got

weaker and slower. The unconscious periods lasted longer, and she no longer shifted restlessly and mumbled.

They were alone when Fiona looked up from bathing Imri's legs and feet and saw that her eyes were open—just slitted, really, but she was awake. "I'll be right back, Miss Imri," she whispered and hurried out.

Across the passage she knocked on the only other door, and Bain immediately wrenched it open. Fiona caught a mere glimpse of a similar bedroom, but Bain hurriedly shoved past her, shutting the door behind him.

He hurried to Imri's bedside, and the woman looked up at him with her liquid dark eyes, now dulled, the light of life almost extinguished. She was too weak to lift her hand, but her fingers moved. He took it and, with an awkward, jerky movement, lifted it to his lips.

"Bain . . ." she whispered.

"I'm here. I'm right here." He leaned eagerly over her.

But her lips merely trembled in the faintest wisp of a smile, and her eyes closed. They never opened again.

Just before six in the morning, Imri died.

Cheney stood and stretched, pressing her hands against her lower back. Her shoulders burned with a hot pain, and a dull ache extended all the way down the backs of her legs. The first traces of dawn, creeping over the eastern ridge, lit the back window of Opal's bedroom. It was just before six.

Cheney stared intently down at her patient, blinking hard because her eyes were gritty but watery. Opal's fever was still high, and she slipped in and out of consciousness, as she had done all night. But somehow she didn't have that air of death about her. Rather stupidly, Cheney tried to analyze this; it seemed it was possible to tell that some patients were better than others. It was also possible to tell that some were dying. What were the indications? She struggled, trying to pin the concepts down to some medical reasonableness, but it was impossible. She was, to put it simply, stupid with fatigue.

And she didn't feel well either. Fuzzily she thought, *I ache all over, my hands and feet and ankles are swollen, my stomach is aching something awful . . .*

Why, that's hunger! I'm hungry—starving! When was the last time I ate? What did I eat?

But it was no use. She couldn't remember.

She had just vaguely decided to see if Opal had anything to snack on in the house when she heard the front door open and close and spry footsteps coming down the hall.

Miss Dekker herself sauntered into the room.

"I'm here, Dr. Cheney," she announced, somewhat unnecessarily. She was a gaunt, bright-eyed elderly woman with sharp eyes and a manner to match. "Rikke says you'll pay me, yes? So I'll stay with her. Go home."

"I don't know," Cheney said tiredly. "I . . . I'm not sure . . ."

Miss Dekker's calculating gaze raked over Cheney. "You're like to fall down, it's silly. I'll take care of Miss White Majesty, there, don't you worry. I nursed two of my husbands with fevers. I'm a good nurse. Go home."

"But . . . do you know about the cold affusions, the ice, the—"

Miss Dekker flapped her skinny arms, alarming Cheney somewhat. "I know all that. I'm no fine white lady, but I know about cold sponges and ice, mmm! I eat it too, since Mr. Locke's giving it out like it's free," she said craftily. "Now go home. But pay me first. No money, no Miss Dekker."

Cheney found that she was actually swaying, the room going around and around sickeningly. "All right, I think I must," she relented, taking a shilling from her medical bag. "But you must promise me, Miss Dekker, to be kind to Mrs. Dekker. She's very ill, and I think, when she awakes, that you might find her attitude toward you is different."

"Maybe so, maybe not," Miss Dekker said,

greedily snatching the shilling piece. "But I'll be good."

Cheney gathered up her things and staggered down to the beach. She had gotten halfway there before she realized she may not have a boat to take her back to *Locke's Day Dream*. But with relief she saw that Calvin Lott was there, sitting stiffly in the jolly boat, just offshore. They exchanged distant greetings and Cheney stumbled into the boat. True to his word, he faithfully rowed Cheney back and forth, but he did keep a safe distance, and Cheney could have sworn that he sometimes held his breath. As they rowed out, even though the bay was calm, her nausea increased, and she felt even dizzier than she had in Opal's bedroom. Her vision was blurred.

Lott pulled the jolly boat up neatly right to the foot of the rope steps, and Cheney stared up at them with dread. They weren't like a Jacob's ladder—they were actual steps, with side ropes, threading up the side of the ship—but it seemed a long, long way up to her. Miles and miles.

"Dr. Cheney?" Lott said worriedly. "Are you all right? P'raps I'd better come help you."

"No! No, keep your distance, Mr. Lott," she said. "I'm fine, I was just . . . thinking." With desperate determination she stood up, grabbed her medical bag—it seemed horribly heavy, how odd—and, practically pulling herself up by her hands, made her way up to the deck of the ship.

It took her a long, long time. Finally she clambered over the side and stood, swaying, just at the four steps leading down to the salon.

She looked down, blinking owlishly. It seemed to be very dark down there. And getting darker . . .

Cheney fainted dead away.

She saw a tiny dim point of light, like a candle flame, very far away. But it grew slowly, very slowly, its edges fuzzy yet warm and white. It got bigger, and her vision was filled with the light. She blinked. And again.

Shiloh lifted his face, and the light fell on it. He was kneeling by the bed in their stateroom. His hands, rough and warm, clasped her cold one tightly. His lips were taut, colorless, his eyes as dark as midnight, his cheekbones stark and sharp. "Cheney . . . Cheney . . ." he whispered.

"I'm right here," she said, confused. "What's wrong?"

"You . . . you fainted," he said, anguished. "I carried you in here."

"Oh . . . I did?"

"Yes, my love, my most precious love," Shiloh answered, his voice breaking. "Are you . . . do you . . ." He swallowed hard, and to Cheney's shock she saw tears glittering in his eyes. She had never seen Shiloh cry.

"Why . . . no, no, Shiloh, I'm not sick," she protested weakly. "I just fainted . . . from exhaustion, I guess. I can't remember the last time I ate."

"Oh, thank God, thank God!" he muttered, again pressing his hot, raspy cheek against her hand. "Cheney, if something happened to you . . . if you . . . got sick . . . got typhus . . ."

"I don't have it," she said gently. "I really don't. Look at me. You'll see."

"I didn't think so," he whispered, "but I was so scared. I think, Cheney, that if something happened to you, I wouldn't want to live."

She caressed his fine golden hair, then ran her fingers down his strong jaw. "Nothing's happened to me, except I've been careless and silly. But if something does, you'll know, Shiloh, that it was the Lord's will, for we both follow His path, always. If my path should take me to heaven before you, you will know where I am, and that you will follow in His good time. And you'll live on, Shiloh, in His joy and peace. Always."

"That's hard," he whispered. "That's awful hard to think of."

"Then don't think of it," she said lightly. "Because we can't know the future; we can only entrust it to Him, each and every day. And today I'm not going to die, Shiloh."

He stayed motionless for a long time, gripping her hand, his breath ragged. When he finally raised his head again, he managed a weak smile. "Okay, you scared me to death, woman! Now here's doctor's orders for you: food, lots of food, in bed, then sleep, in bed, not in a hammock down in the sick bay or at the wardroom table. I'm starting this treatment right now."

Cheney sighed. "You know, I think I'm going to agree with this prognosis and course of treatment."

Shiloh's eyebrows shot up with exaggerated shock. "You are? That's a first."

"Get on with you," Cheney said, waving him away. "Go fetch me some victuals, nurse. I'm starving."

Obediently Shiloh rose and went to the door but turned back to her. "I know I always start making jokes and acting like a big fool," he said quietly, "but, Cheney, you are the reason my heart keeps beating, the blood in my veins is yours, you are the best half of my very soul. I loved you yesterday, I love you today, and I will love you forever. I just wanted to say that . . . and from now on, I'll try to remember to say that. Often. Without dumb jokes." He slipped out and quietly closed the door.

Cheney wept.

———————

It was late in the evening before Shiloh could tear himself away from Cheney to go see about Imri. Cheney had promised to stay in bed and sleep all night—Shiloh would never have left her if she hadn't—but it had taken him all day to see to all of the patients himself. On the island there were now eleven victims, all in various stages of the disease, and on the ship there were nine. Shiloh had been exhausted before Cheney collapsed, but the fear of thinking she might be sick had made him feel as weak as a helpless infant. Now, as he trudged wearily up to the Big House, he stopped for a moment to gather his strength. Straightening his aching shoulders and flexing his stiff fingers, he made himself go on.

Bain answered the door. His tanned face looked gray and drawn, and no fierce tiger's light flashed in his eyes. "She's dead. You're too late." He turned and stumbled, stoop shouldered, down the hallway.

Shiloh dropped his head for a moment, then closed the door quietly and followed him. Bain was sitting, curiously crumpled like an old, old man, in one of the fine leather armchairs. It seemed to dwarf him. The room was dark. Shiloh went to a console table and lit an oil lamp, then wearily sat down in the chair close to his cousin. Bain said nothing. He didn't seem to notice Shiloh was there. He merely sat, staring bleakly into nothingness.

Shiloh thought brokenly, *What can I say? Explain to him that there are people dying on the ship, in the village . . . that Cheney collapsed? That it was impossible for one of us to come? That it prob-ably wouldn't have made any difference if I was here or not, or even whether Cheney was here?*

A sullen little voice whispered into his dark thoughts, *But he wasn't married to her, or any-thing. . . . She was just his mistress, and you know how Bain is. . . . He's not capable of love. . . .*

He shifted restlessly, frowning. *No? Maybe not, maybe not the kind of love that I have for Cheney now, since the Lord has shown me the truth of love . . . but suppose Cheney had died after we'd known each other for a year? I loved her then . . . and back then I really might have chucked myself off a cliff. . . .*

"Bain," he said in a deep, grieving voice, "I know you probably don't believe me, but I am deeply, honestly sorry."

Slowly Bain's head swiveled toward him. Slight wonder passed over his fine, elegant fea-tures, like a twilight shadow falling. "You are, aren't you?" he said dully and turned away again. "But you didn't come. And neither did your wife."

Agonized, Shiloh said, "I . . . I know. It . . . it was just impossible. I know you can't under-stand, but . . . I . . . I honestly don't think it would have made any difference, Bain. This dis-ease"—he made an eloquent, helpless gesture with his big, fight-scarred hands—"the Lord seems to have decided to take some and allow some to live. For reasons we will never understand He must have decided to take Imri."

Bain's head was bowed, his chin almost on his chest. He was huddled up like a scared little child. In a barely audible mumble, he said, "Then . . . then . . . curse Him, and curse you. Get away from me, Locke. You're nothing but a simpering hypocrite, and I despise you and your wife."

Shiloh stood, the muscles in his jaw tensing, and looked down at his tortured cousin. He even tentatively laid his hand on Bain's shoulder. Bain flinched but didn't look up or shake it off. "Bain, you're my family, and the Lord has given me a love for you. Cheney loves you too. Just . . . know that."

Heavily Shiloh left and made his way up the stairs. He thought he heard a strangled sob and hesitated, but then slowly went on. He went to Sweet's room. Fiona sat by his bedside, sponging his face. Sweet lay quietly, very still, as he always was. His face was gray and sweaty, his eyes closed.

"Hello, Fiona," Shiloh said gently. "How are you holding up?"

She'd been crying. "She . . . she died. Miss Imri died."

"I know. Bain told me," Shiloh said quietly. "It wasn't you, you know. Even though Cheney and I are grieved that we couldn't come, I know it wouldn't have made any difference. We're not responsible for who lives or dies, Fiona, you know that. Only the Lord knows those days and hours. All we can do is give them the very best care we can, and you're a good nurse. If I were sick, you'd be a real comfort to me. You're quiet and gentle and kind, and sometimes that eases our pain more than any medicine any doctor can give."

"Is right," Sweet mumbled. "Is right. Miss Fiona is like . . . like calm seas and fair winds. . . ."

Fiona, through her tears, smiled and touched his feverish cheek lightly. He sighed.

Shiloh gave him a quick examination, checking his pulse and respiration and, not wishing to disturb him too much, just gauged his temperature by feeling his lips and hands and feet. He had no rash yet, but he had a high fever. Sweet appeared to be aware of Shiloh's examination, shifting a little in bed, but he seemed to be drifting in and out of consciousness already.

"He's going into crisis, probably late tonight," Shiloh said thoughtfully.

"I know, sir. I'll stay. I know you have to go back, and I know Dr. Cheney can't come, or she would have already been here. I'll stay . . . if . . . you really think I can take care of him," she finished hesitantly.

"I know you can. But—Sweet's a giant, if he gets agitated—"

Vigorously Fiona shook her head. "Oh, he won't. He's not one of those."

"How do you know?" Shiloh asked curiously.

"I just know," she answered firmly. "I just do."

Shiloh, who was himself prone to unreasoned but accurate instincts about patients, understood and believed her. But still, this was a terrible position for an untrained, shy, frail girl to be in. "But look, Fiona, we could give him much better care if we took him back to the ship. And it would be so much easier on you."

Fiona said, distressed, "But . . . but I would hate to leave . . . I . . . it's . . ."

Shiloh's eyes widened. "You would? But why—wait a minute. You're not worrying about my cousin, are you? You're not thinking of him?"

Fiona blushed painfully, then ducked her head and busily sponged Sweet's forehead. "He's been working so hard, helping me with Miss Imri, and of course he was taking care of Sweet all by himself—"

"He was?" Shiloh said, astonished.

"Yes, and then when Miss Imri died he was so sad, so . . . lost," Fiona said, all in a painful little rush.

Shiloh considered for a few moments, then muttered, "Well, he seems to have really changed. Toward some people, at least. But, Fiona," he continued in a sterner tone, "you really don't know my cousin very well. He can be ruthless and cruel, and I honestly think it would be better if you and Sweet just came back to the ship with me."

Sweet spoke up, startling them. "No, sir, Mr. Locke, please. This is my home, here, with Mr. Winslow. I stay here, and please let Miss Fiona stay with me."

Shiloh stared at Fiona, and she pressed her lips together and nodded firmly. "I will stay."

"All right," Shiloh said quietly. "So take good care of him. For my cousin." He patted her shoulder and left.

As Fiona had known it would, Sweet's fever rose and rose and finally the lurid blotches popped out, as if he had been sprinkled with dark blood all at once. He was calm and quiet. He didn't thrash restlessly or even mumble. Doggedly Fiona bathed him, working hard not to wet the sheets, for she couldn't shift Sweet from side to side to change the bedding as she had learned to do. He was much too big and heavy, and as lifeless as a cement block.

She heard Bain downstairs, pacing in the library—the house was deathly quiet—and then, sometime later, up in his bedroom moving around. She had no idea what time it was; oddly, Sweet's bedroom had no clock. It was furnished in the most spartan manner, with his reading nook, a twin of Bain's, precisely lined up at right angles, brush and comb lined up exactly on the chest of drawers, no speck of dust or litter anywhere, not a cobweb or mussed cushion or man's jacket hung negligently over a chair. For the first time, Fiona noticed that there was no mirror in the room.

Bain came in. He still was gray and old looking, but his eyes glittered recklessly. Fiona smelled the brandy on him. Without speaking he went to Sweet's bedside, yanked down the covers, and pulled open his soaked nightshirt. "He's got it," he said grimly. "So he's dead too."

"No . . . no, Mr. Winslow," Fiona protested helplessly. "He's not! He . . . he kept his medication down, and he's so strong—"

"Imri was strong," Bain shot back at her, his jaw clenched.

"But I think that Mr. Sweet is going to be all right," Fiona said in a small voice.

The sardonic eyebrow shot up. "Look at him, you little fool. He already looks like a three-day corpse." Sweet's face was a death mask, glistening gray with scarlet streaks on his cheeks. His lips were bloodless and dry and flecked with spittle. His hands, arms, and neck were covered with the ugly red blotches.

Fiona clasped her hands and started to say something, but Bain made an angry, dismissive gesture to silence her. "He's dead, I tell you. And I'm leaving." He stalked toward the door.

Fiona started to her feet. "But, Mr. Winslow, no, please! He—I swear, I swear to God above that Mr. Sweet's not going to die! Please . . . please . . ."

Reluctantly Bain turned. Some of the reckless anger seemed to have gone out of him, and when he spoke he sounded merely tired and despairing. "Look, Miss Keane, you're a sweet girl and, I suppose, a fine nurse. But you're no doctor, and I think you're just refusing to see that Sweet is just like Imri . . . was . . . in the hours . . . before. I'm sick of death and illness and stench and horror. I'm leaving." He bowed, a ragged, hopeless gesture. "It's been a great pleasure to meet you and have you as a guest in my home. Happily for you, I know that you will not be obliged to stay much longer." Without another look at Sweet, he left, closing the door soundlessly behind him.

Fiona collapsed into her chair by Sweet's bedside, pressing her hands to her temples. *So . . . so Mr. Locke was right. . . . He can be very selfish and cruel. . . . I just never would have believed it. . . .*

She sensed Sweet's small movement and looked up. His eyes were open. They were glazed and perhaps unseeing, but in the depths Fiona thought she saw a terrible sadness.

Swallowing hard, she took his rough, burning hand. "You're not going to die, Mr. Sweet, that I promise you. And he really cares for you, you know. . . ."

Sweet's eyes closed.

Invisible behind the barrier of bulkheads Shiloh had set up, Fausto and Flavio sat on the steps of the main hatch; behind them David Upchurch was playing his fiddle, and behind him Luki Terrio played the flute. Fausto and Flavio, in their twin soaring tenors, were singing "Grace Darling."

> 'Twas on the Longstone Lighthouse there dwelt an English maid,
> Pure as the air around her, of danger ne'er afraid.
> One morning just at daybreak a storm-tossed wreck she spied.
> Although to try seemed madness, "I'll save the crew," she cried.

Shiloh leaned to whisper in Cheney's ear, "I'm surprised they haven't changed it to 'Cheney Darling.' "

"Shush," she scolded. "I want to hear."

The song ended, and weak applause came from the sick bay. At the wardroom table, Cheney and Shiloh and Sketes clapped as hard

411

as they could; Shiloh whistled and stamped.

Fausto or Flavio—their voices were as identical as their faces—yelled, "You sickly little boys hurry up and come back to work! We're sailing as soon as you swabs take a mind to quit your snivelin' and get back to being clipper men!"

Cheney sighed and rolled her eyes. "They are taking more and more liberties with quarantine. They keep sneaking closer and closer every day and staying longer and longer."

Shiloh frowned. "Speaking of taking liberties, you still look like a haint. I think you'd better go back to bed now."

Cheney said, a little petulantly, as sick people can be, "But I slept all day, Shiloh, and I've eaten enough for the whole crew. I feel better, truly I do."

Stubbornly he shook his head. "No, ma'am. It's almost midnight. I let you do rounds, but you're pale and still have great big shadows under your eyes. In fact, I'm going to mix you up a sedative, and—don't you make that face at me, my little cabbage—and you're going to take it and you're going to go right back to bed."

Cheney looked mutinous for a moment, but truth to tell, she did still feel weak and shaky. But she just said in a small voice, "But, Shiloh, my love, I don't think you've slept for three or four days. You can't go on like this either."

He shrugged. "No, I know I can't do it much

longer, but when we get everyone bedded down, I'm going to grab some soup and come up and nap with you for an hour or two. It's fairly calm tonight. We haven't had a new case in four days. Did you know that?" he finished hopefully.

"Why, no, I didn't realize. But these men, and I'm sure many of the villagers, are still very ill, and I know there'll be one or two of them who'll go into crisis tonight."

"The tide's turned, though," Shiloh said quietly. "I can feel it. Just the same, I know we've got some really tough days ahead, so you need to get some rest tonight, Doc, no kidding. And if you're good, maybe I'll let you do some doctoring tomorrow."

"All right," she agreed. "I have to admit I still feel a little shaky."

Shiloh got Cheney medicated and put to bed and then came back down to do a quick check of the men. Everyone was asleep, though he thought that Solly Vaughn might have a bad time later on. But he and Sketes sat down at the table and ate some of Mr. Penrod's plain but good chicken soup, along with fresh-baked bread and a couple of thick, greasy chops that Sketes had wrangled from the cook. Sketes collapsed in the hammock, while Shiloh decided to do one more round before going to the stateroom to sleep.

He was just putting their dirty dishes in the bucket by the bulkhead when he heard the lookout's hoarse shout, far above his head but echoing clearly in the still night. He wasn't too concerned; there had been a surprising number of boats coming into the bay—fishing vessels, friends and relatives of the Bequians from nearby islands. They always turned around hastily, though, on sighting the yellow quarantine flag flying from the ship. But then he heard footsteps pounding across the deck and a hoarse whisper—Calvin Lott's—coming down from the main hatch. "Mr. Locke? Is that you? We need you topside, sir."

"Coming," Shiloh said hastily. He hurried to the rear booby hatch and up to the poop deck. Captain Starnes stood at the railing, his telescope raised to his eye. The night was clear, but there was little light from the slivered first-quarter moon and the fuzzy stars. "What's up, Captain?"

"Mr. Locke, it's that schooner in the bay," Captain Starnes answered, lowering the glass and pointing toward the mouth of the bay just northwest of the ship. "She's making all sail."

"Oh no," Shiloh groaned. "Is it my cousin?"

"I believe so, yes, sir," Captain Starnes said noncommittally. "What are your orders?"

"I don't know," Shiloh yelled back miserably. He was embarrassed—and ashamed for Bain— for he knew the entire ship's company was listening avidly, and he had no choice but to shout. "Uh—what can we do?"

Captain Starnes called back, "I can hail him, sir, and warn him. But if he doesn't stop, the only other thing to do would be to send a crew in the longboat to board him and bring him back." He didn't add "by force," but it was clearly implied in the captain's tone.

Shiloh's shoulders sagged. Send these men— Bain's former employees, many of whom not only hated him but despised him for being a coward—to board his boat and force him back? Shiloh hated the thought, since he had come, in the last dark and difficult days, to understand how his cousin felt . . . and to sympathize with him a little. And once again, here was Cousin Locke, horning in on Bain's little kingdom, bringing death and destruction with him. *Guess I am just like a little black cloud, following him all over the world, raining everywhere he goes.*

With an effort Shiloh brought himself back to the problem at hand. *But what about the quarantine? No new cases in four days, but we don't know what that means, if it means anything at all.*

Suddenly he prayed, quickly and simply, *Lord, what should I do? What's the right, the honorable, the just thing to do?*

"The heart knoweth his own bitterness; and a stranger doth not intermeddle with his joy."

"Huh?" Shiloh said aloud, looking about

him, startled. Captain Starnes watched him curiously. Suddenly Shiloh knew that the Lord had given him his answer, and he repeated the proverb in his mind. He loved the book of Proverbs, and read it over and over, though he didn't understand so many of them—including this one.

Does that mean . . . that I can't help Bain, not really? That I should just . . . let him go? Or, maybe, let go of him. I've been trying to force him into being what I want him to be—my family, my friend—for my sake more than his. I guess I can't know his heart, his bitterness, so I shouldn't interfere with his joys. . . . And if running away is the only joy he can get in this ol' world, then so be it.

"Let him go," Shiloh called.

Captain Starnes was relieved. Getting into family disputes was not his idea of the best way for an employee to further himself with his employer. Besides, he had crossed Bain Winslow once or twice before, and he had no wish to do it again.

As Shiloh went into the stateroom to grab his much-needed nap, he muttered, "All right, Lord, I know I did right. But now you'd better be watching my back, 'cause my wife is going to kill me."

CHAPTER TWENTY-ONE

Death Is Strict in His Arrest

CHENEY SELPT UNTIL nine-thirty, mainly because Shiloh had ordered, on pain of death by hanging from the yardarm, that there was to be no shouting, no scrubbing, no stamping, no loud breathing anywhere near the stern of the ship. The sailors, officers included, had tiptoed and whispered all morning.

When she awakened, she immediately knew that she was much, much better. Cheney was young and strong, and nothing had ever gotten her down for long, much less some silly old vapors. But she did impose upon herself a strict discipline, and assured Shiloh that from now on she would eat three full meals a day and sleep at least five hours, even if people dropped like flies around her. Satisfied, he let her go into the village while he took the ship's sick bay.

Opal Dekker was still lingering in a crisis stage, with delirium and raging fever punctuated with periods of unconsciousness. But Miss Dekker was, as far as Cheney could tell, taking expert care of her: the house was spotless, Opal was always washed, even her hair; there was always fresh water by her bedside, and ice; and Miss Dekker never offered to touch the tempting medications, though she knew they were made with liquor. She assured Cheney that she was giving Opal her medicine faithfully, when she was awake enough.

Four of the villagers, including Elena Verbrugge, went into crisis, all demanding constant care. Their huts were scattered at odd ends of the village, so Cheney went back and forth, up and down, all day long. But she did stop at noon, taking time to sit down in the cool shade at the tavern's by-now familiar table, drinking two ginger fizzes—now with ice, compliments of *Locke's Day Dream*—and eating a fat sandwich with razor-thin slices of *boucan*, the salted and spiced pork that buccaneers had made so famous that they had been named after it.

On the ship, Solomon Vaughn, Billy-O, and Tong Ten went into the crisis stage. Shiloh struggled with the nine sick men on board the ship, but he also grew weary and at times his hope flagged. He had been crushed when Bain had left. Though Bain had given him no great hope of reconciliation, he had really begun to believe that his cousin was changing for the better. But last night that hope had been crushed.

Both Cheney and Shiloh thought often of Fiona up at the Big House alone, taking care of Sweet. They couldn't go. They were too burdened down with other patients. All they could do was pray.

Fiona had fallen asleep sitting beside Sweet's bed. He had been unconscious all night and most of the day, and she had struggled valiantly to bring his fever down. Though last night she had been certain that Sweet would live, after Bain left and the endless darkness wore on, she began to doubt and be afraid. Sweet was so still, so unresponsive, never moving or speaking. His respiration was frighteningly slow and labored. Anxiously Fiona kept laying her hand on his massive chest just to feel it rise and fall. The house was completely silent and had that deserted, bleak feeling. She had not seen Rikke or any of the other Ten Eycks since the funeral. Only the cat had come in once, deigning to sit in Fiona's lap and nap. It had comforted Fiona.

Fatigue had drained her, though, and she kept dozing off. In an uneasy dream she heard something—a rustle, a small furtive sound—and awakened with a start.

Bain stood by her.

Shocked, she looked up at him. He was sun-tanned and smelled of the wind and sea. His white shirt, soiled slightly and the tail somewhat untucked, had lost two top buttons, showing the golden tan of his chest. His fawn breeches were still neatly tucked into dusty black boots. Fiona, in the mad whirl of her thoughts, was thinking that he looked tan and slim and very handsome.

He was watching her and gave her a crooked, exhausted smile. "Good morning, Miss Keane. How's the patient?"

"He's . . . he's about the same," she murmured with confusion. "Maybe just a little better than last night."

Bain studied Sweet, then looked back at her. She dropped her eyes, as always. "Well, you certainly look done in," he said in a surprisingly gentle tone. "You've got dark circles under your eyes and your hair is mussed."

Fiona quickly put a hand to her hair, helplessly patting it. "There's no mirror in here. I thought that was odd, not having a mirror in your bedroom."

"It probably never occurred to Sweet." Bain looked down with a glance that seemed to contain some affection for Sweet, then touched Fiona's struggling fingers. She jumped at his touch. "Here, allow me. Nonsense, girl, I'm not going to strangle you . . . there. All pat and smooth. You have lovely hair, by the way."

"Th-thank you, sir," she said, choking.

"You're quite welcome," he said briskly. "So Sweet's still unconscious?"

"In . . . yes, sir, but . . . he's . . . I mean, he's in and out." She was terribly upset by Bain's nearness, her eyes downcast, her cheeks flaming, her hands fidgeting in her lap.

His eyebrow cocked a little as he watched her knowingly. *Locke would really kill me dead this time*, he thought with arid amusement and moved to sit in the chair on the other side of the bed. Fiona, though she didn't realize it, gave an audible sigh of relief.

Bain continued politely, "He does look better, I think. When I left here, he looked like he was about to draw his last breath."

"I . . . I didn't think you'd come back," Fiona said breathlessly.

Bain waved with one still elegantly manicured hand. "I intended to go to Jamaica, but sailing a schooner all by yourself is too-too much work for a gentleman, and boring at that. I sailed in circles around this godforsaken island all night. Finally I got hungry, realized that there was no steward to fix my breakfast, and decided to come home."

"I'll fix you something to eat," Fiona offered shyly. "If you would stay with Mr. Sweet."

He nodded. "Fix us both something, and we'll eat up here. And then you go to bed."

She nodded and hurried away, but not before Bain had seen the shock and embarrassment on her face. Bain was both amused and bemused. *Is it really possible for a grown woman to be so innocent? She certainly appears genuine, though it is hard to believe.*

At the door Fiona hesitated and turned back

but kept her eyes averted. "I . . . I suppose, Mr. Winslow, if you are planning on staying, that I should go on back to *Locke's*—to the ship, I mean."

"No! I mean, surely you wouldn't leave your patient," Bain said persuasively. "He's still very ill, and you shouldn't leave him now."

She fidgeted, looking distressed, and finally Bain said in quite a different tone, "I would like for you to stay and help me take care of him. Please."

"All right," she said quietly. "But, Mr. Winslow, would you mind—or do you know where Rikke is? Is he still here, at the Big House?"

"They're all here, huddled in their cottages. It's hard for them. Imri . . . Imri was special." He sat brooding, and Fiona came back to the bed- side and slipped into her chair, watching him with compassion glowing in her doe's eyes. He finally sighed deeply and focused on her again. "Why? What do you want Rikke for?"

"I was going to ask him to go tell Mr. Locke that you've come back," she said eagerly. "He'll be so glad, Mr. Winslow, truly he will. And I know that he and Dr. Cheney are worrying about me. And Mr. Sweet."

"Oh? Have they been here today?" Bain asked, his eyes hardening.

"No, but I know that they can't. You just don't know how hard it is for them, Mr. Winslow. With the crew sick on the ship, and all the villagers scattered here and there. They're just working themselves to death," Fiona said passionately.

"No, I don't know how hard it is for them," he said acidly. "Poor, poor Locke."

"He's really a good, kind man," Fiona said, quite firmly for her.

He stared at her moodily and muttered, "Yes, I suppose he is. But, Miss Keane, there are things about our family that you don't know and couldn't understand even if you did. So I'm asking you as a favor not to tell my cousin that I'm back. I deliberately docked the schooner on the eastern side of the island because I don't want—I just can't bear him interfering in my life anymore. So please, I'm asking you. Don't tell him I'm back."

Fiona looked troubled. "But . . . but I can't lie to Mr. Locke. Or Dr. Cheney." She lifted her chin then and managed to say stubbornly, "I'm sorry, but I won't lie."

Bain sighed. "All right then, don't lie. But you don't have to send Rikke to tell him, do you? I'll just send him to find Dr. Duvall and tell her that you're all right, that Sweet's doing better, and that you're going to stay for a few days. And that they shouldn't come, because you and Sweet are managing fine. And that's no lie."

She reflected, then nodded. "As long as they

have word from me, it'll be all right. And it is true, it would be so good for them if they didn't have to struggle and worry to try to get up here." She stood again but faced him with a direct, clear gaze. "Because, Mr. Winslow, Mr. Locke would want to come, not for me, not even for Sweet. For you. Because he loves you, just like a brother."

Now Bain was the one who dropped his eyes with shame. "Fine. But it's better—better for both of us—if he could just let me go."

On the night of the twenty-fourth of May, Solly Vaughn died aboard ship. It hurt Shiloh deeply. *He was only sixteen*, he mourned as he carried the boy's slight body to their temporary morgue—a storeroom with enormous blocks of ice filling it. Solly was the first. Shiloh had ordered that the morgue be set up so that they could keep the bodies frozen until they could return to the deeps and commit their bodies to the sea that they loved.

Shiloh soaked his hands and forearms in carbolic acid, then doggedly returned to the sick bay. Willy Perkins was hanging on somehow, though he still had a raging fever. Thankfully, however, he no longer had wild deliriums, only dull unconsciousness. Shiloh wondered if, perhaps, his brain would be damaged even if he lived.

Tong Ten and Billy-O reached the crisis stage, and Billy-O, unfortunately, was a fighter like Willy Perkins. He was a big, strong man, almost a match for Shiloh. He kept trying to get out of bed, convinced that he was going to miss his ship and needed to report to the docks *right now*. Certainly Sketes couldn't handle him, and Shiloh, hesitant about giving laudanum, had to keep experimenting with Billy-O's dosages in little increments hours apart.

It was late at night when Shiloh, who had been struggling all evening with Billy-O, finally was able to turn his attention to Horatio Seaton, Billy-O's roommate. He checked over the older man, who had been lying quietly during the entire struggle with Billy-O, never complaining, and suddenly Shiloh realized with an unexpected clarity that Horatio Seaton was going to die that night. Sometimes he knew, as now; sometimes he didn't, as with Solly, who had seemed to slip from his grasp without his even noticing it.

Seaton had not been able to keep down his medication and kept vomiting blood. He had a fever, but not a raging one. Yet because of the alcohol's ravages of his body, along with typhus, he was perilously ill, even though he had not yet reached the terrible crisis stage of the fever.

Shiloh didn't think he'd make it an hour into crisis.

Shiloh pulled up an armless chair and sat down close by Seaton's bunk. "How are you feeling, Mr. Seaton?"

"Fine, sir, fine." His voice was weak, already fading.

"I'm sorry I haven't had more time to spend with you."

"That's all right, sir. I know you've been busy."

Shiloh nodded. "Sure have. For now I think I'll just sit and talk to you for a while, if you'd care to. Nice to talk to someone who's not raving for a change."

"Billy-O, he was worried about missing his ship. He's had a bad time of it, hasn't he?" Seaton weakly agreed.

"Yes, but I think he's going to make it," Shiloh said quietly.

Seaton stared at him with bloodshot, sunken eyes. Shiloh met his gaze clearly. Finally Seaton whispered, "I'm not going to, am I, Mr. Locke? Make it, I mean."

Shiloh answered him truthfully. "I don't know for sure, Mr. Seaton. Only God knows . . . for sure."

The older man nodded with understanding. They were quiet for a while. Shiloh sponged his face.

Finally Seaton said, "I'm scared, Mr. Locke." His rheumy eyes filled with tears.

Shiloh gripped his hand. "I know. I can't help you with that, but the Lord can."

Seaton, with a power Shiloh would never have believed in that wasted body, gripped his hand hard in both of his. "Can He? Will He? An old drunk like me?"

"Yes. Jesus loves you, Mr. Seaton, no matter what you've done."

"And . . . and I can . . . He'll save me now? Even though it's . . . I'm almost . . . it's almost too late?" Seaton asked desperately.

"It's never too late," Shiloh said firmly. "Not as long as you draw a breath. Even if it's your very last one, if you call on Him, He'll listen, and He'll forgive your sins and save your soul and take you home with Him."

Seaton nodded, then squeezed his eyes shut, tears streaming down. "Oh, Lord, I'm a wicked old sinner, and now that I'm dying I'm running to you. Will you forgive me for a whole life of sins? Will you save me, Lord Jesus?" He sobbed.

"He will, and He has," Shiloh said gently, wiping his face. "Amen."

Seaton opened his eyes and asked Shiloh pleadingly, "Is that it? Am I saved?"

"Think about it," Shiloh answered. "Look into your heart, Mr. Seaton. The heart's a secret place, and I can't know it. Only you and the Lord can."

Seaton thought, staring into space, and then nodded and smiled a little. "You're right. I'm not scared anymore, because I'm not alone anymore. The Lord Jesus is right here, with me, and in my heart. Oh, how tired I am! I think I could sleep now."

"That would be good," Shiloh said, taking the man's hand again. "Sleep well, my friend."

Shiloh stayed by his side, holding his hand, for twenty minutes. And then he died.

Shiloh carried his body to the dark, cold morgue, but he knew that Horatio Seaton was in a place that was filled with eternal light and warmth and peace and love.

———

Death had come to the village as well. Cheney was at Isaac and Emil Dekker's cabin. Isaac had just died. A young woman named Hasina Dekker had been taking care of the brothers, and Cheney was numbly relieved that she could leave her in charge. Even though Emil was very ill, she thought he might make it. Still, Cheney felt terrible about leaving patients when they were in the last stages of the disease.

I can't be everywhere at once, she thought wearily. She went over the situation in her mind and counted seven more villagers who were in crisis in six different houses.

"At least," she murmured to herself as she gathered her things, planning to go on to the next patient, "Opal is much better." She had come out of the awful raging fevers and delirium of the crisis stage, and had been lucid and even sitting up in bed that afternoon. Miss Dekker was coaxing her to eat some tinned and sweetened pineapple.

Cheney was making her way to the Verbrugges' house when Rikke ran to catch up with her. "Dr. Cheney, Miss Fiona sent me to tell you that Sweet is better, and she's doing fine with him, so you don't have to worry about coming up to the Big House."

"Oh, thank the Lord," Cheney said fervently. Then she told Rikke softly, "I'm so sorry about Imri, Rikke. Are you and your family doing all right?"

He shrugged and gazed at her unhappily. "We miss her."

"I'm sure you must. If you need me for any reason, you come for me, all right?" Cheney said warmly.

"Thank you, Dr. Cheney," he said, turning back to the well-worn old path up to the Big House. "But we live."

Odd thing to say, Cheney thought. *But then again, maybe it wasn't. The line between life and death is not so clearly marked sometimes—but here, in this place and this time, it seems to be obvious: either you're dying, or you live. It's that simple.*

A line from Shakespeare came to her, sharp and clear: *"That fell sergeant death is strict in his arrest."*

Cheney, with firm steps, went to the next house, determined that the fell sergeant, next time, would have her to reckon with before his next arrest.

CHAPTER TWENTY-TWO

God's Hand

JUST AS THE DAYS before had been like an unending storm, when one couldn't tell if it was day or night and it seemed that every moment brought another specter of death, suddenly the world seemed to reach a climax—and then, jarringly, it was calm. So was the twenty-seventh of May on board *Locke's Day Dream*. For maybe the hundredth time since he'd been belowdecks, struggling to understand his place in time, Shiloh looked at his watch. It sang—a solemn, tinny tingling—*When Johnny comes marching home again, hurrah, hurrah . . .*

It was four thirty-seven, and Shiloh yawned and wondered for the hundredth time if it was A.M. or P.M.

"This Johnny's marching home," he said to

Sketes, who was sound asleep in the hammock, slung again in the wardroom. She didn't answer, only snored a little.

Conscientiously he dragged himself around once more to look in on each of the three sick bays. Every man—there were only six of them now—was soundly, peacefully asleep.

He wearily climbed the ladder and went into the salon, taking off his shirt and throwing it down on the floor as he walked. He went into the stateroom and stood staring, stupidly, in the bright orange afternoon sunlight.

"Hi," Cheney said brightly, turning over in the bed and giggling at his dazed expression. "We're married. I'm your wife, Dr. Cheney Duvall."

"Oh yeah," he said, throwing himself into the roomy bed and grabbing her. "I do remember something about getting married. And about a certain promise you made."

"Oh? And what was that?" Cheney teased him as she threw her arms around his neck.

"That you were gonna make up to me for havin' such a lousy rotten plague on my honeymoon," Shiloh grumbled. "And, Doc, you got some makin' up to do."

Cheney, Shiloh, and Sketes were having a late supper down in the wardroom when Fiona

431

came back, quietly slipping in as usual. They welcomed her, and Sketes immediately began filling a plate for her, muttering darkly that it looked like they didn't have no food up at that Big House, did they?

"How is Sweet?" Shiloh asked as he handed Fiona into her seat and Sketes shoved an enormously piled-up plate in front of her.

"Oh, he's much better! He's even getting up. He's so strong, Mr. Shiloh. He's like a bull, and just about as stubborn as one. But not so mean," Fiona added quickly.

Cheney frowned. "The recovery period is so tricky. There's always a chance of pneumonia, even if he is up and around."

"I think he's going to be all right," Fiona said firmly, which surprised them, but she took no notice. "Sketes, four men couldn't possibly eat all this food," she said, taking an enormous bite of fresh-fried pompano fish.

Cheney persisted, "Fiona, are the Ten Eycks taking care of him?"

Fiona chewed, then said carefully, "He's being well taken care of, Dr. Cheney."

Shiloh had been paying little attention—he was eating steadily, for he loved pompano—but now he looked up sharply at Fiona. She glanced at him, startled, for she saw that he knew and understood everything. She didn't know how he knew, but she was sure he did. He winked at her.

Cheney, who was oblivious, went on muttering, "Oh, for heaven's sake, Shiloh, you know that neither of us can just leave him up there. We'll have to start going up to the Big House every day."

"No," he said slowly, "I don't think so. If Fiona says he's okay, then he must be okay. You wouldn't have left, would you, Fiona, unless Sweet was all right?"

"No, sir, I wouldn't," she answered sincerely.

Cheney frowned. "But I feel responsible for him. He is my patient, after all."

"Is he?" Shiloh said mildly. "I seem to recall Sweet asked for Fiona. He was her patient."

"But . . . but . . . she . . . it doesn't work that way!" Cheney protested.

"Why not?" Shiloh asked.

"Why, because . . . because . . . I don't know," Cheney admitted. "I just know that I'm somehow supposed to make myself miserable over it."

"Forget it, Doc," Shiloh said with mock sternness. "I feel like the misery is over, don't you?"

And then Cheney dropped her head, but when she looked up, relief had lit her face. "Yes, I think you're right, Shiloh. The days of death have passed."

They stayed moored in the lovely bay, rowing back and forth to the little island, until the last day of May.

The men on the ship were all steadily getting better, much faster than either Cheney or Shiloh had hoped. But then they were strong men, had led healthy lives for the most part, and had much to look forward to. They had good shipmates, a good and caring captain, and a ship they loved. Somehow they had survived. Out of the nine men who had contracted typhus, only three had died, and Sketes had carefully told everyone that normally five or six of them would have died. The men, of course, thought it was because they had Dr. Cheney and Mr. Locke, the good-luck charms of the world and especially of *Locke's Day Dream.*

In the village, of the twenty-four people who had contracted the fever, only nine of them had died. Cheney was stunned when she calculated the unheard-of low mortality rate of about thirty-seven percent. She told Shiloh, "I've been in agony over what seemed like almost nonexistent medical care. It seems all we did was mix medications and run from one dying person to another."

"But not very many of them died, Cheney," he told her gravely. "And I believe God's hand was in it, every moment. Neither you nor I got the fever, and neither did Sketes and Fiona. All of the men had shore leave, except for Tong Ten, and only nine out of forty-six crewmen and three officers contracted it. Out of over two hundred villagers, only twenty-four got it."

"Yes," Cheney agreed. "There were some hard deaths—neither of us can ever forget little Solly, and sad and bitter Mr. Wooling, and poor Mr. Seaton."

"He died good," Shiloh said quietly. "Real good."

Cheney smiled. "Yes, and just think—some wonderful new chances at life have come out of this. Did you notice those two watercolors in Opal Dekker's living room?"

"Yeah, I did. And there are two more—even better, I think, by the same artist, up at the Big House."

"I know," Cheney said with satisfaction. "And that wonderful artist is Opal Dekker. She just called it 'messing about with paints,' but I think she's very talented, and I told her so. I offered to buy the two at her house, but she refused, saying that she had painted them just for fun, for Willem, and he had loved them. But I told her she ought to paint a few and take them to St. Vincent sometime to put up for sale in the open market. I think her work would sell. She's a little low on supplies, though."

"Ah," Shiloh said, closing his eyes and pressing his fingertips to his forehead, "I think . . . I'm feeling . . . a suggestion coming from my wife . . . something to do with money . . . my money . . ."

"You have enough," Cheney said primly. "You can afford some paints and brushes and canvases."

"Yep," he said cheerfully. "We'll send 'em over from the next stop. But you know what gets me, Doc, is I gave Miss Dekker a bolt of muslin that I'd stashed, from Kingston. I was gonna give it to Mrs. Slopes when we got home, you know. Anyway, did you know that Miss Dekker made dresses out of it—one for herself, one for Opal, and one for Bonnie?"

"I know, she's turned into their guardian angel," Cheney said, laughing.

"Old guardian dragon is more like it," Shiloh grumbled. "Bonnie calls her 'Auntie Miss Dekker.' Uh . . . speaking of my money . . . let's talk about your money."

"All right," Cheney said happily. "How much do you want?"

"None, thanks. What I really meant was, I got . . . a favor to ask you," Shiloh said with uncharacteristic hesitation. "How much would you miss those fancy pistols?"

"Not much," Cheney said easily. "I like playing with my fencing foil better. But Monsieur Bettencourt might require hospitalization."

"Aw, those Frenchies have always got their

braces in a twist," Shiloh grumbled. He frowned and seemed to be having trouble going on.

Gently Cheney prompted him, "The pistols. . . ?"

"Yeah. Hey, you want to go up on deck and talk about it?" Shiloh asked boyishly. "We'll be setting sail before long."

"Of course, my love. I'd like nothing better."

Bain stood at the Overlook. He stared below, his arms crossed, his eyes narrowed against the blazing setting sun. "*Locke's Day Dream*—and Locke—finally sailing out of my bay and out of my life."

He watched the noble ship until she disappeared over the brilliantly lit hills of the northern arm of the bay. Her sails towered, touched with crimson. She was beautiful, and Bain could hardly bear the sight, but he watched until the soaring topmast only nicked the horizon, and then she disappeared from his view.

Bain turned and went slowly back to the Big House. Sweet was waiting. Tonight he would cook them the big fat bonito he had caught himself. Even Fiend might have a little piece, if she wanted.

But Bain Winslow wondered why he felt such a sense of loss.

The next day, Miss Dekker brought him a

package—from the big ship, she said—and demanded payment for delivering it.

Numbly Bain opened the case of the beautiful Boutet pistols he had coveted in Jamaica. Inside was a folded note. Reluctantly he read it.

Dear Bain,
We love you, and we'll pray for you always.

Both of them had signed it.
Bain bowed his head and wept.

PART IV

ALL THEM THAT SAIL WITH THEE

June–August 1869

*For there stood by me this night the angel of
God, whose I am, and whom I serve, saying,
Fear not . . . lo, God hath given thee
all them that sail with thee.*

Acts 27:23–24

CHAPTER TWENTY-THREE

Complete Conversions

"THEY CALL IT 'Kick 'em Jenny,'" Shiloh said.

"I think I see why," Cheney replied darkly.

Rounding the northern tip of Bequia was a big, sharp, black, foreboding rock stuck up right in the middle of the passage. White water frothed at its base; the last rays of the sun tinted the whitecaps a dangerous scarlet.

"I assume we're actually going to make it and not have a shipwr—I mean, an accident. That would just top it all."

"Wouldn't it?" Shiloh said lightly, so lightly that Cheney knew there could be no actual danger. "Nah, guess we're headed right back to Barbados. So, mon chou, you want to go on with the plan we had . . . uh . . . sometime back there in the dim past and go down to Grenada after we check in at Bridgetown for mail?"

"Mmm, not really," Cheney said nonchalantly. "We've been in this part of the world for too long."

He glanced curiously at her, and she looked down and twisted her great ruby ring. It glinted bloodred one last time before the gentle night fell.

"What is it, Cheney?" he asked.

"I just . . . I know you must feel bad about Bain. I do."

"Yeah. Well . . . I gave it my best shot. Not much else to do about it."

She sighed sadly. "I suppose we'll never see him again."

To her surprise Shiloh snorted, and she could hear the tinge of old devilish laughter in his voice. "Huh! I know where that scoundrel lives now. He won't get rid of me so easy as all that."

She tried to see him, but now the darkness was too thick and her eyes hadn't adjusted yet. "Me neither," she finally said, matching his mood. "He owes me for a house call."

Shiloh laughed, and she reveled in it. He had a delightful, deep, most carefree laugh. She went on, "So back to your original question. I know we need to stop at Barbados to check for mail, but why don't we just go on up to Guadeloupe after that? We've already seen Bridgetown, and we haven't seen any of the French West Indies yet."

"Doc," Shiloh said, "I just got two words for Guadeloupe: *Frogs* and *volcano*."

"Posh," Cheney grumbled. "You're as bad as my father. I must remind you, as painful as it is, John Bull, that I'm one-quarter Frog. I mean French. And who's afraid of a volcano? All of the

441

Windwards and Leewards are just volcanoes risen out of the sea."

"Okay, try these two words," Shiloh said with exasperation: "*active volcano*."

"Ohhhh," Cheney said, eyes wide, suddenly having visions of mighty Haleakala on Maui, which had almost killed her, Shiloh, and several of their friends. "Let's stay at the King George Inn in Barbados."

"And how long will you be staying at the King George, suh?"

Shiloh finished signing his name in the guest register with a flourish, then smiled at the hotel clerk. "As long as my money holds out."

Cheney stifled a giggle at the stunned expression on the face of the stuffy British clerk. He typified her image of a British desk clerk: slicked-down thin hair, disdainful expression, long nose stuck in the air. "Shiloh," she whispered reproachfully, pinching his arm secretly, but it did no good because he mumbled, "Ow, Doc, you got a grip like a lobster."

Ignoring him, she told the shocked clerk, "We'll be staying at least a week."

"That's if the cooking is good," Shiloh said. Taking a roll of bills from his pocket, he peeled off several of them and handed them to the bemused clerk.

"And this would be. . . ?" the clerk said, mouth twisted with disdain.

"It's a bribe."

"Suh!"

"A bribe for the concierge, the maître d', and the cooks. I want three meals delivered to our room every day."

He sniffed. "Suh, we have fine dining in the Cavalier and George, and a tearoom, the Queen Anne's Fare."

"Good," Shiloh said, adding a bill to the pile. The clerk took it between two very nimble fingers. "And that's for tea every night at about eleven. And hey, do they have any of those little toasted cakes—whaddya call 'em? Crumbles?"

"Crumpets," the clerk said in an awful tone. "Yes, suh."

"We'll want 'em every night, hot, with butter," Shiloh said, winking at Cheney. She was greatly amused. Shiloh was no respecter of persons, and he cared not a fig for what anyone thought of him. She liked that in him very much. "Here, this is for you, since you've been so helpful." Shiloh handed the man two more bills.

This effected a complete conversion. "Oh yes, suh, we shall certainly accommodate your every need and see that you're not disturbed in any way."

"Good man," Shiloh said with satisfaction. "I

think we're going to be asleep here for a few days."

And they were, practically.

They slept soundly at night, then usually had a nap after breakfast in the cool of the morning; then, of course, siesta after lunch, waking up in time for dinner. They often dozed out on the gallery until tea, and then they were so sleepy they went back to bed. It was heavenly.

Finally on the fifth of June they came out for breakfast, blinking stupidly at the blazing morning sun and the outrageous hues of the tropics. They walked to the post office, a pink building that looked like a planter's cottage, and collected their mail.

They had a surprising stack of letters from Cheney's parents, Victoria and Dev, and Brynn and Walker. They also bought New York newspapers that were only two weeks old, practically hot off the presses for the carefree islanders of the West Indies. They decided that the sun was hot and they could use a nap, though it was only ten o'clock in the morning. Their suite on the ground floor, with a shady patio and the fresh trade wind continuously blowing through like a lullaby, was just as pleasant as any tearoom or café.

And, true, they did want to savor their letters. To Cheney's great gratification, her father had written a long letter just to Shiloh, and so had

Devlin Buchanan. Oddly—for the men were so different—they had formed a solid friendship in the last year after Dev had essentially rescued Shiloh, if not from death, then certainly from a perilous situation. It was most satisfying to Cheney, for she and Victoria Buchanan were best friends, and it made her very happy that she and Shiloh, as a married couple, had such a close relationship with the Buchanans.

Shiloh's cousin Brynn's letter was long and loving and full of news about Winslow Plantation in Hana. But his uncle Logan had not written him, and Cheney knew that his aunt Denise (privately Cheney called her Mad Dog Denise) would never write to him. Or so she thought.

"There's a note from my aunt Denise enclosed with Brynn's letter," Shiloh said with amazement. "Look." He held up a single half sheet of notepaper, monogrammed DCWW (she always used all of her titles: Denise Clare Worthington Winslow), and sealed rather messily with bloodred wax.

"Are you going to open it? Maybe read it?" Cheney asked with amusement.

"I dunno," Shiloh answered. "I think I'll just sit here 'astonied,' as those old guys say in the Bible, and stare at it. Hope it's not poisoned ink or anything." He paused dramatically for a moment, then broke the seal.

"Could be poisoned sealing wax," Cheney

said airily. "Much better method of delivery."

He made a face at her, then read and looked back up—very quickly—and handed it to her. She read:

Hamileia vastatrix found in Ceylon.
Make Caribbean contacts.
Denise Clare Worthington Winslow

Cheney looked back up at him, frustrated. Then she softened, for she saw the pleasure shining in Shiloh's blue eyes—even for this cold, cryptic message from his aunt Denise.

She smiled at him. "We must be sure to thank her for this valuable information. I've been wondering what's been happening in Ceylon."

"Yeah, me too, I can hardly bear the excitement," he replied, his eyes sparkling. "What's"— he took the paper again and frowned—"*hamileia vastatrix*?"

"I haven't the foggiest notion," Cheney replied. "I'm astonied, like those old guys in the Bible."

"Whaddya mean? You know French, Madame Frog."

"It's not French, Shiloh, it's Latin. I think."

"You know Latin too."

"Not this Latin," Cheney said, frowning. "It might be . . . it could be a plant . . . or an animal . . ."

446

"Or a vegetable. Or a mineral," Shiloh said, rolling his eyes.

"I may not know what this is," Cheney said with determination, "but I know how to find out."

———

Across from the Bridgetown Lending Library and Reading Rooms was the dignified Rose and Crown Tea Parlor, the ground floor of a three-story house with wrought-iron balconies, marble staircases, dark paneling, and prints of fox hunting. As the proprietress, Mrs. Sebastian, seated them in a secluded corner table for two, Shiloh ordered high tea, for it was a little past four o'clock. Though this was an exotic Caribbean island, it was vehemently still Little England, and Mrs. Sebastian would have no truck with patrons who weren't interested in traditional teatime.

High tea was almost as varied as a full formal dinner. Mrs. Sebastian brought steaming tea in a no-nonsense Brown Betty teapot, clotted cream, lemon, both Demerara and refined sugar, and honey—the usual trappings for British tea. But Cheney noticed that also on the tea tray were freshly sliced limes, an addition that surely no self-respecting Englishman would countenance, unless he were on an exotic Caribbean island. The bill of fare was also a mixture of British tradition and West Indian spice. For the stiff-upper-lipped Englishman there were scones, an impossibly tall sponge cake, and fig pudding. For loyal Barbadians the sauce for the pudding was cacao-and-ginger sauce, the jam for the scones was papaya-and-nutmeg conserve, the delicate little sandwiches were of tiny spinachlike callaloo leaves, the savories were smoked herring and sweet-hot red peppers on toasted cheese bread.

In between Mrs. Sebastian's deliveries to their table—it took several trips—Cheney and Shiloh talked about their discovery at the library.

"So Ceylon has coffee rust, and Mad—I mean, your aunt Denise wants you to make Caribbean contacts," Cheney ruminated. "I must tell you that I don't know much more than when we started."

Shiloh smiled. "It's a test, kinda. See, most of the coffee imported to England and America comes from Ceylon. You saw the study by that naturalist. Coffee rust is fatal to coffee trees and spreads uncontrollably. So . . ."

"So America and England are soon going to have to import their coffee from somewhere else," Cheney said thoughtfully. "And your aunt Denise expects you to get Winslow Brothers Shipping in on it."

"Yeah. I'm still *astonied* that she put me to work on it. I guess if Uncle Logan had been around, she would have sent him packing," Shiloh said drily.

"Are there coffee growers in the West Indies?" Cheney asked neutrally.

He dropped his eyes and toyed with his china teacup. "Mm-hm. A few."

She watched him curiously, but he said no more and didn't look up. Exasperated, she demanded, "What? Have you bought a coffee plantation or something? Or has your cousin run off and left one to rack and ruin somewhere?"

"No, Doc," he said, "nothing like that. It's just that ... uh ... it's all Troy Bondurant's fault." Troy Bondurant was one of Shiloh's friends in New York. Troy and his father owned Bondurant Banking and Equities, which had both Shiloh's personal and business banking accounts.

"Troy Bondurant? What's he got to do with coffee rust in Ceylon?" Cheney asked, bewildered.

"Nothing. It's just that—aw, the heck with it. I'll never be able to disinclinate with you, woman," he muttered.

"The word is *dissimulate*, and you'd better not."

"Yeah, yeah. Anyway, Troy, see, he got his braces all in a twist because I—we—brought *Locke's Day Dream* down here without the hold bein' stuffed full of 'bout a million pounds of flour or tobacco or sarsaparilla or iron, 'cause he said I could just open the hold doors and sell everything in about two hours. And then, o' course, we're not bringing back anything to sell. No money made on this trip. You know how fidgety bankers are," Shiloh said with amusement.

"So anyway, he gave me this list, see, of Bondurant's West Indies clients and what their business was—they're all planters, of course. Troy said just in case I came to my senses and at least made some business acquaintances down here, I had my tidy little list. So I didn't want it—of course, I don't want to do any business on our honeymoon—but I did just kinda glance at it. There were three coffee growers on it, one in Jamaica, one in Puerto Rico, and one in Trinidad."

Cheney stared at him. "You did more than glance at it if you remember that."

He shrugged. "Maybe. But, listen, Doc, I didn't want to do any business, really I didn't—don't. It's our honeymoon, our time, just for fun. No matter what my aunt Denise says."

Cheney frowned and, looking down, slowly stirred her steaming Earl Grey tea, the tiny silver spoon making musical little clinks against the paper-thin china cup.

Shiloh looked chagrined and leaned over to speak very softly to her. "Don't be upset, Doc. It sounds like it's probably going to be a couple of years before the coffee rust has any real impact on Ceylon exports. I've got plenty of time to deal with this."

"I know," Cheney said evenly. "But . . . why deal with it at all?" She glanced back up at him, her face set in neutral lines.

"Huh? What do you mean?"

She chose her words carefully and spoke slowly. "Shiloh, in the last few weeks . . . you've been . . . you were so . . ." Her cheeks flushed slightly, and she burst out, "I want you to be a doctor!"

He sat back, stunned.

She kept talking, quickly now. "Why, *why* won't you go to medical school and be a doctor? You . . . you're more suited to it, you're so gifted, you're like a . . . it's like you were born to it! You have such a gift!"

Shiloh lifted his cup to his lips, then set it back down and poured more from the squatty brown teapot.

Cheney went on, "I know you love *Locke's Day Dream* dearly, and of course you can keep her and . . . and do whatever you want with her. And of course Brynn and your uncle Logan can handle whatever . . . the . . . shipping . . . routes, or whatever."

He nodded slowly. "Yes, they—and Aunt Denise—have done very well with Winslow Brothers Shipping."

"And . . . and I can't tell you how wonderful it is for me to have you with me, to be . . . my partner, in my life, in medicine. Like we've always been!" Cheney finished passionately.

He watched her, his blue eyes thoughtful. "It means a lot, a whole lot to you, doesn't it?"

"Oh yes!"

He nodded. "Okay, Doc. I'm your man. I mean, I'm your doctor."

CHAPTER TWENTY-FOUR

The Hardest Honesty to Come By

CHENEY DEARLY LOVED their suite at the King George Inn. It was on the ground floor, with French doors leading out to a small, lush courtyard with an immense lemon tree and a lime tree that was almost as big. Banana trees, heavy with fruit, their leaves as big as crates, huddled around their tiny patio. At night they left the French doors open, with the mosquito netting filmily waving in the wind, making the candle flames waver like dancing girls. The fruity and spicy scents drifting in were delicious and gave Cheney good dreams.

But she was oblivious to all this exotic island atmosphere at the moment. She sat at her small dressing table in a luscious peach satin nightdress, brushing her hair. Shiloh sat cross-legged on the enormous four-poster bed with the New York papers spread all around him.

"Hey, Doc, they finished the railroad! Drove the last spike in Utah on May tenth. Now it's only going to take eight days for us to go from New York to San Francisco instead of the old slow ocean route."

"Mm-hmm," Cheney said absently.

"There's an article here that they're expecting to finish the Suez Canal in October, maybe November. And that'll just about finish off the clippers," he finished wistfully.

She put down her brush and stared blankly, unseeing of her soft candlelit reflection in the mirror as her thoughts focused on her husband.

I thought . . . I thought that I wanted more than anything for Shiloh to be a doctor so we could be together all the time, and he could be not only my husband and my closest friend, but also my . . . my partner.

So why do I feel so . . . so dissatisfied?

A tiny, sneaky little voice piped up in the back of Cheney's groping mind. *Ever think about what he wants?*

She made a face at herself. Now Shiloh had lowered the paper and was watching her curiously, but she was unaware of it.

What he wants? Why would he decide to become a doctor if he doesn't want to?

To please you, idiot!

At that instant, Cheney saw clearly what had happened and how momentous it was: Shiloh had, most likely, agreed to become a doctor only to please her!

Cheney hated women who pushed their husbands into life pursuits they didn't want. Of course, she had only observed those situations where women nagged their husbands over making more money, generally making their husbands and family and themselves miserable in the process.

But I was just encouraging him to follow a noble, meaningful calling! It's not the same thing at all!

She stopped and considered carefully what she had just thought. Was it the complete truth? Cheney was an honest person, even to herself, which is the hardest honesty to come by. In thinking about it more carefully, she had to admit that her own motivations were not entirely unselfish. *What difference does it make how worthy the cause is? The whole point is that I shouldn't force him to do anything he doesn't want to do, and the fact that he compromised on such an important thing between us . . . I don't ever want our marriage to be like that. I don't ever want his life to be like that. And most importantly, I don't want to be like that! Forgive me, Lord.*

She ran and threw herself on the bed, scattering papers and throwing her arms around

Shiloh's neck. "Forgive me, my love!"

"Huh? Well . . . here, kiss me a dozen or so times and I'll think about it," he said, drawing her close.

There was silence for a while, and then she pushed him away, though she sat close, her hand stroking his chest. "Shiloh, you're a truthful man, and I'm going to ask you a question, and I know you'll just tell me the straight truth. Do you *want* to be a doctor?"

"Not much," he said, grinning.

She blew out an exasperated breath. "Then why didn't you *say* so?"

"Because, Chency, my love, I'd do a lot more and a lot worse than that to make sure you're happy with me," he said, now somber. "I know it does mean a lot to you. So when I look at it straight on, it seems to me that it'll make you a lot happier than it'll make me miserable. See, I'm not dreading it or secretly shuddering or anything. It's good work, honest and honorable."

"It is," she agreed quietly. "And . . . and though I've been selfish about it, Shiloh, wanting you to be my personal . . . um . . . very personal physician," she said, blushing a little, "you are so talented in the field of medicine. You're intelligent, you have keen instincts . . . and I've never seen anyone with such an ease, such an innate ability as you have with patients."

He shifted restlessly, looking down and

grabbing her hand, smoothing the long white fingers between his own fight-scarred ones. "Yeah, I guess so. That's why I agreed to do it so easy, Doc. I mean, if that's what God wants me to do, then I better do it."

Cheney grabbed his face with both hands and turned him to face her. "Oh, Shiloh, oh, my love, there I go again! It's not God that's nagging you about it, dearest, it's me!"

"It is?" he asked. "But you're so much better than I am! I mean, you've been a Christian all your life, and you know so much more about all this stuff than I do!"

"No, no, Shiloh, I don't know—I can't know the Lord's plans for your life," she said quietly. "You have to find the path that the Lord has set for you. Never, never do what others want until you're sure it's what the Lord wants."

"Even you?" he asked, childlike.

"Especially me," she answered firmly. "I'm much too bossy."

"Yeah, but I'm crazy 'bout you anyway," he said, leaning over to plant a noisy kiss on her lips. "So how do I go about finding out what the Lord wants for me? How do you get in on that?"

She considered him, and he met her gaze clearly and honestly. "Shiloh, tell me this: what is your dream?"

He looked startled. "My dream? My only dream, for years now, has been for you to be my wife." He raised her hand to his lips and kissed it warmly.

She caressed his face. "I think that you do have another dream, perhaps many dreams, and I think that none of them are of becoming a doctor. I think . . . that you still dream of your father and his vision."

Now he stared at her, almost as if he were bewitched. "You . . . you're right. Of course you're right. My father loved the sea, and loved the *Day Dream*, and loved making his way in the world with his ships. He died coming here, the other side of the world, for his dream. . . ."

"But now you're here, and your *Day Dream* is here, and the ocean is wide and filled with your fortunes, Shiloh," she said warmly. "So forget about being a doctor. I'll be the doctor in this family."

He grinned like a little boy on Christmas morning. His eyes lit to a startling cool blue, the V-scar underneath puckered, and his smile creases deepened. "Yeah? You mean it? You'll really be happy?"

"I'll be happy with you if you want to move into a palm-thatched hut and fish for bonito off the side of *Locke's Day Dream*, my love," Cheney said warmly. "Now, why don't you let me have a look at Troy Bondurant's silly old list of business contacts?"

CHAPTER TWENTY-FIVE

Coffee

PORT-OF-SPAIN, TRINIDAD, seemed to Cheney to be dustier, hotter, noisier, and busier than any Caribbean port city they had seen. It was a vast relief to get out of the riotous and crowded city and travel the Eastern Main Road in the shade of the northern mountains to Madariaga Plantation, where they had decided to make the first of several calls to coffee growers in the West Indies.

In the hired carriage, Cheney gave her husband a final once-over with satisfaction. He looked clean and cool in a three-piece tan suit of fine linen. She glowed in a promenade dress of icy green, with a snappy little hat trimmed with flamingo feathers.

"Now remember, these people are Castilians, Shiloh, and Castilians are notoriously proud and haughty and subject to the least offense," Cheney said, fanning herself with a lacy white mother-of-pearl fan.

"Maybe you shoulda given me some fencing tips," Shiloh said mischievously. "In case he challenges me to a duel. And since you gave away my Boutet pistols to my sorry cousin."

"You never liked them anyway," Cheney said, her eyes twinkling.

"How'd you know? I'm the one who knows secret stuff like that."

"I know secret stuff about you," Cheney responded primly. "Lots of stuff. Anyway, don't change the subject. We're still working on your manners and deportment, sir. So I didn't mean that Don Madariaga would actually become violent. I just mean that a gentleman's manner is very important to them. Like my tante Marye, you know. Her mother was Castilian."

"Yeah, but that means that so was Tante Elyse's," Shiloh teased. "But anyway, Doc, I get it. Think I'm fit for such lofty company?"

"Yes, I do," Cheney answered. "You have a natural gallantry and warmth of manner that would endear you to any company. You always have."

Although Cheney spoke firmly, truth to tell, she had some misgivings about their reception at Madariaga Plantation. She had helped Shiloh compose a gracious letter to his possible future shipping customers, introducing Winslow Brothers Shipping, using Troy Bondurant's recommendations as an introduction and hoping that they would be at home when Mr. and Mrs. Irons-Winslow visited Trinidad, for they would like nothing better than to meet Don Madariaga and his wife, and see the widely renowned Madariaga *Plantación.*

It was wildly unorthodox, and she was a little afraid that the former Spanish envoy to Trinidad and Tobago, Don Bartolomé Ramirez y Madariaga, might view them as nothing but upstart vulgar American drummers. Indeed, he might throw them out—of the servant's entrance, of course—and Cheney thought only half jokingly that she hoped Don Madariaga truly wouldn't resort to violence. One never knew about Castilians. Their pride knew no bounds.

She didn't really care for herself, for she had been subject to so much censure since she'd become a doctor that she rarely noticed sly insults from polite society anymore. But she did care for Shiloh's sake. He was not the type of man to feel a snub, but it was important to him, for his business—his dream. She gave him another sidelong glance, but he was, as always, relaxed, interested in the rich landscape outside the carriage windows, alert.

"This is all cacao," Shiloh told her. "See the huge pods? I don't even know when they harvest cacao. Anyway, I don't see any coffee bushes."

"Madariaga Plantation has ninety thousand acres," Cheney said sturdily. "He could have miles of it and we wouldn't see it."

Shiloh nodded. "True."

They drove through black wrought-iron

gates down a long drive bordered on either side by brilliant croton bushes and blazing poinsettias. Madariaga Hacienda was an enormous three-story white stucco building, blinding in the early afternoon sun, with wings extending far out on either side, forming the quadrangle with the enclosed courtyard, the well-loved architecture of gracious Spanish homes.

An unsmiling black footman in startling black-and-scarlet livery let them into the enormous foyer, cool and dark with a soaring ceiling. Shiloh, mindful of his calling etiquette, gravely placed two of his cards and one of Cheney's onto the proffered heavy-beaten silver platter. "Please inquire if Don Madariaga is at home," he said quietly.

Without speaking, the footman slipped out of sight, down the dimness of an apparently unending dark hallway, soundless in his bowed satin pumps.

Cheney and Shiloh looked around, enthralled, for even the foyer of this grand house held such somber antiquities as a faded, immensely old French tapestry, sixteenth-century Spanish battle axes, and a conquistador's suit of armor gleaming in a dark alcove. "Whaddya do when you're waiting for the verdict like this?" Shiloh whispered.

"Try to appear at ease, as if you know you will be received," Cheney said with amusement.

"You know, stifle yawns and look bored with the trivial formalities."

Shiloh was practicing a heavy-eyed, pompously aristocratic disdain, twirling his fashionable ivory walking stick with negligent grace and murmuring in stuffy British, "Wot? Wot? Social calls, such a chore, m'dear, but *noblesse oblige* and all that rot, wot?"

Cheney had to stifle her giggles, for the cavernous great hall was like an echo chamber. Finally a servant appeared who was obviously the butler—a severe black man in black tie with white gloves—and, unsmiling, pronounced in a deep baritone, "This way, if you please, Mr. and Mrs. Irons-Winslow."

He turned and Cheney and Shiloh followed him, exchanging half-surprised glances. He led them down the long hall, past a dark grand staircase that swept up into the dim heights and past many closed doors. He finally opened a door and stepped into gleaming sunshine. "Mr. and Mrs. Irons-Winslow."

Cheney and Shiloh followed him and stood, blinking a little from the brightness. They were, to Cheney's gratification, shown into the gallery, a long, columned, gracious portico overlooking the courtyard. A couple rose and stepped forward to greet them.

Don Madariaga, a tall man with erect bearing and a fine mane of thick gray hair, bowed slightly. "Mr. and Mrs. Irons-Winslow, welcome to Madariaga Plantación. May I have the pleasure of presenting to you my wife, Ynes Padilla y Galvez de Madariaga."

Cheney saw with sinking heart that he spoke stiffly, even coldly, and his disapproval was barely concealed. Doña Madariaga, however, was slightly warmer in her greeting. She was much younger than her husband, a buxom woman with snapping dark eyes and a luxurious black mane of hair.

They turned and walked slowly down the gallery, which was wide enough to allow four to walk abreast. "We were just about to have tea," Doña Madariaga said. "Will you give us the pleasure of joining us?" Down in the courtyard underneath an enormous breadfruit tree was a great round table set with a silver tea service and a glorious arrangement of poinsettias.

Cheney felt anxious and wondered whether she should be rude enough to answer for her husband. She hadn't foreseen this awkward situation and therefore had not instructed him earlier of the etiquette. But he gave the right answer—by instinct, probably.

"With honest thanks we must decline," he said pleasantly. "I'm afraid that my wife and I have been unthinking, calling at this awkward time. I regret we've taken up the British tradition of having tea later in the afternoon, though that is no excuse for intruding on you this way."

Don Madariaga gave Shiloh a slight glance of approval, which Cheney knew he would. The forms must be observed, after all, and the couple would never have received them if they didn't intend them to take tea, which in itself was peculiar. Usually social calls with people one has not formed a previous acquaintance with were a strict fifteen-minute formality, and refreshments were never offered—certainly not a rather intimate event such as afternoon tea. Still, there were four places set.

As she expected, Don Madariaga, with a little less formality, said, "I insist, Mr. Irons-Winslow. I was intrigued by your letter. Young Mr. Bondurant has proved to be a most gracious and accommodating business associate, and I am certain that you have found him, in the course of your undertakings, to be quite as obliging."

Cheney gave Shiloh a heavy glance, and he nodded imperceptibly, understanding the signal. Don Madariaga was receiving them as business acquaintances, not on a social basis. Though it was not, perhaps, the most generous footing, at least Shiloh was free to discuss business, even though the women were present. Cheney suspected that Doña Madariaga's sharp-eyed appraisal of her and Shiloh meant that she might very well be one of those women who—like herself—was involved with her husband's business.

It was a much more common family circumstance for the Spanish than it was for Americans or the British.

They seated themselves at the table, covered in spotless linen, on black wrought-iron chairs with heavy velvet cushions. Doña Madariaga said politely, "We have China and Indian as well as Madariaga coffee. Of course it is not customary to take coffee in the afternoon, but I sometimes do indulge, though my husband does not."

"I'd love coffee," Cheney responded. "It has a wonderful, deep aroma that I can scent even here. It is your own blend, produced here on the plantation?"

"Yes, it is, and I believe it is a superior roast," Doña Madariaga said, signaling the footmen to serve. "We only have two thousand acres of coffee though. Cacao is a much more profitable crop."

At this Shiloh took over, with his easy directness. "Don Madariaga, it is exactly for this that my wife and I wished to call on you. To talk about your coffee."

"Oh?" Don Madariaga said stiffly. "As my wife said, we raise very little coffee. It is more of an experiment, I think you would say. You are interested in growing coffee?"

"No, sir. You see, my family's business is shipping, and we are based in the Pacific, with our routes to the Orient, Hawaii, and San

Francisco," Shiloh explained. "My wife and I are here on pleasure—our honeymoon—and we had no idea of making business calls. But I received word from my family that *hamileia vastatrix*—coffee rust—has been found in Ceylon."

Don Madariaga said with frigid politeness, "Is that so? I was not aware."

"No, sir, and neither is anyone else yet," Shiloh said, smiling. "At least, it hasn't reached the New York papers. And most likely if it hasn't reached the New York papers, no one in this hemisphere knows it."

"The New York papers," Don Madariaga repeated with barely concealed boredom. "Of course."

It was heavy going, for the man seemed supremely uninterested in anything that a commoner would have to say, Cheney reflected. Doña Madariaga's brow was creased in a deep study, but Cheney determinedly turned to her. "I noticed, Doña Madariaga, that you are a Galvez on your maternal side." Cheney knew that the female family name was often denoted in formal introductions as following the precedent *y*, as in the lady's name.

"Why, yes," she answered, a little absently, for she seemed to still be puzzling over Shiloh's words. "My mother was a Galvez, from Salamanca."

"Indeed? Would you be connected to

Bernardo de Galvez, the former governor of our illustrious state of Louisiana?" Cheney asked politely.

"Why . . . yes, the viceroy of Mexico in 1785? He was my great-great-uncle," she answered, puzzled.

Cheney noted that Don Madariaga was paying much closer attention to this conversation than he had to Shiloh.

"My family is also connected to Don Galvez," Cheney said carelessly. "On my mother's side. His sister married my great-grandfather."

Doña Madariaga smiled with true warmth for the first time. "Did you hear that, Bartolomé? Mrs. Irons-Winslow and I are practically cousins! She is a Galvez!"

"The connection is tenuous, I must say," Cheney said, returning the woman's smile, "but I am conscious of the honor every time I visit my great-aunts. Their gracious lineage is easily discerned."

"They are the most gallant of ladies," Shiloh put in warmly.

Don Madariaga suddenly looked at Shiloh through new eyes. "I would like to discuss more of this coffee rust with you, Mr. Irons-Winslow, but I'm afraid we are sadly boring the ladies. Would you care to take a walk around the garden with me, and perhaps indulge in a cigar? I have just received a new shipment from Cuba, and I can assure you that a gentleman with discriminating tastes will agree that they are exquisite."

"I'd be honored," Shiloh said, rising and bowing to the ladies. "If you would excuse us, ladies, though I am sorry to be deprived of such charming company. I won't keep Don Madariaga talking about business for long."

But he did, for Don Madariaga insisted. And Doña Madariaga and Cheney got along very well, trying to discern their family connections, laughing over the intricacies, each telling stories of their Galvez matriarchs. Shiloh and Don Madariaga came back, talking animatedly about horses, and Doña Madariaga sent them away again to see the stables. Truth to tell, Cheney would have preferred to go with the men, as she was an avid horsewoman.

But Doña Ynes—they had worked around to the less formal title—linked her arm with Cheney's, and they went into a delightful drawing room, with comfortable overstuffed satin sofas and gleaming dark mahogany tables and consoles and frangipani everywhere, scenting the air with its heavy, hypnotic fragrance. There Doña Ynes proceeded to interrogate Cheney unmercifully about Winslow Brothers Shipping, about *Locke's Day Dream*, about coffee rust, about the Winslows' cargos from Ceylon, about coffee consumption in America. Cheney grew more animated as they discussed the business implications of Shiloh's news for both their husbands.

When Shiloh and Don Madariaga finally returned, it was getting very late in the afternoon. They, too, seemed to be on a much more cordial basis, with Don Madariaga insisting that they have ices and sorbet after their long, exacting studies of the stables and his forty-eight horses. Then Doña Ynes announced suddenly, "You must do us the pleasure of staying for supper. It is a long time since I have visited with a Galvez kinswoman, and you cannot deny me the pleasure."

Now Cheney, though she was certainly not as concerned with proper etiquette as the Madariagas, was appalled. She and Shiloh were not dressed at all for what would certainly be a formal dinner, and the hem of Shiloh's breeches was dusty. She would feel horribly out of place in the somber, old-world formality of a dinner at Madariagas Hacienda.

"You are much, much too kind, Doña Ynes," she said hastily. "But my husband and I simply cannot impose upon your hospitality so."

"I insist," Doña Ynes said warmly, but with steel backing her tone, as she so often sounded.

"Yes, you must," Don Madariaga said with his new affability. "It is much too hot for you to return to the city now, and it is time for siesta. You must rest—Ynes, the west suite, off the gallery? Yes. I will let your carriage go, and tonight, in the cool of the evening, I will send you back in my coach and four. We will arrange for your clothes to be cleaned while you take siesta, and for dinner tonight we will have such a feast in the gallery. It is much less formal than the dining hall, for good friends."

――――――――――

"Doc, you flat charmed the spit and polish offa those two," Shiloh teased her as they undressed for bed that night after coming back to the hotel from the plantation. "I'm so proud of you. And it's so good, such a good feeling, for you to be helping me. Thank you, from the bottom of my heart."

"Why . . . why, you're welcome, my love," Cheney said, flushing with pleasure. "But you really don't have to thank me. But then again . . . maybe that's a good thing. I've never thanked you, have I, for being so good, so supportive of me in my profession. Perhaps I should. I wouldn't ever want you to think I take it for granted, Shiloh. So please accept my thanks, too, for all you've done for me and all you've meant to me."

"Welcome," he said solemnly. Then his eyes lit up. "It's great, isn't it? Sharing like this, I mean?"

"Yes, it is," Cheney agreed. "Now you know

how I feel, wanting to keep you close, in my professional life too."

"Yeah," he said, taking her in his arms. "How
'bout a deal?"

"I'm game."

"How 'bout if I promise to stick my nose in
your business, and you promise to stick your
nose in mine?" he asked, his eyes sparkling.
"That way we got *two* great partnerships going."

"Deal," Cheney said brightly. "Want to shake
on it?"

"Not hardly," he murmured, pulling her
close.

They sailed languidly to visit coffee growers
in Puerto Rico. The hearty American couple
named Richardson received them with pleasure
and immediately took Shiloh's meaning when he
gave them the news. Mr. Richardson somehow
wrangled Shiloh into helping him figure his new
plantings and how much yield he could expect
in the next five years, and exactly how much of
Richardson's java he could cram into the hold of
Locke's Day Dream. Mrs. Richardson had several
medical complaints, which Cheney gravely and
patiently discussed with her for hours.

They sailed on to Jamaica and had just as
much success with their coffee grower there, an
old Royal Navy captain named Moorer, who

seemed much more interested in *Locke's Day Dream* than in his eight hundred acres of coffee. He toured the ship with evident pleasure and talked to Captain Starnes for hours, then questioned Cheney endlessly about her care of the crew.

"Naval surgeons, some of them were capital fellows, just capital, and others were drunken scrubs," Moorer said stoutly, ruminating over the ship's medical chest and small apothecary's closet that Shiloh had set up. "Never would we have dreamed of having such a physician as you, Dr. Irons-Winslow. The men of *Locke's Day Dream* are lucky swabs." He bowed gallantly, taking Cheney's hand.

When they had said their good-byes, Moorer did take a couple of minutes to discuss business with Shiloh. He said, his still-sharp blue eyes suddenly growing shrewd, "You, sir, you keep in touch with me and let me know how you set up your shipping route. I would be proud for every coffee bean I grow to sail on *Locke's Day Dream*. And by the way, since you've given me this news in such a timely manner, I'll be picking up some properties in Colombia. I can get them for a shilling or two right now. So consider adding Barranquilla to your ports of call."

"I will, sir," Shiloh said, shaking his hand.

As Moorer left the ship, making his way up the crowded wharves of Kingston, he shook his head, smiling. "Fine ship, she is—and a fine figure of a woman. Fine, fine ladies, both of them!"

CHAPTER TWENTY-SIX

Beginning Now . . .

"HOME," CHENEY WHISPERED. "Oh, how I hope Mother and Father will be there."

They were passing Governor's Island, and the madhouse of the South Street Docks was coming into view. Captain Starnes had stiffly declined assistance from the noisome swarm of little pilot boats and tugs that had buzzed around *Locke's Day Dream,* and he was sailing her into the maelstrom proudly, sails billowing, men shining in blinding white ducks and diamond-bright brass buttons, lined up along the quarterdeck as stiffly and precisely as a Roman legion.

Shiloh put his arm around Cheney's waist and pulled her close. "They will be," he said. "I made some arrangements with a fishing boat last night while we were tacking off Breezy Point, waiting for the tide. Had 'em take a couple of telegrams in. The Buchanans will be there too. I hope they bring Dart. He's a cute little scamp."

Cheney hugged him tightly. "You are the most thoughtful person I've ever known. Thank you, Shiloh."

"Welcome."

She kept her arm around his waist and they stood, close together, in the prow of their ship. It was a lovely summer day, but to their eyes, which had been filled with the lush West Indian landscapes and hypnotic turquoise blue of the Caribbean Sea, the looming Manhattan skyline and the rivers seemed washed out and a little forlorn.

"I'm glad to be back too," Shiloh admitted. "Even though the old home place looks kinda ramshackle and gray after where we've been."

"I was just thinking that," Cheney murmured. "I'm just shocked that you read my mind. Mmm, Shiloh—do you really feel that way? That this is home?"

"You're my home, Cheney," he said quietly. "I'll never have another."

"That's the way I feel too, my love," she said, leaning closer against him. "But . . . I was just trying to . . . ask, you see, because we haven't made any plans. None. Zero plans."

He grinned down at her. "We haven't?"

"No, you fool. You know it."

"Okay. So whaddya want to do?"

"Well . . ." Cheney extricated herself from him, with only a slight struggle, to open her reticule and rummage around in it. "I've made a list."

"What? You mean, you've listed our lives from this moment on? That's so like you, Doc.

Gotta have everything all persnickety and organized."

"You had a list," she sniffed. "So I get one."

"Yeah, I did," he admitted, his eyes dancing. "And you helped me with it, so now I'll help you with your list."

"Good," Cheney said crisply. "Now here, item number one: We have no home."

"Sure we do. Did I forget to tell you?"

"Yes, it must have slipped your tiny little foggy mind, Mr. Iron Head," Cheney rasped, propping her hands on her hips.

"Sorry," he said, unrepentant. Then he sobered and took her hands, watching her face carefully. "It's just that Dev's letter had this suggestion in it . . . and I've kinda been thinking about it, but I just didn't know if it would suit you or not—"

"Oh! Of course! Gramercy Park, Dev's house!" Cheney said, her eyes lighting up. "It's perfect, Shiloh! But wait, I thought he had a tenant."

"The lease is coming up for renewal," Shiloh said, still watching her closely. "But, Doc, it's not like . . . like what you're used to. Like Duvall Court."

"Oh, Shiloh, I love Dev's house," Cheney said warmly. "And you and I both have been in much, much worse places than that. Just in the last few weeks, if you recall."

"You'd really like it? 'Cause I like it," Shiloh admitted. "It's really good for a couple, and then it does have the spare bedroom. Just in case, you know."

"In case of guests?" Cheney asked innocently.

"No, in case of some children, of which you've promised me at least eight," he said solemnly. "That's on the list, isn't it?"

"I believe so. Yes, here it is. Item number twelve: *Two* children."

"Huh, that's funny. Oh well, there's lotsa numbers. We'll stick the other six on there somewhere. So what else is on your list, Doc?"

She was laughing, and he thought that no other living creature could possibly look as alive, as glowing, as vital as his wife.

She was saying, ". . . so I did kind of begin it as a to-do list when we got home, but then it sort of turned into a . . . a . . . book of dreams. Yes, that's it, Shiloh. I wrote down all the things I could think of that I want for us."

"You did? And will you let me see it?" Shiloh asked eagerly.

"Of course. But . . . promise not to laugh."

"I promise," he said solemnly. "Why don't you read them to me?"

"All right," Cheney said, blushing a little. "Item number two: Open a private hospital in Manhattan."

"Sounds good. I've always known you wanted to do that, Doc. We'll get to work on it right away."

"Th-thank you, I think I would like to do that," she said. "Number three: Sail to my husband's home in Hawaii and stay as long as he wants."

He turned quickly. "You'd do that? For me?"

"Of course. I loved your home, Shiloh, volcano and all. Truth to tell, I don't think the West Indies can hold a weak candle to Maui."

"Neither do I," he said eagerly. "Maybe next year, do you think?"

"We'll work on it," she answered firmly. "Together."

"I like your list, Doc."

"Thank you, I thought you might," she said. "Now, number four: Follow up on my husband's idea—here, I should have put 'genius.' I'll just add it right now—my husband's *genius* idea of a hospital ship, traveling to plague areas, with a fully equipped laboratory for study and hospital accommodations aboard."

"Whew, Doc, you got things going on into the next century," he said, but he was still grinning. "But you know what? We can do it all. Somehow, someday."

She nodded. "I knew you'd say that. I knew you wouldn't laugh. Here, you'll like number five: Let Shiloh sail around on *Locke's Day*

Dream all he wants and go with him as often as possible."

"Yeah, I love that one, even though the old sea dog is kinda ready for some dry land," Shiloh admitted. "Besides, I don't much want to leave you. I only just got you, you know, and I have to watch you every minute."

"And I hoped you'd say that," Cheney said happily. "But we'll work it out, Shiloh. I promise, I'll figure out a way to share with you and not make you do all the compromising and the giving in. Partners, right?"

"Doubled up," he agreed solemnly.

"Now, for the rest of the things on my list— I think I'll hold back on them for a while," she said, folding the paper and putting it away. "The first five are enough to keep a regiment busy."

"But I wanted to talk some more about item number twelve," Shiloh protested.

"We'll talk all about it later, my love," she said, putting her arm around him again. "In great detail."

"Okay, mon chou. Don't forget," he warned.

"No, never."

They were almost home. They could see the crowded docks, and Cheney thought she could see her father's tall, distinguished form at slip number twelve. "There is one other thing on my list, Shiloh," she said. "Actually, it's the first, and the last. And that is that we'll always follow the

Lord and seek His guidance—in the big things and in the smallest things too."

"Cheney, I can't imagine a life without following the Lord," Shiloh murmured. "I've been there, lost, without Him, in a dry and thirsty land. Never again."

"Never again," Cheney repeated softly. "Forever with Him. Beginning today . . . beginning now."

"I love you, Cheney," Shiloh said, lifting her hand to his lips. "Beginning now . . ."

TWO MUST READ NOVELS
FOR FICTION FANS

A Welcome Return to Lancaster County!

Colorful and quaint, *October Song* weaves together a captivating peek into the lives of Beverly Lewis's most adored characters. Readers young and old will be thrilled by the continuation of their favorite stories, from *The Shunning* to *The Postcard* and more! Featuring Amish barn raisings, walks under the harvest moon, and tea with the Wise Woman, *October Song* overflows with the things of life that make Lewis's novels such delightful reads.

October Song by Beverly Lewis

Will the Light of Truth Direct Her Fight for Justice?

Kit Shannon arrives in Los Angeles feeling a special calling to practice law despite the fact that few in her family understand her burning desire to seek justice for the poor and oppressed. This doesn't detain her for long, however, and soon Kit finds herself working with the city's most prominent criminal trial lawyer and is drawn into a high-profile case. She longs to discover the truth but struggles with her personal doubts about the suspect she must defend.

City of Angels by Tracie Peterson and James Scott Bell

◈ BETHANYHOUSE
www.bethanyhouse.com

11400 Hampshire Ave. S.
Minneapolis, MN 55438
1-800-328-6109